Praise for Joseph LeValley's other
TONY HARRINGTON NOVELS

Danielle —
To my best friend that I
barely know. Regardless,
you have my sincere
appreciation + admiration.
    Best wishes always!
        Joe

PERFORMING
MURDER

12-4-21

PERFORMING
MURDER

JOSEPH LEVALLEY

BookPress®
publishing

Published in Des Moines, Iowa, by:
Bookpress Publishing
P.O. Box 71532
Des Moines, IA 50325
www.BookpressPublishing.com

Publisher's Cataloging-in-Publication Data

Names: LeValley, Joseph Darl, author.
Title: Performing Murder : a Tony Harrington Novel / by Joseph LeValley.
Description: Des Moines, IA: Bookpress Publishing, 2022.
Identifiers: LCCN: 2021909567 | ISBN: 978-1-947305-33-5
Subjects: LCSH Motion picture industry--Fiction. | Hollywood (Los Angeles, California)--Fiction. | Journalists--Fiction. | Iowa--Fiction. | Italy--Fiction. | Murder--Fiction. | Mystery and detective stories. | BISAC FICTION / Mystery / General Classification: LCC PS3612.E92311 P47 2021 | DDC 813.6--dc23

First Edition
Printed in the United States of America
10 9 8 7 6 5 4 3 2 1

*For those who may never know
the difference they made:*

*Wade, Ron, Dave, Sandy, Paul, Steve, Jim, Don,
Roger, Mark, Dean, Dalton, Dick, Bill, Mif,
Raymunda, Corita, Bob, Doug and many others.
To paraphrase Mark Twain, a man who has friends
can never be poor. I am rich indeed.*

"Obviously it's much more fun
to play something you're not than
it is to play something you are."

— *Clint Eastwood*

Chapter 1

Orney, Iowa — Sunday Morning, June 21, Present Day

A dead body is an unwelcome discovery during the heat of lovemaking. Hank Brewster learned this the hard way.

He stood in the grass behind the large, sprawling clubhouse, near the swimming pool. He and Holly Hanover, a former high school cheerleader, stood an arm's length apart, catching their breath after scaling the country club's fence and scurrying across the practice greens to the pool. They were illuminated only by the glow from landscape lighting at the edge of the pool deck and a sliver of moon above.

Hank had wanted Holly since they'd been sophomores at Southern Quincy High School. As a member of the basketball team, he had enjoyed an up-close view of the pixie-like blonde doing flips and splits in her miniskirt and tight sweater in the scarlet-and-black school colors. The fact he had spent his time at games watching Holly instead of his teammates probably explained why Hank had never made it off the bench to the first string. Sadly, the interest had not been mutual. Holly had ignored his efforts to talk with her, thwarting any thoughts of ever asking her out.

A girl as beautiful and smart as Holly was strictly a starter's dating prospect. And even when she had been dating the captain of the team, Holly had earned a reputation for being uncompromising —fun, but unwilling to consider anything beyond kissing.

Now here she was, home for the summer from the University of St. Thomas in Minnesota, apparently excited to be alone with him in near-darkness, and ready to explore more than the shimmering waters of a swimming pool. Or was she? Hank found himself suddenly uncertain, afraid he had misread the signals. But hadn't she seemed genuinely happy to bump into him while waiting in line for ice cream at the local Dairy Queen? Hadn't she said she liked his new look, with longer hair and three days of stubble on his face? Hadn't she suggested they leave her car in the parking lot and ride together in his truck? Hadn't it been her idea to share drinks at the Iron Range Tap until almost 1 a.m.? More to the point, hadn't she whispered in his ear, proposing he bring her here?

Now Hank was frozen in place, staring at the goddess who had been unattainable for so long. He ached to make a move but was terrified he would misstep and spoil the moment. He nearly squeaked when Holly looked him in the eyes and simply nodded.

Hank pulled off his SlipKnot T-shirt, letting it fall to the wet grass. He watched impatiently, and with no small amount of amazement, as Holly maneuvered the straps of her white sun dress off of her shoulders and let it slide to the ground. She stepped out of the bundle of material around her ankles and walked slowly toward him, a mischievous grin on her face. The grin disappeared as she reached him, pulled him tight against her, and began kissing his neck.

Hank slid his hands down her bare back and leaned in to kiss her. Lips parted and tongues entwined. *God in Heaven, this is really gonna happen,* Hank thought as the kiss continued. He felt her hands exploring the lump behind the zipper of his cargo shorts. Clearly Holly Hanover had learned more in college than just quadratic equations and regression analysis.

He broke the kiss long enough to take another look around and make sure no one was watching. Satisfied they were alone, Hank slid his hands further down Holly's back and urged her panties downward. She slipped out of them easily, then unzipped his shorts and pushed them to the ground in a single motion. She then took his hand and pulled him to the edge of the pool. Hank would have preferred the soft grass and a more traditional first time, but he certainly wasn't going to argue with the naked blonde urging him into the water. She dove in first, with Hank only seconds behind. They swam across the deep end to the other side, where Holly turned and faced him, her face flush with exertion, or excitement, or both. As Hank pulled her close, she locked her legs around him and found his lips again.

Suddenly, effortlessly, they were making love, she with her back against the concrete edge of the pool, and he standing on his toes on a narrow underwater ledge. It was the opposite of romance and tenderness, as Hank tried to fulfill seven years of pent-up desire in one explosive session of raw passion.

Holly did indeed like his shoulder-length hair. He fleetingly wondered whether this encounter might have happened sooner had he looked more rebellious in high school, rather than like a close-cropped, all-American boy. In any case, he liked that she liked it. One of Holly's hands gripped his neck tightly, maintaining her ideal position, while the fingers of her other hand continually combed through his locks. The sensation of her fingers on his scalp was wonderful, but still placed a distant second to the other pleasures he was enjoying. When her fingers left his hair, he noticed, but just barely. Suddenly, she seemed to flounder and slip to one side. As Hank reached to steady her, he looked over his shoulder and saw her gripping his hair as it floated beside them in the pool. Floated beside...? *But... no... that can't be,* Hank thought. *What the hell?*

He sensed... No, feared... what he was seeing. To his shame, he didn't want to stop. He desperately wanted to finish before...

Holly screamed in terror, splitting the relative quiet of the night and numbing Hank's left ear. She flailed wildly, desperately trying to climb up his torso and out of the pool, but hindered by the hair in which her hand was now tangled—the hair of a body floating face-down in the Orney Country Club swimming pool.

Chapter 2

Orney, Iowa—Sunday, June 14, Seven Days Earlier

Orney Mayor Tommy Bowman paced nervously in front of the Sapphire Skies Flight Service counter. The guests of honor were late, and everyone was waiting. In this case, the term "everyone" was not much of an exaggeration. The entire city council, the presidents of three international corporations based in Iowa, two state senators, and the governor were joined by nearly a thousand other people in the high school gymnasium, waiting to celebrate the arrival of the director and primary cast members of a movie to be filmed in Orney. *Murder Beyond Them* was a psychological thriller and best-selling novel. It would soon be Hollywood's latest attempt to make a major success *without* featuring superheroes. The twin-engine Gulfstream carrying the cast from Los Angeles to Orney was provided by one of the Iowa corporations, a finance and insurance giant housed in one of the tallest skyscrapers in Des Moines.

"Where the hell *are* they?" the mayor barked at the city manager and two other staffers. Neither expecting nor receiving a reply, he resumed his pacing.

Charles Harrington sat off to the side on one of the vinyl couches near the window, suppressing a smile. He shared the mayor's anxiety, but he was better equipped to deal with it. Harrington was the author of the novel on which the movie was based, as well as its screenplay. He had decades of experience working with Hollywood and knew that the primary activity within the motion picture industry was waiting. Despite this, he had to acknowledge he was anxious for the plane's arrival, not because it was late, but because the director on board was Ramesh Bhatt.

Bhatt and Harrington had been close friends when they'd worked together in Europe many years ago. In fact, Charles had given Ramesh his first job in movies. Both men had been young and single then.

At age 26, Charles already had achieved success as a novelist and screenwriter. He had been on the set of his fourth movie, filming on location in Rome, when Ramesh had approached him. An immigrant from India and a recent graduate of the Paris Film Institute, Ramesh had expressed a willingness to do any kind of job that would get him in the door. Charles had liked Ramesh immediately and had convinced the director to put him to work as a continuity supervisor, one of the people responsible for ensuring consistency in the flow of the story. In other words, if the lead actor's weapon had changed inexplicably from a revolver to an automatic during a lunch break, Ramesh would have found himself back on the street.

Charles and Ramesh had been inseparable for months during the making of that movie, called *Three Nights on Vesuvius,* and had been close friends for a long time after. Sadly, as often happens when separated by thirty years and an ocean, the two friends drifted apart. Charles settled in Chicago with his wife, Carlotta, and continued a successful career as an author and screenwriter, later moving to Iowa to teach. Ramesh lived in Europe while working his way up the ladder in cinema, and later moved to Hollywood, where he earned a reputation as a "can't fail" director of dramas and action films.

Charles had been thrilled when Ramesh had agreed to direct *Murder Beyond Them,* the latest screenplay by C.A. Harker, Harrington's pen name. Charles was even happier the director had accepted his recommendation to film it on location in Iowa. He couldn't wait to see his old friend again. *I should offer to take over the mayor's pacing duties,* Charles thought, allowing a smile to sneak its way onto his face.

Seated to the right of Charles was his wife, Carlotta, known as Carla to her family and friends in the U.S. He had met her in Italy thirty-two years ago while making that same drama, set on the slopes of Italy's most famous mountain. A native Italian, Carlotta had black hair with hints of gray at the temples and olive skin. She had intelligence, grace, and a passionate nature that made her easy to love. Charles had known she was "the one" almost from the first time he'd met her. Likewise, she had fallen hard for the dashing young American writer. They had married in Italy after the filming had wrapped.

Ramesh had been best man at the wedding. His date that night, an American model and actress named Harriet Danziker, had become his wife a few months later.

Sadly, after more than thirty years of marriage, Harriet had died of pancreatic cancer. Charles had called Ramesh to express his sympathies, but the call had been awkward and uncomfortable between the two men who had been living separate lives for so long. Charles hoped Ramesh's visit to Orney would give him the chance to eliminate the awkwardness and put their friendship back on solid ground.

Sharing the portion of the couch to Charles's left was his only son, Tony, a writer for the *Orney Town Crier,* one of the smallest daily newspapers in the Midwest. Tony had inherited his father's boyish grin and writing talent, but had fallen a couple of inches short of Charles's six feet in height. Tony's other characteristics, his dark hair and eyes, the touch of cinnamon in his skin tone, and his passionate nature, came from his mother.

In some ways, Tony was responsible for the airplane full of Hollywood bigwigs who were headed for Orney. When Charles had told his son about the successful sale of another screenplay, Tony had been the first to suggest the on-location shoots be done in Orney. He had pointed out that the story was set in a small, rural city. As a town of 15,000 in northwest Iowa, Orney qualified. As a county seat with a courthouse square, a nearby river valley, and beautiful homes on wide, tree-lined streets, Orney was an idyllic setting. Tony had pressed his dad to do all he could to bring the film project here.

Tony's interest was multi-faceted. First and foremost, he loved Orney and hoped his town would benefit from the financial and perceptual lifts of having the movie based there. Secondly, as a news reporter, he wanted the chance to cover the multiple stories that would emerge during the six to eight weeks of filming a movie involving some of the industry's biggest stars. Lastly, at least two of the lead actresses were gorgeous and single. Tony wasn't foolish enough to think he had any chance at all with them. In fact, he was pretty certain he had no interest in having a relationship with a film star, but that didn't stop him from relishing the thought of meeting and interacting with them as he covered the movie's progress. He, too, was anxious for the Gulfstream to land, if only to see up close the adorable dimples and deep blue eyes that had helped to make Darcy Gillson a star, or to witness the latest outrageous behavior of her co-star, Charlotte Andresson.

The fourth member of the Harrington family was Charles and Carlotta's daughter, Rita. She was absent from the airport in Iowa. As a recent graduate of the University of Chicago's Master's Program in Musical Performance, Rita was busy preparing for and attending auditions. Her dream was to secure a cello seat with a major orchestra.

By the time the announcement came of the Gulfstream's landing, the mayor was nearly apoplectic. The Harringtons were less manic, but were certainly tired, bored, and sore from the unyielding vinyl on the couch. Regardless of disposition, they all moved in unison to the doors separating the flight service waiting room from the tarmac. The private jet taxied up next to the building. The door opened and the stairs unfolded before the engine whine had even subsided.

Suddenly, there they were. Director Ramesh Bhatt, lead actresses Gillson and Andresson, lead actor Kurt Rowsmith, and a mix of additional performers and support staff descended the stairs. Bhatt was first in line, carrying a small leather satchel and moving quickly through the airport's sliding glass doors. He spotted Charles immediately but was headed off by the mayor.

"Mr. Bhatt, welcome to Orney!" the mayor said, beaming. "It's an honor and a pleasure to welcome you here. I'm Mayor Thomas Bowman, but please call me Tommy. Everybody does. I want you to know our entire city stands ready to serve you. While you're here, anything you need, you just ask. I'm your man. Anything at all, we'll make it happen."

Bhatt was polite by nature, but clearly was eager to move on. He shook the mayor's hand, thanked him, and said, "Mr. Mayor, I'd like you to meet my assistant, Witt Silverstein. Whenever I need something, Witt usually will be the person coming to you or whomever with the request. Witt, why don't you and the mayor take a minute to exchange contact information?"

The mayor's smile morphed from warm to forced, but he turned to Witt and repeated his spiel. Bhatt used the opportunity to push past them and hurry up to the Harringtons.

"Charles, Carlotta, what a joy it is to see you again." He embraced and kissed Carlotta and then turned to Charles. He started to speak, stopped, then threw his arms around Charles's much larger frame. After only a moment, Charles, Carlotta, and Tony all realized Ramesh was trying to hide his tears.

Charles said nothing for several moments and simply clung tightly to his friend. Then he said, "It's wonderful to see you, too, Ramesh. I'm so happy we finally got you to Iowa."

As the men separated, Charles said, "Ramesh, this is Tony, my son."

Bhatt's eyes grew large. "It cannot be. You're just… You can't be more than… Goodness, Charles, how long has it been?"

"The last time you saw Tony was when we had our brief reunion in Italy. I think Tony was four or five at the time, so it was a long time ago, my friend. Too long."

"Yes, too long," Bhatt said. "I can't wait to spend some time with all of you." He turned away and rejoined his party.

Charles understood. The director would not want to linger with the Harringtons in front of his cast and crew, considering the emotions the reunion unleashed. Charles also knew Bhatt had a million responsibilities to which he had to attend, not the least of which was getting everyone to the high school gym, where they were expected to glad-hand with everyone from elected officials to students.

Better you than me, Charles thought, just as he heard Ramesh call out, "Come on, Charles, you're riding in the limo with me!"

Charles looked at his wife and son, smiled, shrugged his shoulders, and headed out the door.

Tony and his mother looked at each other and shook their heads, then looked back to watch the entourage climb into limos parked in front of the air service offices. Tony saw Darcy Gillson exiting through the revolving door and realized he had been so caught up in his father's reunion that he hadn't even seen her walk past. All he could see now was her backside as she strode toward the curb.

All in all, still not a bad view, Tony thought, smiling.

As if his mother could read his mind, she elbowed him in the ribs. "Down, boy," she said, trying to look stern but failing.

"Hey!" Tony objected, rubbing his ribcage. "I'm allowed to look."

"Yes, to look," his mother said. "But nothing more. You don't want anything to do with these Hollywood types, believe me."

Tony was ready to agree, but his mother continued. "Remember, I know from experience what a mess that world is." Early in their marriage, Carlotta would accompany Charles to shoots on location. She didn't like being left at home, and it gave her a chance to see some exotic places. However, she quickly learned she wanted no part of it. The combination of big money, bigger egos, high stress, and lack of sleep inevitably led to a lot of bad behavior. But Tony had heard this story many times before, so Carlotta summed it up this time with a simple reminder. "You know most of these people are intolerable."

Tony was tempted to object, still believing his mother was exaggerating, but he held his tongue as she continued.

"There are exceptions, of course, like Ramesh. But they're rare and, even if you found one, you'd have to put up with the nightmare world in which they live and the vultures who surround them."

"Wow. Okay, Mom. I get it. If Darcy Gillson begs me to run away with her, I'll tell her no, she has to quit Hollywood and get a job here. I bet she could make a lot of money as a pole dancer at the

Iron Range Tap."

Carlotta jabbed her son in the ribs a second time and abruptly changed the subject. "May I ride with you to the reception? I'll just leave our car here so I don't have to try to park it at the school. I'm guessing it will be a madhouse."

***

It was worse than a madhouse. Thousands of fans from all over Iowa and elsewhere were waiting at the school for the famous entourage to arrive. Those waiting outside the gym in the early summer heat were sweating and impatient. Many were people who didn't want to have anything to do with the community's formal program. They'd just stopped by to meet their favorite actor or actress, or to get a quick selfie. They were not prepared for the two-hour wait. Compounding their irritation was the fact the mayor was urging the cast and crew to ignore the throng outside, in favor of getting the delayed program underway in the gym.

When Tony and his mother arrived, they found the doors to the gym completely blocked by fans crowded around the guests of honor, waving and shouting for attention. Tony smiled as he heard both men and women expressing their adoration for their favorite stars. He was pretty sure Gillson and Andresson had received multiple proposals of marriage by the time the mayor had pulled them through the doors into the gym. Some fans tried to follow, but the local police officers and sheriff's deputies held firm, explaining that the gym was full.

Tony knew it would be a mistake for him and his mother to wave their VIP passes as they walked past the disappointed crowd. He stopped at the edge of the school's front lawn and took his mother's arm to ensure she did the same.

"Let me text Dad," he said. "There has to be a better way in than pushing through the mob."

A few minutes later, Charles admitted his wife and son into the event through the football players' entrance to the locker rooms behind the gym. With a smile and nod, the elder Harrington led the way through the maze of hallways and across the gym floor to their seats, which were positioned near the center of the basketball court, a few feet to the right of the podium.

Not bad. Thanks, Mr. Bhatt, Tony thought, assuming the seats were courtesy of the director and his relationship with Tony's father. *I guess it's true that it's not what you know but who you know.* Other community and state VIPs were seated nearby, with the movie's crew in similar spots on the opposite side.

The celebrities were nowhere in sight. They had been ushered behind a huge curtain which hung behind the dais.

When Mayor Bowman stepped up to the microphone, the crowd immediately quieted. His opening remarks were remarkably short. Tony assumed Bowman was a good enough politician to understand the crowd was already restless. The mayor quickly got to the heart of the matter.

"Before I introduce our guests of honor, I want to say a word of praise, and of thanks, to Charles Harrington."

Tony's dad gave a quick wave, but didn't stand.

The mayor continued. "In terms of praise, I simply want to congratulate Mr. Harrington on another successful novel and screen-play. Obviously, if Charles Harrington wasn't a great writer, our friends from Hollywood would not be here making a movie."

The crowd applauded politely, and the mayor said, "In terms of thanks, I want to express our community's sincere appreciation for Mr. Harrington's help in encouraging Ramesh Bhatt and his studio to select Orney as the setting for the movie. As many of you know, Mr. Harrington's son, Tony, lives and works here..."

Tony gave a quick, embarrassed wave.

"…and I'm sure Mr. Harrington's occasional visits to Orney to see his son planted the seed that Orney could serve as the quintessential rural city needed for his movie."

The mayor turned and looked at Tony's father, "So thank you, Charles, for everything you've done." More applause.

The mayor turned to Tony, "And thank you, Tony, for letting Mom and Dad come visit once in a while."

The crowd laughed, and Tony smiled.

Then, with great fanfare, courtesy of a quartet of brass instruments from the high school band, the mayor introduced each of the cast members present. As each one passed through the curtain and took a chair on the dais, the crowd roared and applauded its approval. The final two stars, Darcy Gillson and Kurt Rowsmith, were introduced together. They held hands, smiled, and waved for several minutes, as the crowd welcomed them with a standing ovation.

Ramesh Bhatt was introduced last. The ovation was warm and loud, but nothing compared to the welcome the stars had received.

Bhatt stepped up to the microphone, and the crowd sat. Bhatt said, "In case you're wondering, yes, I noticed the smattering of applause I received in comparison to the actors and actresses. I guess if I want to be popular, I'll have to start acting in the movies."

The crowd laughed.

"Of course, if I want to be the boss and make all the money, I guess I'll just keep directing."

The crowd laughed harder.

Now that Bhatt had them hooked, he proceeded with what he was there to say. After thanking the mayor and the horn players, the police and many others, he said, "I would like to get serious with you all for a moment. Since landing at the airport, we have heard from

Mayor Bowman and a dozen other local residents that they are here to help us. If I may paraphrase, we've heard comments such as, 'Anything you need, just let us know.' Well, we all appreciate that, really. One reason we chose Orney is because my friend, Charles, as well as our location scouting crew, told us the residents of Orney would welcome and support us."

More applause.

"Allow me to tell you tonight, on day one, I already know something we need from you." Bhatt paused a long time. It had the desired effect of amplifying the anticipation. The room was as silent as a geometry classroom during summer break.

He finally spoke. "We need your understanding," he said. "Making a great movie is not about receptions and autographs and glamour. Making a movie is hard work. It often involves twelve or fourteen-hour days; days filled with stress and frustration, fears and anxieties. The entire cast and crew will be under tremendous pressure, not only to produce great performances, great images, and great sound, but to do so on a tight timeline and a tighter budget.

"So," he continued, "we need you to be understanding when Darcy or Kurt isn't in the mood to chat or pose for a selfie. We need you to accept the simple truth that when you see me in a restaurant, in a conversation with one of the actors or crew members, that might not be the best time to ask for an autograph. In short, please be respectful and give the cast and crew a little space. If you do that, we'll make sure we create some opportunities along the way for interactions between fans and stars."

Bhatt added, "There's another side to our presence that requires your understanding as well. Please be tolerant of the disruptions we cause. Filming on location can require occasional blocked streets or closed businesses or a host of other interruptions to your normal routines. The more extreme the situation, the more we need your support, like when we're in the streets at 3 a.m., making noise and shining bright lights around. There won't be a lot of late-night shooting, but there will be some. It only makes it harder, and causes it to last longer, when someone opens a bedroom window and starts yelling at us."

Some in the crowd giggled.

"And Mr. Mayor, please be understanding when we crash that dump truck through the front windows of City Hall…" He paused and smiled. "Just kidding."

The crowd laughed. Even Mayor Bowman joined in as the blood returned to his face.

"In closing," Bhatt said, "I want to tell all of you we are genuinely happy to be here and honored to be received so warmly. Obviously, we want you to love us. None of us would have jobs if you didn't appreciate our work and look forward to seeing us. For the next six weeks or so, we're going to be living together. Like any new roommates, we'll need to make adjustments and compromises to make it work. On behalf of my cast and crew, I promise you we'll work hard to hold up our end, and we'll appreciate everything you do to support us. Thank you."

The crowd rose to its feet with an ovation that rivaled the one given to the movie stars. Bhatt smiled and waved his appreciation.

He's good, Tony thought. *It won't help, but he's really good.*

For the next two hours, the stars were surrounded by people seeking autographs and selfies.

***

Later that night, a select group of people sat on padded benches around a fire pit on the backyard patio of Nathan Freed's residence. Freed was the founding principal of Orney's largest law firm. Now mostly retired, Freed was known as much for his philanthropy and community involvement as he was for his prior brilliance as an attorney. He and Tony had become close friends a few years previously, when Tony had dated Freed's daughter, Lisa. A senseless murder had ended Lisa's life, and the two men had grieved together. Later, at Tony's urging, Freed had adopted a daughter, Trina, who had been rescued from an abusive father.

In addition to Tony and Nathan and Trina Freed, the group enjoying drinks around the fire included Tony's parents, Bhatt, the mayor, a few other elected officials, and three members of the cast—Charlotte Andresson, Corky Landers, and Darcy Gillson.

Andresson was beautiful and animated. She was cast as a young wife in the movie—not a faithful wife, but a temptress to the protagonist—and she looked and acted the part. Her jet-black hair and dark eyes seemed to dance around her pale white skin. She had a low, throaty voice that sounded like she was luring you into her lair, even when uttering something as simple as her drink order. Tony almost laughed out loud when the mayor and a state senator jostled for the seat next to hers in front of the fire. The mayor won, so the senator picked the spot opposite Andresson, where he could stare at her while believing he wasn't being obvious.

Landers was funny and loved to tell stories. He was a Hollywood brat. His mother was a well-known costume designer, and his father a popular voice actor in animated movies. Landers had grown up around people like Dana Carvey, Judd Apatow, John Lithgow, Lisa Kudrow, and dozens of other celebrities who came to their home for dinners and pool parties. At age 24, he was pleasant-looking without being overtly handsome. His slight build and receding hairline made him an unlikely leading man, but he was finding great success as a character actor. In this movie, he was cast as the comic relief—the worried husband's wisecracking buddy.

As Andresson smoldered and Landers entertained, Tony barely noticed either of them. Darcy Gillson's presence seemed to overwhelm his consciousness. She was quiet—not moody, but simply content. She smiled at Landers's jokes, and she responded to questions in a friendly, easygoing way. But she initiated no conversation and seemed happy to relax and enjoy her daquiri and watch the flames dance in the fire pit.

Gillson was one of Hollywood's hottest rising stars. *Hot in more ways than one,* Tony thought, trying not to stare. It was hard. She was dressed in a red halter top and white cotton running shorts. She sat on the padded bench with her feet tucked up under her, showing off what appeared to be a mile of lightly tanned legs. Her sculpted chin and nose were framed by blonde locks that fell past her shoulders.

She was well-known as a serious actress and a savvy businesswoman. She had acted in television commercials and sitcoms when she was young but had disappeared from the business for more than a decade. She had turned up again at age twenty-five with dual advanced degrees in theater and history. Once Gillson's agent made it known that this experienced, gorgeous actress was ready to go back to work, she was cast in a Netflix series almost immediately. From there, she was cast as the lead in an action movie, with Ryan Gosling playing the head of her support team. Gillson, and nearly everyone else, loved the role reversal. She worked hard to get into great shape and to be proficient in the required martial arts. As a result, she nailed the role, and suddenly Gillson was the hottest ticket in the industry.

Now she had agreed to make this psychological thriller based on a novel by C.A. Harker, set in a small city in Iowa. Because this was a smaller-budget movie with more drama and less action, many said it was a step backward for Gillson's career. When *Variety* had asked her about it, Gillson had said she loved the story and the role she was cast to play. "She's a strong woman, but in very different ways from my previous characters. She has to win her battles through the strength of her character, rather than the speed of her fists. I'm already learning a lot from her, and I hope other women will too."

To Charles Harrington and Ramesh Bhatt, Gillson's agreement to take the role was manna from heaven. To Tony, it seemed... *Oh my God,* Tony exclaimed to himself, sitting back, eyes wide. *It's almost as if Lisa has come back.*

Tony was shocked the resemblance hadn't occurred to him sooner. He turned and looked at Nathan Freed and saw Lisa's father smiling back at him. *He's been waiting for me to notice,* Tony realized, not smiling back.

Tony had accepted the fact he would never get over Lisa's death. However, he had learned to deal with it and move forward with his life. Having this living, breathing clone working in Orney for the next six weeks wouldn't make his life any easier. The only good news, Tony realized, was that his mother would be happy. *There's no way I'm going anywhere near Darcy Gillson,* Tony vowed privately. He rose, thanked Freed for the hospitality, and excused himself to go home.

𝔗𝔬𝔴𝔫 ℭ𝔯𝔦𝔢𝔯   SPECIAL EDITION

Orney welcomes Hollywood director, film stars, and crew

Tony Harrington, Staff Writer

ORNEY, Iowa – Movie director Ramesh Bhatt requested the patience and support of Orney residents while his cast and crew are in town filming a movie this summer. Bhatt made the remarks during a brief welcoming ceremony at the Orney High School gymnasium Sunday afternoon. Bhatt spoke before a standing-room-only crowd which included community and state leaders in addition to students, residents, and members of the news media.

Bhatt arrived in Orney by private jet with selected members of the cast and crew of the movie *Murder Beyond Them*, which is set to begin filming on location today. Bhatt told the crowd that making a movie is a grueling task and asked Orney residents to understand that the stars and others involved in the film may not always be interested in signing autographs, submitting to "selfies" or talking with fans.

Bhatt promised that opportunities would be made for fans to meet the stars over the course of the estimated six weeks of filming. He stuck to the promise when Orney residents kept him and the stars of the film, including Darcy Gillson and Kurt Rowsmith, busy for more than two hours following the event in the gym. Screenwriter Charles Harrington of Iowa City, who writes under the pen name C.A. Harker, was on hand to welcome Bhatt, a longtime friend. Bhatt acknowledged Harrington's role in convincing him to choose Orney, Iowa, for the on-location shooting.

On Sunday night, the restaurants and taverns in Orney were unusually busy, as residents apparently chose to dine and socialize downtown in the hopes of spotting, and perhaps meeting, one or more of the stars involved in the film.

"Can you believe it?" asked Edna Curlidge, a lifelong resident of Orney who was found sitting on a bench on the town square around 9 p.m. "This is so exciting. I know I'm too old to be acting like a teenager, but I have to tell you, I'm sitting right here on this bench all night if I have to. If I don't get to meet Kurt Rowsmith, I'll just… Well, I'll just die."

Other residents were gathered in…

Chapter 3

Monday, June 15

"You know, Tone-man, I was jealous when I heard you got invited to Freed's party last night. But I gotta tell ya, I think I got the better end of the deal."

Tony looked up from his BLT and fries at the flushed face of his best friend and co-worker, Doug Tenney. They were sitting in a vinyl booth at Willie's Bar and Grill, their favorite spot for comfort food at lunchtime. It was one of several local establishments that had barely survived the dark days of COVID-19, and both men were glad it had.

"Do tell," Tony said.

"Rowsmith was at the Iron Range. Think of that. *The* Kurt Rowsmith, drinking beer and playing pool with me and a bunch of other guys."

"Guys?" Tony probed, amused at Doug's excitement and doubtful that Rowsmith was hanging with a group of men only.

Rowsmith was a popular leading man in movies and a notorious womanizer. He had a boyish grin, sand-colored wavy hair, gray eyes that gave him a mysterious air, and a hard body that Tony couldn't match even if he spent the rest of his life living at a fitness club.

"Well of course, not just guys," Doug said, his enthusiasm undiminished. "That was the best part. He had women all over him. The Iron Range was packed with women, all wanting their chance with him. I've never seen a guy in a situation like that, where he could just point and have any woman in the room."

"But Doug," Tony protested. "You've been with me when I go in there to play piano."

"Very funny. I'm not kidding. I bet he had a dozen offers before he finally left."

"You're right." Tony nodded. "I rarely get up to a dozen…"

"Tony, listen to me. When he left, he was with the Stassi twins. Both of them! Jeez, I'd give a year's salary to have a movie of what went on in his motel room."

"Okay, my friend. Now you're sounding creepy and more than a little pathetic. Just chill out and think about how empty his life is, sleeping with a series of women he doesn't know and won't remember."

"Right," Doug said, taking a bite of a cheeseburger. "I'd like to try living on empty just once."

Tony laughed, knowing Doug liked to be outrageous just to get a rise out of him.

"So tell me, seriously, what'd you think of Rowsmith? Was he an okay guy?"

"I guess," Doug said. "He was nice enough. You could tell he was trying."

"But?"

"But you also could tell he *had* to try." Doug took a sip of Coke and continued. "He couldn't hide his ego, and it was pretty obvious we were just props."

"Props?" Tony asked, intrigued by the reference.

"Yeah, he was putting on a performance in the bar, staging a production to attract flies into his web. You know, female flies. The guys were there to give him a reason to hang around for a while. He clearly wanted to meet as many women as possible before selecting a partner—or partners I should say—for the night. I wasn't fooled by his attention. I don't think any of the guys were. We know we're not gonna get a text from him tomorrow asking us to go fishing or anything."

"Very wise, and very eloquent. You should think about getting a job as a writer." Tony was poking fun at his friend, whose desk was next to his in the newsroom shared by the *Orney Town Crier* and KKAR Radio.

"Nah," Doug said, sitting back in the booth and rubbing his stomach. "I'm happy to let you do all the work while I take credit for half of it."

"Truer words were never spoken."

Tony dipped a fry into a mound of ketchup and took a bite. Doug was about to respond to the dig when both men's cell phones chirped. They had set alarms to remind them to be back in the newsroom in time for the daily budget meeting, news-speak for the discussion of assignments and expected content for the paper being created that day for distribution early the following morning.

"Crap," Doug said. "We have to learn to talk less and eat more."

Tony laughed. "The last thing I need is to eat more. We just need to learn to get out of the office before 1:30 for lunch."

They left cash on the table to cover their tabs and hustled out the door. If the amounts weren't just right, they knew Erma would settle up with them the next time they came in.

***

Ben Smalley, publisher and editor of the *Orney Town Crier,* briefly greeted Tony and Doug as they entered the conference room and took their seats. Five other staffers—two reporters, the sports editor, the photographer, and the head of the copy desk—were already seated. Ben sat at the head of the table and got right to business.

"Needless to say, I've been thinking a lot about our visitors from the West," he said. "My conclusion is simple: the challenges and opportunities accompanying their time in Orney are enormous."

Yeah, no kidding, Tony thought.

Ben continued. "We all know there will be a thousand stories worth reporting, from celebrity profiles to inside looks at movie-making to reports of bad—or good—behavior.

"Let's hope for bad," quipped Shawna Jackson, the new, young photographer. The others chuckled and nodded as Ben carried on.

"In any case, as we're trying to do our jobs, we have to remember we're going to have competition like we've never had before. The state and national media will be here from time to time, and some paparazzi will no doubt be camped here all summer. I've talked with the local police and even the film crew's personal security about giving the local newspaper and radio some reasonable consideration, but I doubt we can count on that."

"So what do you…"

Ben interrupted Alison Frank's question, saying, "Hold that thought. Let me finish, then I'll welcome all your questions. My second conclusion, after realizing the magnitude of this, is that whatever structure and assignments we set around it are likely to change.

We're going to have to be flexible and willing to shift around until we find an approach that works. Thirdly, I want you all to understand my expectations in terms of your personal behavior. You are professionals, and I expect you to behave like professionals both on and off the job."

Doug started to ask what that meant but stopped himself.

Ben picked up on it anyway and said, "For example, do not fawn over the celebrities. I know I don't have to tell you this, but I also know how easy it is to be star-struck in their presence. And make no mistake, if I get a complaint about anyone from the *Crier* harassing or being inappropriate in your interactions with anyone, I will terminate your employment on the spot."

Doug couldn't help himself. He asked, "So if Darcy Gillson asks me to buy her dinner, what am I supposed to do?"

Ben smiled and said, "I suggest you tell her no, then go see a doctor about your hallucinations."

Laughter erupted, and Doug added, "Yeah, I guess I asked for that."

"Seriously," Ben said. "In six weeks, when these folks pack up and head out of town, I want the word on the street to be admiration for the *Town Crier* staff for the way we handled the stories and, more importantly, for the way we handled ourselves. Anyone not understand what I'm asking?"

No one responded.

Ben said, "Okay, so here's how we're going to start. Alison, you're assigned to Darcy Gillson and Charlotte Andresson. You'll do profiles on each. Try to get sit-down sessions with them and find something to tell us about their backgrounds or innermost thoughts that their fans haven't read a dozen times in *People* or on Facebook.

"Doug, you'll do the same with Kurt Rowsmith and Corky Landers. Both you and Alison need to take Shawna with you to get great photos, so be respectful of her schedule. Don't feel like these all have to be done in the first week."

Tony was beginning to wonder what role, if any, he would have, when Ben said, "Tony, I want you to cover the movie-making process. Ask Bhatt if he'll let you hang with him for a few days in the heart of the shoot. Get some real insights into what he and others, like the cinematographer, do to ensure the final product looks fantastic while telling a great story. Take a camera and snap as many photos as they'll allow."

Ben turned to the sports editor. "Jim, I may have to ask you to pitch in, as well, to help with any breaking news or special milestones."

Jim Pulley, a big, elderly man with a voice loud enough to serve as the public address system for the games he covered, tried to look put out. He didn't fool anyone. "Whatever you say, boss."

Ben turned to Tina Crenshaw, a fifty-something fixture at the *Town Crier*. Tina's role was to work days in the newsroom and write stories that came to the *Crier* via telephone or mail. These included obituaries, news releases from local companies and organizations, and a host of other routine reporting.

Ben said, "Tina, you too are going to find your role expanded temporarily. I'm going to need your help covering public meetings, such as city council and the school board, and routine police and fire reports. Are you okay with that?"

Tina's face flushed. She considered the request for a moment, then said, "I'm happy to do what I can, as long as I'm not away from home too many nights. I'm not sure my husband and kids can survive on their own."

Knowing Tina's three boys were in high school, Tony thought Tina's importance at home might be exaggerated, but he also knew the boys were active in summer sports, so she was probably expected to be in the bleachers on a lot of evenings.

Ben simply nodded and said, "I appreciate that. The next few weeks will take a toll on many of us, and I appreciate everyone for stepping up. Oh, that reminds me. I called Evelyn, and she agreed to help us, as well, if we have an especially busy day."

Tony knew Ben was referring to Evelyn Crowder, a semi-retired columnist who now worked nights from home, monitoring the news networks and internet, and posting breaking news to the *Town Crier* website. Though the paper was delivered only once a day, the *Crier*, like all modern papers, had to keep a website current in order to compete with other forms of electronic media. And, of course, it now included a radio station with a twenty-four-hour news cycle. Tony smiled at the thought of Evelyn, who must be in her late seventies at least, chasing an ambulance.

Ben leaned back in his chair. "Okay, now that you have your initial assignments, are there any questions?"

There were dozens. The group talked and debated and resolved issues for another ninety minutes before finally wrapping up with a review of stories scheduled for Tuesday. Tony was barely listening. He couldn't wait to get his work done so he could depart and find his dad. If Tony needed a favor from Ramesh Bhatt, he knew just where to start.

Chapter 4

Lake Como, Italy – March 1989

The young woman knew she shouldn't. She also knew she would. She shouldn't because it was wrong. More importantly, if her boyfriend ever found out, he would be deeply wounded. She couldn't bear the thought of hurting him, nor of having him think less of her.

So why was she here, taking this risk? Why was she sipping wine in a suite in the Villa d'Este with a man who barely knew her and was committed to another woman? Why had she accepted his offer and taken the train from Milan to this paradise nestled between the Alps and the shores of Lake Como? She had no answers to her questions except to acknowledge it was what she wanted—who she wanted—in this blatant act of rebellion and pure pleasure-seeking.

What she was about to do was wicked. Of that, she had no doubt. And it tortured her to admit the wickedness only added to the thrill, serving to exacerbate, rather than deter, her desires. It also baffled her. As a model in Milan, the world's new epicenter of fashion, she had turned down more men than she could remember. Male models who posed with her, photographers who worked with her, business leaders who employed her—men of every type had attempted to bed her. Today, at twenty-three, she was no virgin, but she was proud to have lived by a conservative moral code and to have developed a reputation as one fashion model who refused to sleep her way to success.

As a result, there had been moments throughout the day when she was tempted to turn back, to assert her rational, moral self and not risk everything for this... this... *fling*. However, each time her conscience rose to the surface, she found herself ignoring it and moving forward, getting off the train, taking a taxi to this grand old hotel, ringing the bell of the man's suite, accepting the goblet of Granbussia, sinking into the plush couch cushions next to him, blushing but not resisting, as his fingers gently stroked her cheek.

When his hands moved to the buttons on her blouse, she thought fleetingly of her boyfriend. When his lips found hers, an image of the other woman appeared for a moment. And then, as his hand pushed down beneath the waistband of her skirt, she was gone, lost in the pure animal instincts of lust and passion. She was his. Folly or not, temporary or not, she was his.

She stood suddenly, took his hand, pulled him from the couch, and led him through the double doors into the bedroom. She never looked back. Little did she know that if she had, she would have seen a trail of heartache and death in her wake.

Chapter 5

Orney, Iowa—Tuesday, June 16, Present Day

Tony shifted his bike to a lower gear and pedaled faster, trying to maintain a reasonable pace as he climbed out of the Raccoon River Valley on the S-shaped trail paved for just this purpose. He was tired and winded and sore, and determined not to give in to any of it. *It's my own damn fault. I can't expect to stay in shape when I only get out here once a month.* He had taken a summer break from his weekly training with Pak Junsuh, owner of Jun's Martial Arts. He was sure he could do without the rigors of tae kwon do because he would be on his bike during the summer. *Nice job of planning*, he thought as his muscles screamed at him to stop.

Tony shook his head, mumbled a few other choice words, and forced his legs to keep moving. The sweat slipping into his eyes and the mosquitoes piercing his bare arms added to his discomfort as well as his foul mood. While the evening sun had descended nearly to the tree line across the valley, the temperature had not dropped much from its mid-day peak. It had been a warm, dry June with no signs of changing anytime soon.

Effing attorneys, he thought for the hundredth time as he huffed over the rise and coasted onto the level prairie beyond the trees. The light was better here, and the breeze provided a little relief from both the heat and the parasites, so Tony's mood lifted somewhat. He allowed his pace to slow, though he knew he needed to make it home before the darkness was complete. He had neither packed a flashlight nor mounted a headlamp on his handlebars.

At a time when everyone at the *Crier* was working overtime, Tony was able to carve out an evening for a bicycle ride because the "effing" attorneys had made it impossible for him to do his job. The most frustrating part was the fact that his request to his father, and his father's subsequent request to Bhatt, had gone perfectly. The director had not hesitated to say Tony was welcome at his side at any time while the cast and crew were filming.

Then, inevitably, the attorneys had intervened. They said there were liability issues to consider. What about a non-disclosure agreement? Does he have the proper insurance? What will he do if he sees or hears something we don't want publicized? Could one of the cast members sue the studio for letting a reporter have uncontrolled access? They'd gone on and on about it.

So Tony was here, on a bike trail, on Tuesday evening, instead of on the set watching Darcy Gillson turn the tables on an abusive husband. For two days the cast and crew had been creating movie magic, and for two days Tony had been arguing with security people, local cops, assistants to assistant directors, and lawyers from Los Angeles to New York.

Effing attorneys, Tony thought, as he stood on the pedals and made the final push for home.

***

Wednesday, June 17

At 10 a.m. Wednesday morning, a FedEx package arrived in the newsroom, addressed to Editor and Publisher Ben Smalley. Four minutes later, Ben's voice summoned Tony to his tiny office in the corner of the room.

Tony practically leapt through the doorway. "Is that what I hope it is?"

Ben smiled and nodded, holding out a stack of documents two inches thick. "I'd tell you to read them all before you sign, but I know you won't. Even if you did, and hated every word, I know you'd sign them anyway just to get moving again, so don't bother."

Tony must have looked surprised because Ben added, "Our attorney has been involved in every document, and she assures me they're okay. In the end, it's mostly common-sense stuff related to your safety, your agreement to stay out of the way, and your promise not to sue them, no matter what happens to you. There are no restrictions on what you write, with two exceptions. You have to give the people involved in an article an opportunity to comment, which you would have done anyway. Secondly, you have to honor the non-disclosure related to the script, so you don't give away any movie plot-points."

Tony nodded, and Ben said, "There are four documents. I've already signed them. After you add your John Henry, ask Laurie to make copies for both of us. When she's done, you're back on the clock. Take the originals to Bhatt, and you should be good to go."

Tony beamed. "Thanks, boss. I'm sorry this got so complicated. You probably could have hired two reporters for what you spent on the attorney in the past two days."

"Not at the outrageous rate I pay you," Ben quipped. "Now stop talking, and go out there and earn your salary for a change."

Tony was out the door before Ben finished his sentence.

***

The on-location offices of Prima Racconto Films were housed in the Orney Community Center, a former elementary school gymnasium. The school had been demolished years ago, but the gym was newer and had been spared. After a city-wide fundraiser and the passage of a small bond issue, the community had converted the gym into a multi-purpose facility used for everything from blood drives to craft fairs to weekly service club meetings.

Ramesh Bhatt had taken the mayor at his word and made a request for use of the space. The next day, all previously planned activities in the building were postponed or cancelled, and the staff of Prima Racconto moved in.

By the time Tony drove the few blocks to the center, processed the paperwork, received his lanyard credentials, drove back to the shooting site, and convinced a security guard he was now approved for admission, it was nearly 2 p.m. As he walked up, smiling to greet Bhatt, he heard one of the assistants announce a forty-five-minute break for lunch.

Trying not to groan out loud, Tony shook Bhatt's hand and asked where he should be when the break ended.

"Just stay with me." Bhatt beamed. "Your parents are joining me and some of the cast for lunch. They'll be delighted to have you with us, and so will I."

The two men climbed aboard an electric golf cart, Bhatt in the driver's seat. Ten minutes later, they reached Veterans Memorial Park, the largest city park in Orney. It was well-maintained, with flower beds lining paths of crushed rock, and many stately trees, primarily oak and walnut. Although the park's address was Elm

Street, the trees from which the street had gotten its name were long gone, thanks to the Dutch elm disease that had swept through the Midwest in the 1960s. Tony could also see newer gaps in the foliage, where the more recent plague of borers had wiped out more than a dozen ash trees.

Fortunately, the losses had not overly diminished the park's beauty or utility. It featured walking paths, playground equipment, a ball diamond, nine holes of Frisbee golf, and several open spaces used for kickball, rainbow tag, kick-the-can, or whatever games kids were playing nowadays.

Today the park's largest clearing hosted an enormous white tent, open on three sides. In the shade of the tent, a twelve-foot table was set with china and flatware. Smoke rose from a nearby catering truck.

Bhatt drove the golf cart over the street's curb, into the park, and up to the edge of the tent. Sitting on one side of the table were the movie's four stars, Darcy Gillson, Kurt Rowsmith, Charlotte Andresson, and Corky Landers. On the other side sat Tony's parents. Tony laughed quietly as he climbed off the cart and approached the table. He knew his parents had been dealing with Hollywood types on and off for many years, but the absurdity of the picture still struck him as humorous.

He leaned down to kiss his mother on the cheek, noticing she looked uncomfortable and perhaps even unhappy. As Tony glanced at his father, he could immediately see the source of his mother's irritation. Charles Harrington was engaged in an animated conversation with Andresson. The topic was books. It was Charles's favorite subject. If he was engaged with someone willing to discuss Vonnegut or Twain or Orwell or, God forbid, "Harker's" own work, he might be lost to the rest of the group for hours.

Tony wasn't surprised when his father didn't pause to say hello.

Tony wasn't certain his dad had even noticed him.

Hard to blame him, Tony thought, observing Andresson's famously beautiful eyes riveted on his father, as she nodded in agreement with everything he said. Tony just looked at his mother, smiled, shrugged, and took his seat.

When Charles Harrington finally paused to breathe, Andresson took the opportunity to acknowledge the new arrivals.

"Ramesh, I'm so glad you're actually dining with us today, and not spending another break working. And thank you for inviting your friends to join us. Charles and Carla are just delightful!"

Charles beamed and Carlotta managed a tight smile.

"We've been friends for more than thirty years," Bhatt said. "I couldn't be happier that they decided to stay in Orney for a few days." He, too, kissed Carlotta on the cheek, then took his place next to Charles. "You remember their son, Tony. You met him Sunday night at Mr. Freed's party."

"Of course," Andresson said. "I never forget a handsome single man."

Tony blushed while his mother's face grew even tighter. Across the table, Gillson and Rowsmith clearly were straining not to roll their eyes. As Tony mumbled a polite acknowledgement, the catering staff stepped up and began serving the meal.

Broccoli-cheese soup was followed by a Greek salad, followed by roasted lamb and at least two side dishes Tony didn't recognize. All were delicious, and soon Tony was forcing himself to stop eating. Getting too full was a bad idea, knowing he would likely be standing in the hot summer sun for the next few hours. However, when the white-coated server set the plate of strawberry cheesecake in front of him, Tony couldn't resist. He took a deep breath and picked up his fork.

Through it all, the conversation continued, inevitably turning from books to movies. It didn't surprise Tony that people working in the film industry couldn't escape the gravity well of shop talk. Who's being sought for what project? How much did so-and-so's last picture gross? Is it true Matt Damon turned down the role Ron Howard offered him? And so forth.

Over dessert, Andresson looked across the table at Charles and said, "I think the screenplay you wrote for this film is brilliant. I swear, I'm not just saying that. Ramesh is tired of hearing me thank him for letting me be a part of it."

Charles began to express his thanks for the praise, but Andresson didn't stop to hear it. "Of course, no one has let us see the last twenty pages. We still don't know how it ends. I know it's important to protect the film from spoilers, but all the secrecy drives me crazy. I still don't know if I'm just a victim, like in the original book, or I'm actually the killer."

Ramesh set down his fork and said, "Consider it a compliment. I knew I had to have the most talented cast possible on this shoot because they have to nail the performances without a full understanding of their characters' true natures."

Andresson laughed. "Nice comeback, boss. It's total B.S., but I'll take it. I may even put that quote on my resume."

Kurt Rowsmith apparently had had enough. He said, "Well, it will be a new experience for you to use a quote on your resume that someone actually said."

Andresson laughed again and whacked his arm with the back of her hand, perhaps a little harder than necessary, to make her point.

Rowsmith grimaced but refused to give her the pleasure of verbalizing the pain. She continued her spiel, happy to be the center of attention. When she again turned to Charles, she asked, "So how many of your books have been adapted to film?"

"This one makes eight," Charles said, "if you include the two terrible ones made years ago by small, independent filmmakers."

"Oh, I was just about to ask you if you wrote all the screen-plays, but I guess that answers that. Did you do the other six?"

After a slightly awkward pause, Charles said, "Actually, I wrote them all. I just did lousy jobs with the first two. I didn't know anything about screenwriting, and the company making the films didn't have directors or editors good enough, or perhaps brave enough, to put me in my place and fix them."

Bhatt jumped in. "That's no longer a problem, Charles. I'm plenty brave enough to turn your mediocre script into a masterpiece of a movie."

Everyone laughed, including Charles. "I hope you do, my friend. There's nothing worse than seeing a terrible movie on late-night television and having to acknowledge I wrote it. I'm happy to watch you work your magic."

With that, Bhatt looked at his watch and rose. "Time to go to work, kids," he said. "Kurt, your call is in thirty-nine minutes. Tony, come with me, and we'll go see if the crew is ready."

Tony nodded, rose, and thanked everyone for a wonderful lunch. He hugged his mother and then climbed into the golf cart. As Bhatt backed up the machine, Tony watched Andresson give his mother a polite hug, too, and his father a longer, firmer embrace. Watching his father return the gesture caused Tony to flinch. He wasn't sure why. Jealousy? Concern for his mother? Resentment of a beautiful woman's ability to turn the head of any man on whom she chose to cast her spell?

You're just being silly, Tony thought. *It's just a hug. Nothing's going to come of it.*

He had no idea how wrong he was.

***

Kurt Rowsmith burst through the front door of a mid-century brick ranch house, ran across the neatly trimmed front yard, and stopped in the middle of the street. He paused to take a breath, hands on his knees. He was wearing a tattered terrycloth bathrobe, open at the front, revealing a black T-shirt and boxer shorts underneath. He looked up, gazed down the street, reached into the pocket of the robe, and withdrew a large butcher knife. It glinted in the sun as he raised it. Gazing down the street into the bright sunlight, he screamed, "Go ahead, bitch, run! You see this?" He lifted the knife higher. "Take a good look! When I find you, it's gonna be yours! I'm gonna bury it so deep, they'll have to chop you up to get it out! Go ahead, run! But I'm comin'. Baby, believe me, I'm comin'."

"Cut!" Bhatt yelled. "Hold places, everyone!"

He walked over to the cinematographer, Peter Cristo. The two men had worked together on several films stretching back two decades, so Bhatt didn't need to ask.

"Yep," Cristo said. "Nailed it. The blade caught the light just right, and we got the flash you wanted."

"Good. Kurt did fine too."

"Yep, the kid's good. That's a lotta movement and script to get right, and it gets harder each time."

Bhatt nodded. His desire to catch the light off the knife blade in a very specific way had resulted in numerous takes. Rowsmith had to be exhausted. Bhatt certainly was.

Tony stood about twenty feet behind the camera, watching intently and taking notes from time to time. His attention was primarily on the interactions between the director and cinematographer. He knew it would be difficult to describe the on-camera action without violating his non-disclosure agreement, so he had decided to focus on the two men in charge of the filming. This would make a more interesting story anyway. Everyone would see the action later, in the final cut of the movie. Only the *Town Crier* could show them what was happening off-screen.

Bhatt and Cristo worked together efficiently, almost fluidly. It was like watching a well-rehearsed duet perform. *No*, Tony thought, *more like dance partners. Each seems to read the other's mind. Each anticipates the other's moves.* He realized he had the basis for his first feature article about movie-making in Orney, Iowa.

Town Crier

The dance of the movie-makers

Tony Harrington, Staff Writer

ORNEY, Iowa – Movie director Ramesh Bhatt barely moved. A close observer could see an almost imperceptible shake of his head. Cinematographer Peter Cristo didn't need to ask. He began re-positioning and preparing his camera for another take. The lighting and sound crews drew their cues from Cristo, and soon a dozen men and women were moving in perfect synchronization.

It was like watching a dance, with two featured performers out front, supported by a well-rehearsed and choreographed chorus of dancers. In this dance, Bhatt and Cristo took the lead. Of course, the dance was not perfect. It suffered from occasional stumbles and missed cues, but when it worked well, such as in setting up for filming a particularly dramatic scene for the third time, it was as impressive to watch as the Joffrey Ballet.

For the third take, everything was reset within minutes. They had only to wait for the makeup and wardrobe people to attend to Kurt Rowsmith, ensuring his appearance would be exactly right when the camera began rolling again.

This scene and several others like it played out on Wednesday afternoon and evening as Prima Racconto Films shot portions of a new movie, *Murder Beyond Them*, on location in Orney.

Asked later whether it was typical for crews to move quickly between takes, Rowsmith said, "No, not typical at all. You always hope the director and crew will have it together, but more often than not, you spend 80 percent of your day sitting around waiting for them to get everything set. It's the worst part of making a movie. But these guys are good. I think we're actually ahead of schedule."

After the day of shooting ended, Bhatt gave all the credit to Cristo, the cinematographer. Bhatt said, "He's just the best there is. He knows how to capture those things that are nearly impossible for a director to explain to someone who doesn't get it. Things like the depth and texture and ambiance you're trying to achieve. I can't imagine taking on a major project without him."

In a separate interview, Cristo said he appreciated the compliments, but emphasized the importance of the long-term working relationship. He said, "Ramesh and I have collaborated on, I don't know, maybe eight or nine films. It's true I've learned to read him pretty well. But it's also true he knows exactly what he wants. It really helps me do my job when the director is clear from the start about what he's seeking for the final product. I'm just his eyes and hands. He's the brain that makes it happen."

These thoughts were echoed by sound technicians and others on the set, as they described…

Chapter 6

Orney, Iowa—Friday, June 19

Tony was exhausted. For the past two days, he had risen at 5 a.m. and arrived on location less than an hour later, interviewing makeup artists, lighting techs, and other support personnel as they prepared for the day's filming. He had learned more than he ever wanted to know about the thousands of details and the amazing talents involved in dozens of different fields required to make each frame of film a work of art. After spending each day with the crew, Tony returned to the newsroom to pound out an article for the next day's *Crier*.

The article written Thursday, for Friday morning's paper, had focused on the amazing new technologies being used – digital sound-boards controlled from computer tablets with AI-assisted sound engineering, digital lighting design, and new types of low-heat, low-energy light sources, robotic motion-control trolleys, autonomous drones, and a host of other gadgets large and small. Tony's favorite interview for the article was with Kellie Shanwitz, an "IT nerd" hired to support the hundreds of computers used during the shoot, most of which were embedded in the high-tech equipment.

"I wonder," Shanwitz said during her interview, "how much longer Hollywood will shoot on location. For that matter, I wonder how much longer they'll need actors, or shoot movies at all." When asked to elaborate, she said. "As you know, we've been using CGI— sorry, computer-generated imagery—for a long time now to put actors into whatever setting we want. They film on a sound stage, but appear to be in outer space or at the bottom of the ocean or wherever. They slay dragons that don't exist, conquer worlds that are equally fictional, and often morph into and out of superhero costumes."

She continued, "With the rapid evolution of artificial intelligence, CGI, and editing software, we're now to the point where we can create the images of the people too. One of these days, Hollywood is going to wake up to the realization it's a lot cheaper to create the motion picture on a computer screen than it is to do this." She gave a grand sweep of her arm toward the now quiet movie set. The gesture drove home the point. They were in view of blocks of streets filled with trucks, equipment, wires, and trailers. All would be unnecessary if the movie was created entirely on a computer. Tony had no idea whether Shanwitz was right, but he loved giving the readers of the *Crier* something interesting to contemplate.

Now, at 8 p.m. Friday, Tony sat at his desk writing about several other people he had met. Most seemed nice and remarkably well-grounded. They were just hard-working professionals whose names would never be noticed as the credits rolled at the end of the film. They took pride in their work and were well-paid, but they felt no closer to stardom than Tony did. Many had spouses or partners who also worked in the business. The interviews invariably included lamentations about the difficulties of being away from home while filming on location.

Tony also found the people he interviewed had remarkably diverse, and often surprising, backgrounds. He met a boom operator who had trained as a dancer. A member of the camera crew was a former police officer who had worked security on a film and had decided to stay with Prima Racconto when the company moved to its next location. Eventually, he had trained and been hired for his current role. A third was a lead guitarist for a punk-rock band that was "on a break."

After two and a half days of following Bhatt and his crew around, Tony had only two regrets. One was that the *Crier* would not have the time, money, nor space, to capture in print all of the great stories he was finding. The second was the fact that he couldn't keep his eyes open.

"I was going to invite you out to the Iron Range for a beer after work, but I guess I won't."

Tony sat bolt upright in his chair and opened his eyes to the smiling face of his boss.

"Sorry, Ben. I guess I dozed off."

"Well, fortunately, your drool missed your notes, so I trust you'll finish that piece before you head home?"

"Absolutely." Tony turned back to his keyboard and screen, trying to slow his racing heart.

"Then, when you're done, go home and get some sleep. Do you have to work tomorrow?"

"Yes." Tony nodded without looking up. "But I work the night shift, so I can sleep late in the morning."

"Good. Make sure you do. And Tony…"

He stopped typing and looked up, eyebrows raised.

Ben said, "Thanks. You're doing great work on this, as I knew you would."

"Thanks, boss. I appreciate it. And now that I've had a nap, maybe I should take you up on that after-work drink."

"Nah, let's take a rain check. You'd have to sit around waiting for me to finish editing. You'd probably just doze off again, and this time you might drool on something important."

No clever comeback came to mind, so Tony just smiled and resumed typing as Ben turned and walked back toward his corner fishbowl.

***

At 8:40 p.m., Tony clicked SEND, turning the article over to the copy desk for editing. The paper had his cell number, so he felt no guilt as he cleaned off his desk, packed up his laptop, and prepared to leave.

At the sound of the back door opening, he glanced up to see Alison Frank walk in. She strode purposefully to her desk next to Tony's, dropped her bag on the floor, and flopped into her chair, spreading her arms and legs.

"Problems?" Tony asked, hoping the answer would be no. He didn't have the energy to be the helpful colleague tonight.

"Nah," she sighed, "unless you consider an inability to complete Ben's assignment a problem."

Tony grinned. "Well, he's just the boss, so I wouldn't let it concern you."

She snorted. "Suck it, Harrington."

"Okay, okay, sorry. What's going on?"

"Darcy Gillson refuses to talk to me. That's what's going on."

"Ah." Tony nodded, knowing how frustrating it was to have a primary interview assignment refuse to participate.

"No matter what I say, or the conditions I offer, or the down-right begging I do, she just says no."

Against his better judgment and his brain's pleas for sleep, Tony pursued it further. "So is it Darcy herself, or some handler person?"

Alison sat up in her chair and leaned on her desk with her elbows, two fists under her chin. "Well," she said, "at first it was Norma, that woman who looks like Nurse Ratched, who apparently is Darcy's appointed, or perhaps self-appointed, assistant-slash-bodyguard. But when I persisted, Darcy eventually spoke to me in person and said it's just not gonna happen. God, I hate telling Ben I've failed at this."

Tony knew he was treading on thin ice by offering to help. Alison might really appreciate it, but she might also perceive it as an expression of Tony's ego, thinking he could accomplish something she couldn't. However, as he looked at Alison's dejected face and sagging body language, he decided to try.

"Alison, if you don't mind me offering a little help, I might suggest you hold off on talking to Ben."

She looked up, clearly wary.

Tony continued, "As you know, my family has ties to the director, and I've been hanging near him for the past few days. If you want, and it's totally up to you, I'd be willing to at least ask Bhatt about his willingness to intervene."

"Really? Well, I... Well, yeah, that would be great."

"I'll do it quietly, and it'll still be your interview. I'll just see if he's willing to ask her to reconsider. Can't hurt to try."

"Yeah, for sure. Thanks."

Tony nodded and headed for the door, hoping his offer wouldn't result in anything that damaged his relationship with Bhatt.

***

Tony had stayed long enough at the *Crier* that darkness had settled in by the time he grabbed his bicycle from the storage room near the back door and exited out into the alley. That meant he would be walking home. Similar to most cities, Orney had an ordinance prohibiting riding a bike after dark. While a typical cyclist might ignore this, knowing offenders were rarely cited for it, Tony knew all too well that officers liked nothing better than to write tickets to reporters.

He walked with his left hand on the bike's handlebars, guiding it down the alley beside him. When he reached the street, he turned the opposite direction from his rented two-bedroom bungalow. He hadn't eaten since lunch and was craving a Panucci's Pizza. His weariness had wrestled with his hunger, and his hunger had won. As he reached the end of the block and crossed to the next, he could see a small crowd gathered in front of the restaurant's plate glass window. It didn't take a genius to guess what was happening. One of the movie's stars was undoubtedly inside, and people were gathered hoping to see him or her, or perhaps trying to work up the courage to go inside and interrupt the meal.

After two and half days on the set, Tony was confident he was beyond feeling star-struck. He turned right at the corner, before reaching the restaurant, and guided his bike around to the back of the building. He was one of Mamma Panucci's most frequent customers, so he didn't hesitate to use the back door.

As he leaned his bike on the brick wall and pulled on the door handle, warm Italian aromas washed over him, drowning him in the pleasures of baking crusts, garlic, parmesan, tomatoes, and a host of other toppings and seasonings. Tony smiled broadly as he entered the kitchen, his mouth watering.

"Tony!" he heard Mamma cry from the far corner.

"Hey, Mamma. Sorry about coming in the back. I decided to avoid the crowd glued to your window."

"Can you believe it? You'd think they'd never seen a movie star before. I don't get what they're so worked up about."

Tony looked over to the corner and saw she was carefully arranging two large pizzas on platters polished brightly enough to be used as mirrors. Tony knew it was unusual for Mamma to be in the kitchen at all, and when he saw the fuss she was making over the presentation of the food, he had to smile again.

"Hey, that's beautiful, Mamma. Sure glad you're above getting all worked up over some movie stars."

She looked up at him crossly, but then burst out laughing. "Okay, smart guy. Go find a seat. I'll have your usual ready in a few minutes."

"I'll have mine on a gold platter. I wouldn't wanna be upstaged by these outsiders."

She ignored him.

Tony stopped at the cooler to grab a Diet Dr. Pepper, then pushed through the swinging door into the dining room. He stopped dead in his tracks. Seated at two tables, pushed together to form a table for eight, were Ramesh Bhatt, Kurt Rowsmith, Witt Silverstein, Charlotte Andresson, Corky Landers, and Darcy Gillson. They were seated at the back of the dining room, which meant Tony was only two steps away as he came through the kitchen door.

No wonder there's a crowd outside. They didn't spot a star. This is the whole constellation.

Andresson looked up immediately and said, "Hey, it's Tony!"

Tony smiled weakly, raised the bottle of diet soda in a feeble salute, and simply said, "Hi everybody. Sorry to interrupt. I'm just passing through."

He tried to move past them quickly, horrified at the thought that someone at the table might believe he had been following them or eavesdropping from the kitchen. However, before he took two steps, he heard from behind him, "No, wait. Come join us. Please. There's an empty seat here at the end of the table."

Tony stopped. He turned slowly as he realized the voice issuing the invitation was not Bhatt's nor Andresson's. It had come from Darcy Gillson. *Dear God, Darcy Gillson. Did she just say please? To me?*

Tony could feel his face burning as he came full circle to face the table. What he saw didn't ease his mind. Darcy was standing and pulling out the chair for him. Tony knew he couldn't refuse. Whether professionally or personally, it would be foolish to turn down an invitation to sit with this group. Despite that, every fiber of his being wanted to turn and run.

"Well, I'd be honored," he stammered. "You sure it's okay? I don't want to interfere with anything important."

Bhatt said, "Relax, Tony. We've declared all business off-limits for tonight. We're just enjoying this outstanding pizza, a few not-so-outstanding commercial beers, and some more Hollywood gossip. You'll be a welcome change of pace. Maybe you can share some local stories so we don't have to listen to Charlotte tell us for the third time about her date with Ben Affleck."

Andresson picked a carrot spear from her salad and tossed it at her boss. Everyone laughed and Tony sat, easing the backpack off of his shoulders and onto the floor beside the table.

Tony knew Bhatt could sense his uneasiness and was grateful when the director asked why he was dining so late. Tony explained he was just getting off work, which led to questions about his article for the next day. This gave Tony a chance to tell everyone how impressed he was with their crew and how much he appreciated everyone's cooperation. Once the ice was broken, the conversation quickly found a comfortable groove, and Tony's anxiety eased.

The others at the table seemed sincerely interested in Tony's work, particularly his real-world experiences with criminals and life-threatening situations.

At one point, Rowsmith summed up his reaction, saying, "A corrupt deputy sheriff, a ring of human traffickers, a mafia hit man, all in Iowa? I'm amazed, truly. It's certainly not how I pictured things in the wholesome heart of our country."

"Well, to be fair," Tony said, grinning, "the mafia hitman was in Italy and New York. But I have been shot at and chained to a wall in Iowa."

The group laughed, and the conversation moved on, inevitably returning to the latest news from Southern California.

Well into the conversation, Braden Borden's latest failure at the box office came up. Borden was an action star with a spotty record of successful and not-so-successful films.

"I was surprised this one didn't do better," Bhatt said. "I mostly enjoyed it."

Tony wondered if it was the beer or an ingrained personality trait that drove Kurt Rowsmith's immediate and vocal reaction. "It was a piece of shit!" he spouted, planting his bottle on the table. "For God's sake, Bhatt, you don't always have to be so nice. Borden couldn't act his way out of a wet paper sack."

Bhatt glanced at Charlotte, whose face had clouded at the comments.

Rowsmith grinned and leaned back in his chair. "Ah, crap. Sorry, Char. I forgot you and Borden are a thing. Well, I hope he's better in the sack than he is on the screen."

"Fuck you, Kurt." Charlotte turned to look at him. "He may not be Oscar material, but he does all right. You're not always a picture of perfection either, you know."

Rowsmith clearly intended to respond, but Bhatt shot him a look that would have stopped a grizzly bear in its tracks.

Andresson took advantage of the pause. "Besides, we're not a 'thing' at the moment. If you ever paid attention to any Hollywood news that didn't feature you, you'd know Braden and I split after our trip to Cancun this spring. He's a hothead, and I couldn't take his jealousy any longer."

"Yeah, well, I'm sorry, Char. I should've kept my opinions to myself." Rowsmith's grin contradicted any hint of sincerity in his words.

Tony was glad when the conversation moved on, though it sounded much the same as the cast discussed other famous couples and their lives on and off the screen.

As he finished his third piece of pizza, and almost without thinking, Tony turned to Darcy Gillson and said, "I hear you've declined to be interviewed by the *Crier*." He immediately regretted being so bold and was about to apologize when Darcy spoke up.

"Well, yes and no."

Tony set down his fork and raised his eyebrows.

Darcy continued, "I've declined to be interviewed by Alison."

She apparently could see the surprise on Tony's face. She quickly asked, "Can we speak off the record for a moment?"

"Of course. If that's not clear, everything being said tonight is off the record. I'm your guest, and I'll be very transparent with you all if I hear something I'd like to quote."

"Okay, good," Darcy said. "This may sound silly, and even a little petty, but I never agree to be interviewed by women."

"Really?" Tony was genuinely astonished.

"It's simple, really," Darcy said, "and it speaks directly to my ego, or self-serving nature. But the fact is, I've learned from experience that male reporters simply treat me better than female reporters. The differences are subtle. I don't think women intentionally paint me in a bad light or anything – you know, beyond the trash we've learned to expect from the tabloids and other fringe media. Likewise, I'm sure men don't go out of their way to make me look good. However, I've come to believe there are subconscious forces at work. Men want me to like them. God, that sounds terrible when I say it out loud, but you know what I mean. They tend to downplay the negatives and paint me in a good light. Most women don't have that motivation and may even subconsciously resent me or seek out a flaw or two."

Tony began to object, saying Alison wasn't like that, but Darcy interrupted him, laughing.

"I'm already wishing I'd been less honest. I know I'm stereotyping and generalizing to an unforgivable degree, but it is what it is. Based on my experience, I've decided I only grant interviews to men. Seriously, Tony, if it's important to your paper to have an interview, I'd be glad to talk to you."

Tony leaned back in his chair, his mind racing. He crammed hours of debate—*What would Ben do? Would Alison ever forgive me? How important is the interview to the paper? How would I feel about myself? What's best for Darcy and for Bhatt's movie?*—into a two-second pause in the conversation.

He said, "Thank-you Darcy. It's kind of you to offer, but now I'm the one who has to decline. The article was assigned to Alison, and I wouldn't feel right about stepping in. I know if I asked her, she would tell me to do it for the benefit of the *Crier*. But I also know she would never forget how it felt. If you don't mind, we'll just keep this here, and I'll tell my boss you respectfully declined."

"Okay. I'm good with that if you are. Thanks for understanding."

"No, thank *you*," Tony said. "It was good of you to trust me with an honest explanation."

"Well, a man of principle." Tony turned and saw it was Rowsmith who had spoken. "If we're done here, I'd better get going. I don't want any of Tony to rub off on me before I get to the bar. It's Friday night, and I prefer not to sleep alone. So here's to your principles, Tony." Rowsmith smiled and raised his beer before draining the bottle. "May they forever remain with you."

Groans and chuckles followed the pseudo-toast as everyone stood to leave.

Tony expressed his sincere thanks to Bhatt and everyone for including him in their meal. He picked up his backpack and headed out through the kitchen and into the alley. As he pulled his bike out of the weeds next to the wall, he was surprised to hear his name called. He turned to look and was even more shocked to see Darcy standing in the alley near the kitchen door.

"Huh?" *What a stupid response. C'mon, Harrington. Get your act together.*

"Sorry," Darcy said. "I didn't mean to startle you."

"No, uh, it's okay, really. Was there something else?"

She shook her head. "Not really. I just wanted to tell you I'm glad you joined us tonight. I really did enjoy hearing about your adventures."

"Well, thanks. I'm sure I go on for too long."

"No, really. It was great. I mean, it was nice to get to know someone living in the real world. And what you've accomplished... Well, you know, it makes all this acting stuff seem so silly."

Tony nearly said, "Aw, shucks," but caught himself in time.

"And Tony," Darcy spoke again, quieter.

Every time she says my name, I think I'm gonna melt.

"Kurt made light of it, but he shouldn't have. The fact is, you showed us all tonight that you are a man of principle. Good for you.

It was an honor to spend time with you."

"Miss Gillson, please…"

"Stop. Good grief, it's Darcy. And I've said what I wanted to say. Oh, except one more thing. Tell Alison if she can get free for lunch tomorrow, I'll talk to her. Good night, Tony."

She was gone through the kitchen door before Tony could croak out his thanks. He knew it was just as well.

He was glad he had his bicycle for the walk home. His legs felt weak, and he needed the support.

Chapter 7

Orney, Iowa — Saturday, June 20

The Howdy Stranger Inn on U.S. Highway 26 south of Orney was an older roadside motel, with guest room doors that opened to the parking lot and a small outdoor swimming pool surrounded by a wrought iron fence in an old-world guardian motif. The motel was seventy years old, but the middle-aged couple who owned it took great pride in keeping it meticulously clean and well-furnished. They also offered many modern amenities, such as flat-screen televisions and free wifi. In short, it was a nice enough place, but that didn't help alleviate Charles Harrington's feeling that he was suffocating there. His wife was in a funk and had made it clear she would be staying in the room for the evening. As a result, Charles was faced with a menu of only bad choices. He could stay with her, watching a re-run of *Little Women* on HBO from a vinyl-covered chair; he could unpack his laptop and resume writing his latest short story and get accused of ignoring her; he could go out and leave her behind and suffer her wrath later; or he could try to talk her into coming with him and risk starting a fight. He sighed and chose the last option.

"Honey, this is Orney, not Hollywood. Let's just go find a nice meal. You never know, you might even have some fun."

Carlotta's eyes flashed, but her head never moved from the pillow propped up on the headboard of the king-size bed. Almost without moving her lips, she hissed, "When they're here, it *is* Hollywood. You know it better than anyone, Charles. Hollywood isn't a place, it's a frame of mind, or if it's a place, it's wherever those self-centered narcissists are gathered. And tonight, that's in Orney. I don't even understand why we're still here. It's been a week. Can't we just go home?"

Charles wanted to argue with her, but he knew he couldn't. In the first place, she was at least partly correct. Secondly, defending the mob from California would only escalate the argument. And lastly, he knew the source of her disdain. Charles had a long history of working in the business. He had spent many long hours with the rich and famous, and not always in ways of which he could be proud. But this was different. This was Orney. This was his son's town, and his wife was with him, and their old friend was working here. Those thoughts led him to another tactic.

"How about later? We could call Tony and see if he'd like to join us for a meal when he gets off work."

"At ten o'clock? No, thank you. I'm not hungry anyway. Feel free to call him yourself. You boys can enjoy some time together without me."

Hallelujah, Charles thought. *That's something, anyway.*

"Okay, if you're sure, I'll call him."

Carlotta didn't respond, so Charles pulled out his cell phone and made the call, trying very hard not to get up and dance as his son accepted the invitation for a late dinner at Panucci's.

***

"Another slice, Dad?" Tony hadn't told his dad it was his second night in a row enjoying Mamma P's cooking. He was trying to eat his share, but even a favorite pie gets hard to swallow on the tenth piece in two days.

Charles held up his hand in the universal sign for "Halt."

"If I eat one more bite, I'll explode like a Bob-omb."

Tony's jaw dropped. "How in the hell—I mean heck—do you know about Bob-ombs? That's a reference from Super Mario Brothers."

"Hey, I'm your dad. I'm not a dinosaur." Charles paused, smiled, then laughed heartily. "And to be honest, I don't have a clue how I know about Bob-ombs."

Tony joined in the laughter.

It had been a wonderful meal. And while the food had delighted them with its usual great aromas and flavors, it had placed a distant second to the conversation.

Father and son talked about everything from politics and business to music and art. They reminisced about the past and shared stories of their individual lives in more recent years.

As the meal ended, Tony was glad the conversation continued. While discussing special moments from the past, both good and bad, Tony said, "I still remember the day you walked into our house in Chicago and announced the family was moving to Iowa. I thought you were joking. When I realized you weren't, I thought you'd lost your mind."

"Remind me, how old were you?"

"I had just turned fifteen. I was a sophomore in high school. I was shocked at first. Later, I was just angry and hurt."

"You had every right," the elder Harrington said. "That's a

terrible time to make a kid change schools. I must say, you made it easy on me. After a day or two, it never seemed like you were unhappy or struggling with it."

"Yeah, I tried hard to be a good soldier, but there were a lot of nights I fell asleep plotting how to get even."

"Well, I hope that phase ended," Charles said with a chuckle. "I don't have to keep looking over my shoulder, do I?"

"No, Dad, honestly. Once we got settled in Iowa City, I quickly learned it wasn't so bad. By the end of the first school year, I actually loved it. Living in that great old house by the river, having a yard, being able to ride my bike anywhere—well, almost anywhere—it was all terrific. I met some great friends and had a good experience in school. Then later, when I was at the university, it was cool having you and Mom and Rita nearby."

Charles nodded. "I can see that. I'm pretty sure you never had to wash a load of laundry until you moved up here to Orney."

"That's a point," Tony agreed, grinning, "and treating everyone to Mom's homemade tiramisu once a week made me the most popular guy in the frat house."

Charles waved for the waitress and handed her his American Express Card to pay the bill. She seemed unimpressed by its platinum color. She undoubtedly had seen a number of them already this week. As she walked away with his card, Charles quipped, "Blonde hair, pale skin. She must be *northern* Italian."

Tony laughed. "I think her name is Jorgensen, so more likely she immigrated to this pizzeria from the Scandinavian bakery across the square."

As father and son stood to leave, Tony reached into his pocket and pulled out a gold keychain with a single key dangling from the ring at its end.

"What's this?" Charles asked.

"You mentioned again, on the way over here, how much you admire the Mustang," Tony said, referring to his 1967 convertible. "I picked you up in it tonight just to enjoy the expression on your face when you saw it. Now, I thought maybe you'd like to take it for a spin."

"Seriously? Oh, man, I'd love to. But what if something happened? How could I ever face you again if I wrecked Lisa's beautiful car?"

"Dad, relax. It's just a Ford. Just a beautiful, fifty-year-old Mustang classic in mint condition." He grinned as he watched his father's discomfort grow. "Seriously, nothing's going to happen, and if it does, we'll just get it fixed. Mr. Freed gave me the car so it would be driven and enjoyed. So go enjoy."

"Aren't you coming along?"

"Nah, I'm beat. I've been working my butt off for the past four days. I'm gonna call it a night."

"And the car?"

"Just take it back to the motel tonight. You and mom can drop it off at my place tomorrow. I just had it serviced this morning, and the tank is full, so it's all set to go."

Charles held up the gold ring and watched the key dance in the glow from the ceiling lights. His face was beaming. "Well, if you insist."

"I do, and if you want a recommendation, take it west on U.S. 26, down through the valley, then go north through Viscount and come back east on the county road. It's about a forty-minute trip, so you'll have a chance to air it out a little. The county road back has a series of curves that will test your handling skills. Just be careful through the valley. The deer are thick in there, and they seem to look for opportunities to jump in front of cars."

The two men pushed through the glass doors and walked out

onto the sidewalk across from the Orney town square. "Oh, and Dad." Charles turned to face his son. "Make sure you push the clutch all the way to the floor. I think you know it's a simple four-speed transmission, so it won't be any trouble. But the clutch needs adjusting. If you try to power through the gears too quickly, you're gonna grind 'em pretty good."

"Got it. I'll be careful, I promise."

Charles hugged his son and climbed into the driver's seat of the Mustang parked at the curb a few spaces down from the restaurant. The engine started with a roar. Charles eased it out of its parking space and took the first right, exiting the square.

Tony wasn't worried about his dad's ability to drive it. He had seen him drive a stick shift plenty of times when the family traveled together to Europe. Every couple of years, they flew to Italy to visit his mother's family near the Amalfi coast. Because there was no train service to Amalfi, Charles often rented a car. In Italy, most rentals had manual transmissions. It's where Tony had learned to drive one as well.

"Have fun, Dad," Tony said to the empty street. He smiled and added, "I guess I'll just walk home. It's not far."

***

Orney, Iowa—Sunday, June 21

Tony awoke to the strains of "Small Town Cop" blaring from his cell phone speaker. The song was coded to signal Rich Davis was calling. Davis was a special agent with the Iowa Division of Criminal Investigation. He was a friend and a frequent source of insider information and news tips. The song was an up-tempo rock tune recorded by the Iowa band "West Minist'r" back in the mid-1970s.

Tony liked the beach music vibe of the song, but mostly found it humorous as a signal that Davis was calling.

Tony glanced at the time displayed on the cell phone, 4:56 a.m., and groaned. *5 a.m. on a Sunday. There will be no humor in this call.*

"Hey, Rich. What's up?"

The voice of his friend sounded tired and said simply, "We have a floater in the country club pool," and was gone.

Twenty minutes later, Tony pulled into the Orney Country Club parking lot and stopped his Explorer in the outermost row. It was the closest to the clubhouse he could get. The next row was a makeshift barricade of official vehicles, positioned bumper-to-bumper and tied together with yellow crime scene tape to ensure no unwelcome visitors, such as journalists, could come near the swimming pool located directly behind the building.

Tony thought the elaborate efforts were silly. If he wanted to get a view of the pool, all he would have to do is drive three blocks down the street, walk onto the course from the second fairway, and stroll up to the pool's chain link fence from the back side.

He decided to try the direct approach first. He walked to the end of the row of cars, to where a sheriff's deputy was pulling guard duty over the one gap in the tape.

A deputy sheriff. Tony thought about this for a moment and decided it was possible the country club lay outside the city limits of Orney. That would make it a sheriff's case. Or, alternatively, it was a police case and the Sheriff's Department was just helping out. He hoped it wasn't the latter scenario. He had nothing against the Orney police, but the department was small, and the chief was relatively new. More to the point, Chief Judd Collins was young and inexperienced. The City Council had hired him from a smaller town, where his first four years as an officer had been spent running a D.A.R.E. program in the local high school and writing traffic tickets.

The vehicles in the lot didn't answer the question. Police cruisers joined sheriff's SUVs, a state trooper's car, a DCI crime scene van and Rich Davis's unmarked sedan. Inside the barricade sat an ambulance, the fire chief's car, and the medical examiner's mini-van. At this point, Tony wouldn't have been surprised to see the Batmobile.

Tony didn't recognize the deputy, which was unusual. He assumed it was one of the day-shift officers who spent most of his time serving court documents or ferrying mental health patients around the state to wherever an available bed could be found. Tony put on a smile, which wasn't easy at 5:30 in the morning.

"Good morning, deputy. Can you tell me who's in charge here?"

"I'm not supposed to talk to you."

Tony groaned inwardly. He called officers like this "do-bots." They just did what they were told and often refused to bend, even when common sense overwhelmingly required a little leeway.

He swallowed hard and tried again. "Oh, I understand completely. Sheriff Mackey wouldn't want you to be the source of any leaks to the press. Well, I don't want that either. That's why I'm trying to learn who's in charge. If it's the sheriff, I would simply request you let him know I'm here. Tony fished in his pocket and handed the deputy one of his business cards.

The deputy scowled but pushed the button on his lapel-mounted radio mic and said, "One, this is nine. There's a reporter out here named Harrington. He's asking to see you."

"Ah, son-of-a…" the sheriff's voice broke off, probably as he remembered he could be heard by anyone with a police scanner. "Alright. Tell him to wait there. I'm a little busy right now."

"Ten-four," the deputy nodded and said. "You heard the man. Sit tight for a bit."

Tony nodded his agreement and strolled back out to the edge of the parking lot. He went to the Explorer and pulled a camera out of a bag on the floor of the back seat. He snapped a few pictures of the scene, as the summer sky showed the first signs of dawn to the east, behind him.

He was not feeling as relaxed as he appeared. He was anxious to learn what had happened, to get inside and see what was going on now. He also wanted to get as much information as possible before the competition arrived. If this was a murder, as the crime scene tape certainly indicated, one or more television stations from larger markets could join other print and radio media, in descending on Orney to get the story.

If it had been later in the day, on another day of the week, Tony would be making more of a fuss about having to wait. However, he already knew there would be no scoop for the *Crier* today. Early morning was the worst possible time for news to occur for a morning paper. Early Sunday morning was a disaster for the *Crier*, which didn't normally publish a Monday paper. The paper that would carry this story was almost forty-eight hours away.

Having had these thoughts, Tony immediately scolded himself. He was thinking too much like a reporter from the 1950s, or even the 80s. The fact was, the *Crier* had a website where his story would be published as soon as it was ready. He should also be thinking more about the radio station. Ben hadn't owned it for very long, and Tony was still getting used to the immediacy of broadcast news.

He pulled out his phone and texted Doug with the same brief but clear message Tony had received from Davis. The message would bring Doug quickly, with recorder in hand to get what was needed for radio.

Having just made up his mind to raise some hell, Tony saw Sheriff George Mackey lumbering down the sidewalk to the parking lot. Tony met him at the opening in the barricade.

"Looks nasty, Sheriff. What you got here?"

"Hell, Harrington, I dunno yet. You must know that much by now. These things take time."

"Yes, Sheriff, I get it. But something made you create this barricade and use up five rolls of crime scene tape, so I'm guessing it's not a kitchen fire or people cheating on their golf scores."

"Okay, wise guy. Let me think." The sheriff drew a deep breath and let it out slowly. He said, "So, on the record, you can quote me as saying we have a twenty-eight-year-old female, deceased. She was discovered floating face-down in the Orney Country Club Swimming Pool around 1 a.m. this morning."

"Who found her at that hour?"

"We're not releasing any names at this time, but it appears two young people, a man and a woman, scaled the swimming pool fence to take an unauthorized swim and found the body by accident. Neither of these people is implicated in the death. At this time, we believe they were unfortunate enough to choose the wrong night to trespass on the club's grounds."

"Are there signs…"

"Just hold on, Harrington. Let me finish. We have no specifics regarding the cause or time of death. At this point, the medical examiner has said only that the death appears to have been recent. Because this woman was young and by all accounts in good health, we are treating the death as suspicious. We are being thorough to make sure we get the full story as quickly as possible. Obviously if any of your readers saw anything suspicious or has any knowledge about this cri… uh, incident, we ask them to call the Quincy County Sheriff's Department immediately."

"By all accounts? What does that mean? It would indicate you've talked to people who knew her, which tells me you've identified the victim."

"Sorry, smart guy. That's all you get this morning. Now get your ass outta here. They're gonna be bringing her out soon."

"Thanks, Sheriff," Tony said without looking up from the pad on which he was scribbling notes.

He turned and strolled back to the Explorer as he finished writing. Once at his SUV, he reached into his camera bag again and pulled out a telephoto lens. Snapping it onto the camera, he climbed up onto the hood of the vehicle. By standing there, he had a clear view and excellent perspective of the scene, with the back of the ambulance at the center of the image.

A few minutes later, two EMTs emerged from the pool deck gate, pushing a gurney covered in a white sheet. Tony shot a series of pictures of the crew moving the body to, and then into, the ambulance. Once it drove away, lights flashing but siren off, a traditional tribute to the deceased, Tony climbed down from the hood and packed away his camera.

Tony found himself speculating about Mackey's motives in telling him the body was coming out soon. He knew Sheriff Mackey well. Despite the man's gruff manner, he was smart. He was also savvy when it came to matters of the press. Mackey wouldn't have said it if he hadn't wanted Tony to know. Mackey certainly understood that Tony would stay and take those pictures. *Was he just being nice? Did he want the pictures in the paper for some reason?* Tony might never know. He wasn't even sure he cared. He was just glad he got them. He owed the sheriff one for this.

Ah. That's why. Once he thought of it, the answer was clear. From the sheriff's point of view, there was no downside to allowing Tony to take photos, and now Tony owed him a favor. This was an I-O-U that almost certainly would be called in at some point.

"Hey, Tone-man." Tony stood up and turned around at the

sound of his friend's voice. He saw Doug approaching from the rear of the Explorer. From the corner of his eye, he also saw Rich Davis coming through the parking lot toward them from the other side.

To Doug, Tony said, "I got what I needed from Mackey. He was reasonably talkative. I'm sure he'll talk to you too. Just ask him to repeat what he told me."

"Got it," Doug said, "but what are we talking about here? Is this a murder case?"

"No official word on that yet, but if you ask me, I'd say yes. You don't get this kind of attention for an accidental drowning. Tony swept his arm toward the line of law enforcement vehicles to make his point.

"Okay," Doug said, and headed off toward the clubhouse.

Davis arrived as Doug departed. He motioned his head toward Tony's SUV, indicating they should get in. Once the doors were closed, Davis said, "I heard the tail end of that conversation. There is another reason all these people would be here."

Tony was baffled and about to say so when Davis continued, "Think about it. Whose death is going to bring out every officer in the county, and several from the state?"

Tony's face drained of color. "Dear God, it's one of the movie cast."

"Bingo."

Tony's mind immediately went to Darcy Gillson. The thought of her perishing, especially here, especially after she had...

"Who? Tell me who!"

"Whoa. Easy, my friend. Where's that outburst coming from?"

Tony struggled to get his emotions in check. He needed to remember Rich Davis wasn't just a friend. He was also a criminal investigator. Tony didn't want any misunderstandings to come from his comments.

"Sorry. It's just that I've met and gotten to know the cast. This is horrible. Please, tell me who."

"Strictly off the record, understood?"

"Yes," Tony said, but wished Davis hadn't asked.

"It's Charlotte Andresson."

"Dear God. I just dined with her. She was so animated. So *alive*." Tony realized his sorrow and horror was mixed with a strong sense of relief that it wasn't Darcy. He swallowed that thought and asked, "And now she's been murdered? It was murder, right?"

"Yes, Tony. It's pretty clear. Again, it's not official, and it's off the record, but I'd say someone had sex with her on the floor of the pro shop, and then bashed her skull in from behind with a golf club. I'm pretty sure the M.E. will say she was thrown into the pool after she died."

"Why are you telling me this? I mean, you've been a great friend and occasional source of news tips, but this goes a little above and beyond."

Davis nodded. "Yeah, I like you, but I have to confess, this isn't for your benefit; it's for mine."

"How so?"

"Well, as you said, you just dined with her. So I need to ask you some questions."

Tony immediately tensed. This had gone far too quickly into the realm of an official investigation.

Davis continued. "For example, what was her mood at dinner Friday night? Did anything seem to be bothering her?"

"No, not that I noticed. She kidded around. I would describe her as playful. She tossed a carrot at the director when he made a wisecrack. Oh, but there was one point when she told Kurt Rowsmith to go fuck himself."

"Really?" Davis now was keenly interested. "What led to that?"

"Kurt was shooting his mouth off about what a terrible actor Braden Borden is. Turns out Borden and Andresson are, uh, sorry, *were* seeing each other. Charlotte defended Borden, and the conversation moved on. The whole thing lasted about twenty seconds, so I wouldn't make too much of it."

Davis nodded but continued typing notes on his smart phone.

"And that reminds me," Tony said suddenly. "Andresson said she and Borden recently broke up." Tony's voice inched up a little higher, and he sat up straighter as he recalled the rest of the conversation. "She said she was tired of his jealousy." Tony strained to remember and added, "I think her exact words were, 'He's a hothead, and I couldn't take his jealousy anymore.' That may not be exact, but it's close."

"Is Borden here in Orney with this cast or hanging with her?"

"Not that I know of, but I'd love to know where he was earlier this morning."

"So would I," Davis said. "The difference is, I have the power to find out."

He concluded his interview with some routine questions about times and logistics and other interactions Tony had had with Andresson earlier in the week. Then Davis said thanks and excused himself.

Tony drove straight to the *Crier's* newsroom to write his story for the web. He knew sticking to the Mackey version, without revealing the victim's name, would be one of the most difficult things he had ever done. He fervently hoped some of these key facts would not be released to anyone until Monday afternoon, so they could appear in the Tuesday edition of the printed paper without being too many hours behind other media, including the inevitable buzz on Twitter and other internet sites. If the word got out too soon, the local paper could get beaten by a full day by the statewide and, oh jeez, the national media.

It occurred to Tony, now that he knew who the victim was, that this was going to be big news on everything from CNN to the *LA Times* to, God help us all, *The National Enquirer*.

Chapter 8

Milan, Italy—May 1989

She wished the windows were shuttered. As she waited alone on a single folding chair in an otherwise empty room, she wished she couldn't see the warm spring sun or the glorious flowers erupting from every apartment's window box, balcony, and rooftop in view. She wished she couldn't hear the sounds of traffic, the urgent calls of every honking horn signaling loudly the newborn optimism throughout Milan as it emerged as a center of commerce on the world stage, and as all of Italy found itself finally included in the European economic revival. The earthquake of 1980 had faded into a historical episode shared by old men on park benches, and the future held the promise of a safer world order as the Soviet Union lost control of the Baltic republics and Gorbachev introduced democratic reforms. Outside that window, the world was good and getting better.

It was a sharp contrast to the overwhelming gloom and dread that filled this dreary room. No. *Not the room*, the young woman thought. *The room is just a room. It's my heart that is aching.*

She looked up as she heard a man's muffled voice say, "Miss, I'm ready." The man spoke through a surgical mask. He also wore a surgical gown and gloves, revealing only his eyes to her. They were kind eyes and, combined with the professional garb, they had the effect of easing her anxiety a little.

She knew the man was a medical student, not yet a fully licensed doctor. The mask served to protect his identity as well as the woman's health. It had not been easy to find him—someone qualified to perform the procedure but willing to do it in absolute secrecy. If he was caught, it would be the end of his medical career. But money talks, and the deal was done. They both knew abortion was legal in Italy, but it came with the requirement that all of the patient's data be submitted to the Laboratory of Epidemiology and Biostatistics at the Instituto di Sanita in Rome.

This, the woman could not allow. As a fashion model, her life was too public and her actions too scrutinized. No hint of this must ever be known, by anyone. She could not bear the thought of her boyfriend, her parents, or God forbid, her brother the priest, ever learning of her pregnancy or its termination. So here she was, alone with a total stranger, in an empty apartamento, located in an anonymous high-rise building still under construction, and furnished only with a table, a lamp, and a handful of medical instruments and supplies.

As the man instructed, she removed her clothes below the waist and lay on the clean, white sheet covering the table. There was no small talk, and the woman squeezed her eyes shut as he worked. The discomfort was minimal, and fifteen minutes later, he was done. He left her alone with a bowl of water, a sponge, and some towels. She never saw him again.

Her hands shook as she cleansed herself and dressed, but she was determined not to cry. She was strong, and she had done what needed to be done. Now she could put the whole affair behind her and get on with her life. She was young, successful, and in love with a good man. She had everything she could want and was anxious to explore the future.

She did not look back as she exited the rooms, descended in the elevator, and strode out onto the busy sidewalk.

***

At 3 a.m. the next morning, a young man was awakened by a dampness in his bed. He hated to disturb his girlfriend, asleep beside him, but clicked on the lamp to investigate. He cried out in alarm when he saw the sheet was soaked in blood. He shouted in utter terror when the woman he loved didn't respond to the noise or the light. He shook her and called her name. Still no response. *Dear God, no.* Her face was white and her breathing nearly imperceptible.

The young man jumped from the bed and ran to the kitchen to call for an ambulance.

Chapter 9

Orney, Iowa—Sunday afternoon, June 21, Present Day

"Dammit, I hate this. I mean, I *really* hate this!"

A red-faced Ben Smalley took a gulp of water from a bottle. He turned from the window behind his desk and stared for a moment at each of the three reporters crowded into his office. Less than a block away, and visible from the window, the first network news truck, one from CBS's regional home in the Twin Cities, was adjusting its satellite dish.

Tony, Doug, and Alison remained quiet, wanting to help but not knowing what to say. They all knew Orney could be filled with similar trucks by the end of the day, but Tony was certain of it. He alone knew the actress had been murdered.

Ben said, "Before you ask, the answer is no. We can't get another special edition of the *Crier* out for tomorrow. As you know, we spent weeks planning for the one we just did. I can't get press operators, layout people, or any of the other production staff here in time to put out anything resembling a quality paper. Even if I could, who would deliver it? Our delivery people don't work on Monday mornings."

"So..." Tony began.

"So we're stuck with what we can do online and on the radio," Ben said. "Sorry, Doug. No offense, but you know my heart's always going to be with the printed vehicle. On the other hand, please believe me, for today and tomorrow, I'm very glad to have you and the radio station on our team. We would really be in a jam without you."

Doug just nodded.

The news of Andresson's death had exploded onto all the cable news channels and social media outlets by 10 a.m. that morning. Tony had fervently hoped her name would remain a secret for more than a few hours, but he hadn't been surprised when word had leaked out almost immediately. With that many people involved at the scene, someone was bound to squeal.

Already, the talking heads on television were speculating about what had happened and were running surprisingly thorough stories about her career and her background. Sadly, and predictably, conspiracy theorists already were "revealing" a myriad of scenarios, ranging from a love triangle involving Andresson, Rowsmith, and Borden, to a human sacrifice by a coven of witches.

What's next? Tony pondered. *Talk of an assassination by the CIA to cover up the fact she was an alien from Pluto?*

Ben brought Tony back to the discussion, asking, "So what are we likely to have tomorrow afternoon that'll be big news for Tuesday's paper?"

"Well, we should get an official cause of death by the end of today."

"Yes, of course that's important, but again, the printed paper is going to be a day behind on that. What else?"

Tony pondered the question for a moment before replying. "There will be a lot of investigative activity, obviously. In fact, Rich Davis already interviewed me." He felt, more than observed, the reactions of his co-workers. "It was no big deal. Because I dined with her Friday night, it turns out I was one of last people to see her alive."

"So were you able to help? Did Agent Davis get anything worthwhile?"

"The only tidbit I shared that sparked any interest was the fact Andresson had split up with Braden Borden, saying he was a jealous hothead."

"Well, I can see why that would get an investigator's motor running. Any indication he was involved in this? Is he here?"

"I honestly don't know," Tony said. "I did some internet research and checked *Variety's* website to see if I could find out where, or if, he's working right now. I haven't found anything on him so far. He's a well-known companion of hers, so the fact he's not all over CNN tells me the big boys are having trouble finding him as well."

"Tony." Ben's voice was very soft.

Tony looked up, feeling his face grow hot. "Sir?"

"Don't do that. Don't refer to the networks or any other media as 'big boys.' I don't want you or any of us to fall into the trap of thinking that just because they have more resources and a bigger audience that they're any more important than we are. This is our town. *We* are the big deal here."

"Understood. You know me and my ego well enough to know that I never think of us as second to anyone. But I can see how that sounded. I'll be more careful in the future."

Ben had already had moved on.

"Doug, I want you to camp out on the medical examiner's

doorstep. I want our station and our website to be the first to report the cause of death."

"On it," Doug said, rising and leaving the room.

"Alison, I'd like you to try to get ahold of Ramesh. If you can't get him, find someone who will talk to you about what this means for the production. I assume they'll close it down, at least for a while, but we need to hear that from an official source."

"You'll have it today. I promise," she said, sounding less confident than the words might imply.

"Tony, you're the one who's closest to law enforcement. I know you and Davis are pals, and you even get Sheriff Mackey to cough up a fact or two once in a while. Try to get to one or both of them, or to someone who will give you some insights into the investigation. I'm guessing they've got a full-scale manhunt underway for Borden. That will tie nicely into the efforts you were already making to find him." Tony nodded and stood to go.

Ben added, almost as though he was talking to himself, "I'm going to try to talk with Darcy Gillson or any of the other actors, especially the women. See if I can get some quotes about their reactions. I'm sure they're horrified, but I wonder whether they're frightened, not knowing what happened."

Tony admitted to himself he hadn't thought of that. While the death—the murder—remained unexplained, others working on the film could easily feel at risk.

Ben clapped his hands once. "Okay, that's it. Let's get to it."

As the reporters filed out, Ben said, "Hey, one more thing."

Tony and Alison stopped and turned to face him.

"Be careful. If Andresson was murdered, then we have a killer in Orney. We don't know who it is, or what he or she might do next. Stay in touch with each other, and keep me posted on who you're talking to and where you're going. Take no unnecessary risks." The last sentence was spoken slowly and firmly, for emphasis.

Tony and Alison swallowed hard in unison and went to work.

***

Despite his best efforts, Tony could find no one willing to talk to him on Sunday afternoon. He wasn't overly frustrated, knowing they had to be incredibly busy and under intense pressure to produce results. At 6 p.m., he took a break from the telephone calls and drove over to the Howdy Stranger to pick up his parents. They had agreed to have dinner before leaving to go back to Iowa City.

When his dad opened the door to the motel room, Tony was surprised to see they weren't packed.

"Well, I got a call from Agent Rooney at the DCI," his dad explained. "He asked me to stick around until tomorrow. They want to interview me about this actress's death."

His father sounded anxious, but Tony told him to think nothing of it.

"They've already interviewed me, Dad. They're talking to everyone who knew or interacted with anyone involved in the movie. You spent time with the cast and obviously you know Bhatt well, so I'd be surprised if they *didn't* interview you."

"I know, but still, it feels weird, and your mother and I were certainly ready to go home."

Tony glanced at his mother's tight frown and realized this delay had a "last straw" quality for her.

"One more day to spend with your loving son," he said, trying to brighten the mood. "Let's go find a steak or something."

Chapter 10

Orney, Iowa—Monday, June 22

By noon Monday, Orney looked like Concord, New Hampshire, on primary election night. Satellite trucks and other news vehicles filled the streets around the Law Enforcement Center. The medical examiner had refused to disclose the cause of death, saying he was waiting for the results of laboratory tests. This had only increased the speculation, the tension, and the swarm of journalists descending on this small city.

Most people said they "knew" it was murder, commenting that a healthy young woman doesn't accidently drown in a closed swimming pool while fully clothed.

At 12:11 p.m., standing at a podium on the sidewalk outside the LEC, Medical Examiner Dr. Lance Torgeson confirmed what everyone suspected. "I am sorry to report the findings of the autopsy are conclusive. Charlotte Andresson died of a blunt force injury to the back of her head. In my opinion, she was not alive when she entered the swimming pool. This is based on the fact there was no water in her lungs, and on the results of other tests conducted on the body."

Doug Tenney was taking a few notes and felt his fingers tighten and his pulse quicken as Torgeson made it official—there was a murderer in Orney. He didn't need to run to report the news in order to keep his commitment to Ben that KKAR would have the story first. A direct feed to the station was plugged into the mult box, the device that supplied audio signals to all of the media present. KKAR was carrying the press conference live on the air as well as on the website. He didn't like sharing the news with everyone in the world at the same time, but it was better than getting beaten by someone else's scoop. It was also good for the *Crier* that the press conference had been delayed until Monday.

Dr. Torgeson continued. "I have estimated the time of death at between 11 p.m. Saturday night and 1:15 a.m. Sunday morning. I'm reasonably confident of this because the body was discovered at about 1:25 a.m. All of the factors used to establish time of death, such as internal organ temperatures, the state of rigor mortis, and others, are more accurate when less time has passed. In addition, of course, we were able to measure the temperature of the water in the pool and include it in our calculations. That concludes everything I have to report today. I will not be taking any questions."

The crowd of reporters exploded with shouts of inquiries and demands, as though the doctor's last sentence had not been spoken. The roar subsided as Dr. Torgeson stepped away and Deputy Daniel Bodke approached the microphone.

After introducing himself as the chief investigator from the Quincy County Sheriff's Department, he said, "I have a few other facts to share. We have established that Ms. Andresson was seen in downtown Orney at about 10:30 p.m. as she left a local establishment that serves food and beverages. She was alone at that time. Obviously, we ask anyone from the public who has knowledge of her movements after that time to contact the Quincy County Sheriff's Department immediately."

A reporter in the crowd began to shout a question but immediately stopped when the deputy continued, "The murder weapon... The murder weapon apparently was a golf club taken from the pro shop at the Orney Country Club. At this point, we believe Miss Andresson was killed in the pro shop, then carried to the swimming pool about thirty yards away."

"Why would someone do that?" a voice from the crowd shouted.

Bodke took a deep breath. "I'm sorry, but I can't speculate on why a murderer does or doesn't do anything. I simply have no idea."

"Was she sexually assaulted?" another voice asked, prompting a murmur through the crowd and causing Doug to wince. He knew the question would be asked, and he was as curious as anyone to know the answer, but it still seemed crass to raise the issue in such a public, brazen way.

Bodke stiffened but responded. He too had known the question would come. He said, "We cannot say with any certainty. There were no injuries to the body beyond the crushed skull and scraped skin on three of her toes, apparently the result of her feet dragging on the pool deck as she was carried to the water. There is evidence of sexual activity, but that would be expected of almost any woman her age. And, I might add, I'm only acknowledging this because Ms. Andresson herself was not shy about discussing such things in the media."

A woman whom Doug knew to be a reporter from the *Des Moines Register*, asked, "Does the use of the golf club indicate a crime of passion? I mean, does the fact the killer grabbed a weapon at hand make it less likely it was premeditated?"

Sharp, Doug thought, making a note of the issue on his pad.

Bodke said, "Again, I cannot speculate about what was or wasn't in the killer's mind. I'm sorry."

The questions continued at length, regarding suspects, the status of the investigation, the resources being devoted to it, why Andresson was in Orney, and on and on. Bodke's responses were a series of "no comments," with the exception of assuring everyone that every possible resource was being used to find the killer. He noted the investigation was a cooperative effort of the Sheriff's Department, the Iowa Division of Criminal Investigation, the Orney Police Department, and the Quincy County Attorney's Office. In Iowa, the county attorney was the person who would decide if and when criminal charges would be filed and would prosecute any case that went to trial.

After forty minutes, Sheriff Mackey finally stepped up to the podium and announced he was ending the press conference. When asked if the briefing would be repeated the next day at noon, the sheriff said no. "We will call another press briefing when we have something to tell you," he said with a note of irritation in his voice. "That may not be until we have arrested the perpetrator, which I hope will be very soon but could take days or weeks. Our success will depend, in part, on the public's assistance in reporting anything they saw or heard on Saturday night or Sunday morning that might be helpful to us. Thank you all. Good day."

The television reporters retreated to their camera setups to do their live remotes. The radio reporters, including Doug, stood their ground and finished their live reports, and the bloggers and casual observers dispersed to their cars and businesses. The guy from the Associated Press announced to no one in particular, "It's hot out here. I'm gonna get a beer."

***

Tony stood up from his chair in the newsroom, telephone cradled under his chin, and gave his now-familiar wave to Ben, who was sitting in his glass-enclosed office in the corner. In less than twenty seconds, Ben was at his side.

Tony tapped mute on his smartphone's screen and said, "He's here. Borden is here in Orney."

"You're sure? How do you know?"

Tony held up his hand and unmuted the phone. "Again, thank you. I really appreciate the call. Yes, yes, I understand. No need to worry."

He ended the call and smiled broadly.

"That was a member of the movie production crew. As you know, I've met and talked with some of them. So when I was making my calls looking for Borden, I put the word out to everyone I knew on the crew, asking them to let me know if they heard from him."

"Good thinking. So…?"

"So this guy just called me to say Borden is lying low at the Hampton Inn here in Orney. Borden claims he came to visit Andresson and now doesn't want anyone to know he's here because he's sure he'll be a suspect in her death. He called this gaffer to ask a favor. He wants some food and beer delivered on the Q.T."

"And despite the request to keep it quiet…"

"Apparently the gaffer likes me well enough to call and spill the beans, or more likely dislikes Borden enough to stick it to him."

Ben nodded as Tony added, "And guess what? This guy said he's only going over there because he's afraid of Borden. Said Borden has a nasty temper, so he didn't dare say no to him."

"So are you going to call Davis and tell him you found Borden?" Ben asked.

"Yes, but not until I confirm he's really here."

Ben smiled and said, "Tony, please. Don't bullshit me. The truth is, you're not calling Davis yet because you want to talk to Borden before he's in custody."

"Well, yeah, but…"

"But nothing." Ben was still smiling. "Don't worry. I agree with you absolutely. All I'm going to add is that you can't go alone. If this guy really is dangerous, you have to discourage him from doing anything foolish when you knock on his door."

"Okay, I'll grab Doug, and we'll both go. He's always ready to jump in with both feet when I set out to do something stupid."

"I guess you're talking about me, huh?"

Tony and Ben turned to see Doug strolling into the newsroom.

Tony laughed and said, "How'd you guess? I'm headed out to face down a hot-tempered murderer. I need someone to go through the door ahead of me. You game?"

"Sure. I'm used to being the brave one while you cower in the back."

"Perfect!" Tony exclaimed. "In fact, I may wait in the car, and you can text me updates."

"Same old, same old. When do we go?"

"Right now," Tony said. "He could get nervous and take off at any moment. I don't want to miss this chance."

"Just give me one minute to make a pit stop and grab my cape," Doug quipped.

The exchange ended when Ben said, "Guys."

They turned to look at their boss.

"All joking aside, be damn careful. No more injured reporters, please. My heart can't take it, and my health insurance rates are going through the roof."

***

The Hampton Inn was quiet at 4 p.m. on a Monday. After stepping through the double glass doors into the lobby, Tony looked for and immediately spotted a house phone on a coffee table in the corner. As he headed in that direction, Doug said, "There's no way Borden registered under his real name. Do you know the room number?"

"Yeah, the gaffer gave it to me when he called."

"So why don't we just go knock on his door? You sure you wanna alert Borden that we're here?"

"As you may recall, the last time I went after someone in a motel room, I ended up getting bashed in the head and held at gunpoint."

"Okay, so what's your point?" Doug was grinning.

Tony was not. "I think we invite him down to the lobby to chat. I'm hoping he'll be slightly less likely to kill both of us in a public place in broad daylight."

Tony dialed the number and listened as the phone rang. Six, eight, ten unanswered rings.

"Striking out? Maybe he left already."

"I don't think so. Did you see the Escalade in the parking lot with out-of-state plates? That looks like the kind of vehicle Borden would rent. I think he's just playing hard to get."

Tony dialed and again let the phone ring multiple times.

Finally, someone picked up, and a man nearly shouted, "What?"

"Mr. Borden?" Tony asked.

There was a long pause before the voice said, "Dammit. Who is this? How did you find me?"

"This is Tony Harrington from the *Orney Town Crier*, the local newspaper. My colleague and I would like to talk with you, if you could spare a few minutes."

"This shithole town has a newspaper? Huh. Well, why would I want to talk with you?"

"We are, of course, covering the death of Miss Andresson. She told me Friday night that the two of you were, shall we say, close. I thought perhaps you would share a few thoughts about her. You know, to help our readers get a good sense of who she was."

"You talked to Char? On Friday night? Why were you with her on Friday night?"

Jeez, Tony thought. *The reports of a jealous boyfriend were not exaggerated.*

"I was invited to have pizza with the director and cast. I only spoke with her a little, as part of the larger group, so I thought you could help me fill in some of the blanks. By the way, I'm very sorry for your loss," Tony added, realizing he meant it.

"Yeah. Well, thanks, but that doesn't help me or her, does it?"

Tony didn't know what to say to that.

Borden added, "Do you know what happened? Who killed her?"

"No, Mr. Borden, I don't. But I'm happy to share everything I do know if you'd like to come down to the lobby to talk."

"You're here? At the Hampton? Yeah, okay. Gimme a few minutes."

Twenty minutes later, the three men were seated around a small table in the common area most often used for the continental breakfast served every morning.

Borden was a big guy, over six feet and 200 pounds, all muscle. He had dark, wavy hair parted on the side, a two-day stubble on his face, and piercing, dark eyes. His classic leading man look was blemished today only by the weariness in his manner and some redness in his eyes.

At first glance, Tony wondered if Borden had been drinking, but after shaking hands and sitting, he decided the actor was sleep-deprived and perhaps had been crying.

"You first," Borden said abruptly. "What can you tell me?"

Tony wanted to tell him to read the *Crier's* articles online but decided that would get him nowhere. So he turned to Doug and said, "You were at the Sheriff's press conference. Why don't you share everything you learned?

Doug nodded and began. He laid out all the facts about the crime as he knew them—where and when she'd been found, the nature of the wound, and some other facts Bodke had shared.

"What the hell was she doing at a closed swimming pool?" Borden demanded.

Tony shrugged, "No one knows."

"These two people who supposedly found her, the ones the cops said were just unlucky. I want to talk to them. I want their names."

Tony responded, trying to use his most calming voice. "No one has released their names. You'll have to ask the sheriff for them."

"God, the sheriff." Borden leaned forward and put his head in his hands. "I'm gonna have to answer his questions, aren't I? He's gonna think it was me."

"So was it?" Doug asked. "Did you kill her?"

Suddenly, all hell broke loose. Borden jumped out of his seat, knocking the table over on its side. He leapt toward Doug, his fist pulled back, ready to strike.

Tony reacted without thinking. He bent low and lunged forward, catching Borden's gut with his shoulder. Borden tumbled backward, and both men ended up on the floor. Both were just as quickly back on their feet.

Borden was a trained fighter. One side benefit of starring in action movies was the receipt of considerable instruction in hand-to-hand combat.

Tony stepped back and took a deep breath, glad for the martial arts training he had been doing for the past two years. He said, "Stop this. Doug didn't mean…"

Borden came for him, swinging a hard right. Tony stepped into it, letting the punch fly harmlessly behind his head. However, Borden was quick, and an immediate jab from his left caught Tony in the kidney. It hurt like hell, but as Tony spun, he lifted his right elbow and caught Borden's nose. He heard the crunch and felt the cartilage give.

Borden reared back, grabbing for his face as blood poured out of his nostrils. "You son of a bitch!" he screamed, and he came at Tony again.

This time, Tony stepped back and to the left, grabbing Borden's arm and pulling him forward. Tony brought his elbow down hard as Borden stumbled, catching the actor just below his ear. The big man crashed to the floor, sending two chairs sliding across the tile. One smashed into the coffee cart, knocking the glass carafe to the floor, where it shattered.

Tony was faintly aware of a young woman yelling at them to stop, and of the apparent absence of Doug in the brawl. *Shouldn't this be two against one?*

He didn't have time to dwell on it. Borden was clambering back to his feet. This time, he held a glistening shard of broken glass in his right hand.

"Borden, stop!" Tony said. "This is crazy. All we did was ask you a question."

Borden's eyes had narrowed to slits, and blood covered the sneer on his lips. "You broke my nose, you little prick. Now you're gonna pay for that."

Borden raised the makeshift dagger high, and then suddenly dropped face-first to the floor. Doug was standing behind where Borden had been, holding the tire iron from Tony's Ford Explorer.

Both friends were breathing heavily.

"Is he dead?" Doug asked, his voice shaking.

Tony bent down and checked Borden's breathing and pulse. "Nah, he's okay. Thanks. I haven't gotten to the lesson at Jun's dojang yet about defeating someone who's armed with broken glass and crazier than a loon."

"No problem," Doug said, relaxing a little and lifting the tire iron into the light. "As you can see, I'm a big believer in the martial arts as well. I call this curved end karate and this straight end tae kwon do. I decided to use karate on him today."

Tony choked on a laugh and collapsed into a chair.

***

The EMTs arrived a short time later. As they lifted Borden into the ambulance, the parking lot began filling with half the law enforcement personnel in Iowa and half the news media from the rest of the country. A movie star involved in a fight and taken to the hospital was big news under any circumstances. The fact it had come two days after his former lover had been killed, and in the same small town, made the story a sensation.

At the police chief's request, the motel manager locked the front doors. Only the crime scene technicians would be allowed back into the lobby. Tony managed to call and alert Ben to the news before officers took away his phone and locked him in the back of a police cruiser. Over the next hour, interviews with Tony, Doug, and the motel desk clerk occurred in the backs of separate patrol vehicles.

After giving his statement, Tony was left alone in the car for what seemed like forever. He was on the verge of shouting protests and banging on the window when Sheriff Mackey pulled open the driver's side door and slid into the front seat.

"Hello, Sheriff," Tony said, trying to sound pleasant.

"Harrington…" The sheriff paused, appearing to search for the right words. "Harrington, do you have any idea what a giant pain in the ass you are?"

"Well…"

"Shut up. It was a rhetorical question."

Tony waited.

"So here's the deal. Your story, Tenney's story, and the statement of the desk clerk all seem to match. Lucky for you, son. It would make my day to lock you up for a while, just on general principle."

"Now, Sheriff…"

"Shut up. Based on what the three of you have told us, Mr. Borden is guilty of assault with a deadly weapon. He hasn't been formally charged yet. He's not awake, so he can't acknowledge his Miranda rights. The ER doc tells me it's just a matter of time. The good news is, we now know where he is, and we have in custody a person of interest in the death of Miss Andresson. The bad news is, because of you and Tenney, our suspect is in la-la land and won't be telling us anything for hours, at least.

"And by the way," the sheriff continued, "if he wakes up and claims amnesia about the night of the murder, I'm gonna come back and shoot you myself."

Tony smiled but made no comment.

The gravity returned to the sheriff's voice. "If he does wake up today or tomorrow, we'll hang onto him as long as we can until the judge holds a bond hearing. He'll probably make bail, so you might want to be sure the locks on your doors and windows are good. Any questions?"

"About a million," Tony said, "but for now, just one. When can I get out of here?"

"I'm cutting you loose now," the sheriff said.

"Thanks."

"Don't thank me," Mackey said, clearly irritated. "Just do me a favor and learn a lesson. Next time, call us first, and don't put yourself in these situations."

Tony didn't respond, knowing that wasn't going to happen, and not wanting to lie to the sheriff.

The sheriff opened the car door from the outside, and Tony climbed out.

"Oh, and Harrington," the sheriff said suddenly.

Tony turned to face him.

"You might want to go to the Ford garage and buy another tire iron. Your old one's gonna be in an evidence locker for a long time."

Tony smiled. "Good advice, Sheriff. A guy never knows when he might need to bash someone in the head. Thanks."

𝕿𝖔𝖜𝖓 𝕮𝖗𝖎𝖊𝖗

Film star charged with felony assault

Braden Borden hospitalized after attacking two reporters

Ben Smalley, Editor

ORNEY, Iowa – Braden Borden, famous for numerous roles in Hollywood action movies, was hospitalized Monday afternoon at the Quincy County Medical Center and charged with a felony assault after attacking Tony Harrington and Doug Tenney, both staff writers for the *Orney Town Crier* and KKAR Radio, according to Quincy County Sheriff George Mackey. The sheriff reported Borden is in stable condition with a head injury and a broken nose. He is under guard at the medical center.

Once released from the hospital, Borden will be held at the Quincy County Jail until a bail hearing can be set, the sheriff said.

According to Harrington, he and Tenney were interviewing Borden in the lobby of the Hampton Inn on Highway 26 when Borden became agitated and attacked Tenney. Harrington attempted to intervene and found himself engaged in a fight with the actor. A glass coffee pot was broken in the scuffle.

"Mr. Borden threatened me with a broken piece of glass," Harrington said. "That's when Doug Tenney struck him in the head."

The incident occurred while Tenney and Harrington were interviewing Borden regarding Charlotte Andresson, the actress who was found dead at the Orney Country Club early Sunday morning. Borden and Andresson had previously been in a relationship, according to multiple sources who knew Andresson.

It is not known why Borden was in Orney, Sheriff Mackey said at a press briefing Monday night.

Borden is not part of the cast for the movie currently being filmed in Orney, according to the movie's director Ramesh Bhatt.

The lobby of the Hampton Inn was temporarily closed Monday while crime scene technicians from the Iowa Division of Criminal Investigation (DCI) collected the weapons used in the fight and other evidence.

Mackey said the two reporters will not be charged with any wrongdoing. "It's clear from all the evidence and from a motel clerk's eyewitness account, that the two reporters were defending themselves from an unprovoked attack," the sheriff said. "We're just glad there were no other injuries and..."

Town Crier

Mystery surrounds murder of Hollywood actress in Orney

Sheriff George Mackey says "every available resource" will be used to find killer

Doug Tenney and Tony Harrington, Staff Writers

ORNEY, Iowa – Authorities have no suspects and no known motive in the brutal slaying of Charlotte Andresson, 28, a well-known motion picture actress who was found dead at the Orney Country Club early Sunday morning, Deputy Sheriff Daniel Bodke said at a press conference Monday afternoon. Speaking from the steps of the Quincy County Law Enforcement Center (LEC), Bodke said Andresson was last seen alive in downtown Orney Saturday night.

Her body was discovered several hours later, floating in the swimming pool of the country club. She had been killed by a blow to the head with a golf club and was thrown in the water afterward, according to County Medical Examiner Dr. Lance Torgeson, who also spoke at the press conference.

Bodke asked that anyone with knowledge of Andresson's movements after 10 p.m. Saturday please call the Sheriff's Department Hotline.

Andresson was in Orney as a member of the cast of the movie *Murder Beyond Them*, being filmed on location in Orney. Director Ramesh Bhatt said he and all members of the cast and crew are "devastated" by Andresson's death.

"She was a wonderful person and solid performer," Bhatt said. "She had a long career and a long life ahead of her. It is just impossible to think we'll not have the pleasure of working with her again, or of seeing that magnificent smile, or of hearing that infectious laugh."

Regarding the impact of the death on the filming, Bhatt said, "Well, of course everything will be on hold for a while. The authorities have asked everyone to stay in town, at least for a few days, to expedite the investigation. So we'll be here. After things settle down and we get over the shock, we'll start looking at options for changing the script or re-casting the role. It makes me indescribably sad to even contemplate that. Charlotte was a perfect choice for the part."

Quincy County Sheriff George Mackey said every available resource from the county, the City of Orney, and the State Division of Criminal Investigation (DCI) is being employed in the search for Andresson's killer. "We are determined…

Chapter 11

Milan, Italy—June 1989

The young man stared across the kitchen table at the woman he loved. She looked pale and thin, almost fragile. She was wearing a light blue terrycloth robe brought with her from the hospital. Her hair was down and uncombed. She looked resigned, defeated. It was a far cry from the vivacious fashion model he was used to seeing in that chair. Her eyes were cast toward the table, eyeing her tea as if searching for a magical answer in the swirling, dark liquid. In the brief moments when she glanced up, he could see her eyes were red. She had been crying again.

The man knew they were at a crossroads—one of those times in life when the words spoken, or left unspoken, would determine everything that followed. Which path to take? What choice to make? Quite literally, what life did he want?

His heart had been shattered and his confidence shaken. He had been scared shitless, and then, when he had learned what had happened, he'd been devastated. Later, the devastation turned to anger. He wanted to lash out, to scream at someone, at her. Then he would see her, and the anger would melt away. When he asked himself that last question – What life do I want? – the answer was clear.

He spoke her name, and she looked up. "I love you," he said.

"You can't…"

"Please, hear me. I love you. I wish you hadn't done this. Of course I do."

"I didn't think… I didn't know… I…"

"My love, please. Be quiet and listen." He reached across the table and took her hands in his. "What's done is done. I love you. If you still love me, then we must pledge to put this in the past and never talk of it or think of it again. We must start over and build the life we dreamed of… before."

Tears inched down the young woman's face. "You are such a good man. You know I love you. I do. More than you could ever know. I loathe what I have done. I can't understand why or how it happened."

"Shh, enough. It's done. It's history. Now we move forward."

Suddenly, the woman was sobbing. She shuddered and said, "But you don't know the worst."

The man could not imagine what could be worse than knowing the woman he loved had cheated on him, had become pregnant with another man's child, had terminated the pregnancy, and had nearly died.

"It's fine," he said. "Whatever it is, we'll get over it—I'll get over it—and we'll move on."

The tears continued. Between gasps for air, the woman said, "At the hospital… in the hospital, the doctor… the doctor told me…" She struggled to compose herself. Finally, she drew a deep breath, looked into his eyes and said, "I will not have children."

The young man looked down, squeezing his eyes tightly closed, still gripping the woman's hands. After several long seconds, he looked up. "Do you love me?"

"Yes, I swear."

"Do you pledge your faithfulness to me?"

"Yes."

"Do you want to marry me and build a life together?"

"Yes."

"Then it matters not. We choose a future together. Nothing can stop us. No one can hurt us again."

The woman's lips stopped quivering, and just a hint of color touched her cheeks. A spark of light returned to her eyes.

"There is only one thing I ask."

The light faded, and the woman tensed.

The man said, "I must know who it was."

"But why? What good can…?"

"Please don't question me. I swear to you he will never know that I know. It is simply that we cannot have secrets between us. You cannot share a secret with him from which I am excluded. That I could not bear. So I must know. Who was it?"

She told him.

Chapter 12

Orney, Iowa—Tuesday, June 23, Present Day

"So did Borden do it?" Charles Harrington asked, spearing a lump of scrambled eggs on his plate. He and Tony were enjoying a late breakfast at Willie's.

Tony swallowed a bite of pancakes smothered in maple syrup and said, "Who knows? He certainly has the disposition for it. He attacked Doug and me for almost no reason. Having seen him in a rage, it's easy to imagine him attacking an ex-girlfriend."

Charles nodded. "Motive, means, and opportunity. All three components are there. I'm just surprised he stuck around after the deed was done. He had to know that if he was discovered in Orney, he would be at the top of the sheriff's list of suspects."

"Good point, but on the other hand, he was at the top of the list anyway. Maybe he thought if he ran, the authorities would find him anyway, and his running would only make him look more guilty."

The two men contemplated that as they chewed. Tony added,

"On the other hand, when I first met him, I could tell he was exhausted and had been crying. Of course, that doesn't mean he's innocent. He could be grieving her death equally hard whether he killed her himself or someone else did it."

"Hmm," Charles mumbled as he chewed another mouthful of hash browns. He swallowed and said, "God, if he did do this, I hope they string him up."

Tony looked up, eyebrows raised. It was an unusually blunt and aggressive thing for his father to say. As Tony studied the lines in his dad's face, it dawned on him that his father was mourning.

"Dad, I'm an idiot," Tony said, setting down his fork.

His father looked surprised at the sudden change in subject.

"It hadn't occurred to me until just now how devastating this whole incident must be for you."

"For me? No. Well, yes, but no more than anyone else."

"Well, you knew and liked Charlotte. But even more heart-breaking for you personally is the impact this is having on your friend Ramesh. And you have a big stake in what happens to the film. It's your screenplay that's at risk, so it's only natural that this whole thing is getting you down."

"Really, Tony, I'm okay. Well, except for being stuck in a road-side motel with a cranky wife." Charles smiled and took a swallow of coffee.

"Okay, Dad, I get it. But please, remember you can talk to me. Don't keep everything bottled inside."

Charles smiled. "Okay, Dr. Freud. I promise to visit the couch before I do anything crazy."

***

As Charles's sedan disappeared around the corner of the town square, Tony mentally slapped himself in the forehead. "I forgot to ask him why he's still in Orney," he said aloud to the empty street.

Tony shrugged it off and headed to the *Town Crier* building. He was unsure what kind of day it would be, filled with unanswered questions and lots of waiting, or the rush of breaking news as deputies and DCI agents interviewed Braden Borden, now awake in his hospital bed and perhaps charged with the murder of Charlotte Andresson.

To Tony's disappointment, it was very much the first scenario. At 6 p.m., he could wait no longer, either in terms of his growing desire to hear *something*, anything, or in terms of the looming deadline for the morning paper.

He called Davis's cell phone.

"Hey, Tony."

"Hey, Rich. Just checking in."

"Yeah, I figured. Sorry to disappoint you, but I got nothing."

"Nothing-nothing?"

"Well, nothing I can share with you at this time."

"Do you want to go off the record? I'm dying, here."

"I understand that, but no. There's nothing worth telling even if we did."

"Can you at least confirm you've talked to Borden? Is he saying anything?"

"Well, I prefer you get it from the sheriff, but yes, he and I interviewed Mr. Borden today. He acknowledged he lost his temper and threatened you and Doug, but denies he attempted any physical harm."

Tony snorted, but otherwise didn't respond.

"He also denies he killed Miss Andresson. Said he arrived in Orney Saturday evening and never saw her. Said he was as shocked as everyone else when he heard the news."

"What do you think? Are you buying it?"

Davis chuckled. "How do you do this to me? Okay, Tony, *now* we're off the record. Between you and me, I'm unsure what to think. I'm certainly not ready to just take his word for it that he's innocent, but I'm not picking up big vibes that he's lying. Granted, it's hard to know what to think when your interview subject is lying in a hospital bed loaded up with pain killers. Not to mention the fact he's a trained actor. Obviously, we'll keep digging, hoping to find an eyewitness or some kind of direct evidence to tie him, or anyone, to the crime. Back on the record, I would say simply that we talked with Mr. Borden, he was cooperative, and the investigation continues."

"Thanks, Rich. You're the best," Tony said, leaning back in his chair.

"Remember what I said, Tony. I prefer you get your report from the sheriff. It's his case, and I don't want to piss him off."

"I'll do my best, I promise," Tony said and ended the call.

When he called the Sheriff's Department and identified himself, Marlys, the evening dispatcher and jail matron said, "Oh, Mr. Harrington, I have a message for you from Sheriff Mackey."

Tony was surprised, but he scooted his chair up to the keyboard to take down whatever it was. He could hear Marlys shuffling some papers.

"Here it is," she said. "Sheriff Mackey told me to expect your call and to tell you that whatever you got from Rich Davis was fine. He didn't need to talk to you."

"That's it?"

"Yessiree. That's it," Marlys said, her smile reaching him through the phone line.

Tony thanked her and hung up, grinning. Mackey always found a way to surprise him. He had known Tony would talk to Davis first, and he trusted the two of them to agree on a story that would support, and not harm, the investigation.

The little journalist conscience that lived in the back of Tony's brain wondered in passing if there was such a thing as being too predictable, or too close to a source, or too collaborative. On the other hand, if he did his job any other way, he wouldn't have the information Rich had just shared, information no other media outlets would have.

In the end, it didn't matter. Tony was terrible at suppressing his instincts or changing his own behavior. He was who he was. It got results, and his boss liked him. That was good enough.

***

Just after 7 p.m., Tony's desk phone rang.

"Tony Harrington. Can I help you?"

"Tony, it's Darcy. Darcy Gillson."

As if there's any other Darcy on the planet right now. Tony took a deep breath. "Oh, hi, uh, Darcy. Hello. What's up?"

"Well, to be honest, I was wondering when you get off work tonight."

Tony's heart stopped cold. His mind went blank. What had she just said?

Darcy waited a beat. When Tony didn't respond, she said, "I'm sorry. This must sound terribly forward, or maybe even inappropriate in light of what's happened. But the fact is, we've been asked to stay in town, and the only people I know around here, except you, are the cast and crew from the movie. They're all morose and going stir crazy, and I can't bear the thought of another night of whining and moaning. I thought maybe you and I could have a meal together and just talk, you know, about normal stuff." She waited. "Tony? Are you there?"

"Uh, yeah, of course. Sorry. You just took me by surprise. I would be happy... *honored*, in fact, to buy you dinner. I've filed my big story for the day, so I can leave anytime. When and where can I find you?"

"Tony, please don't say honored. I'm just a woman looking for a night out. If you try to treat me like some kind of princess, I'll... I'll scream. I swear I will."

"Okay," Tony laughed. "I get it. I promise to be rude and self-absorbed."

It was Darcy's turn to laugh. "Perfect," she said. "Eight o'clock at the Hampton Inn. I hear you know where it is."

"Do I ever," Tony said as his phone beeped that the call had ended.

***

When Tony pulled into the carport of the motel, Darcy was waiting outside the front door. She was wearing jeans and a blue Oxford shirt with the sleeves rolled up. She wore sandals on her otherwise bare feet. Her blonde locks were brushed out and falling to her shoulders. To Tony, she looked perfect—not overtly sexy or flamboyant, just simple, down-home gorgeous.

He had planned to hop out and play the gentlemen, opening the door for her, but she beat him to it. She was in the passenger seat of the SUV the moment it stopped.

"Hey," Tony said. "You look great."

"Thanks. You, too." She leaned over and kissed him on the cheek. "And thank you so much for doing this. You'll never know how excited I am that you said yes."

"Oh, I think I can imagine," Tony said with a smile.

"I'm not too casual, am I?" she asked, looking down at her

jeans and sandals as she snapped her seatbelt into place.

"In Orney? Are you kidding? You might be the best-dressed person we see tonight, except, of course, for Gretchen. She always wears a sequined low-cut top to the Iron Range Tap."

"Does that work for her? Maybe I should have tried it."

"Well, I can assure you, it would work better for you than for her. I'm guessing Gretchen tips the scales at about three hundred and ten pounds."

Darcy whistled. Tony wondered when he had last heard someone actually whistle. It was a nice sound.

"Trust me," he said, "your attire is perfect. Nothing could be better for a night on the town."

"Except for what you're wearing, of course."

Tony blushed a little. He hadn't been sure what to wear, so he was in charcoal gray dress slacks and a maroon polo shirt. "You just got lucky. I'm required to wear these pants at least once a year, and tonight was the night. If anyone sees me in these, they'll think we just came from a wake."

Darcy giggled.

Speaking of nice sounds, Tony thought. He put the Explorer in gear and asked, "So what kind of food do you like?"

"I'm not particular, really. It's your town, so you choose."

"Tell you what," Tony said. "I'll name two places I love, and you pick between them. Deal?"

"Deal," she said.

Tony named a popular Tex-Mex restaurant that served margaritas in glasses as big as bowling balls. His second suggestion was The Acropolis, a family-owned Greek restaurant. He said, "The food there is wonderful, but I have to warn you that the owner will make you eat every bite of what you order. He's a bit of a local character. Umm, maybe total looney-toon would be a better description."

"Oh, let's do that," Darcy said. "It sounds fun and unique."

"Yep, it certainly is that," Tony said, turning toward the west edge of town.

The Acropolis sat on top of a hill a few blocks north of Veterans Memorial Park. The entrance faced the side street on the north, and the entire west wall was windows offering a view down into the wooded valley that eventually reached the Raccoon River. As Tony and Darcy entered the restaurant, the summer sun was just dropping below the trees, filling the dining room with an orange glow and casting an intricate pattern of shadows on every surface.

"Do you want to see a menu first?" Tony asked as they approached the maître d' stand.

Darcy leaned in and squeezed his arm with both hands. "No," she whispered. "It looks wonderful."

Tony felt his temperature rise about fifteen degrees. He wasn't sure if it was from her words or her grip on his arm—probably both.

Gus Ariti burst through the swinging door at the back of the dining room and came charging toward the front.

"Tony!" he cried. "My friend. Welcome back. It has been too long. Look at you. You're practically skin and bones. You need to let Gus take better care of you, and... My, my, who is this lovely creature on your arm? By the gods, I swear you've brought Aphrodite back to the Acropolis."

Darcy smiled broadly and held out her right hand. "I'm Darcy," she said. "Tony has told me of his great fondness for the Acropolis and for its owner."

Gus beamed. He ignored Darcy's outstretched hand and placed his hands on her shoulders. "Miss Darcy, welcome." He kissed her once on each cheek, then turned and offered her his arm. "I have a very special table for goddesses right over here by the window."

Darcy giggled and took his arm. Tony followed. As they walked, Gus made one motion with his free hand. By the time they reached their table, just a dozen paces into the dining room, a young man and woman were there to greet them with menus, warm bread, olive oil, and a bottle of wine.

Once seated, with the wine poured, Gus took a deep bow and said, "Miss Darcy, as Tony knows, my place is in the kitchen. I will leave you in the capable hands of Amara. But if you need anything, anything at all, you ask for me, okay?"

Darcy nodded. "I promise."

Gus smiled and bowed again. "And in return, I promise to give you the best meal of your life. Before you finish, you will be begging Gus to come back with you to Hollywood to be your chef."

As he strode away, Darcy laughed and said, "Well, I guess that answers the question about whether he recognized me or not."

"Even if he didn't, he undoubtedly thinks it's a safe guess. He knows just about everybody in town. If he sees me out with someone new while there's a movie filming in town, it's pretty easy to put two and two together. Especially when that someone new is beautiful enough to be a movie star."

Darcy's face flushed a little. She said, "Thanks, Tony. I'm happy to take that as a compliment. But please, let's have that be the last reference to stardom or movies tonight. Remember, I invited you out to talk about other things."

"That's right," Tony said brightly. "So, how 'bout them Hawkeyes!"

Darcy stared at him blankly, and Tony burst out laughing. "Well, you can't say I didn't try."

The evening progressed ideally from there. The food was outstanding, the service from Amara was exceptional, and the conversation was completely engaging. At one point Tony asked about her advanced degrees.

"I understand the master's in theater, but tell me about the history degree. How did that come about?"

"No great story to share," she said. "I've always loved history. When I finished my theater degree, I was seeing someone, so I wasn't ready to leave Pittsburgh."

"Carnegie Mellon University, right?"

"Yes, that's right. You've done your homework."

"It's what journalists do."

"Well, don't dig too deeply. I don't want a follow-up article about my time with Jake."

Tony made a typing motion on an invisible keyboard. "Note: no articles about that bastard Jake."

Darcy nearly choked on her moussaka. When she managed to swallow, she was still laughing. She finally said, "Anyway, I was there, I could afford it, and I needed something to do, so I went back to grad school. CM has a small but excellent history program in the College of Humanities. One of the tracks is an emphasis in African studies, so I signed up."

"African history?" Tony prompted.

"Well, I think I surprised them a little. The Africa I wanted to study was Egypt. I pretty much created the curriculum I wanted. Finishing school roughly coincided with finishing Jake, so I came back west and went to work."

"I have to admit, I don't know squat about Egypt," Tony said, not wanting to hear anything more about the former boyfriend. "Tell me something about it."

"Okay, here's a factoid you can use to win a bar bet now and then. Take a guess at the answer to this: When King Tut was the ruler of Egypt, how old was the Great Pyramid?"

"When King Tut…"

Darcy interrupted him. "Picture this. You're Tutankhamen. You're a teenage pharaoh. You gaze across the plains of Giza at the gleaming white Great Pyramid. How old is the building you're admiring?"

"Gleaming white?"

"Yes. If you didn't know, for most of the pyramid's existence, it was covered in smooth, white limestone. It's only been in relatively recent history that the limestone was removed by vandals, looters, and even those needing materials for other projects. Now stop trying to change the subject and answer the question."

"Well, since you hinted the answer will surprise me, I'm going to guess it wasn't new. I think I read somewhere that whoever started it was one of the earlier rulers of the Egyptian Empire, so I'm going to guess it was pretty old. Maybe a hundred years old or more at that time."

Darcy smiled triumphantly and vocalized a game show buzzer. "Nope," she said. "When King Tut ruled Egypt, the Great Pyramid was one thousand, three hundred years old."

"Wow."

"Hell yes, wow. Think about that. He was ruler of a kingdom that had existed for more than two thousand years. He was admiring buildings and monuments that were awe-inspiring feats of engineering and construction, created by people who were as far in his past as Jesus is in ours, or nearly so. Surrounded by such achievements and wealth and military power, I bet neither King Tut nor any of the pharaohs ever conceived that there could be a day when Egypt wouldn't rule a huge part of the known world." Darcy was becoming more animated as she talked. "I think it's so important for people— for Americans, especially—to understand this. We get so caught up in how great our country is, and how invincible we are, but we're just starting out. Civilizations and cultures that lasted ten times longer than we've existed still declined and fell into oblivion. It's an important lesson in why we should never take things for granted, why we must always be proactive in preserving our democracy."

"I can't argue with you," Tony said. "It's a great point. Of course, I work in the newspaper business. Someone's always challenging freedom of the press and suggesting we need to be more regulated, or more liable for the consequences of reporting the news. In other words, journalists are constantly reminded of how fragile our freedoms are. We never take them for granted."

"I hadn't thought about it from your perspective," she said, and then suddenly changed subjects. "Do I really have to eat all of this?"

"You might escape Gus's wrath, being a goddess and all, but I can't promise. And don't forget, dessert is coming."

"Dear God, I'm gonna explode," she groaned.

Eventually they finished, paid the tab, thanked Amara, exchanged more kisses and hugs with Gus, and escaped into the warm night air.

"That was wonderful, but I really am uncomfortably full," Darcy said. "Can we walk for a while?"

"Sure. The park isn't far from here. Let's walk there."

As they strolled, they talked some more about Egypt and about Tony's work, but eventually the conversation ebbed. Darcy reached out and found his hand and clutched it to her side as they walked. Tony felt as if his fingers would burst into flames any moment.

Once they entered the park and followed the path into the trees, the darkness was nearly complete. Only a trickle of moonlight found its way through the maze of branches.

"It's kinda creepy," Darcy said.

"I think you're safe in Orney," Tony said, pulling free of her hand and putting his arm around her shoulders.

"Normally, I'd agree, but in light of what happened to Char..."

Tony was embarrassed. "Jeez, you're right. I should have thought of that. Do you want to go?"

"Just one thing first," she said, turning to face him in the dark. She reached up, put her arms around his neck, and kissed him. This was no peck on the cheek. It was a long, warm, passionate, wonderful kiss.

When they separated, Tony said, "Darcy, I…"

She put a finger to his lips. "Shhh."

She turned him around and headed back on the path toward the entrance to the park. She said, "I'd like to see the newspaper—the building, I mean. Can you take me there at this hour?"

"Absolutely. It's only ten o'clock. People will still be working in the production areas. The newsroom will be winding down, but we'll have no trouble seeing whatever you want."

Tony parked in the alley behind the building and took Darcy in through the back door. It wasn't the most attractive first impression of the building, but it's what he experienced every day. Once through a storeroom, they emerged into the newsroom. Only one person was immediately visible, and she was working on the copy desk, probably doing some final proofreading or page layouts for the latest news. She waved but didn't look up. All the reporters were gone, and most of the lights were out.

Tony soon noticed the glow from Ben's glass-enclosed office in the corner. His boss was leaning back in his chair, his feet on the desk, reading large printouts of something.

"Come on. We should say hello," Tony said.

Ben apparently noticed the movement outside his office because he sat up and waved them in before Tony could reach the door to knock.

"I hope we're not intruding," Tony said. "Ben, I'm sure you remember Darcy Gillson from the gathering at Freed's a couple of weeks ago. Darcy, Ben Smalley, owner, publisher, and editor of Iowa's finest newspaper."

Ben stepped around his desk and shook her hand. "Intruding? Hell, no. I'm reading financial reports from our accounting department. It's about the most depressing thing I do every week. I'm glad to have the diversion, and I'm certainly glad to welcome one of Orney's most esteemed visitors."

The three of them settled into a brief, comfortable conversation. Darcy asked about Ben's past, and after hearing he had been a reporter in Detroit and Baltimore, asked how he had ended up in Orney.

"It's pretty simple, really," Ben said. "I'd been to Iowa a few times, covering the presidential caucuses, and came to love the place. When I decided I didn't want to be bossed around anymore, that I wanted to own my own paper, this seemed like the obvious place to do it. The *Crier* was for sale, and as they say, the rest is history."

Tony knew the real story behind Ben's departure from the East Coast had been more dramatic and painful than what he had just revealed, but also knew Ben shared those details with very few people. Tony felt honored to be one of them.

Ben said, "I'm truly sorry about Ms. Andresson. This whole situation must be horrible for you and your castmates. Were you close to her?"

"Thanks," Darcy said. "We were friendly, but not really friends. I enjoyed her company and admired her work, but we never really bonded. As you may know, she was very outgoing and sometimes outrageous. She loved being in the public eye. I'm pretty much the opposite. I look at acting as a craft. I make a wonderful living doing it, and I take pride in my work, but when we wrap for the day and go home, I strive to live as normally as possible, which is difficult most days."

"I understand completely," Ben said, "which, by the way, makes me all the more grateful that you gave that wonderful interview to Alison Frank."

"I was happy to do it. I thought she did a very thorough and professional job. If all the reporters were like her, being a successful actress would be a much more tolerable life."

"Thanks for saying so. I'll pass the compliment along."

Tony said, "Darcy asked to see the *Crier*, so I'm just going to show her around for a few minutes."

"That's about all it will take. Knock yourselves out. I think there's some six-hour-old coffee left in the pot if you want some."

"Thanks, but no," Darcy said, rubbing her stomach.

"We just ate at Acropolis," Tony explained.

"Ahh, you gave her the Gus treatment. That's a little cruel on a first date, don't you think?"

Tony and Darcy looked at each other. Neither had thought overtly about the fact it was a first date.

"Gus thinks she's a Greek goddess, so he went easy on her," Tony chuckled.

Darcy said, "I can barely walk. I can't imagine how he could have forced any more food into me."

"Trust me, he can," Tony and Ben said in unison, and laughed.

When Ben had retreated to his office, Tony walked Darcy across the room to his desk.

She said, "So this is where it all happens? It seems too modest for a man of your talents."

"Modest, yes, but just right," Tony said, unsure if she was being serious or sarcastic. His arm swept across the room. "It's no ivory tower. There are no trappings of greatness or honor. Even the awards we've won are not displayed here. It's a very functional, practical place. Everyone has what they need to do their jobs, and when collaboration is required, there are very few walls, few barriers of any kind. The focus is on the importance of the task, not the importance of the people doing it."

Darcy seemed to understand, and Tony continued.

"Do me a favor. Close your eyes."

She did.

"Take a deep breath, through your nose."

She did.

"Do you smell that? It's a hundred and twelve years of ink, paper, paste, darkroom chemicals, tears, and more than a little sweat permeating every surface. More to the point, it's the aroma of a hundred and twelve years of reporting the news, of informing, entertaining, and challenging people to think. It's a century of freedom, and of protecting that freedom."

Darcy opened her eyes. "Very eloquent, Mr. Harrington."

Tony didn't acknowledge the compliment, but said, "When I come in here alone, late at night, and hear the old wooden floors creak, or feel the rumble of the presses in the basement, I have no trouble seeing this room as it was a century ago, with manual typewriters clacking away and copyboys scurrying between writers and editors. It's a magical place, an *important* place."

He took a deep breath and looked at her. "Nowadays, with laptops and wifi, I can write anywhere. But I choose to write here whenever I can. When I sit here…" Tony placed his hands on the back of his desk chair, "I am reminded of all those people who came before me, and who sit around me today, who have worked so hard to make the *Crier* a great community newspaper. Especially him." Tony nodded toward Ben's office. "I have the greatest boss in the world of journalism, maybe the greatest boss in the world, period. Sitting here, I'm not allowed to forget that. I simply must do my best work."

"That sounds awesome, Tony. I envy you."

He smiled. "Well, then there are the days he makes me cover the county supervisors' discussions about which particulate to put on the gravel roads, and I want to kill him."

Darcy laughed.

Tony gave the rest of the tour, keeping it light and not delving again into the historical or philosophical sides of the newspaper world. When they walked through occupied rooms, such as the production room and the press room, Tony introduced her to everyone at once. People looked up from their tasks long enough to wave or shout a greeting, then returned to their work.

He did comment on the challenges of keeping the news media financially viable in an age when huge portions of advertising revenue had moved to online services. Craigslist, eBay, Pinterest, and Etsy have replaced classified ads, for example. "A few years ago," Tony said, "the desks in the ad department and even the newsroom had shrunk to a third of what they had been two decades before. Then the pandemic hit, and the paper really suffered."

"I didn't notice a lot of empty spaces or empty desks now," Darcy said. "Has something changed?"

"Yes, actually. Two things. First, the community rallied as best it could to support us. Even those who don't read us can't imagine Orney without a daily paper. The second thing was that Ben had the brilliant idea to buy the local radio station. He kept the best people from each company and combined them all in this building. By doing so, he kept the ad revenue from both, but dramatically reduced what it costs to sell and produce the ads, as well as cover the news."

"And the FCC and the anti-trust people are okay with Ben owning both?"

Tony was impressed by the astuteness of the question.

"We're holding our breath. So far, no one has challenged it. Ben thinks as long as the local community supports it, the feds will leave it alone. Also, it seems to me the feds would look a little silly, opposing a tiny operation like this when they've approved multiple mergers between huge media conglomerates."

"In case you haven't noticed," Darcy said, "being silly or outright unfair doesn't seem to factor into our government's thinking very often."

"Sad but true. So keep your fingers crossed for us."

As they strode out the back door and climbed into the Explorer, Tony said, "Thanks for putting up with my rambling in there. I must have sounded like a pompous ass."

"Not at all," Darcy said. "I was just thinking the same thing about my rant on the lessons of history. So, if you're a pompous ass, then I'm a doubly pompous-ass goddess, or something like that."

They both laughed, then locked eyes. Tony quickly looked away. "So do we call it a night?" he asked. "Take you back to the Hampton?"

"If you must, but to be honest, I was hoping for a nightcap. Can we get a drink somewhere?"

"Well, sure..." Tony said, sounding uncertain. He looked at his watch.

"I'm sorry, do you have to get up early?"

"No, no, nothing like that," Tony said quickly. "I'm just thinking about the fact that, at this hour, the people in the Iron Range are going to be full of beer. If I take you in there, you'll cause a sensation. If you were serious about not relishing the attention, then I don't think that's a good solution."

Darcy said, "The motel doesn't have a bar. Maybe room service or something..."

Tony said, "I have a better idea, if you won't think me too forward. We could go to my place. I'm not much of a drinker, so I don't have hard liquor on hand, but I do have beer and wine."

"A glass of wine sounds wonderful," she said, "and I would love to see your place."

"I can't promise it'll be clean. I wasn't expecting guests."

"All the better." She smirked. "We'll see how the real Tony Harrington lives."

"Great," Tony groaned, and started the vehicle.

***

Tony lived in a rented two-bedroom bungalow in a well-established neighborhood of Orney. It was about as solidly middle class as living could get in small-city Iowa. He used the second bedroom as an office and base for his hobbies, such as music. It held a relatively new Yamaha keyboard, called a Clavinova, and a Bedell six-string acoustic guitar. The keyboard was made possible by a trust from which he received an annual payment. The guitar was found in a pawn shop in Des Moines.

Tony was a decent pianist, but he could barely play the guitar. He still loved owning it, knowing the founder of the company was from Iowa and knowing a little about the company's environmentally-friendly practices in harvesting wood. It was an exquisite instrument. Even with the help of the trust fund, Tony could not have afforded to buy it if the pawn broker had charged anything close to its actual value.

The house had a one-stall garage, accessible from the alley behind, and a carport next to the side entrance that Tony used for a patio. Knowing they would be leaving again soon, Tony parked the Explorer on the street and took Darcy in through the front door.

His prediction was correct. The house was not clean; it rarely was. However, it was tidy. Tony liked to keep things picked up and orderly, so he wasn't overly embarrassed for Darcy see it.

"This is nice," she said, noticing the leather furniture and the abstract art on the living room wall.

As she studied the two paintings, Tony said, "Don't ask about the artist. I don't have a clue. I bought them at the Des Moines Art Festival several years ago and promptly lost the artist's card. I can't make out the signature, so it's a mystery. I'm tempted to start telling people I did them."

Darcy moved on, following Tony into the kitchen. "I like them. You have good taste."

"Thanks. Let's hope it carries over to my wine selection."

He let Darcy choose, and she decided on a Moscato from California. "Very drinkable and unpretentious. Not at all what you would expect a goddess to choose, right?"

"I never question the wisdom of goddesses." Tony chuckled. "Also, if you want a pretentious wine, you might have to look somewhere other than my cupboard. Probably somewhere other than Orney."

They took their glasses to the living room. Tony turned on the sound system, selecting a playlist that included some of his late-night favorites—Norah Jones, James Taylor, and Bonnie Raitt. They sat together on the sofa, listening and sipping wine.

Eventually, Darcy said, "Tony, this is perfect. The whole evening has been exactly what I'd hoped."

"For me too," he said. "I hate to see it end."

Darcy set her glass on the end table and turned to face him.

She said, "It doesn't have to, you know."

Tony swallowed hard and set down his glass as well.

Darcy said, "I'm sorry to be forward again, but you're such a nice guy, and I'm… Well, I'm Darcy Gillson. I'm pretty sure you're not going to make a move. So let me say it straight out. I would love to have you take me by the hand and lead me into the that bedroom over there, and… and, well… You know."

Tony stared at her. His mouth was instantly dry, and his heart was pounding.

Almost in a whisper, he said, "Darcy, that may be the most amazing and unexpected thing anyone's ever said to me. And trust me, you cannot imagine how much I want to do just what you said."

"But…?"

"But I'm scared shitless. You're so perfect…"

She started to object, but Tony stopped her and said, "Don't deny what we both know. You're smart, you're charming, you're funny, you're talented, you're well-grounded, you're successful, and you're so… you're so damn beautiful. I want you desperately."

"But…?"

"But then what? In a few days, you fly away, and I'm left in Orney, Iowa, reminiscing for the rest of my life about the time I made love to that movie star who eventually married Chris Evans or some other leading man. I can't fall in love and get left behind again. I'm sorry. I just can't."

She looked at him for a long time, her eyes growing moist.

"Dammit," she said softly, shaking her head. "I don't have a thing I can say to you. You're right. I don't want to hurt you. I don't want to get hurt, either, by the way. So you're right. We shouldn't let this go any further."

She reached for her wine glass, took the last swallow, and stood.

"I guess it's time to go," she said, forcing her voice into a cheery tone. "It was still a wonderful night. I'll always be grateful to you."

She moved toward the front door, but Tony remained on the couch, staring at her.

She turned back to him. "Tony?" She waited. "Tony?"

"God help me," he said, standing, walking to her, reaching one arm behind her shoulders and bending to cradle the backs of her legs with the other. He picked her up in his arms, marched into the bedroom, and kicked the door shut.

Chapter 13

Orney, Iowa—Wednesday, June 24

Sunlight clawed at Tony's eyelids. He rolled over and opened one eye. The clock on the nightstand said 9:23.

Good grief. He opened the second eye and reached his arm across the bed. Darcy was not there. He heard no sounds in the house. He was pretty sure she was gone. He was curious whether she had walked or had called for a car to pick her up. Acknowledging that Darcy was a grown woman who could take care of herself, Tony didn't worry. In fact, a large part of him was glad she had left. If she had been there, he would have been utterly clueless about what to say to her. Last night had been fantastic. Tony still didn't know what it meant or what would happen next, but he was pretty sure he was capable of screwing it up in the first five minutes of their next conversation.

He showered, shaved, and dressed in record time, grabbing a bagel and a banana on his way out the door. Despite the effort, he was late for work. When he walked into the newsroom, Ben was sitting at his desk, reading the morning's *Des Moines Register.*

"Hey, Tony. I was just about to call you. Late night?"

Tony was relieved to see his boss smiling.

"Sorry, yeah. I overslept. I mean, I really overslept. It just occurred to me that I'd promised Jun I would come to the dojang this morning for a workout. He read about my altercation with Borden and was concerned I was out of shape. He seemed to think Doug's tire iron to the back of the head should not have been necessary."

"No worries from me, but you might want to get an apology to Jun post-haste. You don't want him pissed at you the next time you spar."

"Good point. So what's up?"

"Sheriff Mackey called here first thing this morning to let us know Borden made bail. He's being released at noon today. I didn't call you right away 'cause I figured you'd be here by noon, regardless of what happened with Darcy last night."

Tony could feel his face warming.

"Yeah, about that..."

"Hey," Ben interrupted. "I don't want to hear about it. I'm a single guy, too, remember? I haven't had a date in months. I don't know how you do it, but whatever magic dust you're sprinkling on your clothes, I want you to share a little with me."

Tony didn't know what to say. He'd spent years admiring and looking up to his boss. It felt awkward to have the roles reversed, to have Ben envious of him. He decided to get back to business.

"On a serious note, I hope you don't mind that we went out. It looks like I ignored your 'don't fraternize' request, but I didn't plan it. She called and asked me to take her to dinner. I couldn't say no."

Ben nodded. "I wouldn't expect you to. I appreciate the explanation, but after what's happened, I'm not sure what the rules are anymore."

Tony sighed in relief and asked, "Have they set a preliminary hearing date? When does Borden have to be back in court?"

Ben laughed and said, "I'm pretty sure that's your job, to find out and report what's going on with his case."

"Obviously they haven't charged him with Andresson's murder. If they had, they wouldn't be letting him go. I wonder why. He's here, he's demonstrated his violent temper, he had a motive, and the means was sitting in a display at the pro shop."

"I did ask Mackey if they were still looking at Andresson for murder one. He clammed up, as he often does, but he was kinda hinky about it."

"Hinky?"

"Yeah, I don't remember his exact words, but he basically said there's a reason why they haven't taken action."

"An alibi? Another suspect? Fingerprints or a DNA mismatch?" Tony wondered aloud.

"Again, that's your job. Work your magic with Rich or someone, and see what you can find out."

"Roger that," Tony said.

Ben folded up the paper and rose from Tony's chair.

Smiling as he walked away, he said, "About last night... I hope you did what I think you did. Now call her up and ask her if she has an older sister, or even a mom, a grandmother, somebody!"

Tony grinned, sat in his chair, and picked up the desk phone. Before he could dial, he spotted Rich Davis coming into the newsroom through the back door. Tony hung up the phone and stood to greet the agent.

"I was just dialing the phone to try to reach you."

Davis looked tired and drawn. He obviously had not had much sleep. The nature of the murder case, amplified by the constant pressure of national and international media, was taking a toll. He said, "Yeah? Well, good. Can we talk?"

"Of course. Let me get a chair."

Davis grabbed Tony's arm as he started to move.

"Someplace private. The conference room?"

Something about the grip on his arm and the tone in Davis's voice turned Tony's blood cold.

"Sure, Rich. If it's busy, we can always take a walk, or even ask Ben for the use of his office."

They walked down the hall and found the conference room dark and empty. Tony clicked on a light and motioned to the row of chairs on one side of the oval table. "Take your pick. Can I get you coffee or a soda?"

"Coffee would be great. Thanks."

Once the men were settled, Davis with the ultra-strong brew from the *Crier's* break room and Tony with his standard drink, a Diet Dr. Pepper, Davis got right to it. He pulled out his electronic tablet and said, "We're going to do the official business first. Then we can chat if you like."

"Official business?"

"Please, Tony, don't make this harder. You know how it works. There are things I can't tell you about some investigations, especially when you're in the middle of it."

"The middle of what? What are we talking about here?"

"Official business first," Davis said tersely. He punched a couple of buttons on his tablet and said, "This is DCI Special Agent Rich Davis. It is… ten fifty-two a.m. on Wednesday, June 24. I am interviewing Mr. Tony Harrington of Orney, Iowa. Mr. Harrington is speaking to me voluntarily and has not requested an attorney be present. Is all that correct, Mr. Harrington?"

"Yes, but I don't know the topic of the conversation," Tony said defensively, "so I have no way of knowing if, or why, I would need an attorney."

"Please understand, Mr. Harrington, you may stop this interview at any time and request an attorney be present before you answer any questions, okay?"

"Of course," Tony said, anxious to get on with it, to understand what in the hell this was all about.

"Mr. Harrington, please state for the record your actions and whereabouts on the evening of Saturday, June 20, and the morning of Sunday, June 21."

Holy Mother of God, Tony thought. *That's the night of the murder. He's asking me what I was doing the night of the murder.* He suddenly felt sick and clammy. Intellectually, he knew he shouldn't be worried. Rich knew him well enough to know he was no killer. Emotionally, it was devasting to be in a position where his longtime friend was talking to him as though he was a suspect. *I'm one of the good guys, for God's sake*, he wanted to scream.

Tony took a deep breath and said, "Starting when?"

"Anytime during the day or early evening is fine," Davis said, "unless you believe something you did or saw or heard earlier would have any bearing on the case of Ms. Andresson's murder."

Tony knew that Davis was aware of his pizza dinner with the cast on Friday night. Davis hadn't asked him to start his account there. *So what is he after?*

Tony leaned his elbows on the conference table, looked his friend in the eye, and said, "I worked here at the *Town Crier* on Saturday, from about 1 p.m. until nearly 10 p.m. I wrote several routine news articles and one longer piece about the movie production that's underway in Orney. The computers here at the paper timestamp articles when they're forwarded to the copy desk, so you can easily see what work I did, and when. You have my permission to look at that log if you wish. I'm sure Ben, uh, Mr. Smalley, the publisher, would be happy to provide you with a copy if necessary."

"Thank you. Please continue."

"Sometime before ten, I'm not sure of the time, I left work and drove over to the Howdy Stranger Inn to pick up my dad. He had called earlier in the evening and asked if I would like to have pizza with him when I got off work."

"What time was that?"

"I think I already said I'm not…"

Davis interrupted. "I'm sorry. I meant what time did your dad call?"

Tony was baffled by the question, but said, "I'm not sure. Probably around eight or so. Why?"

Davis ignored the question and asked one of his own.

"What were you driving?"

Again, Tony was surprised, but said, "I had my Ford Explorer here at the office. However, on the way to the motel, I stopped at my house. I left the Explorer there and got my Mustang out of the garage."

"Why is that?"

"Well, my dad loves that car. It's a nostalgia thing for him, for people of his generation. I mean, I love it, too, but for different reasons. I thought it would be fun to be driving it when I picked him up."

"So taking the Mustang was your idea?"

Tony realized Rich was asking a question, not making a statement.

"Of course. Whose idea would it have been?"

Again, Davis didn't respond.

"So you picked up your dad, and then what?"

"I drove to Panucci's Pizza. I parked the car at the curb, just a couple of spots down from the front of the restaurant. We went inside and had a very nice meal. We talked about all kinds of things. It was a great father-son evening."

"Were any topics discussed that could have any bearing whatsoever on Ms. Andresson's murder?"

"No, of course not. There was no murder at that time, and Ms. Andresson was just one of dozens of interesting people we had met in the course of the week as the cast and crew of the movie were working in Orney."

"You or your dad didn't have any special interest in Ms. Andresson? No mention was made of how attractive she is or anything like that?"

"Not that I recall. Rich, what in the hell is this about?"

"Please, Mr. Harrington, just a few more questions."

Davis's all-business demeanor was starting to piss Tony off.

Davis said, "After dinner, did you drive your father back to the motel?"

"Actually, no," Tony said. "I handed him the keys and suggested he take the Mustang for a drive. He drove off, and I walked home."

Davis didn't respond. He looked at Tony hard for a few moments, then scribbled a couple of notes on the pad's surface.

Tony sensed, was certain, something had just happened, but he wasn't sure what.

"Why did you do that, hand over the keys to your dad?"

"I don't know. It just seemed like a nice thing to do. As I said, he loves that old car. He'd ridden in it a few times, but had never driven it. I thought it would be fun for him."

"You didn't go with him?"

"No, I was beat, and I knew he'd have more fun if he could air it out a little. You know, out in the country, without me looking over his shoulder."

"So then you walked straight home and went to bed?" Davis asked.

"Well, I played my Clavinova for a little while, watched a couple of short YouTube videos, then went to sleep."

Davis asked some questions about when Tony was awakened by the telephone call alerting him to the body at the country club, then asked Tony to walk through his movements at the crime scene and throughout much of the morning.

Suddenly, Davis said, "Can you describe the car, please?"

"The car? What car?" Tony was genuinely puzzled.

"Your Mustang. Please describe it."

Even though Davis knew it well, Tony told him it was a 1967 baby blue Ford Mustang convertible, equipped with a small V-8 engine and a four-speed manual transmission.

Davis then asked when Tony had seen the car next, and Tony explained that his dad returned it to him later the next day.

"When your dad took the car, was the top up or down?"

"The top was down," Tony said. "What's the fun of driving a convertible in the summertime if the top isn't down?"

"When the car was returned to you, was the top up or down?"

Tony had to think. "The top... was... up. I suppose dad put it up when he parked it for the night. He would be like me, I'm sure. That is, reluctant to leave the interior vulnerable to vandals or animals or the weather while sitting in a motel parking lot."

The interview lasted nearly an hour. When it finally was over and the recording shut off, Tony leaned back in the padded chair and said, "Okay, Agent Davis, what the fuck is going on?"

Davis sighed and said, "You know I'm not supposed to tell you a thing."

Tony started to object, but Davis held up a hand and said, "I can't tell you much, but I am going to tell you why I'm here. Understand, Tony, I could get fired for sharing this with a person of interest in the case. I could maybe even be charged criminally. So I'm trusting you with my life, and I'm only telling you this because I know with absolute certainty that you didn't kill Charlotte Andresson. You don't have the kind of out-of-control passion it took to beat that young woman to death with a golf club."

Tony's emotions had just taken a ride on the Vomit Comet. At the reference to "person of interest," his heart had sunk quickly; then hearing Davis say he knew he didn't do it, his spirits had risen to a remarkable high. Also, Tony found himself thinking he was lucky that Davis hadn't witnessed his time with Darcy the night before. *Out-of-control passion might be more up my alley than you think.* He smiled to himself and said, "Okay, so spill it. Why are you here?"

"I'm here because we've found a witness who saw Andresson downtown Saturday night."

"Okay..."

"She saw Andresson crossing the street, when a blue Mustang convertible stopped in front of her. The top was up, which is unusual on a warm summer evening, and Andresson's body blocked the witness's view of the driver. Andresson leaned down and talked to the driver through the passenger-side window. Then she opened the door, climbed in, and left in the Mustang. So far, that's the last anyone has reported seeing her."

Tony swallowed hard, immediately understanding the point of Davis's questions. *How many blue Mustang convertibles are there in Orney, or in all of Quincy County? Could it have been my car? Could someone have stolen it from the motel lot and used it in this horrendous crime?*

Davis reached into his suitcoat pocket. He handed Tony an envelope clearly containing several sheets of paper.

"I'm sorry," the agent said. "This is a search warrant for the Mustang as well as your Explorer and your house."

"Jesus Christ, Rich. C'mon."

"I know. I know. I'm sorry, but it has to be done. We have to know if she was in your car. You can understand it's a vital piece of the puzzle in this case."

"Sure, but my SUV, my *house?*" Tony was thinking about the sheets on his bed, soaked with sweat and still clinging to the scent, and probably more, of Darcy Gillson.

"If we find traces of her in your car, then checking your house is an obvious move. We have to do it all at the same time to prevent any chance of evidence-tampering."

Tony was growing more frustrated and angry by the minute. He knew from his years as a reporter how thorough the crime scene techs could be, and what that could mean to people's personal property.

"If they damage one single thing…" Tony began.

Rich said, "Relax. I'll be there with them to make sure everyone behaves. And it's not like we're looking for stolen property or secret spy stuff. We'll be checking the surfaces for hair, fingerprints, and other traces that she was there. No one's gonna be tearing up any floorboards or ripping open the furniture."

Tony said, "Just so you know, I did have sex in my bedroom at home."

Rich looked up sharply from his pad.

"Relax. It wasn't Saturday. It was last night, and it wasn't a brunette. She's blonde. I just thought you might want to warn your techs that they're gonna get a mountain of meaningless samples."

"Great," Davis said, sarcasm thick in his tone. "I've been married for seven years, and I swear you get more action than I do."

"Oh, sure," Tony said, "Once a year or so, whether I want to or not."

Davis smiled and said, "One more thing."

Tony waited, wondering what else could possibly be on Davis's mind.

The agent said, "I need you to promise that you will not say a word of this to anyone. Do you understand? We're at a very delicate point in the investigation, and I can't have anyone else knowing what you know."

"What about the people executing the warrant?" Tony asked, believing no one could really keep this a secret, which meant he had to talk to Ben about how the *Crier* would cover it.

Davis said, "Believe it or not, we're going to keep this search under wraps. I'm using a small team from our Des Moines lab. They won't be driving the van, and they won't dress until they're inside your garage or your house. I'm not telling Mackey or anyone else. We will keep this secret, at least for now. We must. Which means, again, that I'm trusting you. Tell absolutely no one."

Tony was skeptical, but he welcomed the idea of not being in the national media as a person of interest in a murder case, so he agreed.

Davis approached him and extended his hand.

Tony was about to shake it when Davis blushed and said, "Sorry. Keys."

Tony was taken aback but quickly realized what the agent was asking. He reluctantly reached into his pocket to retrieve his ring of keys. After removing the key to the *Town Crier* building, he handed the ring to Davis.

"It's all there—the house, the garage, and the Explorer. The keys to the Mustang are in the knife drawer in the kitchen."

"Thank you." Davis seemed unsure what to do next. He turned and headed for the conference room door, stopping as he gripped the handle. "I am truly sorry for all of this, my friend. Let's hope it comes to nothing."

"Thanks," Tony said, and Davis left.

Tony was unconvinced it would come to nothing. He could tell that Davis thought it was something, and that was enough to scare Tony to his core.

***

The remainder of the day was one of the longest Tony could remember. It was difficult to concentrate knowing a team of techs was rifling through his house and vehicles. He agonized over what the results of that work might reveal. These thoughts were interrupted periodically by thoughts of Darcy Gillson. *Should I call her? If I do, what will I say? If I don't, what will she think?*

Occasionally, Tony was forced to do some work. Fortunately, it was a slow news day, and with production of the movie at a standstill, there was no point in writing his next feature story on that topic.

Near the end of the day, Ben stepped out of his office and waved at Tony to come join him. Once both men were seated inside with the door closed, Ben said, "You want to tell me what's up?"

"Uh, I'm not sure what you mean."

"Come on. Don't shit me. You haven't been able to stay in your chair for more than five minutes at a time all day. I think you've consumed nine or ten Milky Way bars, and at least that many diet pops. I even saw you drink a cup of that steel-melting brew we call coffee. In other words, you've been a total wreck ever since Rich Davis was here this morning."

"You're right. I have. And yes, I want to tell you all about it. But I can't. I'm sorry."

Ben leaned back in his chair and looked Tony squarely in the eye but stayed quiet.

"Believe me," Tony said. "I have no desire to keep secrets from you, but Rich made me promise to tell absolutely no one what he's doing. I swear, as soon as I can tell you, I will."

"Well, I don't like it, but that's mostly because I'm worried about you. And I suppose if I'm being honest, I'm curious to know what could be going on that has you so tied in knots. I have no doubt about your judgment or your loyalty to the *Crier*. Just be sure to come to me if you need help."

"Thanks, boss. I appreciate your understanding and support. I'll push Rich to let me talk with you soon."

"Speak of the devil," Ben said, nodding. Tony turned and saw Davis entering the newsroom.

Tony stood and said, "I guess I'd better go see what he wants."

Moments later, Tony and Davis were back in the newspaper's conference room with the door closed. Tony's hands had a barely perceptible tremor as he pulled out a chair to sit.

Davis sat across the table from him and said, "Well, I have good news and bad news." He didn't ask Tony which he wanted first. "The good news is, we're done. Here are your keys."

He slid the ring of keys across the table and said, "I parked your Explorer in the back. Rooney's waiting outside to give me a ride." Special Agent Dan Rooney was Davis's partner, also assigned to Quincy County. "I don't think you'll even be able to tell we were in it. Your house, either."

"And the Mustang?" Tony asked.

Davis grimaced. "That's the bad news. We've impounded it. You won't be getting it back for a while."

"Dammit," Tony said. "Do you have to? That's not just any car, you know."

"Of course I do," Davis said patiently. "I know what she means to you, but I have no choice."

Tony felt the muscles in his stomach twitch and tighten.

"I'm sorry, Tony, but her fingerprints are in your car. We also collected hair from the seatback. It looks like hers, but we'll do a DNA analysis to confirm it."

Tony fought hard to not start crying. "Charlotte's fingerprints? But... But how in the hell... How could that be?"

"I don't know, but obviously that's now the primary focus of our investigation."

"Dear God." Tony leaned toward the table, his face in his hands. He worried he might faint. "So I'm a suspect now? Do I need a lawyer?"

"Sorry, I can't advise you about the lawyer question, but I can tell you that you're not necessarily a suspect—at least not any more of one than you were this morning."

Tony looked up, and Davis continued. "Your dad's account of Saturday night matches yours. It's pretty clear you didn't have the car. I suppose you could have taken it back later, when it was parked at the motel, but so could a lot of other people. A car made in 1967 isn't exactly difficult to hotwire. Almost anyone could have been driving it."

Tony felt a little of his anxiety ebb. He was glad the authorities understood that. More importantly, he was grateful for Davis's efforts to put his mind at ease. He thanked him for it.

Davis said, "My advice is, go home and get some rest." He grinned. "Based on what you've told me, I'm guessing you didn't get much sleep last night."

Tony groaned. "If you're trying to make me feel better, references to last night aren't going to do it. I'm as confused about that as I am about your murder case."

"That's a shame, but don't expect me to feel too sorry for you.

I might be okay with a little confusion in exchange for a night in the sack with Darcy Gillson."

"Bite me," Tony said.

Davis chuckled and went out the door.

A short time later, Tony took the agent's advice. He told Ben he was headed out, drove home, ate half an Italian sub left over in the refrigerator, and climbed into bed. As he tried to sort out all the issues that had emerged in his life in the previous twenty-four hours, he finally fell into a deep sleep.

It was the last good rest he would get for a while.

Chapter 14

Orney, Iowa—Thursday, June 25

It was nearly lunchtime on Thursday when Tony's cell phone buzzed in his pocket. He sat back from the laptop on his desk, where he was writing an article about a teenager who had created a successful internet business during the COVID-19 quarantine period. The sixteen-year-old girl was now making a seven-figure income selling everything from discount cosmetics to kitchen appliances to video games. She bought them in bulk from the manufacturers and resold them online, making a margin on every product. As a virtual wholesaler, she never even saw the products themselves. She simply made the connections between sellers and buyers and collected her money.

Tony pulled the cell from the pocket of his Dockers and saw it was his mother calling.

"Hi, Mom. What's up?"

"Tony! Oh my God, Tony. Your dad. They…"

Tony was immediately on his feet. His mother was hysterical. "Mom, what's wrong? Slow down. Tell me what happened."

"Your father. They came and took your father. He just called me. They're not going to let him go."

"What?" Tony asked. "Who's not going to let him go? I don't understand."

"The police!" his mother screeched. "They're charging him with murder! They think he killed that girl, that actress."

Tony felt the air go out of his lungs. He headed for Ben's office as he said into the phone, "That can't be right, Mom. You must've misunderstood. I just talked to Rich Davis last night..."

"Stop it! Don't tell me I misunderstood. Your father just called me. He told me! He said to call you—that you would know what to do. My God, Tony!" She was sobbing uncontrollably.

Tony realized he was inside Ben's office, his boss staring at him. He also realized he didn't know what to say to either Ben or his mother. He took a deep breath and tried to think. Into the phone, he said, "Okay, Mom. Please try to relax. I'll get over to the sheriff's office and try to get to the bottom of this. In the meantime, you have to take care of you. I'm sure this is just a mistake. We know Dad hasn't done anything wrong, so there's no need to worry. Try to hang tight for a little while, and I'll call you back as soon as I can."

He heard his mother sob what sounded like agreement, so he ended the call.

To Ben, Tony said, "You won't believe this, but my mother says they've arrested my dad and are charging him with Andresson's murder."

Ben's eyes widened, and his jaw dropped. "Your dad? You're sure?"

"Well, my mom said he called her. He..."

Tony's cell phone began playing the song, "Small Town Cop." He looked at it and said, "This is Davis. Maybe he can clear it up." Ben nodded and bent an ear to listen as Tony answered. "Rich, I'm glad you called."

"Yeah, I wanted to get to you right away," Davis said. "It's about your father."

"My mom just called me. Is what she said true? They're charging him? This is a mistake, right? You're gonna fix this, right?"

Davis said nothing for a moment, then, "Yes, it's true. He was interviewed for the second time this morning. Then the county attorney filed the charges. He's been taken to the Law Enforcement Center where he'll be held until a hearing is scheduled."

"My dad's in jail? In *jail*, Rich? *My* dad?"

"I know. It's hard. I'm sorry."

"But you know him! You have to know he didn't do this."

There was no response.

Tony pushed. "Rich, c'mon. You know he didn't do this."

Rich finally said softly, "I'm sorry. Really, truly sorry, but the evidence says he did. I never would have let it get this far if I wasn't convinced."

Tony collapsed into one of the two chairs in Ben's office. "I can't believe this. You think he did it. Has the world gone crazy?"

"Please understand, I don't want to believe it either. But my job is to trust the evidence. When you see it, you'll understand."

Tony's face flushed and his voice rose. "The hell I will! There is nothing on Earth that could make me understand something as ridiculous as this! My dad wouldn't hurt a fly! He sure as hell did not kill Charlotte Andresson!"

"Tony, I…"

Tony ended the call, leaned forward in the chair until his elbows rested on his knees, and fought back tears. After what seemed like hours, he composed himself and looked up at his boss sitting across the desk from him. He started to speak, but Ben stopped him.

"My advice is simple," Ben said. "Focus on what you need to do next. Let's talk about what we both need to do."

Tony nodded, hoping Ben would continue because he had no idea where to start.

Ben said, "First, you should think about your mother. She's as upset as you and alone in a motel room."

Tony nodded again, and Ben continued, "You need to call Rita right away. She needs to be warned before your mom talks to her."

Ben was right. *If my sister gets a call from mom like the one I just got,* Tony thought, *it will send her over the edge.*

"Another thing," Ben said, not slowing down. "You need to think about calling an attorney for your dad. Does he have one you could consult? You don't want him stuck with a public defender. If you're going to help him and minimize the damage from any bad publicity, the early legal moves in the case are important."

Tony nodded, fighting to control his thoughts and emotions. "You're right, of course." His brain was churning now, engaging in the challenges facing his family.

Ben said, "I'll give you a leave of absence starting now so you can focus on doing what you need to do. I'll assign the story to Doug, unless you prefer someone who's not so close to you."

"No. If you're okay with Doug doing it, so am I. I know he'll be accurate and fair. Jesus, I hate the thought of seeing this in the paper."

"Tony…"

"I know, I know. It won't just be the paper. This will be international news. A big celebrity's murder, and now a minor celebrity is the culprit—the *alleged* culprit. It's gonna be what we in the media like to call a shitstorm."

"Yes, that's very likely. So I suggest you get going. I'll talk to

Doug and get him over to the LEC. Once he has a copy of the formal charges, I'll make sure he scans and forwards the document to you.

"Thanks."

"You okay? You know what you're going to do?"

"Yes. I think so." Tony rose to leave, then stopped and turned. "Before I go, I have to say thanks again. I don't know how I would cope with this if you weren't so... so..."

"Just shut up and get moving. I love you too," Ben said. "Good luck."

***

Tony grabbed his laptop and shoulder bag and headed out of the office as fast as he could. He didn't want to see Doug, or Shawna Jackson, the photographer, as they scrambled to get their gear and head out to the LEC—to the *jail*.

Once in his SUV, Tony called the one person that, only minutes ago, he never would have dreamed of calling in this situation.

"Tony!" Darcy Gillson said when she answered her cell phone. "I'm so glad you called."

"Darcy, I... I'm sorry, but I'm calling for something else. I mean, something not really related to... I mean, I need a favor."

"Oh. Well, sure. What's up?"

Tony told her what had just happened. By the time he finished, his voice was shaking, and his eyes were moist again.

She said, "My God, I'm so sorry. That's... That's unbelievable. Your dad is such a nice guy. Nobody can really think he did this."

"Yeah, I wish that was true. Sadly, one of the people involved in the investigation—someone I know and trust—is apparently convinced he did it, so I'm scared out of my wits."

"So what's the favor?" she asked. "How can I help?"

"I hate to ask something as big as this, but you said you're not busy, and my mom is alone at the motel. She's a total wreck. I can't go there because…"

Darcy interrupted him. "I get it. Enough said. Give me ten minutes to get myself together and find a ride, and I'll head over there. You're right. She shouldn't be alone. Will she let me in?"

Tony found a smile and said, "She's Italian. Just tell her you're hungry, and she'll start cooking you dinner in the room's microwave. Tell her you're single and you like me, and she may start writing you into her will."

"Well, I am single, and I do like you, so if that'll get me in the door, then we're set. I'll do whatever I can to help her."

"Darcy," Tony waited a second to be sure she was listening. "Thank you. From the bottom of my heart, thank you. You're an angel."

"No, remember, I'm just a woman who wants a meal and to talk about normal things. I'll call you later and let you know how she's doing." She ended the call.

Tony didn't have time to dwell on the conversation. He was certain Darcy would be a great comfort to his mother. With that important issue addressed, he dialed Rita's number. He could talk to her while he drove. He was anxious to get moving because he knew where he needed to go next.

***

Tony parked the Explorer in front of the single-story brick building at the corner of 1st Street and Truman Avenue. The glass window at the front of the building was adorned with simple blue and white letters: Lawrence Pike, Attorney-at-Law.

When Tony stepped into the front lobby, he saw Pike's

receptionist/secretary behind a desk and one man sitting in a chair in the waiting area.

"Can I help you?" the gray-haired, stocky woman asked with a wide smile.

"Is Mr. Pike in?"

"Yes, he's here today, but I'm afraid he's busy. He only works part time now, so you'll need an appointment to speak with him. Can I ask what you need to see him about?"

"I'm sorry, but it's urgent. I really must speak to him as soon as possible. My dad is in trouble, and I need some help today."

"I'm sorry sir, but someone is with Mr. Pike now, and as you can see, there's another gentleman waiting to see him."

Tony turned and looked toward the man in the chair for the first time. It was Howard Brown, owner of the local hardware store. Tony nodded toward him and smiled. He turned back to the woman. Before he could speak, he heard Brown rise behind him.

"Lyla," Brown said, "if it's okay with you, I can come back another time. My business with Larry isn't urgent. This young man can have my time."

As Tony tried to express an adequate thank you, Brown was out the door. *Only in Iowa*, Tony thought.

"Well that certainly was thoughtful. Have a seat, Mr. uh... I'm sorry. I know I should know your name, but I'm having trouble pulling it out of this rusty brain of mine."

Tony told her and took a seat. He was grateful that only minutes passed before Pike emerged, escorting an elderly woman to the door.

When Pike finished parting company with the woman, he turned to Tony and said, "Mr. Harrington. I don't recall seeing you on my schedule for today."

Tony and Pike were well-acquainted from an incident four years previously, when Tony had covered a murder trial in which

Pike had represented the defendant. Tony had been impressed with the elderly attorney's abilities in the courtroom, though he hadn't won the case.

Pike, who was pushing seventy, was a widower. He continued to practice law part-time because he loved it.

The receptionist spoke up, saying, "Mr. Brown graciously offered to come back another time so Mr. Harrington could meet with you. Apparently it's urgent."

"It is," Tony assured them both.

"Very well," Pike said, gesturing for Tony to come with him.

Tony followed the portly, white-haired attorney down a hallway to his office in the back. Once settled into their respective seats, Pike took out a legal pad and pen and said, "So tell me. What brings you here today?"

Tony proceeded to recount the morning's events, concluding with a request that Pike go see his father to somehow help him out of this mess.

Pike squeezed his eyes closed for a long minute, set down the pen, and said, "You can probably guess what I'm going to say."

"Probably," Tony said with a morose nod. "You're going to say you only work part time, that you're a sole practitioner, that this case is going to be huge, that you don't do criminal work anymore, that you don't need the pressure of a case that's being covered by dozens of national and international media outlets, and that you can name twenty attorneys who would do a better job with it."

"So if you know all the reasons I should decline the case, why are you here?"

"Because," Tony said, leaning forward from the edge of his chair, "It's you I trust. It's my dad. I know with every fiber of my being that he's innocent. You're the person I trust to help him."

"That's very flattering, Tony, but it doesn't change the list of reasons why I should decline it."

"I'll tell you what. Let's make a deal. You go over to the LEC, talk to my dad, find out from the authorities what's going on, and then decide what to do. If you'll go today and try to stop this freight train before it leaves the station, I'll abide by whatever you decide after that."

Tony wasn't sure whether it was the reasonable nature of the compromise or the pleading in his voice that moved Pike, but the elderly lawyer stood up, walked to a coat rack in the corner, and slipped on a blue blazer.

"Alright, Tony. I'll talk to him."

Tony also stood, elated.

"But I have to warn you," Pike added, "the freight train is already halfway to the coast. You and I both know the county attorney would not have filed charges against a high-profile person like your father unless he had some rock-solid evidence in his pocket. And now that he's made this move, he's not going to back down unless he's forced to do so by some very clear proof in the other direction."

Tony's elation quickly faded. He said, "I know you're right, but there has to be a hole in whatever it is he thinks he has. My dad simply could not have done this. Mr. Pike, this isn't just a son's wishful thinking. I know my dad. I know he's not capable of this kind of violence."

"I'll take your word for that, for now. Let's go see what your dad has to say, and what nonsense Mr. Garcia in the County Attorney's Office has assembled that he thinks is evidence."

***

Pike was well known to the deputies in charge of the jail, so he was admitted with a minimum of hassle. A quick peek into his briefcase to ensure he carried no weapon, and a pass through the metal detector, and he was in. Tony's admission was another story. It was rare for an attorney to bring a member of the family along for a visit. The deputies' anxiety was exacerbated by the fact they recognized him as a member of the press. Because the sheriff had anticipated Tony would come, and had instructed them to allow him in, they couldn't say no, but that didn't stop them from thoroughly searching every item of clothing he wore and requiring him to leave his belt and shoes in a storage cabinet outside the first set of locked doors.

Their behavior irritated Tony, but he was determined not to give them the pleasure of seeing him upset. He clamped his jaws shut, silently endured every prod, and followed every instruction. Eventually, stocking-footed, he was following Pike down the hallway to the conference room used for attorney-client discussions.

For Tony, the fact that the jail was relatively new and clean, with a reasonable amount of daylight streaming in through high, narrow windows in nearly every room did little to lessen the blow of seeing his father in the standard orange jumpsuit and handcuffed to a metal table in the small meeting room.

Charles stood as they entered and threw his free arm around Tony.

He said, "I'm sorry I can't hug you properly. Thank you for coming."

"Of course," Tony said. "Dad, this is Lawrence Pike, a local attorney. I've asked him to help you out."

Charles raised one eyebrow, realized what he had done, then quickly made his face passive.

As all three men sat, Pike said, "I saw your reaction, Mr. Harrington, and it's quite alright. I've already told Tony that I'm too

old and ill-equipped to represent you in this case. But I did agree to
talk with you, as well as the county attorney, so I can give you and
Tony my best advice regarding how to proceed."

"Fair enough," Charles said. "I apologize if I looked, uh,
surprised. I trust Tony's judgment. I'm sure he went to you first for
a reason. And by the way, call me Charles. It's simpler, and it'll save
any confusion between addressing me and Tony."

He continued, "Before we start, I need to ask you, Tony, how's
your mother? She pretty much lost it when I called her. I've been
sitting here wishing I had called you first."

Tony said he assumed she was doing as well as could be hoped,
given that he had asked Darcy Gillson to go to the motel to look after
her.

"Darcy? Really! That's a surprise. I didn't know you two had
become friends."

"I'm not sure we have," Tony began. "It's complicated. We'll
talk about it another time. The important thing is, I think Darcy will
be a great help to Mom. So how are you doing?"

Charles said, "Well, mostly I'm in shock. I can't quite believe
I'm in here. As the shock wears off, it's replaced by frustration,
confusion, and anger. I haven't done anything wrong, so why am I
here?"

Pike didn't respond immediately. From his briefcase, he
extracted a hand-held Dictaphone, a yellow legal pad, and a pen. He
turned on the recorder and said, "So what have they told you? Tell
me about your interactions with the authorities from the beginning."

Charles explained that he had been interviewed on Monday
afternoon by Rich Davis from the DCI and a sheriff's deputy. "I don't
even recall his name," Charles said. "They told me they were talking
to everyone, and I didn't think anything of it. They asked about a lot
of things, like did I have any idea who might have done it? Had Ms.

Andresson said anything indicating she might have been nervous or scared? You know. That kind of stuff. They knew I had eaten lunch with the cast on Wednesday, the week before Andresson's murder, so they asked me about that."

Charles said all the questions had seemed pretty routine— questions they might ask anyone. "The only exception I can recall was their question about why I'm here in Orney. I told them I had written the screenplay for the movie, and that Ramesh, the director, is an old friend. They seemed to know this, but it led to questions about my prior relationships with anyone else involved in the movie, and what my role was in choosing Iowa as the on-site location for the film.

"I told them I had suggested Orney to Ramesh. I did it as a favor to Tony and his newspaper, thinking it would be exciting to have a movie filmed here."

"Did they ask you about the night of the murder?"

"Well, sure," Charles said. "Again, it sounded like a question they were asking everyone. I told them I'd had dinner with my son at that pizza place downtown, then took his Mustang for a drive and ended up back at the motel, where I joined my wife and went to sleep."

"If necessary, we can cover the details of that first interview later," Pike said. "Just tell me if any of your answers seemed to spark their interest. Is there anything you said, or they said, that might have hinted you were a suspect in the crime?"

"No. Not at all. As I said, it all seemed pretty routine. Oh," he said suddenly. "They did ask if they could take a blood sample. I thought that was a bit much, but they said it would be just a quick fingerstick. They said they were drawing from everyone who would allow it, so they would be able to use DNA testing to eliminate suspects in the future. I consented to it."

"Okay. Then what happened?"

"Well, as it relates to this," Charles looked at his wrist and rattled the chain on the handcuff, "my next interaction was the next day, on Tuesday. Deputy Bodke called and asked me to stay in town a while longer. He said they were re-interviewing a lot of people, and he would appreciate it if I stayed nearby so I could answer any follow-up questions. I told him that would be fine. I enjoy Orney, and it's been great spending some extra time with Tony. It's summer break, so I'm not teaching right now. Again, I didn't think much about it. He was very pleasant, and I was happy to oblige."

"He didn't ask you any questions during that call?"

"I don't think so."

"And then?"

"Then this," Charles said, sweeping the room with his free hand.

"Tell me about it."

"Okay, let me think. At about ten or ten-thirty this morning, we heard a knock on the door of the motel room. I assumed it was the maid. I went to answer it, to tell her we'd like a little more time before she came in to clean. I was shocked when I opened the door. Deputy Bodke was standing there with three other deputies. He asked me to come with him to the Law Enforcement Center. I asked why, and he said I was going to be questioned again, this time as a suspect in the killing of Charlotte Andresson. I told him I thought that was ridiculous. He didn't respond to that, but simply demanded I go with him. I asked if he was placing me under arrest. He said no, but he would if necessary. By that time, of course, Carla was at my back wanting to know what was happening. I told her not to worry, the deputy was just asking me to come to the station to answer a few more questions. I realized it would be easier on my wife if I just went along and didn't make a fuss, so I went with them."

Pike snorted and said, "I just love this no arrest-arrest game they play. But no matter. What then?"

"They put me in a room similar to this, but larger, and spent the next two hours asking me questions."

"Did you answer them?"

"Yes. Yes, I did. I watch enough TV to know better—hell, I write enough interrogation scenes to know better—but dammit, I haven't done anything wrong! I really thought this whole mess could be cleared up by simply telling them everything I knew."

Pike shook his head, but said, "It's an easy mistake to make, even for someone who knows better. So I assume the nature of the questions was different this time?"

"Oh God, yes. Now everything was asked from a whole different point of view, one from which they assumed I killed her. The questions were things like, 'Why did you take her to the country club?' and 'What did she say that made you angry enough to kill her?' Things like that."

"And you said?"

"I just kept saying they were wrong, that I didn't take her anywhere, that I didn't kill her. This is all just so crazy. Why would anyone suspect me of such a thing?"

Pike set down his pen and said, "I haven't talked to the county attorney yet, so I haven't heard or seen anything about their case, but Tony has shared one fact with me in confidence, as your attorney."

Charles sat up a little straighter.

Pike continued, "An inside source has told your son that Andresson's fingerprints, and possibly her hair, were found in the front seat of Tony's Mustang. I'm guessing that's a big part of the reason they're looking at you. You've told them you were the one driving the Mustang Saturday night. Do you have any idea how that could have happened? Was she in the car?"

Charles looked wide-eyed at Pike, then at Tony, then back to Pike. He composed himself and said steadily, "I swear to both of you, I have absolutely no idea how that could be true. I never saw her Saturday night, and the car was never out of my sight. I took it for a long drive, ending up back at the motel, where I parked it in the lot and went inside to bed. I locked it up and kept the keys with me."

Tony said, "When you say, 'locked it up,' are you saying the top was up?"

Pike didn't look happy at the intrusion, but he must have assumed Tony had a good reason for asking. He made no objections.

Charles said, "Yes, I put the top up. I couldn't imagine leaving a classic car like that outside all night with the top down."

"When?" Tony asked. "When did you put up the top?"

"When I got back to the motel, of course. Why?"

"No reason, Dad. I'm just trying to be sure we have a clear picture of everything."

Pike asked, "Was your wife awake when you entered the room and got ready for bed?"

"No," Charles said. "She was sleeping. I took a shower, brushed my teeth, all the usual stuff, and then climbed into bed with her. I kissed her goodnight and got a mumbled acknowledgement, but I doubt she knew what time it was, if that was the point of your question."

Pike nodded to agree it was the point, then said, "You showered? Is that normal? You always shower at night before bed?"

"Not always," Charles said, "but sometimes. Saturday night I smelled like garlic and pepperoni from the restaurant, and after driving the route around the county Tony had suggested, with the top down on the convertible, it felt like my hair was full of mosquitoes. A shower seemed like a good idea."

"Tony suggested a route?"

Tony jumped in, saying, "Yes, I suggested he drive the highway west, then north to Viscount, and then back on the county blacktop. I thought that would be a good forty-or-so-mile trek, you know, to really let him enjoy driving the car."

Pike turned. "Thank you, Tony, but please, let your dad answer my questions. I can talk with you later."

"Sorry," Tony said, feeling his face redden.

Charles said, "I have nothing to add to that. That's exactly what Tony recommended, and it's exactly what I did."

Pike said, "Forgive me for being redundant, but let me ask you one more time. Were you alone the whole time?"

"Yes," Charles said, gritting his teeth. "I swear, I was alone every minute. I never saw Andresson or any other woman, except an occasional pedestrian as I drove out of town. I never spoke to anyone, I never saw anyone, and I sure as hell didn't give anyone a ride in that car."

"Very good," Pike said. "That seems pretty clear. If all they have is the girl in the car, it's not enough to hold you. It means they jumped too quickly, and we could have you out of here tomorrow morning."

Charles and Tony both smiled.

"But," Pike said, "as I told Tony, I doubt that's all they have. You're too well-known, and quite frankly, well-liked, to put you in here facing murder charges unless they're sure. I'm guessing they have more. Just try to keep your chin up throughout this ordeal. And Charles…"

The man in the orange jumpsuit looked at his attorney.

Pike said, "Two critically important things. First, behave yourself in here. No matter what someone says to you, or even does to you, do not react. Do not get in trouble. They have cameras everywhere, and they would love to catch you on film behaving badly. Second, do not talk to anyone about anything. Just shut up and trust me to do my job."

Charles actually smiled. "That sounds like a speech you've given a few times before."

"A few too many times," Pike agreed. "And you'd be surprised at how often my clients have ignored it. Those clients are assholes. Don't be an asshole, Charles."

Pike rose and walked to the door, pressing a button and announcing, "We're done here."

As a guard punched a code into the lock from the other side, Tony gave his dad a hug.

"I love you. Try not to worry. You know I won't let you down."

Tears were streaming down Charles's face as Tony and Pike left the room.

Tony was nearly overwhelmed with helplessness and grief, but it was tempered by his determination to get to the truth and set his father free from this nonsense.

Sadly, Tony didn't know the worst was yet to come.

Town Crier

Oscar-winning screenwriter charged with murder

Charles Harrington, aka C.A. Harker, denies killing actress

Doug Tenney, Staff Writer

ORNEY, Iowa – Charles Harrington, better known as author and screenwriter C.A. Harker, was arrested and charged with first-degree murder on Wednesday, in the death of actress Charlotte Andresson, 28, of Santa Clarita, Calif. The arrest and charges were announced Wednesday evening by Quincy County Sheriff George Mackey and County Attorney Alejandro "Alex" Garcia.

Harrington, 57, of Iowa City, denies the charges, saying he never saw the actress on Saturday night or Sunday morning, according to his attorney Lawrence Pike.

Andresson's body was found floating in the Orney Country Club swimming pool early Sunday morning. Authorities believe the evidence shows Harrington drove Andresson to the country club late Saturday night, and broke into the Pro Shop inside the clubhouse, Sheriff Mackey said. While inside the shop, Andresson was apparently struck in the head from behind and killed, and then dragged to the

outdoor swimming pool and thrown in, Mackey noted, repeating what had previously been reported by Quincy County Medical Examiner Dr. Lance Torgeson.

The University of Iowa in Iowa City, where Harrington currently teaches, issued a statement expressing "shock and dismay" at the news of Harrington's arrest.

Harrington is a longtime friend and colleague of Ramesh Bhatt, the director of the movie currently being filmed on location in Orney. Bhatt said, "I have never been more astonished than I was when I learned Charles had been arrested. Next to the death of Charlotte, this is the most devastating news I've heard in a long, long time. I hope and pray this is some kind of mistake. I know Charles well and can't believe he would commit an act of violence like the one of which he's accused."

Those sentiments were echoed by others in Orney, where Harrington is relatively well-known. He is the father of one of the employees at the *Town Crier*, and he visits Orney regularly to spend time with his son.

Sheriff Mackey said Harrington is currently being held at the Quincy County Law Enforcement Center. He is expected to appear in court later today to enter a plea to the charges and request a bail be set.

Lawrence Pike, who is currently representing Harrington, is a well-known defense and general practice lawyer in Orney, now semi-retired. Pike said he could not comment on the case beyond sharing his client's absolute denial that he was involved in any way.

Mackey refused to detail the specific evidence gathered which led to the charges against...

Chapter 15

Orney, Iowa—Friday, June 26

Tony sat at the small, round table in his kitchen. The morning newspaper was lying in the center of the table, still tucked into the traditional "newsboy fold." He didn't want to look at it.

On the kitchen counter, coffee was brewing in the expensive, but rarely used, Moccamaster. Tony was sipping a Diet Dr. Pepper. The coffee was for Darcy.

He stared at her from behind as she filled her cup. He was so damn glad she was here. The situation was horrendous, but it would have been utterly unbearable to face alone.

Knowing this would be the case, Tony had urged his mother to come stay with him. She had declined, saying she was comfortable at the motel and pretty sure the maid would do a better job of cleaning up and taking care of her than Tony would do on his best day.

Darcy had offered to stay there with her, but again, Carlotta had declined. She had looked at Tony and said, "You and your lovely new girlfriend need some privacy. You go. I'll be fine, really, especially if I know you're not alone."

Tony had been too exhausted and anxious to appreciate what she was saying. He also had been too tired to argue. So he had come home, and Darcy had come with him. They had spent a long night together filled with tears, questions, pacing, ranting, and more tears —everything except romance.

Looking at her now, Tony found himself surprised at how natural it had all seemed. She had listened when he'd ranted, had responded when he'd asked a question, had held him when he'd needed it, and had been there when he'd lapsed into brief periods of sleep.

Now here she was, making coffee and looking relaxed, rested, and beautiful. It was a stark contrast to his own appearance, which he had been forced to admit appeared to be a total wreck of a human being, when it had stared back at him from the bathroom mirror a short time ago.

"How do you do it?" Tony asked.

"What's that? How do I do what?"

"You seem so calm and put together. You must have gotten less sleep than I did."

She smiled and said, "Perhaps. But remember, I have a job where I often have to get up at 4 a.m. for makeup and wardrobe. Working on little sleep is a way of life for an actor."

"Still…"

Darcy sat, setting the cup on the table and letting the coffee's steam warm her hands.

"You have to remember, Tony, he's not my dad. My heart aches for him, and for you and your mom, but I can't possibly feel it to my core the way you do. I'm just happy someone could be here for you when you needed it."

He didn't respond, and she quickly added, "No, that's not right. I'm happy I could be here when you needed it."

"I'm glad, too," Tony said. "I don't know how I would have made it through the night without you."

"So what's next?"

Tony looked at his watch, a Tissot his parents had given him as a present when he'd graduated from the University of Iowa.

He said, "My dad's preliminary hearing is in ninety minutes. I'll go there, learn what I can, and hope they set bail so he can get out of there. You're welcome to join me, but please don't feel obligated. You've done enough."

Darcy looked a little pained by the comment and said, "No, I don't think I should join you. Not because I'm too busy or don't want to, but because I don't want to make this worse."

Tony wrinkled his brow.

She said, "Think about the media frenzy. The courthouse is going to be packed with everything from CNN to European paparazzi. If I show up, it only fuels that fire. Another Hollywood starlet in the middle of this case."

"Jeez, I never even thought of that. I'm sorry I keep forgetting you're famous. I don't think of you as a movie star."

"God, don't apologize," she said, reaching over and squeezing his arm. "That's just about the best thing I've ever heard."

Tony stood. He needed to get cleaned up and over to the courthouse. Darcy had just reminded him that the media would be gathering there already.

Darcy stood as well, and Tony pulled her close and wrapped her arms around him.

My God, she feels good, Tony thought.

Aloud, he said, "If circumstances were different, I bet I could come up with a few other things to say that you wouldn't mind hearing."

She looked up into his eyes and put her arms around his neck. "I'm sure you could, and when this is all over, I'm going to hold you to that." She kissed him hard, and then pushed him away toward the bathroom. "You'd better hurry."

When Tony came out of his room thirty minutes later, dressed in a sport coat and tie, he announced he was ready, then quickly realized the house was empty.

How does she keep doing that? He shook his head and went out the back door to climb into his SUV.

***

The scene at the Quincy County Courthouse on the west side of the town square was absolute pandemonium. Satellite trucks, TV cameras, microphone booms, and a large crowd of people pushing and shouting filled the street and sidewalk right up to the front steps. There, a row of deputy sheriffs blocked the entrance. Deputy Tim Jebron was moving from media outlet to media outlet, taking names of principles and handing out press passes, explaining to each that there would be no cameras or microphones allowed, and that there was room for only one person from each organization.

As Jebron reached the end of the row, Tony was there with his hand out.

Jebron said, "I'm sorry, Tony, but Doug Tenney is already inside."

Tony gritted his teeth and said, "Tim, think about it. I'm on a leave of absence from the *Crier*. I'm here as a member of the family."

"Oh, of course. Sorry."

Tony held out his hand again.

Jebron hesitated. "Passes for family members are done through the attorneys' offices. I don't think I can…"

Tony hissed, "Just give me the fucking press pass."

Jebron looked startled. He probably had never heard Tony curse before. Certainly not using that word.

"Well," he said. "I guess it'll be alright."

Tony grabbed the pass from his hand and marched past the other deputies and up the courthouse steps. *God save us from do-bots.*

Inside the courtroom, he walked up the center aisle and sat in the first row behind the defendant's table. He was surprised to settle in next to his mother. He had debated bringing her and had decided it would be too unpleasant.

Court was not yet in session, so he said in a quiet, but relatively normal tone, "Mom, you surprised me. I didn't think you'd want to be here."

"Honey, please. Don't be ridiculous. He's my husband. I have to be here for him. Mr. Pike was kind enough to call this morning and ask if I would like to come with him before all the media craziness started, and I'm glad he did."

Tony leaned over, hugged her, and kissed the top of her head. "Yeah, I should have done that myself."

"No matter," his mother said. "I know you were busy with your new girlfriend. She's wonderful, by the way. She reminds me a lot of Lisa."

Leave it to his mother to come right out with it.

"Really, Mom? I hadn't noticed."

Tony's sister, Rita, had wanted to come to the hearing as well. Speaking with her on the phone the day before, Tony had discouraged her, saying, "The whole thing will last less than an hour. If the judge lets him out on bail, I'm sure he'll be headed home right away. It'll be easier for you to visit him there."

What Tony had left unspoken was the possibility that his father would be held without bail. If that happened, he would be here for Rita to visit whenever she found a more convenient time.

Tony had concluded their conversation by saying, "There's really no need to disrupt your schedule and race over here. Plus, it's better if you never see him like this—in custody, I mean. It's... it's disorienting and distressing."

In the end, she had relented, but only on the condition that Tony promise to call her immediately when the outcome of the hearing was known.

Tony glanced over and saw Doug seated in the first row on the opposite side. It was the preferred spot for reporters. From there, they could get a slightly better view of the defendant. The two men acknowledged each other with the slightest of nods.

Everyone's eyes turned to the front as Lawrence Pike came through a door, followed closely by Charles, still wearing the orange jumpsuit but sans any hardware. Following Charles was one of the deputies Tony had seen in the jail the day before. Once Charles and Pike were seated, the deputy moved to a discreet spot at the side of the room.

The bailiff then entered and commanded, "All rise!"

They rose.

"Hear ye, hear ye. The District Court of the State of Iowa is now in session, Judge Arnold Schroeder presiding."

Tony groaned. Schroeder was not a man known to be kind to accused murderers.

Schroeder sat, banged his gavel once, and instructed everyone to sit.

They sat.

He then addressed the room in a very matter-of-fact tone. "Ladies and gentlemen. We are here this morning to conduct a preliminary hearing in the case of the State of Iowa versus Charles A. Harrington. Mr. Harrington has been charged by the State with the crime of first-degree murder. Please remember, this is not a trial. No guilt or innocence will be established today, and many of the procedural rules you may have observed in trials of other cases, or on TV, are not followed here. But just because this hearing will be conducted in a less formal way than a trial, do not think for one minute that it is unimportant. This is a vital step in our judicial process, and I expect everyone to treat it with the gravitas it deserves."

The judge paused and looked from one side of the room to the other. "Before we begin, let me be clear about two things. First, the defendant, Mr. Harrington, is innocent until proven guilty. That is one of the foundational principles of our democracy, and it will be observed in my courtroom. I expect everyone in this room, and outside of this room, as well, to treat Mr. Harrington and his family in a respectful manner."

Tony was shocked. He'd been in several court proceedings over which Schroeder had presided, and he'd never heard the judge speak in support of a defendant. *He must be really concerned about this crowd of outside media people in his courthouse,* Tony mused.

The judge continued. "Secondly, I expect everyone in this room to remain silent. If I hear a whisper or an outcry, or God help you, a ringing cell phone, you will be removed from the room immediately. I don't care if you're Joe the Plumber or Wolf Blizter. Hear me on this—silent means silent. We are going to do our business quickly and quietly and without interruptions from the gallery."

The judge turned to the first of the two attorney tables. "Mr. Garcia, I assume you are here representing the State?"

"I am, your honor," the county attorney said.

"Mr. Pike, welcome back. It's been a while. Are you representing Mr. Harrington?"

"Yes, your honor, for the purposes of today's hearing."

"Very well." The judge turned back to the first table. "Mr. Garcia, I believe the floor is yours."

Garcia stood to address the judge but remained behind his table. He was concise and professional. He knew Schroeder as well as Tony did, which meant he knew any grandstanding or flamboyance would result in a banging gavel and a reprimand.

The county attorney read the formal charges, which were relatively brief. He then laid out some basic facts of the case.

Tony knew from experience that the State would not want to share too much. This was a very early stage in the process after a relatively short investigation. Garcia would not want to say anything that could come back to haunt him later.

Tony glanced around the room at the unbelievable number of reporters, thinking the media presence would pressure Garcia to be especially brief. Any fact he revealed in court had the potential to arouse the interest of the press. If he mentioned a witness or a piece of evidence, two dozen reporters could leave the courthouse determined to find and interview the witness or confirm or debunk the evidence.

Trying to sound formal and fully-grounded in the evidence, Garcia basically said Tony's dad had known and had demonstrated an interest in the victim, and had admitted to driving the car that had picked her up on the night she'd been killed.

None of that surprised Tony, but Garcia's next bombshell did.

"The State also has evidence that places Mr. Harrington at the scene of the crime."

What? What in the hell could that... Well, shit. It's a Pro Shop.

Of course dad's been there. This is bullshit.

Tony wanted to scream. Remembering his mother, he turned to reassure her, but she sat stoically, as motionless as the marble statues out in hall.

Next, he looked across the rail to his dad's back. He, too, was motionless.

Garcia was still speaking, "In conclusion, your honor, the State believes it can prove beyond any reasonable doubt that Mr. Harrington had a motive, had the opportunity, had the means, and in fact did, strike Ms. Andresson in the head with a golf club, killing her. We respectfully request that he be ordered to stand trial and be held in the Quincy County Law Enforcement Center or a similar secure facility until such time as his trial can be held. Thank you."

"Thank you, Mr. Garcia. Mr. Pike, you and your client have heard the charges read and the remarks by State's counsel. Are you prepared to enter a plea?"

"We are, your honor."

"Very well. How does the defendant plead?"

Charles rose. Pleas were almost always entered by defense counsel on behalf of their clients. However, it didn't surprise Tony to see his dad standing, apparently ready to speak. Tony could imagine his dad begging Pike to let him do this himself.

Charles said, "Your honor, I swear to you and everyone, I did not commit this crime. I respectfully enter a plea of not guilty."

"Thank you, Mr. Harrington. You may be seated. Mr. Garcia, would the State like to be heard on the issue of bail?"

"Yes, your honor." Garcia stood. "As I mentioned, we respectfully ask that Mr. Harrington be held in custody pending his trial. If I wasn't clear, we are requesting bail be denied to ensure he remains in custody."

Schroeder asked, "Would you care to elaborate?"

"Well, your honor," Garcia shifted his feet, giving the appearance the question had taken him by surprise, "we are talking about a defendant in a heinous and violent crime. Mr. Harrington is also a man of considerable means and experience traveling the world. We believe the evidence is clear regarding his commission of this crime, and we believe the combination of these factors makes him a considerable flight risk. For the sake of justice, the preservation of the State's resources, and the safety of the community, Mr. Harrington should remain in custody."

Tony was dying to speak up. He had a comeback to every argument Garcia had made. He bit his tongue.

Schroeder said, "Thank you, Mr. Garcia. Mr. Pike, I assume the defense would like to respond?"

"Oh, indeed, we would," Pike said, standing. "Your honor, for starters, there is no doubt in my mind Mr. Harrington is innocent."

Tony knew this comment had absolutely no bearing on the judge's decision about bail, so he assumed Pike was making it for the benefit of the journalists in the room. Thank you, Tony thought, trying to transmit his appreciation to Pike's brain telepathically.

The attorney continued. "More to the point, Mr. Harrington has absolutely no record of violence in his fifty-seven years. In fact, he has no record of any kind of criminal activity. Except for a couple of speeding tickets, he's never done anything to cause law enforcement or the State of Iowa any concern. He is a well-respected writer and teacher with deep ties to our community and our state. He adamantly professes his innocence, which means he wants to be here for his trial, if it comes to that, in order to prove it. Mr. Harrington has a wife and son here in Iowa, both of whom he loves. He is not a flight risk. He is an innocent man who wishes to stay here and fight until this nonsense is put to bed. We respectfully ask he be released without bail pending trial."

"Your honor!" Garcia was on his feet, and someone in the gallery choked back a laugh.

Schroeder's gavel crashed to the bench immediately.

"Quiet! Sit down, Mr. Garcia. Even Mr. Pike knows it's unlikely Mr. Harrington will leave the courthouse today without posting bail."

Garcia said, "Your honor, if I may…"

"No, Mr. Garcia, you may not. I've heard enough."

The judge looked sternly at Charles. "Mr. Harrington, I don't know who's right. As I mentioned at the outset, guilt or innocence cannot be established today. Unfortunately, because of the nature of the crime and the evidence alleged by the State, I am hereby ruling that you stand trial on the charge proffered by Mr. Garcia."

Tony could see his father's shoulders sag. He was glad he couldn't see his face.

The judge continued. "However, I also mentioned that you are considered innocent until proven guilty. Your lack of a criminal record speaks well for you, as do your successes as a teacher and as a parent."

The judge glanced at Tony.

Holy shit, Tony thought. *He's alluding to me.*

"So here's what I'm offering. I'm going to release you from custody pending trial on three conditions. First, you must post one million dollars in cash bail. This must come from your personal resources, not a third-party bail bondsman. Second, you will wear a secure GPS tracking device at all times so the State can monitor your movements. Third, you will promise to appear in court at each and every required step in the process. You will be on time—no, you will arrive early—at every appearance and will cause the court no reason to regret its generosity. Are those conditions clear?"

Pike rose and said, "They are, your honor."

"And do you agree to them?"

"We do, your honor," Pike said.

"Mr. Pike, I believe the defendant demonstrated earlier a willingness to speak for himself. If you don't object, I'd like to hear from him."

Pike nodded, and Charles stood. "Your honor, I understand your ruling and its conditions completely. And while you apparently think I'm a lot wealthier than I am, I fully and unconditionally agree to your conditions. I swear, I will be here as needed."

"Thank you, Mr. Harrington. My order will be typed up and signed before I leave for lunch. I'm instructing the sheriff and his deputies to do everything reasonable to expedite your release."

The gavel banged again.

"This court is adjourned."

The judge disappeared through a door behind the bench, and the courtroom erupted. Reporters scurried to file or record their reports, spectators grabbed their phones to tell their neighbors or family members what had happened, and Charles Harrington turned and hugged Lawrence Pike. He then spun farther to his right and leaned over the rail to embrace his wife and son. All three were shedding tears.

Garcia walked over to Pike and shook his hand. He said, "Jesus, Larry, what just happened here? Does your client have pictures of the judge in a brothel or something? I've never seen Schroeder act like this."

"Don't ask me," Pike said. "I haven't talked to him. Maybe he just agrees with me that the evidence is wrong, and Mr. Harrington is innocent."

Garcia, a tall, lanky attorney, looked down at Pike and said, "Larry, I'm sorry, but that's just not the case. When you see what we have, you'll understand why I speak so definitively. This time, there is zero doubt your client is guilty."

"Well, then I guess we'd better get to work. When can I meet with you to review this so-called airtight case?"

The two men made arrangements to meet in Garcia's office Monday morning.

Pike then turned back to the three celebrating Harrington's minor victory and said, "It was remarkably nice of judge Schroeder to urge your immediate release, but there is still the matter of the million-dollar bail. Do you have that kind of money?"

Charles shook his head and said, "Hell no. Not in cash. I have more than that in assets, or even in retirement funds I've accumulated over the years, but I hate to cash those out. I'd have to pay taxes on the money, and it would take several days to process the request and get a check."

"How much cash do you have available?"

The group turned toward the new voice. Ramesh Bhatt had walked up to them from the courtroom gallery.

Charles looked at his friend and said, "I'm not sure. Perhaps two or three hundred thousand in cash accounts and savings. I might be able to get another hundred thousand from my publisher. They haven't given me an advance on a book in years, but I think they will if I ask."

Bhatt said, "See what you can pull together by four o'clock. However much you're short, I'll cover it."

Charles looked astonished. "Ramesh, that's incredibly kind of you, but I couldn't…"

"Nonsense," Bhatt said. "You can, and you will. You're my friend. These charges are ridiculous. I have no doubt you're innocent, and I have no doubt you will appear in court. So I'm happy to put up the money. You can call it an advance on your movie royalties if it makes you feel better."

"Actually, that would make me feel better," Charles said. "If we can sign an agreement to that effect, for whatever money you contribute, then yes, thank you, I'll gratefully accept your help."

Pike interjected. "That works better for me too. The judge made it clear he wants the bail to come from Mr. Harrington's own resources. By showing it's coming from his movie royalties, we won't have to worry about playing loose with the judge's orders."

"It's done, then," Bhatt said. "I'll come to the jail at four, and we'll conclude the payments and paperwork. With any luck, we'll have you out of there by the end of the day."

Charles reached out, grabbed Bhatt's arm, and pulled him to the rail. Wrapping his arms around the director, Charles said again, "Thank you, my friend. I'll never forget this."

***

At 4:47 p.m., Charles Harrington was escorted to the front door of the Law Enforcement Center by Deputy Jebron. Tony, his mother, Bhatt, and Pike were right behind them. They paused at the glass doors and looked at the zoo assembled outside. Reporters, well-wishers, movie cast members, and curious bystanders were crowded onto the sidewalk and front lawn.

"You sure you wanna leave?" Jebron asked, smiling. "It's a lot more peaceful back in that cell."

Charles looked at the deputy and said, "No offense to your wonderful hospitality, but I'll take my chances with the outside world." He pushed open the door and walked into a sea of cameras and microphones.

The group had decided in advance that no comments would be made this afternoon. As the press shouted questions, they pressed forward to the parking lot, where Tony's Explorer and Pike's Lincoln sedan were parked and waiting.

As they reached the edge of the mob, still several steps from the vehicles, Tony's eye caught movement off to his left. He turned and saw a tall, dark-haired man with bandages on his face moving swiftly toward them.

Oh no... "Dad!"

Tony's warning came just as Braden Borden screamed, "Murderer!"

Time slowed to a crawl. Tony could sense his parents turning toward the sound of the scream. He heard the rest of the crowd grow quiet. He saw Borden charging forward, now just steps away. Then he saw it, the glint of gray metal in Borden's hand. The hand was rising, pointing, aiming the barrel of a revolver at his father's chest.

Tony reacted, lunging forward, his right arm lashing out toward the gun. His hand felt cold steel just as an enormous sound erupted near his head.

Now half deaf, Tony kept going, crashing into Borden and tackling him to the ground. As Borden thrashed and pushed, trying to free himself from Tony's grasp, all Tony could think about was the gun. *Where is the gun?*

As his hearing returned, Tony heard screams, cries for help, deputies shouting orders. *The gun. Where's the gun?*

Then he felt it. The metal was scraping across the back of his head. The gun was still in Borden's hand, and he was holding it against the back of Tony's skull. Again, Tony reacted, even before thinking about it. He released his grip on Borden, flipped over on his back, and lashed out with his foot, catching Borden in the kidney, one of the most painful places to take a punch. Borden screamed, wriggling on the ground, trying to roll onto his side to face Tony.

As Borden's hand with the gun swung over and across his body, Tony spun a quarter turn on the ground and kicked again, this time connecting with the side of Borden's face. The man screamed again, then suddenly, it was over.

Sheriff's deputies and bystanders swarmed Borden, pinning him to the ground and prying the gun from his fingers.

Tony sprang up from the ground, turning to see whether his father had been shot. Relief erupted from every pore as Tony saw his dad clambering up from the ground and brushing the dirt off of his charcoal gray suit. Behind his parents, Tony noticed a knot of people on the stairs. Several were bent low, apparently helping someone who had been hurt.

A siren wailed from a couple of blocks away. Because most of the law enforcement officers in the county were already on site, Tony assumed the siren was an ambulance. He pushed through the crowd to see who had been injured. Sprawled on the concrete, blood oozing from a hole in his shirt, was Doug Tenney.

Town Crier

Town Crier reporter shot in courthouse attack

Braden Borden charged with attempted murder and assault with a deadly weapon

Ben Smalley, Editor

ORNEY, Iowa – Doug Tenney, 31, of Orney, was listed in serious but stable condition at MercyOne Medical Center in Des Moines at press time Thursday night, following a shooting incident at the Quincy County Law Enforcement Center (LEC)...

Thursday afternoon.

Motion picture actor Braden Borden, 38, of Anaheim, Calif., was arrested at the scene and charged with assault with a deadly weapon, according to County Attorney Alejandro "Alex" Garcia. He said Borden was also charged with the attempted murder of Charles Harrington, 57, of Iowa City, an author of books and screenplays who is charged with murder in the death of Charlotte Andresson.

The incident occurred when Harrington was being released from the LEC after posting a $1 million cash bond, the amount set by Judge Arnold Schroder in a hearing at the Quincy County Courthouse Thursday morning. Harrington denies he committed the crime.

During the hearing, Garcia told the court the State of Iowa has evidence that Harrington had an interest in Andresson and had been at the Orney Country Club where the young woman's body was found early Sunday morning.

Sheriff George Mackey said Borden had a relationship with Andresson in the past. Borden arrived outside the courthouse shortly before 5 p.m. Thursday carrying a revolver, the sheriff said. Several journalists and others in the crowd outside the LEC heard Borden shout "Murderer!" and saw him point the revolver at Harrington.

Harrington's son, Tony Harrington of Orney, reached out and knocked Borden's arm to the side, causing the shot to go wide and strike Tenney, the sheriff said.

Tenney was at the LEC observing the release of Charles Harrington on assignment for the *Town Crier*.

"Mr. Tenney was very unfortunate to be standing in just the wrong spot when Mr. Borden fired his gun," Sheriff Mackey said. "The young man suffered one gunshot wound, plus some minor injuries to his arm, shoulder, and face related to his fall to the sidewalk."

The sheriff credited the deputy sheriffs on site with reacting quickly, subduing Borden, and preventing any further injuries.

"No one could have expected a violent incident like this at something as simple as a man being released on bail," the sheriff said. "But my men are trained to be ready regardless of the…

Chapter 16

Des Moines, Iowa—Saturday, June 27

Tony stirred and sat up. Every part of him ached. He glanced left and realized he had been leaning against Darcy as he slept on the waiting room couch. Her eyes were closed, but she didn't appear to be sleeping.

"Sorry," he said in a whisper, noting that others in the room were still sleeping. It was a large and comfortable room just outside one of the medical center's three intensive care units, but no matter how comfortable a waiting room was designed to be, it was always a lousy place to spend the night.

Tony glanced at his watch—4:36 a.m. "Any news while I slept?"

"No. I would've woken you if anyone had come around."

Tony reached into his pocket and pulled out his phone. A text from Doug's dad said he would arrive before noon. Harold "Hoppy" Tenney was a big rig truck driver. He had been in Colorado when he had received Tony's call about the shooting. He was pulling a trailer full of fresh fruit from California, so he'd skipped a night's sleep and had kept driving. It would get him to Des Moines within an hour of what the airlines could have done, even if there hadn't been an all-too-likely delay.

They had called Doug's dad shortly after arriving at the hospital the previous evening. They had wanted to know Doug had survived the helicopter ride to the medical center before reaching out to his father.

By the time Tony and Darcy had arrived in Des Moines by car, Doug was in surgery. Because of its urgent nature, the surgery had begun without the usual permissions and background information. Two hours later, as Doug was moved to the recovery room, one of the hospital staff had come to Tony and Darcy and had asked them to follow her to a consultation room. The surgeon, Dr. Gina Becker, had been waiting for them there. She'd asked if Tony could put her in touch with Doug's family. She needed to give them an update, as well as ask about Doug's medical history.

Tony had explained that Doug's only family was his father. At the surgeon's request, Tony had made a second call to Hoppy's cell phone, putting the call on speaker so all could hear.

The surgeon's first question had been whether it was okay for Tony and Darcy to be there. Because they weren't family, the surgeon couldn't share any information with them unless she had permission. Hoppy had assured the doctor it was fine, saying "Tony's the closest thing to a brother Doug will ever have. Please include him in every-thing until I get there." Doug's dad went on to say, "I don't know Ms. Gillson, but if she's with Tony, then she's fine with me too."

With that out of the way, the surgeon had proceeded to tell them Doug had been shot once with a .38 caliber bullet. The slug had entered his body just below the rib cage, miraculously missing any vital organs except for tearing a small piece from the edge of his liver. As it exited the body, it had torn a nasty hole in his right side.

The doctor had said, "I was told he was an unlucky bystander in a shooting, but I can tell you, from my perspective, he was extremely lucky. We repaired the damage, and barring any complications, he should recover with few, if any, lasting consequences."

Dr. Becker had then asked a series of questions about Doug's health history, after which she had excused herself, hurrying to scrub in and prepare for her next surgery. Tony had felt a mixture of relief and anxiety. He'd been thrilled to hear the positive news, but had known he wouldn't feel good again until Doug was on his feet and headed home.

Now in the waiting room, Tony stood. "I'm going to check on him. You want to come?"

"You go," Darcy said. "If you need me, just whistle, and I'll come running."

Tony stopped at the door to the ICU. He washed his hands thoroughly at the sanitizer station, and then pulled on a gown, cap, and mask. Hand sanitizing had been a standard precaution in hospitals for many years, but the gown, cap, and mask were new precautions since the days of the pandemic.

As Tony entered Doug's room, the pungent odor of serious medical care washed over him. The abundance of pharmaceuticals, plastics, body fluids, and cleaning solutions combined to create an unmistakable scent. The lights in the room were low to promote rest. The darkened room had the additional effect of accentuating the dizzying array of flashing lights, display screens, and alert messages on the stacks of high-tech equipment. Tony was pretty sure NASA had used less gear to launch the latest Mars rover.

A young female nurse was using a penlight to check wire leads or tubes or something beneath Doug's gown. Tony hung back, not wanting to interrupt.

Without looking up, the nurse said quietly, "It's okay. As long as you approach from the other side of the bed, you won't bother me."

"Has he been awake?" Tony asked hopefully.

"Not yet, but it's still early. He's only been out of surgery for a few hours."

Seeing Doug lying there strapped to the bed and tethered to the machines was almost more than Tony could bear. *This is my fault.*

Intellectually, Tony knew he couldn't be blamed. It was Borden's fault, and that of dumb, stupid, bad luck. But emotionally, Tony couldn't shake it. *This is my fault.*

He slid a small chair to the bedside and sat. He took Doug's hand and began praying silently. He didn't notice when the nurse slipped away and left him alone in the room.

***

At 9:30 a.m., Tony happened to be back in the room, once again holding Doug's hand, when suddenly his friend coughed, groaned loudly, and rasped out, "What... the... hell?"

Tony stood, elated. As Doug's eyes focused on Tony, Doug croaked, "Tone-man. You shot me!"

An older male nurse who was changing IV bags shot Tony an alarmed look.

Tony laughed and said, "I did not shoot you! Braden Borden shot you. I just helped him aim."

Doug coughed and groaned again. "Dammit. Do not make me laugh. Whoever shot me did a good job of it. This hurts like a son of a bitch."

The nurse finished his task and asked Tony to step back. He

used the penlight to check Doug's eyes, then asked him to squeeze his hand.

"What's with all the hand-holding around here? Jeez, can't you at least find a woman to do that?"

The nurse smiled and asked Doug to rate his pain on a scale of one to ten.

"Two hundred and twelve," Doug said. "Shoot me up with something before I start screaming."

Tony left the nurse to it and stepped outside the room. He fished his phone from underneath the gown and texted Darcy to come join him. A few minutes later, she was at his side, looking silly in a gown that hung loosely on her slender frame.

The nurse came out of the room and simply nodded as he went by, indicating he was done with Doug for the moment.

"I love this," Darcy said.

Somewhat surprised, Tony asked, "Love what?"

"Sorry, I mean the gown and mask. I love being anonymous. Today I'm just another loved one visiting a patient. No one can recognize me."

Tony was again reminded of how irritating it must be to always be recognized, to always have to think about what you're saying or doing, knowing that someone is probably photographing you. He made a mental note to talk to her more about the subject later, then put it out of his mind.

They walked into the room and up to Doug's bed.

Doug opened his eyes and said quietly, still in a raspy voice, "Hey, Darcy, thanks for coming."

"So much for anonymity," Tony said.

"I recognized the bumps on the front of her gown. I'd know that shape anywhere."

"Jeez, Doug…" Tony said.

"Mr. Tenney, if you weren't tied to that bed, I would slap you silly," Darcy teased.

"Go ahead," Doug said. "After what that guy just gave me, I wouldn't feel it. Besides, my best friend shot me. Why shouldn't his girlfriend beat me up?"

Tony could tell Doug was going to ride him relentlessly for months, maybe years, about the gunshot. At the moment, Tony was so happy his friend was awake and doing well, he didn't care.

Chapter 17

Orney, Iowa—Sunday, June 28

Sunday was the first time in days Tony had felt at ease and able to keep at bay the looming storm clouds. His parents were back in Iowa City, Doug was out of intensive care and expected to be released from the hospital in a couple of days, and the state and national media had dissipated. They would be back for his father's trial, if a trial actually occurred, but for now, Orney had resumed its quiet Midwestern vibe. Even the movie cast had mostly left town, while Bhatt sorted out how to proceed.

Bhatt kept his room at the local Marriott, saying he could work from anywhere. His permanent home was in the mountains east of L.A., but he didn't want to return there until the movie was finished. As a widower with no children, he was happy to stay in Iowa where he had friends and could work without interruption.

The other person who stayed in town was Darcy Gillson. She told Tony she wanted to spend some time with him and help with the efforts to exonerate his father. Tony couldn't find the words to resist, marveling at the star's continued interest in him and his family.

They spent all of Sunday together, beginning with Mass at St. Mary's Church at 11 a.m. Like many young people, Tony had mixed feelings about religion. He believed there was something larger in the universe than just happenstance, and he believed in the power of prayer, but he wasn't big on jumping through all the hoops put in his path by the organized church.

However, he still enjoyed going to Mass when his schedule allowed. There was comfort in the ritual and a community spirit among the churchgoers that attracted him. He also enjoyed much of the modern music being played and sung. Lastly, there was the benefit of not having to lie to his mother when she asked him whether he had been to church on Sunday.

Tony loved the priest currently serving at St. Mary's. Father Gregory Benedict believed faith was a journey in which everyone was called to serve others and explore the richness of God's creation, rather than a set of rules to be obeyed. That seemed about right to Tony.

He had been surprised and happy when Darcy had readily agreed to join him.

The service was followed by a bike ride and picnic lunch. They first drove back to Tony's place, where they changed into shorts and casual shirts. Tony left his bike shorts in the drawer, knowing Darcy didn't have formal riding gear. It seemed ungentlemanly to dress for his own comfort when he couldn't see to hers. So he wore a pair of cut-offs and an NPR t-shirt he had won as a door prize at the annual Firefighters' Pancake Breakfast. Darcy wore yellow shorts and a navy sleeveless top.

When she came out of the bathroom after changing, Tony said, "You look great."

"Thanks."

"No, I mean really, really great."

She stood on her tiptoes and kissed him quickly. "We'd better let that go, or we're never gonna get out of here."

Tony couldn't argue with that, so they headed out and climbed into the Explorer. Tony's bike was in the back. They drove to Ben's house and borrowed his bicycle for Darcy. He had left it for them on the front porch of his single-story ranch. Built in the 1960s, it was a prairie school design, with sleek lines, a stone front, and a walkout basement to the sloping backyard. The bike was an old Schwinn ten-speed, but it had new tires and was meticulously maintained. Tony was pretty sure it would outlast his new Cervélo without much trouble.

Next, they stopped to pick up the picnic lunch, which Tony carefully "prepared" by handing a teen at the drive-through window a credit card for a bucket of KFC, original recipe, a side of mashed potatoes, and a side of beans. Already in the Explorer, waiting to be added to the feast, were two diet sodas and a bottle of wine.

The next stop was Veterans Memorial Park. After parking at the curb, they unloaded the bikes from the Explorer. Tony bundled the food, drinks, plates, and utensils into a large vinyl tote and strapped it to the handlebars of his bicycle. To Darcy's he tied a large quilt, rolled up and secured with a short bungee cord.

They strapped on their helmets and headed through the park to its southwestern edge, where they found the head of the trail leading down into the river valley.

It was a perfect June day, warm and sunny with a slight breeze. The woods were lush and green from the spring rains. They rode in silence for twenty minutes or so, enjoying the sunshine, the buzz of insects, and occasional birdsong. As the path turned downward to begin its descent into the valley, the views across to the other side were spectacular.

"Not the miles of cornfields we picture when we think of Iowa!" Darcy called out from behind him on the trail.

"Who's we?" Tony shouted back. "Some of us think of this view first."

"Touché!"

For several minutes, almost no pedaling was required. Tony enjoyed coasting down the winding trail but knew all too well that the payback would come later when they had to ride back up.

As they neared the river, they came to the old bridge that spanned the water. It had been a railroad trestle at one time, now converted and paved for cyclists and joggers to enjoy. Tony braked to stop short of the bridge, and Darcy slowed to a stop beside him.

"Remember that story I told over pizza about being shot at?"

"Of course," she said.

"That's the spot, right up there." He nodded toward the bridge.

"Kinda gives me the willies."

"Well, you can un-willie, because we're not going to cross today."

"No?"

"Nope, we have a lunch to eat. Follow me."

He turned his bike to the left and took a steep gravel trail down beside the bridge toward the riverbank. The path curved back under the bridge and continued for two or three hundred more yards, following a bend in the river. It ended at a large clearing. The thick grass was shin-deep and ran all the way to the water's edge. About a third of the way into the river, a sandbar formed a bright crescent.

"Would m'lady care to dine on grass or sand?"

"Methinks grass, kind sir," Darcy said, giggling. "Methinks sand makes a poor condiment for chicken."

"An excellent choice. I believe we have just the spot you're seeking right over here." Tony bowed and made a sweeping gesture toward the edge of the clearing where the grass was level and enjoyed some shade from the forest. There they spread out the quilt and sat on it cross-legged, the tote between them.

When they had enjoyed their fill of the Colonel's cooking, Tony opened the wine. He then looked around and realized glasses or cups had not made the journey.

"My apologies, dear lady. Methinks I royally screwed up."

"No worries, fine sir. The court jester once demonstrated how wine can be consumed without the aid of such accoutrements."

Darcy took the bottle from him, raised it to her lips, and drank two large gulps. "Ah, a very fine vintage."

Tony stared at her. His open mouth slowly drew into a smile. He grabbed the bottle and took a swig.

Darcy said, "I noticed I drank two full swallows, but my companion had but one. Is there a method behind such madness?"

"Yep," Tony said, dropping the Shakespearian mannerism and adopting a southern drawl. "I prefer my women to be exactly twice as drunk as me. That way they don't find me so damn unattac... unattrac... uh... ugly."

Darcy grinned and set the bottle down on the quilt. She spotted the cork and returned it to the open neck with a firm pop of her hand. She then reached out and pulled Tony to her. She kissed him hard, then moved her lips to his ear.

The sensation of her tongue flicking across his lobe was exquisite. She whispered. "You, Mr. Harrington, are anything but unattractive. I think you're wonderful, and I don't need more alcohol to want you inside me."

"Works for me," Tony said, pulling her down onto the quilt. He was on his back, with Darcy pressed against him. He wrapped his arms around her and kissed her. Their mouths opened and tongues entwined as their breaths became faster and shallower.

He rolled over onto his side and let Darcy slide off of him onto her back. With his head propped up on one arm so he could look at her, he ran his hands lightly over her breasts, down across her stomach, and stopped between her legs. Her shorts already were unsnapped and unzipped.

How did she do that? he wondered as he pushed his fingers deeper.

She gasped and raised her hips. Staring into Tony's eyes, she said, "Can we do this? Here? Will someone see us?"

"Probably not," Tony said softly, "but you never know. Someone in a tube or a canoe could float past, or some hikers could stumble across us." He moved his finger up and down in two quick motions. She gasped again.

He said, "Or some couple as horny as us could come looking for this same spot."

Darcy leaned up and kissed him. When she drew back, she said, "No one on planet Earth is as horny as I am right now. Take me, Tony. Now. Please."

"Works for me," Tony whispered.

***

It was wonderful but didn't last long. The combination of their urgent need for each other and their nervousness about being seen caused them to hurry through the lovemaking to its conclusion. In addition, the occasional mosquito bite on bare skin didn't encourage them to linger.

They quickly dressed, picked up the trash and re-rolled the quilt. Tony caught Darcy looking around in all directions, then doing so again.

"You're dressed now," he said. "Seems like an odd time to be nervous."

"Do you have any idea what a picture of us—of me—doing that..." she nodded at the matted grass where they had just been, "would bring a member of the paparazzi?"

"Nope. Not a clue."

Darcy froze for a moment, then laughed. "Actually, I don't either, but I'm pretty sure it's a lot. And God help me if some fisherman's iPhone movie made it onto the internet."

"Hey, a video like that made Paris Hilton a star. Maybe we should stick around. I've got a phone here somewhere..."

"Very funny. You forget, I'm already famous. More importantly, I'm respected. I need to protect that at all costs."

"Just kidding," Tony said, mildly irritated at her mood swing. "I understand, really. I'm not too anxious to star in an X-rated video either. My mother would have a heart attack."

"Of course. I'm sorry. I know it's not just about me. I think I warned you in our first conversation that my desire to protect my self-interests drives a lot of my decisions."

"Again, I understand. You have a lot riding on your image. One misstep could cost you a lot more than it would cost me or anyone of less interest to the public."

"Let's change the subject," she said. "Let's talk about how the virile and gallant young man is going to carry me and my bike back up to the top of that long hill."

"No problem," he said with a grin. "As soon as I spot that guy, I'll be happy to talk with him about it."

"Ugh. I guess that means I'm on my own. Oh, well. If I have to pedal myself, then I might as well show off a little and beat you to the top."

"Is that a challenge?"

Before Tony had finished the question, Darcy was off, pedaling furiously back toward the bridge. Once she made the first turn and was out of sight, Tony never saw her again until he reached the summit. As he crested it, huffing heavily and sweating even more, he spotted her sitting cross-legged at the side of the path, sipping the bottle of Diet Coke he had wrapped in the quilt for her.

"Nice of you to join me," she said, smiling broadly.

"Bite me," he said, riding past her and continuing east toward the park.

***

Once back at Tony's house, they plopped into kitchen chairs, not wanting to get dirt and sweat on the living room furniture. They chatted about the ride, and the river valley, and other mundane things, but eventually the conversation turned back to Charlotte's murder and Tony's father.

"It had to have been Borden," Tony said. "I don't know how or why he dragged my dad into it, but Borden's the one with the temper and the jealousy. My God, he didn't come all the way to Iowa just to sit in the Hampton Inn. Nobody could possibly believe he didn't go looking for her when he arrived Saturday night."

Darcy appeared to disagree. "Tony, think about it. If Borden did it, why did he try to shoot your dad? Now, instead of getting away with something, he's back in jail on serious felony charges."

"Maybe it was part of his plan all along. By faking his rage at my father, he convinces everyone he didn't commit the murder. He knew he was a suspect, so he had to divert attention from himself."

Darcy looked skeptical.

"Well, c'mon. It worked on you. The fact he attacked my dad has convinced you he's not the killer."

She shrugged an acknowledgement.

Tony continued. "So he ends up doing a couple of years in prison for assault but gets away with first degree murder. Or…" He paused, then snapped his fingers. "Maybe he never intended to hit my dad. Maybe his intent was to miss. When I intervened, I caused the shot to hit Doug. If Borden was going to miss on purpose—if no one was injured—he almost certainly would have been able to plea the charge down to something less serious."

"Maybe," Darcy said. Her voice betrayed that she was still unconvinced.

Tony looked at her and noticed a bead of sweat at the hairline, just above her temple. He lifted his hand and swept it away with his thumb. Before he could retract his hand, Darcy reached up and grabbed it in hers, turning her face to kiss his palm. "We don't want to talk about crimes and suspects anymore, do we?" she asked.

"No, probably not," Tony said, his voice low and his mouth dry.

"We should probably clean up."

"Yes, probably."

"It's probably best if we take one shower instead of two. Cheaper and better for the environment and all."

"Yes, probably," Tony was barely able to croak out.

They stood and walked into the bathroom together. The combination of warm water, liquid soap, and bare skin had the predictable effect. Later, after an hour on Tony's queen-sized bed, they needed another shower.

***

While Darcy was drying her hair, Tony was back in the kitchen fixing salads for dinner. He had turned on the television in the living room, tuned it to Comedy Central, and turned up the volume so he could hear it while he worked.

When Darcy came out of the bathroom, she stopped in front of the TV. She called out, "Do you mind if I change the channel?"

"Of course not," he said.

She switched it to Entertainment Tonight, which was just beginning. "Occupational hazard," she said as she came into the kitchen.

Tony didn't think much about it or pay much attention to the show until he heard his name. He and Darcy both froze, looked at each other, then hurried into the living room. On the screen was a picture of Darcy and Tony, standing next to their bicycles near the park. It was evident the picture had been snapped after their ride, because they both looked terrible – sweaty, dirty, and with helmet hair.

The announcer was saying "…seen with her new beau in the town of Orney, Iowa, where he lives, and she has been on location filming a new movie for Prima Racconto Films. Orney has been in the news a lot lately, due to the brutal murder of one of Gillson's castmates, Charlotte…"

"Turn it off," Darcy said.

Tony did.

She sank down onto the sofa. "Dammit, dammit, dammit."

Tony had no idea what to say, so he waited.

Darcy stood. "Well, it was bound to happen." She headed for the kitchen.

Tony followed, "So what does it mean? Is it so bad to have people know we're, we're… well, whatever the hell we are?"

"Exactly," Darcy said, exasperated. "It just complicates a situation that's already too complicated. Just what *do* we tell the press, now that they're going to be asking about our relationship?

And how does this affect what we can do, where and when? Now the word is out, everyone will be watching for us, taking pictures and speculating about what every pose and move indicates."

She looked at him and added, "Think about it. What if the person who took that photo had seen us at the beginning of the ride instead of the end? What if they had followed us to get more pics? This could have been a disaster."

Tony's anxiety rose as he realized she was right, not only about what had almost happened, but about what would happen in the future. Now there was every possibility the paparazzi would be following them. Photographers might be at his doors and windows at some point. He found himself unable to resist turning and looking out the kitchen window. Even without the full-time vultures lurking around, every person with a smart phone, which was just about everyone on the planet, was now a potential photographer for celebrity news.

Tony turned to Darcy, reached out, and pulled her to him. Looking down into her eyes, he said, "Hanging with you is turning out to be kind of a pain."

She looked down and he pulled her closer, whispering in her ear, "And you're so worth it."

Chapter 18

Orney, Iowa—Monday, June 29

Tony was at his desk in his home office, typing out some notes to himself about potential avenues to investigate for his father, when his cell phone began playing Big Head Todd and the Monsters. It was his father's ringtone.

"Hey, Dad. I was just thinking about you. What's up? You and mom get settled in at home okay?"

"Yes, thanks. But I'm headed back to Orney now."

Tony glanced at his watch. It was nearly two in the afternoon. "Now? How come?"

"Your lawyer friend called me and said it was urgent that I meet with him. Sorry, I guess I should call him my lawyer. In any case, he asked me to drop by this afternoon, and I said I could. You know, it's not like I'm too busy or anything."

"Did he say why?"

"No, just that it was urgent. I'm calling because I'd like you to be there with me if you can get free."

"Of course, Dad. No problem. What time?"

"Four o'clock. Pike's office. If I push it hard, I'll just make it, so I'll meet you there, okay?"

"Yes, I'll be there."

Tony was baffled. What could be so urgent that Pike would pull his dad back from Iowa City so soon? Any trial would be months away in all likelihood. He found his hopes rising as it occurred to him that maybe the county attorney had admitted his mistake and had dropped the charges. Maybe they'd found the real killer.

Suddenly Tony couldn't wait until 4 p.m.

***

When Pike escorted the father and son into his office and shut the door, his first words were, "Charles, I'd like to suggest that we ask Tony to leave. I'm going to be discussing some key issues of your case with you, and it might be best if you hear them one-on-one before deciding when and how you communicate them to your family."

Tony's father reacted immediately and negatively. "No," he said. "I won't ask Tony to leave. I trust him completely. I thought you did too. I want him to know everything I know."

Tony said, "Dad, I don't mind. If Mr. Pike thinks…"

"No," Charles said firmly. "I've already said I want you here. Let's get on with it."

"Very well," Pike said. "Please take a seat."

Tony and his dad sat in armchairs facing Pike, who sat behind his desk. The attorney opened a drawer, took out a file folder, a USB drive, and a yellow legal pad. He said, "Charles, I want you to understand you have some options in terms of how we move forward.

There are some things we can try to mitigate the end result."

Charles looked at Tony and back at Pike. "What are you talking about? Mitigate what?"

Pike ignored the questions and said, "You have some options, but continuing to lie to me is not one of them."

"Now just a damn minute. Lie to you? I haven't lied to you. Every word…"

"Just stop!" Pike roared.

Tony jumped in his seat, agog at the lawyer's outburst.

"Mr. Harrington," Pike continued in a strong but less angry voice, "I have seen the evidence. I've seen these reports." He held up the file folder. "And I've seen this video." He held up the USB drive. "I now know what the authorities know, and what you know. So let's be adults here and talk about your options. And stop all the nonsense."

"Dammit Pike, I don't care what you've seen, or think you've seen. I am not a liar, and I'm sure as hell not a killer. And if you don't want to represent me and prove my innocence, then I'll just find someone who will."

Pike was about to respond, but Tony interrupted. "Dad, Mr. Pike, can we just turn everything down a notch?" Tony looked at the lawyer and said, "Maybe it will help if we could see what you've seen. Then perhaps we can figure out where the disconnect is between what you and the authorities think you know and what my dad knows."

"Of course," Pike said. "Charles, this is why I suggested Tony not be here. Are you sure you want me to go into this with him present?"

"Yes, I'm sure," Charles said testily. "Get on with it."

Pike did, and within minutes, Tony and his dad were wishing he hadn't.

Pike began by reiterating what they already knew. Charlotte Andresson had been seen getting into a blue vintage Mustang convertible at about midnight Saturday night. Later, her fingerprints and hair had been found inside Tony's car. She had not ridden in the car with Tony. Charles had been driving the car, or had been the last known driver of the car, shortly before Andresson entered it.

Tony and his dad were impatient. They had heard all of this, and there were reasonable explanations as to what had happened. But Pike continued. "The state also has witnesses regarding the fact you and Andresson were flirting with each other and embraced in public after a luncheon on the Wednesday before her death."

"We weren't flirting, and it was a simple hug, a goodbye gesture between friends."

"That may be, but they have witnesses saying it appeared to be more than that." Pike paused and cleared his throat. "And they have witnesses saying this is not the first time your head has been turned, shall we say, by a beautiful young woman."

Charles suddenly looked stricken.

Pike said, "You can see, Charles, why I kept asking about Tony's presence here. Do you want me to continue?"

Charles hung his head but said, almost in a whisper, "Yes."

"The DCI has dug deeply and has outlined at least three instances in which you allegedly had affairs with women who were not your wife. Is this true?"

Charles lifted his head and turned to his son. "Tony, I…"

Tony was stone-faced. The accusation was world-shattering for him. He had always admired and respected his father. He had felt so blessed to have grown up with parents who were not only smart and kind and supportive, but were in a stable, loving marriage.

He shook his head once, swallowed hard, and said, "Dad, it's a conversation for another day. Let's stay on task here."

Pike smiled at Tony, but spoke to Charles. "You should be very proud of the young man you've raised. Not many would have his poise in this situation. Let's move on. Unfortunately, from a criminal defense perspective, it gets much worse."

Jeez, Tony thought. *What could possibly be worse?*

Pike said, "You'll recall Mr. Garcia's comment that they could place you inside the pro shop at the golf course?"

"Yes, but..." Charles began.

Pike interrupted him. "It's not just that. Ms. Andresson was killed by a blow from a Mizuno seven iron. The weapon was left at the scene. Her blood and hair are on it." Pike looked up at his client. "So are your fingerprints."

"What?" Charles rose out of his seat.

Tony felt his throat constrict. His heart pounded in his ears. What?

"Sit down, Charles. Your fingerprints are on the murder weapon. And I'm not through."

Pike set one report aside and picked up another from the file. "The autopsy results show that Ms. Andresson had unprotected sex prior to her death. Semen was found inside her body. It's yours."

"Bullshit!" Charles snarled, back on his feet. "That's a lie! That's not possible!"

Pike looked stern. "Please sit down. These aren't my findings. I'm just telling you what the prosecutor is going to bring into court if you let this case go to trial."

Tony pulled himself together enough to speak. "How is it possible?" he asked. "I mean, if my dad wasn't there, if he didn't do this, then how could they think it's his semen they found?"

"Gentlemen, according to this report from the lab, the DNA match with Charles's blood sample is a lock. It's your semen, Charles."

"I'm sorry," Charles said, "but you're wrong. They're wrong. It can't be mine because I was never with her. I didn't see her that night, I didn't have sex with her, and I didn't kill her."

Pike shook his head and stood, grabbing the USB drive and walking over to a flat-screen television hanging on the office wall to the right of his desk.

"You say you weren't there. Perhaps you'd like to explain this."

He plugged in the drive, returned to his desk, and punched a few buttons on the remote control. A video appeared on the screen. A time stamp at the bottom of the picture read *Sunday, June 21, 12:19 a.m.* The picture was of a sidewalk, flower bed, and lawn. The sidewalk was long, leading down to a parking lot.

Tony recognized the area immediately. It was the front of the Orney Country Club. From the angle of the video, it was clear it had come from a camera placed over the front door.

As the time scrolled by on the bottom, a woman came into view, followed by a man. The woman was immediately recognizable. It was Charlotte Andresson. She was dressed in a very short skirt, sandals, and a tube top. Even in black and white, she looked fantastic. She was smiling. The man behind her was dressed in slacks and a button-down shirt. He wore a baseball cap, pulled low over his eyes.

Please, God, no, Tony pleaded silently.

When the couple reached the door, Andresson stepped to the side, and the man approached the door. Only his back was visible for a few moments. Then he took a step back, grasped the door handle, and pulled. As he did so, he looked up for a moment. Into the camera stared Charles Harrington.

"How in God's name…?" Charles slumped back in his chair.

Tony felt like he was going to pass out.

Pike grabbed the remote control and keyed the USB to resume playing at 1:09 a.m. One minute later, into the view of the camera, came the head, shoulders, back, and legs of the man in the cap. He strode out of view into the parking lot.

The view changed again. This time, the video was from the parking lot surveillance camera. It showed the man in the cap getting into a car and driving away. The car was a powder blue 1967 Ford Mustang convertible. The license plate was clearly visible. It was Tony's car.

Pike said, "Remember when the couple paused at the front door in the first video segment? Garcia said that is when you took a lock pick—one of the sophisticated electric ones—and unlocked the door."

Charles appeared to be catatonic. He didn't respond.

Pike continued, "After they arrested you, they searched your car. At that point, they had probable cause and didn't need a warrant. They found this."

He slid a photograph across the table. Charles glanced down but didn't seem to register what he was seeing. Tony looked over and saw it was an eight by ten-inch photo of a KLM Professional Lockpick Tool.

Pike said, "They found it stuffed between the seat cushions in the backseat of your car. So, as I said," he continued, "we need to talk about options. We know things can happen. Maybe it was an accident somehow, while you played some kind of lover's game with the golf clubs. Maybe there was an argument, and you lost your head. If you killed her in a moment of rage, then that's not premeditated murder. It's a lesser crime. In fact, I'm pretty sure Garcia only charged you with first-degree murder because he knows you're going to plea bargain to something less."

Tony's father finally moved. He leaned forward in his chair and said, "But it wasn't me. I swear, I wasn't there."

Pike said, "Please, Charles. This isn't helping."

Tony felt like he was in a nightmare—an actual nightmare in which things he knew couldn't be true suddenly were.

He stood, his legs unsteady beneath him. "I'm sorry. I have to go."

Neither his father nor Pike said a word as he walked out the door.

***

Tony's house was nearly dark when his cell phone buzzed for the fourth or fifth time. He finally fished it out of his pocket and turned it off. He was curled up on the sofa, staring at nothing. He had barely moved in more than four hours. *Dad, how could you?*

His brain was in turmoil, and his heart had turned to stone. The man he loved and respected, the father he admired and thought he knew, a serial adulterer, a liar, a cheat, and… and a murderer. *Daddy, how could you?* Tony began to sob uncontrollably.

He had spent nearly eight years at the *Crier* writing about, and sometimes pursuing, evil people, men and women who committed terrible crimes like assault and murder. Now, Charles Harrington, his own father, his rock, was one of those people. Tony couldn't cope. He didn't know what to do. How could he ever face his mother? How could he tell Rita? How could he go on in Orney, or anywhere, after a sensational trial showed the world his father's true character?

"Tony."

He knew the voice, and he knew the scent. It was Darcy. He must have dozed off.

He opened his eyes, and she was there facing him on her knees in front of the sofa. "Tony, I was worried. Are you okay?"

The house was completely dark. "What time is it?"

"Almost eleven. You didn't answer your phone."

"How did you get in here?"

"I called Alison. I had her number from when she interviewed me. She put me in touch with Ben. He drove me over here and showed me where you keep the key hidden. In fact, he's waiting outside. Give me a sec and I'll tell him it's okay to go."

"You should go too," Tony said. "You shouldn't be here."

"Sorry, pal. You're stuck with me." She pulled open the front door, gave Ben an okay sign with her fingers, and returned to the sofa.

"Sit up. My knees are getting sore."

Tony sat, and Darcy settled in next to him.

"Can you tell me what happened? Besides standing me up for dinner, I mean?"

"Oh shit. I'm sorry," Tony said, beginning to cry again.

"Hey, it's okay. I only jabbed you a little because, you know, nobody stands up a movie star and gets away with it."

Tony looked at her, wanting to join in the banter but unable to bring himself to do so.

"Okay," Darcy said. "Let's grab that half-finished bottle of wine from your refrigerator. If you're not gonna feed me, the least you can do is give me something to drink."

Tony allowed her to pull him up from the sofa and lead him into the kitchen. When the wine was poured, they sat at the table.

Tony said, "I want to talk about it, but I don't want to talk about it."

"Well, I want you to talk about it, so that makes the vote two to one. Spill it."

Tony took a deep breath, fought to still a quivering lip, and began talking. He walked her through the whole list: the flirting, the history of cheating, the car, the fingerprints, the semen, the lock opener, and the videos. By the time he had finished, he was overwhelmed again. There could be no doubt. His dad really had killed her. As he wept, Darcy remained silent.

After several minutes, she said, "Take a drink of your wine. I have some questions."

Tony took a large swallow and waited.

"Do you think of your dad as dumb? Hang on. It's a serious question. Is he mentally deficient?"

"Don't be ridiculous. No."

"Second question: what does your dad do for a living?"

"He teaches…"

"Don't be an ass. What has he done his whole life?"

"He's a writer."

"What does he write?"

"Novels, screenplays, an occasional short story? What's the point of this?"

"Shut up. I mean, answer the question. What kind of novels and screenplays?"

"Mostly murder mysteries, thrillers. You know, popular fiction."

"About crimes and criminals, right?"

"Well, yeah." Tony was beginning to sense where Darcy was headed.

She quickly proved him right. "So what are the chances that an intelligent guy with a long history of writing crime novels is going to pick up a victim in an easily-identifiable one-of-a-kind car, drive to a place with surveillance cameras, look into the camera, then kill the young woman inside, leaving his body fluids inside her and his fingerprints on the murder weapon when he leaves the scene?

"By the way," she continued. "In that second video, does the man run away? You know, does he appear to be in a panic, like he was frightened away?"

"No," Tony said. "He calmly walks to his car—*my* car—and

drives away."

"So he calmly leaves the body where it will be found and calmly leaves the murder weapon at the scene. Does any of this sound reasonable to you? Even possible?"

"It sounds incredibly stupid and unlikely," Tony admitted. "But that doesn't change the fact that it's true. I can imagine the prosecutor arguing that Dad's so clever he's using this reverse psychology— doing these dumb things to make it look unreasonable."

Darcy shook her head. "I know I wasn't in Pike's office with you. I didn't see the reports or the videos, and maybe that's helping me react less emotionally, but I'm telling you, I don't buy it. Your dad's a brilliant writer of crime stories, which in many ways makes him a brilliant criminologist. I don't believe he would leave all these things in plain sight that tie him to the brutal murder of a young woman."

"If you're thinking it's a frame-up, I love you for suggesting it," Tony said. "But I think it's naïve to believe that. In the first place, who would want to frame him? In the second place, how in the hell would they produce things like fingerprints and… and… you know, what they found in her?"

"I don't know. It seems impossible, I agree. But let's also agree that we now have two impossibilities—we know your dad couldn't have done it, and we know there's no way he could have been framed. Doesn't it make sense to at least keep digging until we find out which impossibility turns out to actually be true?"

"Nice thought, but where would we start? If someone in the crime lab is fabricating results, how are we supposed to flush that person out? If Dad has an identical twin producing similar DNA, or, hell, I don't know, if aliens are coming down from Neptune and… and…" Tony realized he was shouting, stopped himself, and swallowed. "Forgive me."

Darcy said, "Tony, it's easy to forgive your emotional outbursts. I'm going to struggle more with forgiving your surrender."

He looked at her, and she continued. "More importantly, when this is all over, you're never going to forgive yourself if you let him be convicted without a fight. I've read enough about you to know about the Ralph Wells case. Prosecutors thought that evidence was overwhelming too."

Tony took her hands in his and said, "Darcy, that case was orders of magnitude different from this. Ralph Wells was a slow-witted introvert who was easily manipulated by a whole conspiracy of powerful people, and the evidence against him was all circumstantial. There was nothing at the crime scene, nothing tying him directly to the victims or the act. Surely you can see this is a whole different ball game."

"Yes, I can, which is why we need to get started."

"Okay, you convinced me. I'm Superman, and you're..." he almost said Lois Lane, then realized that could be perceived badly. Instead, he finished with "...you're Wonder Woman. We're going to debunk the clear-cut evidence, exonerate my father, find the real killers, and win my second Pulitzer Prize. Anything else on the list?"

She leaned across the table and kissed him. "I can think of a few things, but we'll leave that discussion for another day."

They went into Tony's office, where his computer still held the notes he had been making before going to Pike's office. Tony woke up the screen and suggested she sit and read what he had written.

He said, "It's mostly a recap of what I knew at the time, but there are a few new thoughts in there.

After reading through it, she said, "You suggested getting the names of other guests at the motel and interviewing them. That's a good idea, but what about surveillance cameras?"

"Nope. None on site. As you know, it's an older roadside

motel."

"Yeah, and if I remember the doors, they have the old-fashioned keyed locks, so there's no electronic system keeping track of what time your dad came in."

"Right."

"What about your mom? Have you asked her what time your dad returned?"

"No. I figured, why bother? If she testifies he was with her at midnight, it won't carry any weight with Garcia, and probably not much with the jury. It's what she would be expected to say."

"Yes, but it would carry weight with you and me. If she says he was there, it would help strengthen our conviction that we're on the right track."

"A fair point," Tony said. "I'll ask her."

They were quiet a moment before Tony said, "I wish I could examine my Mustang. I wonder how closely the forensics team looked for evidence of the car being hotwired?"

"Good question. That's one we should have Pike raise with Garcia."

"Holy shit!" Tony exclaimed. "I just thought of something."

Darcy smiled. "Whatever it is, I like it. Your face finally looks like there might be a little blood flowing to it."

Tony ignored the jab and said, "We need to see the odometer. I had my car serviced Saturday morning. The sticker on the windshield will show how many miles were on the odometer. We should be able to demonstrate that my dad drove the exact route he said he did."

"It's not conclusive, but it would be a nice piece to put in the puzzle. Do we add that to the Pike list?"

"Hell no," Tony said. "We go."

Darcy didn't ask and didn't argue. She simply followed him

out the side door to the Explorer.

***

Tony parked two blocks from the Law Enforcement Center. He said to Darcy, "Orney doesn't have a formal impound lot for vehicles. They just park them in the back of the LEC lot and put a band of crime scene tape around them. I won't be able to open the car, but I should be able to walk up to it and get what I need."

"And if you get caught?"

"If I get caught, I'll probably get arrested for trespassing or evidence tampering. But hey, do Superman and Wonder Woman worry about such trivialities?"

Darcy smiled. "Absolutely not, but perhaps you should choose Harry Potter as your alter-ego, so you can take your cloak of invisibility along."

Tony smiled and kissed her. "I'm plenty invisible. Just ask any girl I tried to talk to in high school."

Darcy laughed, and Tony went out the door.

Tony knew the LEC lot had cameras in place in addition to police officers and deputies coming and going as part of their regular duties. In other words, the only way to get away with this was to be fast. Knowing his cell phone could see in low light better than he could, he decided not to try to read the odometer and window sticker, but to simply snap pictures and leave.

He pulled the phone from his pocket, jogged across the lot, snapped a total of four photos, and jogged back out of sight. The whole episode had taken less than fifteen seconds. Even if he'd been caught on film, it would only show that he never touched the car.

Back in the Explorer, he pulled up the photo storage and compared the pictures. In the first, the window sticker clearly showed the mileage recorded on Saturday morning: 63,014. Tony held his breath and pulled up the photo of the odometer. Despite being partially obscured in a shadow, the reading was clear: 63,028. *Wait. Fourteen miles?* He went back and double-checked the first photo to be sure he'd read it correctly. Then he noticed something else. The windshield was clear. No bug splatters.

"What the fuck?" he said aloud. "Dad, what have you done?

Chapter 19

Orney, Iowa—Wednesday, July 1

Tony and Darcy spent the next two days in a jumble of agonizing, debating, speculating, and trying to forget. Wednesday morning, Tony dragged himself out of bed early and went to the dojang, thinking a workout with Jun would help ease his anxieties. It didn't.

Now it was evening, and he and Darcy were lying side-by-side in Tony's bed, each scrolling through social media and websites on their phones, trying to avoid another pointless conversation about Tony's dad. Occasionally, one of them would find a funny bit on Dry Bar Comedy or a clever tweet and would share it with the other. It was mindless passing of the time, and it felt pretty desperate to Tony.

"Did you hear that?" Darcy asked, sitting upright in the bed.

"Hear what?"

"Listen."

Tony shut off the rerun of a Graham Norton show he had been

watching and pulled the ear buds from his ears. "I see what you mean. Now I hear it. Stay here."

He was wearing jeans and a tan T-shirt that proclaimed, "Bookmarks are for quitters." He pulled on his loafers, shut off the bedside lamp, and opened the bedroom door a crack. He could see a light on in the kitchen. He inched the bedroom door back closed and whispered, "Did we leave the kitchen light on?"

"No," Darcy whispered back. "I'm sure I shut it off after we finished the dishes."

"Lock this behind me when I leave," he said, then opened the door just wide enough to slip into the hallway and closed it again. He stood there silently until he heard the lock click.

The older bungalow had hardwood floors that tended to creak as you walked on them. To avoid detection from a potential intruder, Tony stayed to the far-right edge of the hall and moved agonizingly slowly.

When he reached the end, he could see a small slice of the kitchen but not enough to see who or what was there. However, the noises were distinctly louder from here. There was no question someone was in his house.

Tony inched along the wall to the kitchen doorway. He slipped his phone out of his pocket and dialed 911, holding his thumb above the send button, but not pressing it.

He moved his head slowly to the left so just one eye could see past the edge of the opening. A man of average build in shorts and a hooded sweatshirt was standing at the counter, his back to Tony, digging through one of the kitchen drawers.

Looking for a knife? Tony wondered. He decided to act quickly, before the intruder could find what he was seeking. He called out. "Don't move! I've got a gun and I've already called the police!"

The man turned around and said, "Jeez Tone-man. Where do

you keep your bottle opener? How's a guy supposed to drink your beer?"

"Doug!" Tony yelped and nearly ran the four steps to embrace his friend.

"Hey, take it easy. That hurts. You shot me, remember?"

"Jesus, Doug, what are you doing? I really do own a gun, you know. I could have killed you."

"Bullshit," Doug said. "You keep your gun in the car, and even if you didn't, you couldn't shoot anybody."

"What are you doing here?"

"I came over for a beer. It turns out nobody's stocked my fridge in a while because, you know, my best friend shot me."

"Yeah, okay, but I mostly missed, and by the way, I'm starting to regret that. Hang on."

Tony walked back down the hall, knocked on the bedroom door, and told Darcy she could relax. The intruder was just some totally inept drunk looking for booze.

"Hey, I heard that," Doug bellowed.

Back in the kitchen, Tony opened Doug's beer, encouraged him to sit, and grabbed a Diet Dr. Pepper for himself.

Joining Doug at the table, Tony said, "I didn't recognize you from the back. My God, you lost a lot of weight while you were spending all of Ben's insurance money."

"Of course I lost weight. Have you ever eaten the crap a hospital calls food? I mean, what they serve you tastes okay, but they made me eat healthy stuff. I swear I would kill for a thick-crust sausage pizza right now."

"That could probably be arranged," Darcy said, walking into the room wearing Tony's bathrobe and a wide smile. "It's good to see you, Doug."

As she approached him, Doug said, "Hang on a minute. If I'm

gonna get a sympathy hug from Darcy Gillson, I'm gonna enjoy it."

Using his arms on the table and the chairback to assist himself, Doug rose out of his seat, grimacing as he moved.

Darcy's brow wrinkled as she spoke the obvious. "It still hurts."

"Yeah, but not enough to pass on this." He held out his arms and Darcy embraced him tightly.

"Man, that feels great," Doug said. "Really awful, but great."

Tony and Darcy laughed.

Darcy grabbed another beer from the refrigerator and joined the two friends.

Tony said, "So you could have called to tell us you were coming, or even knocked on the door."

"Aw, hell. I figured you two were doin' it. I didn't want to interrupt. Y'know, seeing as how Tony finds it impossible to get laid. Was he a virgin, Darcy? He never would admit it to me, but I wouldn't be surprised."

"Bite me," Tony said, then turned to Darcy. "He's been talking to me like this since the day we met. Try to forgive him, or better yet, try to ignore him. I suspect he was raised in the Catskills by a family of out-of-work comedians."

Darcy shook her head at both men, then grinned.

"Anyway," Doug continued, "I figured the two of you would come up for air eventually. I was just gonna sit and enjoy a beer or two until you came out. If you never did, no big deal. I get free beer and go home."

Getting serious for a moment, Tony and Darcy asked Doug what he needed and how they could help him until he was more fully healed. As they talked about groceries and laundry and other mundane tasks, Doug suddenly said, "Oh, by the way, I almost forgot. Did you know some guy with a camera is sitting outside?"

Tony and Darcy looked at each other, then back at Doug.

"No..." they said in unison.

Tony asked, "Outside here? In my yard?"

"Not exactly. He's across the street, leaning against your neighbor's garage, in the shadow of the house. At least he was when I drove past. If he saw me pull into the driveway from the alley, he might have taken off."

Tony rose and went to the back door. As he put on a black windbreaker and zipped it up, he said, "Do me a favor and call the police. Tell them what you saw. The guy might not have trespassed here, but he sure did over there. Tell them I'm going outside to find him, so try not to shoot me when they arrive."

Darcy said, "Tony. If he's doing what we think he is, please don't confront him. I've had a lot of experience with these guys, and they dream of being attacked. It's how they get their best stories."

Tony nodded his acknowledgement and said, "Don't worry. That's Doug you're thinking of. He's the one who takes a tire iron to the backs of guys' heads."

"Not tonight, Tone-man. If I raised my right arm high enough to hit someone, the stitches in my side would never forgive me. You're on your own."

"Got it," he said and exited through the side door to the carport.

Once outside, he looked around quickly, determined no one was watching, and trotted the four steps to the fence separating his back yard from the neighbor's. He hopped the fence, ran through the neighbor's yard, and turned up the driveway which ran along the side of the house. When he reached the front, he knelt and peered around the corner.

From his current position, the angle allowed no view of the space between the garage and the house across the street from his. Tony didn't mind. If he couldn't see the guy with the camera, then the guy with the camera couldn't see him either.

Tony sprinted across the street, worked his way behind the first house, then to the back of the second. Moving as quietly as he could, he reached the corner closest to where the photographer supposedly was hiding, and peeked around. He quickly spun back out of sight, astonished by what he had seen. This was no ordinary hack looking to grab a quick photo. He wondered if his brain had misinterpreted the darkened images captured by his eyes, so he stole another quick look.

Again, moving silently, inch by inch, Tony backed away from the corner. Once a safe distance away, he pulled out his phone and selected the camera function. He then inched back to the corner, held the phone so just the camera lens would be visible from the man's position, and snapped a series of pictures.

The man was kneeling in front of a piece of electronic gear. As Doug had reported, the man was facing Tony's house. He was totally outfitted in night camouflage gear.

How in the hell had Doug spotted this guy?

The man's ears bulged under his hood, causing Tony to assume he was wearing headphones. The camera was like nothing Tony had ever seen.

Despite what Darcy had said, Tony decided he couldn't just let this go. This was surveillance, or more accurately, intrusion, on a ridiculous level.

Tony pushed the phone back into his pocket. He could examine the photos later. He stepped around the corner and said, "Hey! What do you think you're doing?"

The man stood and spun around in one motion. Seeing Tony, he calmly walked over with his hands in front of him, palms out, in a universal "no harm meant" gesture.

Tony wasn't in the mood to be gracious. He opened his mouth to speak, but suddenly the man lashed out. Tony's head took a serious blow, immediately followed by a second one as it slammed into the siding of the house. He fell to the ground. The man took one long step toward him and kicked him in the temple. The world instantly disappeared into a sea of blackness.

***

"Mr. Harrington? Mr. Harrington! Can you hear me?"

"Stop shouting," Tony groaned as he opened his eyes. The beams of flashlights were in his face and he squeezed his eyes closed again. "And put away the lights, please."

Tony could feel hands on him. A blood pressure cuff on one arm, a stethoscope pressed to the skin under his shirt.

He said, "Is it safe to open my eyes?"

"Yes," a man said. "Sorry about that. We were worried about you. Can you tell us what happened?"

"Yeah, sure," Tony said, squinting at what obviously were two EMTs fawning over him. "I got my ass kicked by some guy in a Spider-Man suit. Not the red suit, but the black Evil Spider-Man version." He could hear mumbling. He smiled and said, "Relax, everyone. I'm okay. I'm exaggerating about the suit, but not by much."

One EMT said, "We've spotted what appear to be signs of three blows to your head."

Tony thought for a moment. "One… then bam… then… yep. I'd say that's right."

"Do you have pain anywhere else?"

"No, I'm fine. Really."

A new voice said, "Guys, if you're finished, I'm going to need to talk to Mr. Harrington to get a statement."

"Agent Davis, how the hell did you get here so fast?"

"I was at the Law Enforcement Center when the call came in. I got here almost as fast as the police officer did. Once I confirmed it was you, I told him this related to a state case and asked him to let me handle it. He was only too glad to oblige."

"Thanks. You probably saved me from having to spend two hours or more in a hard plastic chair at the LEC."

"I'm still going to need a statement."

"Of course," Tony said, "but now I can give it from the comfort of my own living room, with a beer in one hand and a beautiful babe massaging my injuries."

"If you mean me," Darcy's voice said from behind him, "I'm right here. I appreciate the compliment, but if you call me a babe again, I'm gonna kick you somewhere other than your head."

Tony grinned sheepishly. "Oops. Blame it on the injuries. My brain isn't working right."

One of the EMTs said, "His vital signs are strong, and he's communicating and seeing clearly, so we think he's fine. It would be smart to have the hospital ER check him out, but he certainly doesn't need an ambulance." The man turned and addressed Tony directly. "If you notice any dizziness…"

"Let me stop you right there," Tony said. "Unfortunately, this isn't my first blow to the head. I know the list. Thanks guys, I'm going home now to sit somewhere comfortable and drink a beer."

"But you don't drink beer," Davis said.

"I do now."

***

They all sat in the living room with the lights dimmed and The MonaLisa Twins singing quietly in the background. Rich had his electronic pad on his knee, taking notes and recording, as Tony described what had happened. Next, Doug described how he and Darcy had become concerned when Tony hadn't returned to the house. Darcy had stayed inside, assuming the photographer was trying to get pictures of her, and Doug had walked over to where he had seen the man earlier.

He found Tony lying unconscious in the flower bed between the driveway and the house. He was about to make a second call to 911 when the police arrived. They checked to be sure Tony was alive, then called for the EMTs while Doug ran to get Darcy.

Darcy smiled and said, "I'm not sure that loping movement with one hand pressed to your side could be called a run, but I do appreciate you for coming to get me."

"You mentioned taking pictures of the guy," Davis said. "That was really smart. Let's take a look."

"It was dark, and I was shooting around a corner, so no promises," Tony said as he pulled out his phone and began scrolling through the dozen or so shots he had taken.

"There," he said. "This shows pretty much everything I saw from the corner." He handed the phone to Davis.

"What the fuck?" the agent blurted. Everyone looked startled. "I'm sorry. Forgive the language. What is this all about?"

Darcy said, "We assumed it was a star-seeker or the paparazzi. What are you seeing?"

Davis shook his head and said, "This isn't a camera. This guy is using a military-grade parabolic microphone. It's pointed right at your bedroom window that faces the street. He could probably hear and record everything you said in there tonight."

"Hmm, everything they said or *did*," Doug prodded, grinning.

"Shut up, Doug," Tony said, as his mind scrambled to recall his and Darcy's conversations.

"My God," Darcy said. "What…? Why…?"

Davis turned to Tony and asked, "Any idea why someone would do this? I can't believe it's the paparazzi. In the first place, this equipment isn't easy to buy, and for those who find a way to, it sets them back a hell of a lot of money. Secondly, I've never heard of anyone having success selling just audio recordings of celebrities. This almost certainly has to be something else. What are you working on that would attract this kind of attention? You have some big secret story coming up?"

Tony shook his head. "I'm not working on anything right now. I'm on leave from the paper. All my time is being spent with Darcy or working on my dad's case..."

The room grew quiet.

Tony looked at the agent. "Do you think this could be related to that? Maybe my dad really was framed. If so, whoever did it is remarkably resourceful. Maybe the same person found out somehow that I was looking into it. Considering my history, that would be reasonable to assume."

"I don't have a clue," Davis said, "but I'm still not ready to buy the idea your dad is innocent. I find it hard to believe this is related to that. Send me the picture, and I'll see what I can find out about it."

Davis looked at the photo again. "Look at his getup. He's nearly invisible. You're lucky he wasn't sitting on your front porch." Tony rubbed his throbbing temple. "Yeah? I don't feel so lucky somehow."

Davis asked about Tony and Darcy's conversation in the bedroom that day and evening.

Tony said, "Well, if he was only there this evening, that's really good news. We spent the night looking at random videos online and making sure we talked about anything *but* my father's case. I'm guessing our camera... uh, microphone guy is one frustrated dude at the moment."

When Davis rose to leave, Tony tried once more to introduce some doubt in the agent's mind about Charles's guilt. After pushing the likely tie to the surveillance guy outside, he brought up Darcy's argument regarding his father's intelligence and understanding of criminal evidence. Darcy jumped in, explaining her belief that it was preposterous to think Charles Harrington would have left the trail of evidence found by investigators.

"Sorry my friends, but it just doesn't wash. If it was just the flirting, or just the car, we'd be having a different conversation. But you can't explain away things like the fingerprints and the video." He went on, touching on each of the other pieces of evidence. He concluded by saying, "I'm sorry, Tony, but you have to man up and accept the truth."

With each word from Davis, Tony grew more irritated. The "man up" comment nearly put him over the edge. If Darcy hadn't been there, Tony might have done or said something he would have regretted later. However, he held his anger in check and simply said through gritted teeth, "That's enough. I think you'd better go now."

Chapter 20

Orney, Iowa—Thursday, July 2

"I can't believe it," Ramesh Bhatt said, reaching for another piece of warm bread from the basket at the center of the table. "It's outrageous the way people have turned on your dad. From adoring him one minute to assuming he's guilty the next."

Tony nodded glumly. Bhatt had invited Darcy and him to dinner. They had agreed on Italian food, so they were at the only restaurant in Orney that served a variety of dishes beyond pizza— Papa Sal's in the shopping mall on the south end of town. It was never going to make the Michelin list, but the food was better than passable.

In addition to the three of them, Bhatt's assistant, Witt Silverstein, had joined the party. Bhatt had invited them out to discuss plans to resume filming the movie, but the conversation had quickly turned to Tony's father.

Darcy said, "I still don't believe it, but there's no question the evidence is damning. If we don't poke some gaping holes in it, I don't see any way Charles is going to be exonerated in court."

"He's toast," Witt said through a mouthful of cavatini. The table grew silent as everyone turned to look at him.

"Sorry, Tony. I know he's your dad, but c'mon, facts are facts. Everybody makes mistakes. This time your dad made a big one."

"Witt, zip it," Bhatt said. "I'm sorry, Tony. Having an assistant who speaks his mind is a great asset to a director most of the time. Then sometimes, it's a giant, inappropriate turd in the punchbowl."

"It's okay," Tony said, "He's only repeating what I've already said. It's clear my dad lied to me and to everyone. He absolutely took her for a ride in my car and had sex with her. It's almost as certain that he killed her. Let's change the subject."

Bhatt nodded and began talking with Darcy about the logistics of getting everyone back to town, scheduling locations, arranging caterers and a myriad of other details related to movie production.

Tony assumed Darcy was just a sounding board. Because she was the lone remaining cast member in Orney, Bhatt didn't have anyone else to tap, besides Silverstein, to hear his thoughts and provide some input.

While they chatted, Tony's mind returned to his father's case. His prints were on the murder weapon. Her blood, too. Pretty cut and dried, right? *Okay, Tony. Open your mind. Assume dad didn't do it. How could this have happened? Wait. Who says the prints were put on the club in the pro shop? What if the club…?*

Tony sat bolt upright in his chair. Who could he call to ask? Not his dad. He couldn't alert anyone involved. Even asking the question might give someone a chance to tamper with the evidence. Tony hated thinking like this, but he knew he had to be careful, or the potential for finding what he was seeking, for getting the first real evidence in his father's favor, could be lost.

He took a swallow of his diet soda and said, "Ramesh, Darcy, Witt, I'm sorry. I have to go."

"Wait. What?" Bhatt asked.

"Tony, what is it?" Darcy added.

"I have to check on something. It means a long drive, so I need to get going."

"A long drive?" Darcy said, rising from her seat alongside him. "It's late. Are you sure? If it has to be now, you shouldn't go alone."

"I'm fine," Tony said. "I don't want to interrupt your dinner."

"Don't be silly," she said. "I'm nearly done with my meal, and considering how I've been eating lately, I can afford to skip dessert."

Bhatt stood and shook his hand. "I'm sorry to see you rush off. I hope everything is okay."

"Everything's fine, really. I just had an idea, and I need to check it out. I'll be back in the morning."

"Can you tell us about it before you go?" Bhatt asked. "Now you have us curious."

"I'd like to, but it probably won't amount to anything. I'll be sure to call you if it turns out to be anything more than a wild goose chase."

"Okay. Thank you again for joining me. Be careful driving."

Tony thanked him again for dinner, then nearly sprinted from the mall to his SUV. Darcy was right behind.

"Where are we headed?" she asked.

"Solon, Iowa," he said, grinning.

"Where?"

"Exactly," he said. "It's not nowhere, but it's next door to there. We'll stop at your motel so you can grab an overnight bag, then at my place so I can do the same. While we're there, we can grab sodas and a blanket and pillow. You'll want a soft place for your head when you fall asleep."

Darcy reached over and took his hand. "Did I mention I'm a movie star, and don't want anything to do with your normal, boring life?"

Tony chuckled and squeezed her hand. "Too late. You're trapped. You're just going to have to stay bored and normal, right up until the day we catch a killer."

***

Once they were on the highway, Tony pulled out his iPhone. "Siri, call Rich Davis."

The DCI agent answered on the second ring. "Hey, Tony! I wasn't sure you were still talking to me."

"I wasn't sure, either, but now I need something, so I decided we're friends again."

Rich chuckled. "At least you're honest. You know I'll help you if I can. What's up?"

"Tell me the specifics about the murder weapon. I mean, I already know it was a Mizuno seven iron, but tell me where it was found, and whether or not you know where it came from."

Rich didn't hesitate to share the information. It would all be released to Pike soon anyway. He did pause to think. "Hmm, the club was found on the floor of the pro shop, in the middle of the aisle where the new sets of clubs are on display. You know, there's a full wall on one side, and a half wall on the other. Both sides of the aisle feature new woods and irons."

"Did the murder weapon come from one of those sets?"

"No, none of the sets was missing a club. Our assumption is that the club came out of a tall barrel at the end of the aisle. It has miscellaneous used clubs stuffed into it at random. We asked about them, and the club pro told us that sometimes when someone trades in an old set of mismatched clubs, they put them in the barrel and sell them individually. Other clubs in the barrel were found on the course. If no one claims a found club for a year, the pro shop adds it to the barrel and puts it on sale."

I knew it! Tony wanted to shout. Aloud, he said, "Thanks, Rich. That's really helpful."

"You gonna let me in on what this is about? It sounds like you're onto something I should know about."

"Maybe, but I'm trying not to get my hopes up. I'll call you tomorrow and let you know."

"Okay, my friend. I'll look forward to it."

The call ended, and Tony returned the phone to his pocket.

Darcy said, "Golf clubs?"

"Yep," Tony said, smiling, "but more importantly, clues. And if we're lucky, a get-out-of-jail-free card."

It was after midnight when Tony turned into the driveway for the Lake Brindle Golf Club. Darcy was asleep as predicted, but she had placed the pillow over the center console of the SUV so she could lean across it comfortably and place her head on Tony's shoulder. He didn't mind. He liked feeling her warm breath on his arm as he drove.

He still had no idea where their relationship was going, or even where he wanted it to go, but for the moment, he was happy to have her company.

When he stopped the vehicle, she immediately awoke. "Are we there?"

"Yep."

"And where, again, is there?"

"Lake Brindle, just outside of Solon, Iowa."

"East, right? We went east."

"Yep. Just a short drive south of us is Iowa City, where my

parents live, and by the way, the home of the world's greatest public university."

"I wouldn't know about public universities," Darcy said. "I went to a real college."

Tony smiled and jabbed her in the ribs. "You'll pay for that later, movie star. Let's go."

They climbed out of the vehicle, and Tony marveled again at Darcy's trust in him. *Jump in the car, drive forever, get out in the dark, in the middle of the night, follow me, don't ask questions. She is as amazing and tolerant as I am headstrong*, he thought.

She looked around and said, "We're at a golf course."

"Yep."

She then proved she was even smarter than he realized. She said, "Let me guess. This is where your dad is a member. This is Iowa, so I bet he leaves his clubs here. You are here to get a look at your dad's golf clubs."

"Bingo."

"So how do we do that at…" she looked at her Apple Watch, "…12:19 a.m.?"

"We talk to Geoff. That's Geoff with a 'G.' We use my powers of persuasion and your adorable smile and other… uh, attributes… to charm him into helping us."

"Just make sure to keep Geoff-with-a-G's eyes, and hands, off my other attributes," Darcy said.

Geoff Warbler was a caretaker and night watchman at Lake Brindle Golf Club. The manager of the course had employed Geoff to ensure no vandalism occurred at night, and to keep the teens' keggers and other late-night encounters on the dark fairways to a minimum.

As Tony and Darcy walked up the sidewalk to the clubhouse, a golf cart with headlights came around the corner of the building and stopped in their path.

"Howdy," said an elderly man in cargo shorts, tennis shoes, and a Grateful Dead T-shirt. He had a skinny face and bony knees but sported a pot belly that hung over the front of his belt. "I thought I saw a car pull into the lot. How can I help you folks?"

Tony explained to him what he wanted.

"You just wanna look? You won't touch anything?"

"Right," Tony said. "Not touching is very important, in fact."

"Well, I guess it'll be okay. Can I see some ID first?"

Tony and Darcy took out their driver's licenses. Geoff impressed them both when he took a picture of each license, then attached the photos to an email and pressed send.

Geoff said, "Now you won't get any ideas about doing me in and robbin' the place. Your info is in my boss's inbox."

"That's very smart, Geoff," Darcy said. "But I'm pretty sure you were safe without that."

"I don't know, young lady. If I spend much more time around you, I may die of a heart attack."

"Don't do that," Darcy quipped. "If you collapse, I might have to give you mouth-to-mouth resuscitation."

The old man choked and spit into the grass beside the sidewalk. "Now I *know* I'm gonna die of a heart attack. C'mon, let's go before I get a woody."

Darcy turned to Tony and asked, "What is it with Iowa men? You all act like you've never talked to a woman before."

Tony shook his head, smart enough not to engage in that conversation. A few minutes later, they were inside the storage area beside the pro shop. Tony gazed at the mass of bags on racks, on hooks, and standing on their own in the middle of the floor.

"Each bag has a tag with the member's name, the current year, an' the year he joined. Sorry miss, I mean the year he or *she* joined.

As you can see, there's lotsa bags. And there's no real system to it beyond what's in the members' heads, so you'll just have to look at them one at a time 'till you spot it."

"It may not be that hard," Tony said. "I've been here with Dad before, and I think he favors that back right corner. He doesn't play very often, so I'm guessing his bag is buried pretty far back."

He was right. After examining just five bags, Tony found the one with the tag that read, "Charles Harrington."

"Do you have a pair of clean gloves or even a couple of spare towels?" he called out to Geoff, who was standing in the front of the room, staring at Darcy.

Geoff turned. "Thought you said you wasn't gonna touch nothing?"

"That's why I need to cover my hands. I need to move the bag out into the light, and I don't want to touch it with my bare skin."

Geoff looked at Darcy and said, "I knew this wouldn't be as simple as you said. It never is."

"Please Geoff," Darcy said, "help us out here. Tony's dad is in a lot of trouble, and it will mean a lot to Tony, to both of us, if this turns out to help him."

"Yeah, I heard about Harrington's troubles. Ain't every day a member gets arrested for killin' a movie star. I figgered this had somethin' to do with that."

Moments later, the men had the golf bag under the lights in the clear area of the room where caddies cleaned and repaired members' equipment.

"Well, well," Tony said, smiling. "Look at this."

Darcy approached and peered at the bag. Charles Harrington's clubs were a well-used set of Callaway woods and new Mizuno irons.

Tony took some photos with his phone, then turned to Geoff. "Sir, I need... I should say we need to ask you a couple of other favors."

"Of course you do," Geoff said wearily.

"These are pretty simple, I hope. First, do you have a big garbage bag or tarp or something we can use to cover and protect this bag?"

"Sure. We got sixty-gallon lawn and leaf bags we use when cleanin' up around the clubhouse grounds. One of them ought to work nicely. What else?"

"Do you have a place you can lock up the bag?"

"It's locked in here."

"No, I mean a separate space that can be locked, where no one but you has access."

"That's tough," Geoff said. "I'm not the only employee here, ya know. Anyplace I can open can also be got to by a dozen other guys… and gals. Sorry, miss. Course, I could just lock 'em in the trunk of my car. I live alone. No one but me can get in there."

"It's not ideal, but it may be the best we can do. It will only be for a few days, or maybe only a few hours. We need to keep track of what's called 'chain of custody.' You might have to come into court and testify that no one tampered with the clubs between the time we looked at them tonight, and the time the sheriff or someone comes to pick them up."

"Yeah, I know about chain of custody. I watch TV too. I even seen one of this lady's movies once. I think you were a zombie or some damn thing."

"Oh, good," Darcy said, "You saw me in my Academy Award performance." The sarcasm in her voice was heavy enough that even Geoff caught it.

"Ah, not so proud of that one, eh? I thought it was okay." He grinned. "I liked what you were wearing."

Darcy turned to Tony, to explain, but he said, "Never mind. I can guess."

He looked at Geoff and said, "There is one more thing."

"Of course there is."

"This one is easy. Would you let me take your picture with the bag, as it sits here now, to ensure we've documented that link to you tonight? Then I'd like to take one with your phone, as well, and have you send it to me. That way I'll have your contact information."

"Fine," he said, "but only cause I got so much pleasure out of that young lady's movie, if you know what I mean." He winked at Darcy. She just shook her head.

Once the pictures were taken, the men carefully placed the heavy paper sack over the golf bag. Geoff dug some duct tape out of a tool drawer. The men held the bag up, while Darcy drew the sack around the bottom and taped it multiple times, ending by wrapping the tape around the base in a circle until the tape ran out.

"It ain't goin' nowhere," Geoff said.

At Tony's request, they all signed and dated the tape. Then he took more pictures, including one of Geoff loading the bag into his trunk.

"Keep your car keys in your possession at all times until the cops come for that," Tony said.

"Yeah, yeah, I get it. What are you hopin' to find, anyway?"

"Geoff, if you don't mind, I'll tell you that after the DCI techs have examined the bag. The less you know, the less chance there is of someone crying foul over this. By the way, I'd like to give you something for all your trouble and pay for the sack and the duct tape."

"Nah, put your money away. I'll take care of it. You wanna do somethin' for me, I'll settle for one more photograph." He handed Tony his phone. "Take one of me and this-here movie star. The boys at the Legion Hall ain't never gonna believe me without it."

Darcy cuddled up next to the elderly man, and just as Tony

snapped the photo, she leaned over and kissed him on the cheek. "You're the best," she said.

"Yeah, well, maybe I used to be. But thanks for sayin' that. A man can always dream."

***

It was nearly 2 a.m. when Tony and Darcy arrived in Iowa City. They found a room in one of the Marriott-affiliated motels along Interstate 80. Once inside, they dropped their bags, took turns using the bathroom, and crawled into bed. The large flat-screen, the mini-bar, and even the reading lights, went unused.

As they cuddled, the idea of making love naturally occurred to Tony, but he didn't bring it up. It somehow felt even more intimate this way, holding Darcy close, hearing her breathe, taking in her scent, feeling her reach back in the dark to find his hand and hold it tight.

He nestled his face into her hair and quietly said in her ear, "Thank you."

"No problem. It was fun. Geoff was quite a character."

"No, I mean thank you for everything. For being there when I needed you, for believing in my dad, for believing in me. I don't know if a bag of golf clubs will make any difference in what happens, but it has made a huge difference to me. I will love you forever for what you've done."

Darcy pressed herself tighter to Tony but surprised him when she spoke in a voice mimicking Geoff's raspy drawl, "Thanks for sayin' that. A girl can always dream."

Chapter 21

Iowa City, Iowa—Friday, July 3

Tony and his father sat in the home office/library of the Harrington family home in Iowa City. Tony had fond memories of the room. Here is where he and his dad had discussed the most critical issues of Tony's high school years: cars, dating, sports, and school. As he had grown older, the subjects had changed to politics, religion, current events, and other weighty issues. And throughout it all, books.

They loved to talk about writing and writers, about great literature and mindless fantasy, sometimes in the same book. Tony glanced over and saw the beautifully bound copy of Jules Verne's *20,000 Leagues Under the Sea*, looking just as it had when he'd first discovered it on the shelf of their home in Chicago at age twelve. His father's copy was published in 1956 by the Limited Editions Club, with illustrations by Edward A. Wilson. Tony had read that novel over and over, amazed and thrilled by the adventures told within its pages as well as by the author's unparalleled foresight in terms of the science and technology of the future.

Tony had been sitting in this same overstuffed leather chair when he had first told his father he wanted to be a writer and, later, when he had revealed he wanted to pursue journalism rather than literature as a career. It was here they had celebrated many of Tony's successes and had mourned his painful losses.

Today, the subject was his father's golf clubs. Tony explained what he had done and that he was about to call Rich Davis to ask him to have the clubs retrieved from Geoff Warbler and examined by the forensics team.

"I wanted you to know so you wouldn't decide to play a round of golf and find your clubs missing," Tony said. "Also, I probably had no right to do what I did without your permission. I didn't call you in advance because I didn't want the prosecutor to be able to claim that you had time to tamper with them."

"Just what do you expect to find?"

"I'm not sure exactly. But I find it pretty remarkable that the club used to kill Charlotte was the same make as the clubs in your bag. It could be a coincidence. Or it could indicate a host of other possibilities. I'm trying not to speculate, or get my hopes up, before I hear what the DCI lab has to say."

They talked a while longer about the case, his father reiterating his innocence and continued inability to understand how the evidence compiled by the state could exist.

"Tony, I swear to you, I wasn't with her Saturday night, or any night," Charles said. "Besides one hug, I never touched her."

"So where were you Saturday night?" Tony asked, his expression turning grim.

"What do you mean? You already know that. I went for a drive in the country. I followed the exact route you recommended."

"No, Dad, you didn't."

"What do you mean I didn't?" His father's voice rose a little in pitch and volume.

"Dad, my Mustang drove a total of fourteen miles on Saturday and Sunday. I had it serviced Saturday morning. I checked the odometer against the mileage on the sticker. The car went fourteen miles. I don't know what's going on here, but I wish you would level with me. I have to believe I could help you more if I knew the truth."

Charles got out of his chair and walked over to Tony's. He then dropped to one knee, looking Tony in the eyes and reaching out to put his hand on Tony's arm. Tony was astonished at his father's demeanor.

Charles said, "Tony, I don't know what's going on either. All I can do is swear to you again that my actions Saturday night and Sunday morning were exactly as I have described them. Maybe the garage made a mistake in noting your mileage. Maybe whoever took the car was smart enough to mess with the odometer. I don't know. I only know this: my life is on the line, and you are the only person on Earth I can hope to convince of my innocence. You must believe me."

"I want to, Dad. You know I do. But there's so much…" he let his voice trail off. He didn't want to rub his father's face in the long list of evidence once again. However, he did desperately want to raise the other issue, the elephant in the room. His dad did it for him.

As Charles got up and walked back to his chair, he said, "I'm sure it doesn't help that you heard about my… That you heard some things about my past that were a surprise to you."

"I think 'world-shattering' was the phrase that occurred to me at the time," Tony said.

"I'm sorry you ever heard about it. Like any father, I want my son to look up to me. I know that's going to be hard for you now.

I'm willing to tell you more about it, but I don't want to sound like I'm making excuses. There is no excuse for the things I did."

"I do want to hear it. As I said a moment ago, I need to know everything if I'm going to help you. I also want to know the truth so I can try to somehow process what it means to me, to you and Mom, to all of us."

"Assuming you don't want names and places, there's not a lot to tell," Charles said. "When I was younger, I was on the road a lot, doing book signings and giving speeches. Then my fourth screenplay enjoyed remarkably more success than the first three. When it got nominated for an Oscar, I found myself in big demand in Hollywood. I became a minor celebrity. To make a long story short, young women suddenly wanted to spend time with me. I loved the attention. It was like a drug to have a college coed or a young starlet come up after one of my talks and ask if she could buy me a drink. Sometimes they were even more forward, more explicit, than that." Charles hung his head. "For a long time, I resisted all offers. Then I accepted a few invitations for drinks or meals. Eventually I caved. I was in Miami. We took a walk on the beach and… it just happened."

Tony found himself hoping he would hear no more details than that, but his father moved on.

"After the first time, it got easier. Of course, because of my ties to Hollywood, I had opportunities with some very beautiful and accomplished women. I succumbed to temptation with a few of them as well."

"That explains Mom's distaste for the cast."

"Yes, well, distaste isn't quite a strong enough word for what she thinks of the whole movie-making industry. Anyway, the inevitable happened. Your mother found out about one of my affairs. When she confronted me, she quickly realized it wasn't a one-time thing. I nearly lost her over it. To be more precise, I nearly lost everything. She told me she was taking you and Rita and moving back to Italy."

Tony looked up, wide-eyed.

His father said, "I couldn't let that happen. I begged her to stay. I swore it would never happen again. She reluctantly agreed to give me a chance to prove myself, but only on the condition that I change my lifestyle completely. That I find a way to be at home and engage with her as a full-time husband, and with you and Rita as a full-time father."

"Holy crap," Tony said. "That's when you took the job here in Iowa City. That's why we moved from Chicago!"

"Yes," Charles said, nodding, "and it's the best thing I've ever done in my life. I have been faithful to your mother—one hundred percent faithful—ever since that confrontation. I have loved rebuilding my relationship with her, and finally building a real relationship with my children. I'm proud of what we, as a family, have accomplished here. Most of all, I'm proud of how you and Rita turned out. You're better people, and you're more grounded and principled than I'll ever hope to be. All of it—my happiness, my success as a teacher, my success as a parent—is because your mother gave me a second chance. I would never throw all of it away for one night with Charlotte Andresson or anyone else. I hope you can see that."

"I can," Tony said, "but it's a damn tough sell to a jury."

"Believe me, I get that. You saw my reaction in Pike's office. I know Garcia will paint me as exactly the type of philandering asshole who would have my way with her, then kill her to shut her up."

Charles had said it exactly the way Tony had framed it in his mind. It made his stomach hurt to imagine the courtroom that day, and the explosion of press that would follow.

When Tony looked at his dad, he saw an odd expression flit

across his face. He realized his dad was waiting for a reaction, perhaps hoping for some kind of absolution from his son.

"Dad, you know me well enough to know it's going to take some time for me to come to grips with all this. I'm about to turn thirty. I didn't expect to be learning now that my fundamental understanding of my parents, of our family's dynamics, was off by about eighty degrees."

His father started to reply, but Tony didn't let him.

"However, I'm glad you told me. Just knowing the full story feels like a big step in the right direction. And it's not like I can point fingers. I've had my share of, uh… relationships. The bottom line is, I still appreciate and admire you. And I still love you with all my heart. Nothing will ever change that."

Before Tony finished speaking, his father was out of his chair and pulling Tony out of his. He threw his arms around his son and held him tightly.

***

When father and son had composed themselves, they left the library and strolled into the kitchen. What they saw put smiles on their faces. Tony's mother and Darcy were in chef's aprons and covered up to their elbows in pale, white muck. Spots of flour were everywhere. They stood over the kitchen table, which was covered with a plastic sheet. The plastic was covered with flour, eggs, and strips of dough. In the center was a chrome device with a crank on one side.

Tony said, "Making pasta? Really, Mom? Darcy's first visit here, and you have her cooking for us?"

"Shush," his mother said. "I told you and your father we would fix lunch, so we're fixing lunch."

"I thought maybe a sandwich, or a salad…"

It was Darcy's turn to interject. "As your mother said, shush." She giggled. "I like that word. I'm going to make a mental note to keep it handy."

Tony groaned.

Darcy added, "I'm having a great time. The bad news is I'm really terrible at this. Lunch may not be served until eight o'clock."

"Not terrible," Carlotta said. "A little slow, yes, but you're doing fine. The boys can wait for their lunch. It will be worth it."

"Besides," Darcy said, "Your mother is telling me all about you. We're going to need a lot more time together."

"Kill me now," Tony said.

"No worries," his mother said. "I'm only telling her the good stuff. I haven't even brought up your challenges playing sports. Or that middle school dance. Now *that* was funny."

"Ooh, I can't wait," Darcy said with another giggle.

***

Later, as they dined on homemade fettuccini with chopped tomatoes, mushrooms, and peppers, Tony steered the conversation back to his father's situation. "I don't want to spoil dinner, but there's a question I need to ask you both."

It grew very quiet, and Tony forged ahead. "Think about what we're all saying about this case. Dad's innocence means this has to be a frame-up. All these pieces of evidence didn't just happen by coincidence or divine intervention. And if we accept that Dad's being framed, it means someone has gone to extraordinary lengths to do it. I need you both to think about who would do such a thing. Who hates you, Dad, or is obsessed with you enough that they'd want you arrested and convicted of murder?"

Charles looked at his wife, then back at Tony. "I can't imagine," he said. "I don't get involved in casting the movies, so it's not likely to be some rejected actor. I pay my bills and treat my students fairly and with respect. I've never been in a fight in my life. I haven't cheated anyone I can think of."

At the word "cheated," Charles glanced at Carlotta. "The fact is, the person I've hurt the most in this world is your mother, and I'm pretty sure she's not doing this."

"I'm not," she said, "but there was a time when I might have, if I hadn't had the kids to think about." Her face turned serious. "Your father's right. Except for what happened between us, I can't think of a soul your father has wronged. I know of no one who would want to hurt him. In fact, just the opposite. Everyone's always adored him and has gone out of their way to help him."

Tony nodded and took a sip of diet soda. "Well, think about it. The easiest way to get Dad out of this, and maybe the only way, is to find the real killer."

Carlotta's face grew taut, her right fist clenching her fork until the knuckles were white.

Charles said, "Your mother and I are concerned about you. We all know from past experience that when you go looking for the truth, it can trigger real danger. Whoever really did this is still out there and doesn't want to be caught. If you get close…" He stopped, realizing his wife was on the verge of tears.

Darcy reached over and laid her hand on Carlotta's arm.

Tony said, "I swear, I'll be very careful. And I'm pretty sure there's no risk at the moment. Whoever did all this is probably feeling pretty smug right now." He glanced toward his father. "You've been ordered to stand trial, and the evidence against you is overwhelming. No one even knows we're looking into it further." Tony didn't believe this, in light of what had happened with the surveillance guy, but he hoped it would put his parents' minds at ease. It didn't.

Charles pushed back, saying, "Please, don't make assumptions like that. You never know. You need to watch your back every minute."

"You're right, Dad. I promise."

Carlotta raised her arm from the table, and used her hand to touch the side of Darcy's face. She said, "You be careful too. We don't want you to get so much as a scratch. After all, this is the first time Tony has been in love since Lisa died."

"Mo-ommm…"

***

It was 4 p.m. before Tony and Darcy were back in the Explorer and headed for Orney. Almost before they were out of the driveway, Tony turned to Darcy and asked, "Did my dad's concerns scare you? I agree that I can't put you in danger. When you want to distance yourself, you just need to say so."

Darcy slipped the shoulder harness off and leaned up over the center console to kiss him on the ear. "Don't be silly. This is the most exciting thing I've ever done. I'm not going anywhere. Besides, I barely heard your dad. I was rather distracted by that part your mother said there at the end."

"Well, uh… sure, but, uh… You know, it's Mom…"

Darcy laughed. "Relax, farm boy. I get it. I had a mom too."

"Had?" Tony asked, realizing with some degree of horror that he had never asked about her family or much of anything about her past beyond Jake, the "bastard" boyfriend.

"Yeah, she's gone. She died from an antibiotic-resistant infection when I was in grad school. She went from a young, vivacious, Hollywood mom to a hole in the ground in less than a week."

"I'm so sorry," Tony said softly. "That must have been horrible."

"It was. It was also what ended things with Jake. He said he was too busy to go with me to California to be with her. He didn't even come to the funeral."

"Were you close? You and your mom, I mean."

Darcy laughed. "You don't want to hear how close Jake and I were? C'mon, it'll be fun to tell you all about it."

"As much as I would love that, why don't you tell me about your mom first?"

Darcy thought for a minute before answering. "Losing her saddens me. I miss her, of course. But we were never really pals. I always felt like I was her trophy rather than her daughter, and sometimes just her source of income. She was the ultimate stage mom, celebrating each of my successes far more than I ever did. I feel terrible for her now. She loved living in L.A. and had the world on a string. She would be going crazy over the new success I've had post-graduation. But I have to tell you, if she had lived, I probably wouldn't have gone back to work. It's hard to explain."

"I think I get it," Tony said. "What about your dad?"

"Oh, Mom left him behind a long time ago. I grew up in Buffalo. He's a dentist there. Mom used to take me to New York City for auditions and lessons and things. That's no small trip, by the way. That's like driving from here to Chicago."

"Yeah, I know the geography."

"Once I started getting hired, Mom and I stayed in the city for longer and longer periods of time. I was just a kid. I was having fun, and it was exciting. When my agent suggested we go to L.A., Mom had the plane tickets bought before we had left her office. My career kept moving, and so did my mom. Before long, she had a boyfriend, and... Well, you get the picture."

"Yep, I do. It makes me sad. It also reminds me how lucky I am that my parents hung in there after what my dad did. Sorry, this isn't supposed to be about me."

Darcy smiled and said, "Well, that's about it, anyway. Dad's still in Buffalo, remarried to a younger woman. They have two sons, so I have a stepmom and two step-brothers, ten and fifteen years younger than me. The boys are smart, and cute, and spoiled rotten. I like them."

Tony didn't ask about the stepmom. He figured Darcy had a reason for stopping short of telling him more. He wasn't going to pry.

They rode a long time in silence. Traffic on I-80 was thick. After passing the third enormous boat being towed down the highway on a fifth-wheel trailer, Tony turned to Darcy and said, "Friday of a three-day holiday weekend. Lots of people are heading somewhere fun. Tomorrow's the Fourth of July."

"Good point. I haven't given the holiday much thought."

"As much as I hate the traffic, I'm glad to see people are getting out. It wasn't that long ago we wondered if life ever would get back to normal."

"I'm not sure what normal is," Darcy said, "but I'm certainly glad they're going to movies again. I like to be working."

Tony abruptly reached into his pocket for his phone. "Jeez, I told Rich I would call him. The day is almost over."

"It's a holiday weekend. Shouldn't you give him a break?"

"I told him I'd call. I'll leave it up to him."

Once connected, Tony asked his friend if he wanted to talk or preferred it wait.

"Are you kidding?" Davis said. "I've been dying to know what trouble you're causing now. Let's hear it."

Tony explained how he had found and examined the golf clubs

at Lake Brindle, noting the iron used in the killing was the same brand as his dad's. He described how they had carefully handled the golf bag and clubs and had documented how they wrapped and sealed them, finally putting them into Geoff Warbler's car trunk.

"Okay…" Davis said, haltingly. "And how does that help your dad? Won't Garcia be glad to hear it?"

"Rich, dad's bag isn't missing a club. The seven-iron is there."

"Okay, fine. I still don't get it."

"Pick up the bag and check the seven iron for dad's prints. Check the iron itself and see if it really came from that set."

"Ah, I think I see where you're going with this. You're saying if the seven iron in the bag doesn't match exactly, and doesn't have your dad's fingerprints on it, then maybe the person who framed him took your dad's club from the bag and replaced it with another just like it. Then he used your dad's club to kill Charlotte, benefitting from the fact it already had your dad's prints on it."

"Exactly."

"But think about it," Davis said. "Even if we find what you hope, the prosecutor will just say your dad took his own golf club to the pro shop, killed her with it, then put a new one in his bag to replace it."

Tony wasn't daunted. He said, "You saw the video. Was the man who entered the clubhouse carrying a golf club?"

"No," Davis acknowledged.

"So the prosecutor would have to argue that my dad pre-planted his own golf club in the pro shop filled with readily available clubs. Why would anyone do that? The only reason to plant my dad's club in the shop in advance would be to have it there later so it could be used to frame him."

"There's some logic to that, I guess, but it's pretty weak. That alone won't get him off the hook."

"That's why I bundled the whole bag, and not just the seven-iron. You need to check it all for prints. Maybe the real killer's are there."

"Shit. Tony, c'mon. The lab's gonna chew my ass into mush if I ask them to do that. Do you know how many people have probably touched that bag? Golf partners, caddies, people in the storeroom moving it around? We'd get dozens of prints, maybe hundreds."

"Please, Rich," Tony pleaded. "This is my dad, who's looking at life in prison. He didn't do this. We have to try."

"Okay, okay. I'll get the clubs to the lab and ask the techs to try. Don't get your hopes up."

"Too late," Tony said, smiling. "Thanks."

He stuffed the phone back into his jeans and gave Darcy a thumbs-up.

She said, "Very clever, Mr. Harrington. So which piece of evidence are you going to debunk next, the video of your dad, the mileage on your car, or the sperm inside the dead actress?"

"I'll take the first two, you can figure out the third one."

"Gee, thanks. Unfortunately, I only know one way to inseminate a woman, and your dad swears he didn't do that."

The word "inseminate" reminded Tony of something important. He said, "At the risk of offending my most beautiful new girlfriend, I'm pleased to say you're wrong. There *are* other methods. Artificial insemination is done all the time. Here in rural America, for example, using tubes and syringes to inseminate cows is a way of life."

"Yes, but that doesn't explain…"

"Yeah, I know. That's why you got the assignment. I'll never figure it out."

***

"Are you afraid of heights?" Tony asked. He and Darcy were

back together at about 9:30 p.m., after taking a break to clean up and change clothes in their respective lodgings. Tony had picked her up at the motel and had driven her back to his house. They were walking through the back yard from the alley to his house when he glanced at the sky and asked about heights.

"Not particularly," Darcy said. "I can't imagine anything in Orney tall enough to scare me, unless we're going to climb up the water tower and spray paint our initials on it."

"Hmm, not a bad idea, but no, not tonight. Wait here."

Tony unlocked the garage, disappeared inside, and emerged carrying an aluminum extension ladder. He walked to the side of his house, planted the ladder's feet in the grass, and pulled on the rope until the ladder extended six feet or so above the eave.

"After you, m'lady."

"And we're climbing to the roof why?"

"As I said, tomorrow's the Fourth of July! The annual fireworks are starting any minute."

Darcy removed her sandals and climbed the ladder in her bare feet.

"Smart girl," Tony said as he watched her legs and feet climb past his face. He looked up at her from below and said, "Smart and, uh, well-built."

Darcy gave her backside a little shake and said, "Bite me, farm boy."

Tony grinned and said, "In your dreams," and began to climb.

Once balanced on the sloping shingles, they carefully made their way up to the peak.

"Which way?" she asked.

Tony pointed west and they sat. The roof radiated the heat it had collected from a day in the sun. The warmth of the shingles, complemented by the cool breeze and the moonless sky, created the perfect perch. Within ten minutes, the sky was ablaze with color, and waves of explosive sounds rocked them.

"My God," Darcy said. "It feels like they're putting on this show just for us."

"That's why I like to watch from here. We could go to the park, but there would be a big crowd. Here, we can enjoy that!" He pointed and shouted as red and blue stars exploded above them and turned to white as they cascaded toward the Earth. "And we can enjoy it without distractions."

Darcy ran her fingers up the inside of his thigh.

Tony swallowed hard and said, "Experience that without unwanted distractions."

Darcy grinned, and Tony continued, "Also, up here we'll get ninety percent fewer mosquito bites, and a hundred percent fewer instances of three-year-olds dropping their sno-cones in our laps."

Darcy's hand moved higher.

Tony shifted his position. "You really need to stop that. Having your clothes torn off while sitting on the roof is kind of an open invitation to those nosy photographers we discussed before, don't you think?"

"I'll tell you what I think, farm boy. I think this is fantastic. The setting, the show, and the company. I also think it's time we go inside and make some fireworks of our own."

Tony had never descended a ladder so fast.

***

It was nearly midnight. Darcy was sound asleep, curled up against him. Tony lay staring at the ceiling, trying to imagine scenarios in which the other evidence against his father could exist. He was stumped.

"Small Town Cop" started blaring from his phone, still in his pants which were lying in a heap on the floor.

"Sorry," he said as he extricated his arm from under Darcy's head and rolled out from under the covers. He answered the phone as he grabbed his robe and walked through the living room into his office. "What's up?"

"I'm sorry, Tony," Davis said. "Something's happened." He sounded as worn down as Tony had ever heard him.

"Tell me."

"I called the number you gave me for Warbler. He never answered."

Tony sat in his desk chair as dread filled his chest. "And?"

"I felt it was important that we get the golf clubs as quickly as possible to eliminate any potential issues with chain of custody. So I tracked down the course manager to see if Warbler was working. The guy told me Warbler didn't come on until eleven, but he agreed to drive over to the old man's house to check on him."

"And?" Tony clenched his jaw so tightly his teeth hurt.

"On the way, the manager came across the scene of an accident. There's a bridge over Mill Creek, just outside of Solon. Apparently, a car struck the bridge abutment, flipped over, and rolled down to the creek. It was an older car and was completely mangled. The driver was trapped inside, dead at the scene."

Tony thought he might vomit. "It was Geoff?"

"Yes, it was Geoff Warbler. I'm sorry."

"Dear God. I'm sorry to ask, but were... are the golf clubs okay? Were they damaged in the trunk?"

Davis said, "I called the dispatcher and asked to be put through to the state trooper at the scene. He said the trunk sprang open in the crash."

Tony could feel his heart sink. "They're damaged, aren't they?

They went in the damn creek or something."

"Tony," Davis said. "There's no sign of a golf bag anywhere. The trooper said the trunk was empty, and they've found no evidence of anything like a golf bag at the scene. It's a shallow creek. There's nothing there."

Chapter 22

Orney, Iowa—Saturday, July 4

A cell phone clattered a generic tone. Tony opened his eyes. The room was dark.

Darcy stirred beside him. "Is that yours or mine?"

"What time is it?" he asked.

He felt her lift her head to see the clock on the nightstand.

She groaned and said, "It's 4:52 a.m."

"Probably me," he said, climbing over her and searching for his jeans in the dark.

She clicked on the lamp. He turned and motioned it wasn't necessary.

"I don't mind," she said. "I don't want you to trip and fall. "Your head has too many lumps already. Do you get these a lot? The late phone calls, I mean, not the lumps."

"Nah, only about twice a week," he said, grinning. "Twice a night is a bit over the top." He pulled out his phone. "Harrington."

No one spoke, but he could tell someone was there.

"Hello?" he repeated. "This is Tony Harrington. May I help you?"

"Sir? Sorry… so early." It was a woman's voice. She spoke quietly and with an accent Tony couldn't place.

"It's okay," Tony said, trying to sound like he meant it. "May I ask who's calling please?"

"No," she said simply. There was no defiance in her voice, just the statement of a simple fact. "It is your father, yes? The one the police took?"

"Yes," Tony said, walking down the hall to his office and sitting in front of his computer in case he needed to take notes. "What about my father?"

"Does father's trash matter?"

"What?" Tony was stupefied by the question. *Did I hear her right?*

The woman said, "I not know how to say." She paused. "Does his trash do his trouble?"

Tony had to stifle a laugh. "Are you asking me if trash somehow affects his case or is involved in the evidence against him in some way?"

"Yes! Yes, just so," she said, clearly relieved he had understood.

"Not that I know of," Tony said, turning on his phone's record function. "But there are many aspects…" He stopped himself, remembering the woman's struggle with English. Speaking more slowly and articulating carefully, he said, "There are many things we don't understand. Anything is possible. Tell me why you ask. Maybe that will help to answer your question."

The woman was silent a long time. "I cannot."

Tony groaned. *Don't call me at 5 a.m. if you're not going to tell me anything*, he thought, wanting to shout it at her. He held his tongue.

She said, "I cannot be know this me. I am illegal. No papers. Understand? No papers, no police."

Tony did understand. She was an undocumented immigrant. She couldn't report what she knew to the police. She couldn't let this come back on her. Tony sympathized with her plight. On the other hand, his dad was facing life in prison. He felt compelled to press her.

"Please, miss, whatever you know, if it's related to my dad's case, it could be important. Please tell me."

"Is why I called," she said. "No sleep with worry. I want tell. I no want lose job or lose America."

"I understand," Tony said. "I'll be careful. I promise. Now please tell me."

"I gave man the trash each day."

"I'm sorry, I don't understand."

"At motel. Each day. Man want his trash. Pay me much. One hundred dollar. Four days."

Holy shit, holy shit. Tony stood, trying to control his excitement.

"You work at the motel, here in Orney? The Howdy Stranger Inn?"

"Yes..." Tony could hear the hesitation creeping back into her voice. It was dawning on her how easily she could be found.

"It's okay," Tony said, "I'm very glad you called me. Please, tell me how it happened."

After an agonizing pause, she said, "Man in parking lot at end work. Give me money. Twenty dollar. He say he give more if find what he want. Only want trash from room one-one-two. You father room, yes?"

"Yes," Tony said. "This man, can you tell me what he looked

like?"

"Not so much. Taller me. No fat. Normal. Wear hat, sunvisor."

"Hat and sunglasses?"

"Sunglass, yes. And... long coat. Not see much."

Tony understood. The man had been careful to cover what he could, to mask his appearance. "So what did you do?"

"Each day, four days, put trash in bag. Take when end. Leave by mailbox."

"So each day, you put the trash from Room 112 in a separate bag, took it with you when you left work, and left it by the mailbox."

"Just so."

"What mailbox? Where?"

"Two blocks, by chicken."

The mailbox next to KFC. "Okay, I understand. What then?"

"Day four, man is there. He say no more. Give more money. Lot more. He say tell no one."

"When was this?"

"Two days, girl die."

"Two days after he met you the second time was the day Charlotte Andresson was murdered?"

"Yes," the woman said, her voice quivering. "So much sorry. Did I do bad? Am in trouble?"

"No," Tony said. "Please, try not to worry. You did the right thing to call me. You may have saved my father's life."

"I hope. I wish good for you." She was gone.

Tony shut off the record function and stared at his phone.

Fuck a duck and the truck that made it buck. I know how my dad's sperm found its way into Charlotte.

***

"You do understand that I work for the State, right?" Rich Davis asked. "I'm the investigator for the prosecution, not the defendant."

"That's B.S., and you know it," Tony replied. "We're friends because we both care about the truth. I've never known you to think of it as taking sides. In any case, I know you well enough to know this lead is just too crazy to not follow up. I would do it myself, but I don't have the authority to ask the motel for her name or to subpoena videos from private surveillance cameras."

"If the guy wears a hat and sunglasses, what do you hope to find?"

"C'mon, Rich. Don't play dumb. There are cameras everywhere these days. Maybe we'll get lucky and catch a license plate number or be able to judge his height from his proximity to the mailbox, or maybe we'll just document that the woman who called was telling the truth. If this man exists, and he's picking up my dad's trash each day for four days the week before the murder, don't you think we should know it? That Garcia should know it?"

"Of course I do," Davis said, but he sighed heavily. "I'll get on it right away. Could you just do me one favor?"

"Anything."

"Someday could you just once conduct an investigation that proves I'm right about something?"

Tony laughed. "If you're ever right, be sure to let me know, and I'll jump all over it."

"Stick it up your ass, smart guy."

Tony chuckled, but quickly grew serious. "Rich, please do what you can to protect the hotel maid."

"I'll try, but if we're going to use this evidence, she'll almost certainly be taken in to give a statement. It's gonna be hard to stop Garcia from turning her over to INS."

"Well, do what you can. But also, I meant protect her physically. Think about what happened to Mr. Warbler. If this killer finds out she talked to me, she could be in real danger."

"Good point. I'll get Rooney over to the motel to find out who she is and to keep an eye on her. If the *alleged* other killer tries something, maybe we'll get lucky and catch him in the act."

Tony thought, *Great. Now she's not only facing deportation; she's being used as bait.*

He said, "Thanks, Rich. Despite your ineptitude as an investigator, you're a hell of a nice guy."

"I think you may have missed it, but a few moments ago I told you to stick something where the sun don't shine. Now I suggest that something be a boat anchor."

"Ouch," Tony said, and hung up.

It was 11 a.m. on Saturday. Because of the holiday weekend, he had resisted calling Rich earlier. He had just dropped Darcy off at her motel and was planning to head to the grocery store.

Before doing any shopping, he knew he had another call to make. This one to Nathan Freed. The retired attorney and long-time friend answered his office phone on the second ring.

Tony said, "For a retired guy, you spend an awful lot of time in that chair."

Freed chuckled. "Just looking at the firm's quarterly statement. Making sure I'll be able to afford whatever favor Tony Harrington asks of me next."

The comment made Tony cringe, knowing that's exactly why he had called. "Oh man, I hate being *that* guy."

"You know it's fine. One of your favors brought me a stepdaughter I've grown to love. How can I help?"

Tony explained about the hotel maid, how she may have just saved his dad, and the troubles she was going to face because of it.

Freed understood immediately.

"Have her ask for me, and I'll be happy to help," Freed said. "That's no guarantee she'll be okay, but I think I can call in a few favors with the powers that be."

It was what Tony had hoped to hear, but Freed's agreement was no surprise. He knew him to be an exceptionally compassionate man.

"And by the way," Freed said, "congratulations. It sounds like you're making real progress in helping your dad. I wouldn't have thought it possible."

"Thanks, but we're not home free yet. Let's pray Davis finds some corroborating evidence and that Garcia is willing to look at it."

"Alex is an honorable man. You bring him the goods, he'll be interested."

***

After shopping and fixing himself a sandwich, Tony went looking for Lawrence Pike. He found him right where he expected he would, sitting on the deck at the back of his house, reading a book.

As Tony came around the back corner of the house, Pike looked up. Tony said, "That doesn't look anything like the latest edition of *The Annotated American Law Reports*."

Pike glanced at the cover of the latest John Grisham novel in his hands and said, "Mr. Harrington, the amount of trivia stored in your head is beyond belief. And no, I'm not working. In case you've forgotten, it's a holiday weekend."

"Would you prefer I leave and not share the breakthrough developments in your case?"

"Is anyone going to shoot at me while you're here?"

"I don't think so."

"Okay, come up and join me. Grab something to drink from

the house before you sit."

Tony didn't find Diet Dr. Pepper in the refrigerator, so he grabbed a bottle of water and joined Pike on the deck. Pike noted the page he was on in the novel, closed the book, and set it on the redwood table. After a few minutes of small talk, Tony turned serious and took Pike on the roller coaster ride of the past two days' developments—the golf clubs, Warbler's death, his father's history of affairs, the man with the parabolic microphone, and of course the trash collected from his father's motel room.

Pike said, "Jesus. Unbelievable. I don't even have a pen out here. I assume you're documenting all this?"

"Of course. I'll bring you the photographs, notes, and recordings on Monday. I just thought you'd like to know right away that all hell is breaking loose."

"Well, yes, absolutely."

"I also want to ask if there are things I should be doing between now and Monday. Can you think of anything?"

The old man pondered the question for a moment, then said, "I'll have to think about that. In the meantime, there are a couple of things *I* need to do."

Tony waited, watching Pike's features morph through a variety of expressions as his mind churned.

Eventually, Pike said, "First, I'm going to call Alex and give him a heads up about some of this. He won't like it, but our formal meeting with him later will go much better if we don't drop this on him like a bomb."

Tony nodded, but he wasn't keen on the idea.

Pike must have seen Tony wince. He asked, "What? You disagree?"

"No, no. I trust your judgment completely. It's just that someone must have tipped off the killer about the golf clubs. I find it impossible to believe that Warbler just happened to have an accident the next day, and the golf clubs just happened to have been stolen from the scene. Very few people knew about them. Our killer is close to someone on the inside. Please caution Mr. Garcia about that."

"I will, but be careful you don't assume too much, or perhaps a better way to say it, be careful to consider all the possibilities."

Tony was all ears.

Pike continued, "For example, maybe you were followed to Lake Brindle Thursday night. Or maybe someone is tracking your cell phone. That guy with military-grade surveillance equipment might also be able to do that. Or maybe Warbler told the wrong person."

"You're right. We need to be careful in a whole bunch of ways we haven't been before."

Pike nodded and said, "The second thing I'll do is get the medical examiner's report of Charlotte's autopsy and really look at the details of the findings related to the semen. Your theory, that the sperm came from the bathroom trash at the motel, will hold up better if there were only traces of it found in the body."

Tony could see the logic in that.

Pike continued, "I'm happy to report I don't know anything about collecting, storing, and transferring semen. I know it can be done, but I don't know whether evidence of those activities can be spotted. I should have thought to ask before."

Pike grew quiet and closed his eyes. Tony sipped on his water, wanting to give the attorney plenty of time to think.

When Pike opened his eyes, he leaned forward and looked hard at Tony. "Something else just occurred to me. Something important. We've talked at length about the extraordinary measures someone has undertaken to frame your father."

"No argument there. It's unbelievable."

"If this is a crime against *him* and not against her…" Pike's voice trailed off as he thought for another moment. He then said, "I think you understand me, but let me be clear. If your father is innocent, there are two possibilities. First, the murderer may have intended to kill Miss Andresson and frame your father to get away with the crime. The second is that the murderer wanted to hurt your father, and only killed Andresson *in order to* frame him for murder. If the second scenario is the truth, then the killer must be obsessed with hurting him. Enough to kill over it."

"Right…"

"So if the killer senses the frame-up is coming apart, that all of his efforts aren't going to get the results he planned, he may seek an alternative course of action."

Tony leaned back in his chair, feeling the blood drain from his face.

Pike said, "I see you get my drift. If your father's going to get exonerated on these charges, then the killer might go after him in some other way—perhaps try to hurt him physically or even go after you or another member of the family."

Tony groaned for what seemed like the thousandth time in the past two weeks. "You're saying we need to warn my family that someone very diabolical, someone who has already killed one young woman and perhaps one old man in cold blood, might decide to come for them? This is incredible. Do you know how many times my sister has been in danger because of me, because of the work I do? How am I going to…?"

Tony pulled his phone out his pocket and said, "I'll call dad, but I'm texting you Rita's number. I'll pay you ten thousand dollars to make that call for me."

Pike smiled and said, "It's on the house."

***

At 6:30 p.m. exactly, Tony pulled his SUV into the carport at the Hampton Inn. Once again, Darcy was waiting in front. This time, she was signing autographs for a small group of people crowded around her.

She waved at Tony, signed her name a few more times, and made her way to the vehicle.

As she climbed into the passenger seat, Tony's breath caught in his throat. She was wearing a short, black dress with a pattern of large, red blossoms. It had spaghetti straps and was cut low in front. Darcy had accented it with a wide white belt and a white-and-red scarf.

"You like?" she asked, smiling wide enough to serve soup from her dimples.

"You look stunning. You look better than stunning."

"Thanks. And look at you! You told me you only wore those slacks once a year."

"Well, twice, if I really like the person I'm dating. I'm glad you like them. Gretchen hardly noticed."

"Gretchen...?" Darcy's brow furrowed. Then, as she remembered the conversation about the three-hundred-pound barfly, she burst out laughing. "You didn't tell me you and Gretchen had a history! So that's why you didn't want to take me to the bar that night."

"Busted," Tony nodded, grinning.

He and Darcy had agreed to dress up to attend a performance of *The Music Man*, the classic Meredith Willson musical set in small-town Iowa. The Orney Community Theater was doing weekend performances of the play throughout most of the summer in celebration of its return to live productions following the pandemic. The theater company was one of many not-for-profit organizations that nearly hadn't survived the shutdown.

The OCT owned a small building with a performance venue appropriate for the dramas and comedies normally produced. However, because of the size and scale of a musical that included a full marching band, the OCT had rented the Pixley Center, a beautiful tiered theater that held up to six hundred spectators.

As they entered the hall and walked down to their seats in the sixth row, Darcy turned to Tony and said, "Wow. This is spectacular."

"It's oversized for the town," Tony whispered. "It's here because a very generous donor wanted Orney to have the biggest and best theater in Iowa for performing arts. It's not the biggest—that would have been crazy—but it probably is the best. It has all the latest sound and lighting equipment in addition to great acoustics and a whole bunch of comfortable seats."

"Who would've thought you could find this in Iowa?"

"Some of us think of this first," he said with a wink.

Darcy laughed and squeezed his hand as they settled into their seats.

Before the lights dimmed, Tony was surprised to see the director step out in front of the curtain. "Good evening, everyone," she said. "My name is Cynthia Lanthro, and it is my privilege to serve as the director of this summer's musical. The cast and crew have worked incredibly hard, and I think you'll be impressed when you see and hear what they have for you tonight."

Tony found himself squirming in his seat. Curtain speeches were tacky in his opinion, and it embarrassed him to have Darcy see the OCT doing one. He soon found out why the director had chosen to do it.

Lanthro said, "As you all know, a lot has been happening in Orney this summer. It's been exciting to have a major production company in town filming a movie. We've enjoyed seeing and, in some cases, getting to know the cast and crew from the movie. For those who haven't noticed, I'd like to point out that one of the stars of the movie, and one of the most talented and accomplished actresses in Hollywood, is here with us tonight. I didn't warn her I was going to do this, but Darcy Gillson, would you mind standing so the people of Orney can acknowledge and thank you for being here?"

Darcy stood, nodded to the director, and turned and waved to the crowd. The applause was thunderous. As it diminished, Darcy turned back toward the stage. In a loud voice, she said, "Break a leg!"

Everyone laughed.

Lanthro said, "Thank you, Miss Gillson. I hope you enjoy the show." She looked up into the crowd. "I hope you *all* enjoy the show, and I hope our ovation at the end is a fraction of what you shared with our guest."

The crowd laughed again, and the director disappeared.

Tony turned and whispered into Darcy's ear. "I'm really sorry about that. I didn't know."

"Don't be silly," she whispered back. "I should have expected it, and I really don't mind. Don't you know we movie stars feed off of the adoration of the masses?"

Her smile was wide and warm. It took all of Tony's strength not to lean over and kiss her right there. He forced himself to turn back toward the stage.

The curtain opened to the sights and sounds of a train filled with traveling salesmen chugging across Iowa and into River City.

***

Later, enjoying the nostalgic mood set by the musical, Tony and Darcy agreed that burgers and shakes at the Dairy Queen would hit the spot. They sat at an outdoor table under the neon lights and enjoyed another warm summer night.

"It really was an impressive performance," Darcy said. She paused a moment, then started to chuckle.

Tony looked at her quizzically.

She said, "I almost made the mistake of saying, 'Who would have thought you could find that in Iowa?'"

Tony smiled. "I was impressed too. I'd heard great things about it, but it exceeded my expectations. So how would you compare it to the movie? Have you seen it?"

"I did a long time ago," she said. "It was featured in our local theater on one of those classic movie nights. Dad took me to see it. I was probably in middle school, and I couldn't see how a girl like Marian could fall for an old guy like Harold Hill."

Tony chuckled, "One of the great musicals of all time, and that was your takeaway? That the love interest was too old?"

"What can I say?" Darcy grinned. "I'm shallow."

Tony shook his head and shifted gears. "I almost always like the live version of musicals better than the movies, but *Music Man* was one where a few of the original Broadway cast members were allowed to play their parts on screen, including Robert Preston. I think that made it special."

Tony paused to sip on his shake, then added, "The other advantage to the movie, of course, is the magic at the end. It's such a great illusion, when the local kids are transformed into a band with fabulous uniforms and instruments and talent."

"I can't argue," Darcy nodded. "It's what we do best in movies, create illusions."

The conversation moved on. Tony was commenting on the unusually great weather they had enjoyed for days when Darcy suddenly said, "Tell me about Lisa."

Tony looked up from his straw and wiped the chocolate from his lips with a napkin. He swallowed hard and said, "There's not much to tell. She was great. I fell in love. She got killed. End of story."

Darcy looked at him, clearly wanting to know more.

After a long lull, Tony said, "I'm sure you know by now that you remind everyone of her. Not just because you're blonde and beautiful, but because of your intelligence, your humor. A lot of things."

"Is that why you're with me? Are you trying to fill that void?"

"Hey, you asked me out, remember?"

Darcy smiled. "Touché."

"Seriously, though, that's not it. Lisa's death was years ago. I've had a couple of other semi-serious relationships since then. I've stopped dreaming about Lisa. I still miss her, sure. I visit her grave and talk to her sometimes, but it's not an obsession. I know she would want me to move on, to be happy, and I want that too. So I've put her in the part of my brain where you park beloved grandparents who have died. You love and appreciate them. You never forget them. But they're no longer a part of your life."

"Hmm, I wonder…"

"A more pertinent question," Tony said, "is why are you with me?"

She looked surprised by the question.

He continued, "I mean really, you could have almost any man on Earth."

"Well, let's not talk crazy…"

"You know what I mean. Men everywhere dream of being with you. They follow you on social media, buy your posters, your action figures, go to every one of your movies. When you have the pick of the litter, why hang out with me?"

"You're the only single guy I know in Orney, Iowa," she said.

"Oh, God. I knew it," he said with an exaggerated pout.

"Tony, shut up," she said. "You know I'm joking. With everything you've accomplished, with the courage and talent you demonstrate every day in your job, and even with your experiences with wonderful women like Lisa, it astonishes me that you have this inferiority complex. Look, I've dated my share of guys…"

"Do I want to hear this?"

"I told you to be quiet." She tried to sound stern, but she was smiling. "I've dated losers like Jake and movie stars like… Well, nevermind. Movie stars. None of them have been as interesting, or as fun, or as attractive as you."

Tony snorted. "Speaking of crazy talk…" he said, taking the last pull of milkshake from his straw.

"I mean it, Tony. I'm crazy about you, and… and…"

He looked up and saw a tear in her eye.

"Hey, I didn't mean to upset you." He wiped the tear away with his thumb.

"See what I mean?" she said. "You're just so damned… nice."

Tony heard some commotion and looked to his right. Near the door to the DQ, four teenagers had gathered and were looking at them.

"Uh-oh," Tony said. "Get out your pen."

Darcy sat up straight and smiled as the group approached.

When the teens reached the table, one of the girls held out a copy of the *Orney Town Crier*. She said, "Excuse me, but aren't you Tony Harrington? Would you sign this for me?"

Darcy shrieked with laughter.

***

That night, their lovemaking was different. Still intense and physical, but somehow elevated. Thinking about it later, Tony realized the intensity had come from emotions beyond desire. He hadn't just wanted to experience the pleasure, he had wanted to give himself over to her completely, and to possess her in return. He had not wanted to let her go. He never wanted to let her go.

Something in Tony's heart had turned a corner. It terrified him.

Chapter 23

Orney, Iowa — Sunday, July 5

"We go back to work tomorrow," Darcy said, dipping a wedge of pancake into maple syrup.

"You go to work tomorrow? Here in Orney?" Tony asked, mildly irritated that she was raising it now, while they were having brunch with Doug and Alison. The four of them had agreed to meet at Willie's for the Sunday buffet.

"Yeah, Bhatt says he's finished his rewrites, and that we can resume filming while he searches for Charlotte's replacement. A bunch of cast and crew will be showing up in Orney today and tonight for an early start tomorrow."

Doug asked, "What does that mean for you, Tony? Will you be coming back to work, or are you still on leave?"

"I don't know," Tony said. "So much is happening in my dad's case right now, I had assumed I would stick with that. But with the movie gearing up again, I hate to leave Ben short-handed. I guess I need to talk to him before I decide."

Darcy said, "I'm sorry, Tony. I forgot how much our presence affects your job too. I should have told you yesterday when Bhatt texted me."

"No big deal," Tony lied. "We'll figure it out."

Darcy looked across the table at Doug and Alison. "So what's the deal with you two? Are you seeing each other now?"

As Alison turned beet red, Tony said, "Don't mind Darcy. She's been around my mother too much lately."

The group laughed, and Doug said, "Well, you can relax. This is a sympathy date only. If I wasn't nursing a bullet wound, Alison would have told me to take my brunch invitation and... never mind."

"Don't be so sure," Alison said, raising eyebrows around the table. "As long as you're paying, I might agree to do this again. After all, it's broad daylight, and two other people are here to protect me."

The banter continued through the meal. Later, after the bill was paid and the four were preparing to go, Tony said, "I've been thinking a lot about last night."

Darcy grinned and said, "Well I should hope so."

It was Tony's turn to get red-faced. He said, "Not that. I've been thinking about what you said about movie magic, about how illusions are what movies do best."

"Yes, I remember. Thinking about it in what regard?"

"Think about the framing of my dad. What is a near-perfect frame-up if not just another elaborate illusion?"

The others may have found the thought interesting, but no one commented.

Tony continued, "So if the murderer did it to get at my dad, is it a coincidence it happened when a movie he wrote was filming here, or did the murderer wait until one of his movies was in production to implement his plan?"

Darcy nodded. "I think I see where you're going. If this person was out to get your dad, maybe Charlotte wasn't just a convenient victim. Maybe the killer wanted the victim to be an actress for some reason."

Tony was growing more animated as he thought about the possibilities. He said, "Yes, but even beyond that, maybe the killer is a part of the movie business. That's why he or she was able to do all these things. The killer knows how to create illusions, to match and swap props, to manipulate things like blood and semen and car odometers."

"I'm not sure the two sets of skills correlate that precisely," Darcy said, "but I think what you're saying is possible. Especially if the person had plenty of time to plan."

Tony nearly jumped out of the booth. "And, oh my God, of course! Videos! Who can take a video of a killer entering and leaving the Orney Country Club and insert my dad's face into it? Someone in the movie business! Why didn't I think of this sooner? I just had a conversation with a woman on the crew who described how film-makers can create almost anything digitally now. Someone inside the business would know how to make it look absolutely authentic."

They all agreed he was onto something important.

He turned to Darcy, "Can you keep this under your hat for a while? I don't want our killer to know this has occurred to us."

"Please, Tony," she said, rolling her eyes a bit. "If you all can keep it out of the media, I think I can keep the secret too."

"No offense," he said. "I'm just frightened about what might happen. As Lawrence Pike told me, the killer might try something else if he learns his plan is falling apart. Please be on your guard everyday."

"I promise," she said, "but I have to ask the same of you. I know your history. It seems to me the bad guys are more likely to be aiming their guns, knives, tanks, or whatever in your direction, not mine."

The four exited Willie's and said their goodbyes. Tony and Darcy watched as Alison helped Doug into the passenger seat of her car. She leaned in to be sure his seatbelt was fastened, then walked around to the driver's side and got in.

As the car pulled away from the curb, Darcy said, "There's something going on there."

"Yep," Tony said with a smile.

Tony and Darcy had walked to the diner from Tony's house. As they began the return trip, strolling east along a wide, tree-lined street, Tony pulled out his phone and called Rich Davis.

"Holiday weekend," the agent said when he answered. "H-O-L-I-D-A-Y, defined as a day of rest and…"

"Okay, I get it. I'm a pain, and you're starting to wish that sniper had taken my head off."

"Not quite, but you're getting there. What's up this time?"

Tony explained his latest theory, then made a request. "Can you get me a list of every member of the cast and crew of the movie? I mean everyone who was here the week Charlotte was killed? Maybe not just a list. Can you get me the background information you gathered? Even copies of the interview notes?"

"I don't know, but I doubt it. That's a huge amount of material, and most of the people who talked to us weren't expecting their information to be shared outside of law enforcement. Especially not with a member of the press."

"How about with the accused? Doesn't my dad have a right to see it?"

"Well, sure…" Davis said reluctantly. "If his attorney requests it, we'll have to turn everything over to him."

"That's great. It's really my dad who needs to see it anyway.

Can you expedite the process? Get it to us, uh, him quickly?"

"Is that important somehow? What's got your underwear in such a bundle?"

"Think about it," Tony said, exasperated. "If someone involved in the movie is also involved in framing my dad, maybe he'll spot some connection in the information. Maybe it's a former lover he jilted, or… God forbid, a child he left behind without realizing it. Someone involved in the movie may be the person who hates my dad enough to plan and carefully execute this near-perfect crime. The more I think about it, the more positive I am. The person who killed Charlotte, and maybe Geoff Warbler, is on that list."

Davis sighed audibly. "Okay, okay, you convinced me. It's important. I'll get on it right away.

"Oh, and one more thing."

"You're kidding, right?"

"Sorry, but can you have someone—no, not just someone, a real expert—take a super-close look at the videos from the country club? If the killer is in the movie business, he or she could have created the video with my dad in it."

"We always check to be sure the video is authentic."

"I'm not surprised, and I didn't mean to question anyone's abilities, but now it's almost certain the video is a fake. I'm hoping there's some way to spot it if the right expert knows the situation."

"I'll ask, but I'm not sure there's a 'next level' of testing for that. Now remind me, is that nine or ten assignments you've given me that need to be done by end-of-day tomorrow?"

"You're wrong," Tony said. "The deadline is noon."

"To quote a young reporter I know, bite me."

Tony grinned and said, "Thanks, Rich. You're the best."

***

Tony and Darcy spent the rest of Sunday working on his house. Not, as Tony pointed out more than once, because he was an ogre, but because Darcy wanted to do it. She insisted she wanted to take the lead in thoroughly cleaning the interior, including washing the bedding and scrubbing the sinks.

"Is it really that bad?" Tony asked.

"Not at all. I just want to do something ordinary for a day. Something domestic. Assuming you'll let me crank up the stereo with tunes recorded more recently than 1980, I won't mind the work at all."

"If you're gonna choose Imagine Dragons or Twenty One Pilots over Jimmy Buffet and Bonnie Raitt, I may just have to go outside and mow the lawn."

"Perfect," she said, clapping her hands. "I can have my way with your house, and I won't have to hear you whine about the music."

"I never whine," he said as she shooed him out the door.

***

Once it was dark and the chores were finished, Tony and Darcy enjoyed a light supper of cheeses, summer sausage, crackers, fruit, and wine.

"The house looks great," he said.

"Thanks. The yard looks nice too. I noticed you even trimmed the bushes in front of the porch."

"Yeah, I like to give them some attention once every three years or so, whether they need it or not."

She giggled.

"God, I love it when you laugh."

"I'm glad, because I seem to do it a lot when I'm with you."

"So tell me why you really did all this work. You spotted something gross you were compelled to remove? You wanted a chance to check my closet for another woman's clothes? What?"

"Nothing of the kind. It was just what I said. I wanted to do something for you."

Tony searched her face for tell-tale signs that there was more.

"And," she said.

"Ahh, I knew it."

"And," she said, "I wanted to show off just a little. It seemed important for you to know I'm willing to get my hands dirty—to be something more…" She hesitated. Tony held his breath, hoping she would continue. "I can't explain it. I just wanted—desperately wanted—to share a piece of your everyday life."

"And was it what you hoped?" he dared to ask.

"I'll tell you later. But right now, I need to get cleaned up."

"Care to share the shower? I'm really good at scrubbing those hard-to-reach places."

"Hmm, we know from experience where that can lead."

"Exactly," Tony said, standing up, taking her hand, and leading her into the bathroom.

***

Later that night, they lay in a jumble of twisted sheets, entwined limbs, and matted hair.

"I'm afraid I've wrinkled the nice clean sheets you put on my bed," Tony said.

He could feel her smile in the darkness. "It's not just the bedding that needs to be cleaned again."

"It can wait till morning," he said. "I don't want to let go of you."

"Morning comes early for me tomorrow. Remember, I'm expected back on the shooting location before seven."

"Will you want breakfast? I can get up and fix you something while you shower."

"You would do that for me? You hate getting up in the morning."

Tony nearly dismissed her question with his typical attempt at humor, but he changed his mind. He had something else to say. He took her face in his hands, able to just make out her eyes in the darkness. "Darcy, I made a big mistake once a long time ago. I never thought I would be in a position to make it again, but here I am."

He could feel her tense up and realized she might be misunderstanding where this was going. "I don't know how this happened, what it means, or where this relationship is going, but I want you to know something important." He gulped and took a deep breath. "I am completely, utterly, hopelessly in love with you."

He heard her breath catch, felt her face warm under his touch, then felt her tears drip down to his fingers. Finally, she said, her voice trembling, "Oh, Tony. I've never been happier in my life. I've dreamed of hearing you say that. Don't *ever* let go."

She kissed him long and hard.

Tony wasn't naïve. He noticed she stopped short of saying "I love you too." He knew the happiness she'd found with him, in a two-bedroom bungalow, in a small Iowa community, couldn't last. He doubted he would be able to hold onto her for long.

He didn't care. He was with her now, he was in love, and he had told her how he felt. No matter what happened, no one could take that away from him. He was happy.

Chapter 24

Orney, Iowa—Monday, July 6

With Darcy at work, and with Rich Davis and Lawrence Pike following up on their respective tasks related to his dad's case, Tony found himself in an empty house with nothing to do.

I can't even decide to clean something, he thought, looking around at floors, counters, and furniture that were more spotless than he ever had seen them.

At 10 a.m., he walked into Ben Smalley's office at the *Crier*. Smalley looked up, surprised, then smiled broadly.

"I know you. You're that guy who used to work for a living."

"Yep, that's me. Scoop Harrington, reporting for duty."

"So you're ready to go to work? I haven't heard that your dad's case is settled."

"It's not, but I honestly believe we're getting close. If you have time, I'll tell you all about it."

"Absolutely. Let me grab a coffee, and I'm all yours."

Once settled in, Tony walked his boss through the recent events as well as his theories about the two deaths and the mystery man or woman behind them both.

"Wow," Ben said. "I think you may be right. I hope you are. I can't wait to publish the headline telling the world your dad is innocent."

"You and me both."

"And to be honest," Ben added, "I can't wait until we can publish this whole story. Once it's over and the facts are corroborated, it's gonna be one hell of a piece. Maybe a whole series."

"Wouldn't that be nice? Let's hope. Meanwhile, we—and by 'we,' I mean primarily my dad—have to figure out who hates him enough to do all this."

"You know, not all obsessions are well-grounded. It could just be some nut he cut off in traffic once."

Tony nodded, but said, "I hope not. If that's the case, we may never figure it out. So let's assume this person's rage is well-founded. What could cause that?"

"Your dad has confessed to these affairs you mentioned. Could one of those women have been married? Maybe some guy got jilted because his wife or girlfriend fell for your dad."

"Maybe. That's the kind of thing he'll look for when he has the list of cast and crew. With luck, some name or piece of information in someone's background will ring a bell for him. But I don't know, the level of ire we're describing almost feels like it could be associated with a bigger loss. Maybe a death? Someone's daughter or sister got run over by a bus as she was leaving an encounter with my dad? Something like that?"

"The loss of a child would do it," Ben said, "but I doubt there's anyone in the cast or crew old enough to have been a parent to one of the women your dad dated fifteen or twenty years ago."

The mention of a child triggered something in the back of Tony's mind. He was just talking about children with someone. *Wasn't I? Or was I thinking about them? When was that?* The answer hit him like a thunderbolt. No, not an answer, but an idea. A crazy, impossible idea. *But could it be?*

He must have gone still in his chair because Ben said, "Tony? Are you okay?"

Tony stood. "Yeah. I just had a thought about someone my dad might have hurt a long time ago. I need to check it out. I'll let you know if it turns out to be anything."

Tony exited the office and walked through the newsroom to his desk. He dreaded his next task, but knew it had to be done. He dialed his dad's cell phone number.

"Hello. I was hoping you'd call," his dad said brightly. "Any news yet?"

"Are you alone? Can you talk?"

Charles Harrington immediately picked up on the serious tone in Tony's voice. He said, "Sure. Just let me shut the door to my study. Has something happened?"

"Not exactly," Tony said, taking a deep breath. "I need to ask you a difficult and embarrassing, but hugely important, question."

His father sighed. "Go ahead. I can't imagine anything that would be worse than the things we've already discussed."

"Did you sleep with Harriet Bhatt?"

The phone was silent for a long time, confirming Tony's suspicions.

His father said, "Well, yes and no."

"Sorry, dad, but I'm pretty sure that question has only one answer."

"Well, the truth is, yes, I had a fling with Harriet. It was just one night, and it happened before she was married. She was Harriet

Danziger. I may have been a playboy in my youth, but I wasn't a total scoundrel. I never would have slept with her if she had been married. Why do you ask? You can't think Ramesh had something to do with all this?"

"Actually…"

His father cut him off, saying, "Well, you can forget it. Ramesh and I have been friends for more than thirty years. He would never do something to hurt me or anyone. Besides, he never knew about Harriet and me."

"You can't know that, Dad. You don't know what Harriet may have told him. You don't know how that fling might have affected her or them as a couple."

"Well, sure, but if Ramesh knew, and resented me for it or worse, why did he remain my friend all these years?"

"I don't know. Maybe he learned about it later. Maybe he promised Harriet he would. By the way, do you know why Ramesh and Harriet never had children?"

"What are you…?" Charles stopped himself, seemingly resigned to follow the conversation wherever Tony took it. He sighed and continued, "Not precisely. I remember once when we all met in Europe, Harriet was having great fun playing with and entertaining you and Rita. Later, when Ramesh and I were alone, I nudged him a little. You know, like friends do, saying, 'Hey, pal. It's about time you took the plunge.' That sort of thing. He told me then that Harriet couldn't have children. It seemed to sadden him, so I didn't pry any further."

"Thanks, Dad. I appreciate you being honest with me. This is helpful."

"Tony, please don't go and accuse Ramesh of something. Think about how supportive and generous he's been to me throughout this whole ordeal. I would still be in jail if not for him. He's a true friend, and I don't want to offend him."

"I promise. I won't even hint at a thing until I'm sure of it or until I've shared whatever I learn with you."

"Very well," Charles said, sighing again. "Be careful, and don't waste too much time on this. The real killer is still out there somewhere."

After the call ended, Tony sat at his desk, tapping a pen rapidly against the black surface. He had a suspicion about Harriet Bhatt's childbearing issue, but he was completely baffled about how to get the next piece of information he needed. He racked his brain.

Then he had another crazy idea. He looked at his watch, did some mental calculations about time zones, and picked up his phone. He called for a taxi driver in Amalfi, Italy.

The happy voice of Montay Ricci answered the phone on the first ring. "Tony! I did not know you returned to my beautiful land. Where can I take my favorite rich American tonight?"

Montay and Tony had become friendly the previous year, when Tony had stayed in Amalfi, his mother's home town, to attend the funeral of Tony's young cousin. Montay had driven Tony everywhere for several days, and had helped Tony find the man suspected of killing her.

Tony was about to protest the comment about being rich, then realized how absurd it would be in light of what he was about to ask. "Montay, my friend, I'm sorry to say I am at home in America. Unless you've learned to drive even faster than the last time I saw you, I'm afraid you won't be taking me anywhere tonight."

"I am sorry to hear it. So why a call from America? Perhaps you wish to tell me of the man you chased last year? I never heard what happened beyond you, as you say, getting your ass kicked in the bus station." He cackled at the thought.

"That man disappeared," Tony said. "No one's seen him in a

year. It's a mystery."

"Yes, I'm sure," Montay said. "Disappearing seems to be a common mystery for the Camorra."

Tony winced at the memory and the reference to the Italian mafia.

"I'm calling because I do want to hire you, just not as a driver."

"But driving is what I do."

"Yes," Tony said with a warm smile, "I remember. Unfortunately, I need someone to do detective work, and I can't do it myself. Even if I came to Italy, I think I would fail. I don't think an American could ever get the information I need. Would you be willing to take a trip up to Rome for me, and perhaps to Milan? I'm not sure where you'll find it."

"Detective? Like the movies? Roma? Really? But no, I…"

Tony interrupted. "I'll pay you, of course. I'll pay you for a full week, so you'll have time to travel as well as gather information."

"I also will have the loss of my regular income."

"Of course." Tony braced himself. He knew where this was headed. "How much will it take?"

Montay named a figure. It was about three times greater than the sky-high figure Tony had predicted he would hear.

"Jesus, Montay! I hope you threw that out as a starting point for our negotiation."

"No, I named that price because you are rich," Montay said, his smile leaking through the phone connection, "and because you are desperate. And you shouldn't use the Savior's name to curse at me. Your mother wouldn't like it."

In the end, the two men agreed Tony would pay half Montay's price in advance. The other half would be paid only if Montay succeeded in finding what Tony sought. Tony adored Montay and considered him a friend, but that didn't stop him from assuming the young man needed an incentive to actually do the work, and not simply take the money and enjoy a leisurely vacation somewhere.

In exchange for the exorbitant fee, Montay also agreed to leave the next day. Tony instructed him to start at the Instituto di Sanita in Rome. He gave him Harriet Bhatt's name, and told him her maiden name had been Danziker.

"The fashion model?" Montay asked.

"Yes, but that was thirty-five years ago. How in the world did you know that?"

"My father. He liked beautiful women. Every year, he bought a calendar with pictures of a beautiful model and hung it on the wall of his motorcar repair shop. He never took down the old ones. Just found a spot to... How do you say?... squeeze in the next one. I grew up with Harriet Danziker wearing a swim suit, smiling down at me from the shop wall. She was one of his favorites."

"My parents knew her for many years before she died, and I can see why. She was a lovely person."

"Person, yes," Montay said with a laugh. "That's what my papa and I always admired in that picture, her, uh... person."

"Okay, enough, my friend. Not get your ass in gear and find what I need. And please be careful. We don't want to harm Harriet's good name, and we don't want the next bad guy coming after you."

"Wait. What?"

Tony ended the call.

***

On Monday evening, Tony felt like he was making real progress in clearing his dad's name. Pike had called earlier to say the autopsy confirmed that only small amounts of semen had been found in the body of Charlotte Andresson, making it possible it had been transferred there in some way other than intercourse. Pike had also said County Attorney Alex Garcia had agreed to meet with him and Tony's dad on Thursday to review any new evidence and developments in the case.

As Tony and Darcy were fixing BLTs and preparing to watch a movie, Davis called with some updates as well.

"First," the agent said, "we quickly confirmed the seal is broken on the Mustang's odometer."

"I knew it!"

"Before you get too excited, remember how old the car is. The odometer could have been tampered with at any point in its long life. It's not difficult."

"Still, it's one more piece in the puzzle. At least it doesn't refute my dad's assertion that the mileage must have been turned back. What else have you got?"

"The hotel maid is an immigrant from Bosnia. I'm not sure why she's illegal. A lot of people fled to the U.S. from Bosnia during the war there. It should have been relatively easy for her to come legally, once she could identify the people she was joining here."

"Maybe that will help Freed's efforts to prevent her deportation."

"It won't hurt," Davis agreed. "Her name is Marija. I'm not going to try to pronounce her last name. She related her story to us exactly as she told it to you. That allowed us to get warrants to look at cameras from the stores and branch bank near the KFC, including the bank's ATM camera. A couple of agents will start looking at those tomorrow."

"Boy, I hope they find something. That would be a huge help with Garcia, if he could actually see someone else who's involved in this."

"Lastly, a couple of our folks spent the day over in Solon, looking closely at Warbler's fatal crash."

"And?"

"Nothing definitive, of course. He was an older man, and he could have gotten distracted or had a seizure or any number of things, causing him to veer into the bridge abutment. However, one of the agents did find and document some paint scratches on the driver's side of the car—the kind you would expect to find if someone had bumped him while passing."

"Unbelievable. Who would…?"

"Again, don't read too much into it. The damage could have been a result of the accident. It was pretty mangled in lots of places. And, before you ask, yes, we looked at your pictures from Thursday night. They only show the rear portion of the car, and it was too dark to see anything anyway. We can't tell if the damage was already there. The good news is that if we find a suspect, we'll be able to check his car for damage. We might get lucky and get a match on the paint samples."

"What about the video from the country club?"

"Gimme a break, Harrington. It's only Monday."

"I know. I just thought I should ask."

"If you must know, I called and asked Agent Tabors in Chicago if she would have the digital experts at the FBI take a look at it."

Tony knew Agent Anna Tabors from a previous case on which the FBI had assisted the Iowa DCI. In addition to being in charge of the FBI office in Chicago, she was an extremely capable and determined investigator. She would know whom to go to for the best opinion about the videos. Tony wanted to reach through the phone and give Davis a hug. "Thank you so much," he said. "Have I mentioned you're the best?"

***

After finishing their sandwiches, accompanied by boiled corn on the cob and fresh watermelon, Tony and Darcy curled up together on the sofa. The flat screen TV remained off.

Outside, flashes of light and long, rolling rumbles told them a summer storm was approaching.

Darcy said, "I'm glad I was right about your dad, and that people are starting to listen. I can tell you're going to succeed. You're going to prove he didn't kill Charlotte."

"You realize, of course, it's looking more and more like someone involved in the movie is the killer. It might be someone you know and trust. Someone you like."

Tony wasn't sure why, but he wasn't ready to tell her that Ramesh Bhatt had risen to the top of his list of suspects. He knew she liked Bhatt and was excited to star in his latest movie. She would be hurt in more ways than one if Tony's suspicions proved to be correct.

"I can't imagine," Darcy said. "It's horrible to think I might be working side-by-side every day with someone capable of doing that to Charlotte, and to Geoff."

"Just be careful every minute, and don't give anything away. You could be in real danger if this person feels threatened."

"You forget, I'm a great actress." She gave him an elbow to the ribs. "No one will know I suspect a thing."

The lightning flashes grew brighter, and the rumbles morphed into loud claps of thunder. Soon, heavy rains were pounding on the roof. He took her into his arms, and a gentle kiss grew more needful. One pleasure led to another, and soon they were back in Tony's bedroom, the sounds of their lovemaking accented by the furies of the thunderstorm.

Chapter 25

Orney, Iowa—Wednesday, July 8

Wednesday afternoon, Tony was back on the set of *Murder Beyond Them*, watching Bhatt, Cristo, the actors, and the crew create their magic. Bhatt seemed relaxed and completely in control, enjoying the great performances being created by Rowsmith, Landers, and Darcy.

As Tony watched the director work, it was nearly impossible to imagine him as a cold-blooded killer filled with hate. Only a true sociopath could so completely appear to be something he wasn't. Tony had to admit the more likely scenario was that he was simply wrong about Bhatt.

The filming lasted into the evening. Bhatt had chosen Wednesday to film two night scenes, an encounter between Landers and Darcy on a downtown sidewalk, and a portion of a car chase.

By 9 p.m., Tony was tired and bored. He would have called it a night, but he had promised Darcy he would stay until she was finished. He hoped it wouldn't be much longer.

He felt his cell phone buzz in his pocket. He stepped back, away from the filming, and stole a look at the screen. It was his dad texting to say he had arrived at the Howdy Stranger, where he was staying for the night before meeting with the attorneys the next morning.

Tony replied with a thumbs-up emoji.

Before he could put his phone away, it buzzed and lit up again. This time it was a call coming from Montay in Italy.

Tony looked at the time on the screen and did the math. It was 3 a.m. in Rome. He quickly strode to the back where ropes restrained a crowd of onlookers. He ducked under the ropes, pushed his way through the crowd, and found a quiet spot in a building doorway on the next block.

"Hey, Montay. What's up? You need bail money or something?"

"Or something," the taxi driver retorted. "I'm calling to tell you I have it. I am a great a detective! Better than your Sherlock Holmes."

"Sherlock Holmes was British," Tony said, as excitement crept into his voice. "But it's great to hear you succeeded. How did you do it so fast? More importantly, what did you learn?"

"The good news is, I found a man who works there, at the Instituto, who has, shall we say, a greater desire to be rich than to be honorable. I'm still awake because he said he could retrieve and copy old records only after hours. He just brought me the reports. He was very thorough. It's all here."

"It sounds like there might be some bad news?" Tony prompted.

"The bad news is that it cost me—no, it cost you—two thousand Euros."

Tony swallowed hard but didn't complain. If it helped to exonerate his father, it was worth it. "You'll scan and send me the reports tomorrow? I mean, later today, your time?"

"Of course."

Tony quickly said, "Before you go, can you tell me what it says? What have we learned?"

"We learned you were right. In May 1989, Harriet Danziker terminated a pregnancy. She did it illegale... uh, not follow the law. She didn't need to do that. It was allowed in Italy at that time. She probably wanted to keep it unreported because of her fame, so she had it done by an anonymous doctor outside of a clinic."

"So why did the institute have a record of it? You lost me."

"She was injured in the procedure and nearly died from blood loss. The hospital reported her, so it all ended up in the official records anyway."

"Thank you, Montay. This is a tremendous help. Don't forget to send me your bill."

"You are welcome, Mr. Tony. Don't forget to send me money. A lot of money."

***

The shooting wrapped a little before 11 p.m. Darcy went to her trailer to change, and Tony sat on a bench in the town square, watching the crew pack up and cover equipment for its short rest overnight.

At 11:30, Tony was growing impatient. Darcy had said she would only be a minute. Nearly everyone had dispersed, and Tony was alone except for the mosquitos and gnats that were all too happy to focus their attention on him now that everyone else was gone.

He was about to call her when he noticed Bhatt walking down the street toward him.

"Still waiting for Darcy?"

"Yes. I wish she'd hurry. I'm getting eaten alive here."

Bhatt sat on the bench a couple of feet from Tony and leaned back.

"A good day, don't you think? Everything seemed to be back on track. I was worried it would take longer for the cast to shake off the delay and their grief for Charlotte."

"Yes, a good day," Tony said, his anxiety rising. "You're doing a phenomenal job."

Bhatt smiled. "Thank you. I think I'm forced to agree." He chuckled as he turned and looked around the square. "I'm going to miss Orney. It really is a lovely little town. Very much as your father described it to me. I owe him a lot, you know."

"Yes, I think I do," Tony said, his senses on high alert.

Bhatt turned toward him and asked, "So level with me Tony. How much do you know?"

Suddenly the fun and games were over. No more façade. Bhatt was admitting it was him.

Tony couldn't resist being honest. After all, he wasn't in any danger sitting here in the middle of the town square. He said, "I think I know it all."

"I was afraid you would say that."

"It's over, Ramesh. I know you killed Charlotte, and I'm pretty damn sure you killed Geoff Warbler. I'm guessing it was you who hired the sound technician to listen outside my house, but I'm not guessing about how you created and planted all the evidence. My dad's golf club, the semen lifted from his motel room trash, the CGI-altered video, the heist of my car—all of it. It was genius on your part, but I'm confident we've solved the puzzle. And now the DCI and FBI are about to help prove I'm right."

"The FBI? Really? My, my."

."And as of a couple of hours ago, I know why you did it."

For the first time, Bhatt's smile faded, and his face grew dark. "What do you mean by that?"

"I mean, you have a very good reason to hate my dad. It doesn't justify two murders and a false arrest, but it explains your anger."

Bhatt's voice took on a hard, pointed tone. He nearly spit out his words. "You couldn't possibly know how your father destroyed my life. Nothing, *nothing*, I could do to him would atone for the pain he caused me and those I love."

Tony sighed and said, "I do know, Ramesh. I know he slept with Harriet. I know Harriet was pregnant, probably with my father's child. I know she…"

"Stop it!" Bhatt screamed. "You have no right to speak of her. Just stop it." His face was red and his eyes bulging.

Tony glanced down to reassure himself Bhatt wasn't holding a weapon and saw the director's hands clenched into fists.

Astonishingly, the moment passed quickly. Bhatt took a deep breath, leaned back on the bench again, and said, "We should go."

"But…"

"Don't be an ass. Darcy's not coming. I have arranged for her to be… umm… tied up for the evening."

Tony felt the blood drain from his face. He wanted to stand, but he feared his legs wouldn't hold him. "You bastard," he managed to croak. "If you hurt her…"

"I haven't, but I might. That all depends on you. Come with me, do what I tell you, and I promise Darcy will be fine."

Tony wanted to scream. He wanted to lash out. He wanted to pull out his phone and call 911. His knowledge of Bhatt was all that stopped him. He knew the director was brilliant, diabolical, and determined. Tony had to assume Bhatt had worked out in advance what he was doing. Darcy's life would indeed be in jeopardy if Tony didn't do what he was told.

He said, "Let her go. Prove to me she's safe, and I'll do whatever you say. I promise."

Bhatt stood, turned, and started walking. Over his shoulder, he said just loud enough for Tony to hear, "Fuck you, Tony Harrington. Come with me now, or she dies."

Tony took a breath and rose with reluctance. He had no choice but to obey.

Chapter 26

Orney, Iowa—Thursday, July 9

Charles Harrington had been asleep for less than an hour when he was awakened by his mobile phone. He had plugged it into the outlet in the motel's bathroom to charge, so he had to climb out of bed to answer it. He was more alarmed than irritated. It was not yet 1 a.m. Calls at this hour were never good news.

"Hello?"

"Charles, it's Ramesh."

"Hi. What's happened? Are you okay?"

"Yes, my *friend*, I'm fine."

Something in Bhatt's voice told Charles his longtime friend wasn't fine.

"So why are you calling? I don't mean to be rude, but I have an important meeting with my attorney this morning."

"I'm calling because Tony is in danger."

Charles's blood turned to ice. He thought about Tony's

suspicions regarding Bhatt and fought to keep the panic out of his voice.

"Tony? What's happened to Tony?"

"He's about to die," Bhatt said, "and only you can save him."

"Dear God, Ramesh, please, no. What have you done?"

"I've done what I do best, Charles. I have taken your work and rewritten it to make the drama more intense, to make the pleasure and pain more realistic."

Charles felt as if he might faint. He unplugged the phone from the charger and grabbed his slacks from the hook on the back of the bathroom door. He put the phone on speaker and began dressing as he talked.

"Don't hurt him, Ramesh. Please. He's done nothing to you. It's me you want."

"Well, you're half right," Bhatt said. "It's you I want. Unfortunately, your son's meddling has forced a change of plans."

"Ramesh…"

"Maybe it's not so unfortunate," Bhatt continued. "I actually like the new plan very much."

"Dammit! Tell me what you want." Charles sat on the stool and pulled on his socks.

"Of course. That's why I called. Here's what I want. First, do not call anyone. I swear to you, the only chance you have to save your son is to come to me alone. I only have to push this button…" Suddenly the speaker was blaring a loud, grinding noise. Just as suddenly, it stopped. "I just push this button, and in minutes, your son is gone. He's in a place where rescuers cannot reach him for hours. Do you understand? No calls. Come alone."

"I understand. You have my word."

"Good. Do you recall the location we chose for filming the murder scene?"

"I'm not sure." Charles hesitated. "You mean the site we chose for the current movie? The farm?" Terror seized Charles's heart. He now had an idea—a horrific idea—of what the grinding sound had been.

"Exactly. I want you to come to the farm we chose together. You remember? We worked closely together on our movies because we were such good friends."

"I remember. Please Ramesh. We *are* friends. I love you like a brother."

"Lancelot loved Arthur, too, but it didn't stop the gallant knight from fucking over his king, did it?"

Charles had no idea how to respond. He didn't want to say or do anything that would trigger Bhatt to act on his threat.

Bhatt said, "Just come to the farm. Come alone. You have ten minutes. Not one second more." The call ended.

Charles raced into the other room, found his shoes, and pulled them on. He grabbed a sweater from his bag and pulled it over his head. He remembered his glasses from the nightstand. His wallet and keys were in his pants pockets. He tried to calm his panic enough to ask himself what else he might need—what else he might have with him—that would be helpful. He couldn't think of a thing.

He ran out of the motel room, letting the door slam behind him. He jumped into his Lincoln, started it, and charged from the parking lot, leaving tire tracks of burned rubber in his wake.

The farm they had chosen was six miles northeast of Orney. Charles had only been there once. He hoped he could find it again in the dark. They had chosen the spot because it had all the equipment they'd needed for the murder scene, but did not have a family living there.

Like many family farms, this one had been purchased years ago and merged into a much larger farming operation. The farmhouse had been demolished, but the farm buildings were still on the site and in use. In fact, the site had been expanded and the equipment modernized. It now hosted two giant Sukup galvanized steel grain bins, each at least forty feet in diameter and twenty-five feet tall. They were connected by a catwalk. A steel staircase wound around the side of one bin to reach the catwalk, which led to the hatch at the top of each bin.

The murder scene Charles had written involved the victim being thrown into one of the steel bins full of corn. In the scene, the murderer turns on the auger, which removes the grain from the bottom of the bin through a channel under a false floor. As the grain is pulled out, the victim is pulled down, leading to suffocation beneath thousands of bushels of shelled corn. It was a realistic way to die. There were documented cases of men and boys dying by accident in just this way.

Charles gritted his teeth. He had no doubt about the origin of the sound when Bhatt had pushed that button. It was the sound of the auger being activated. If Tony was inside the bin... The thought caused Charles to begin to weep. He fought to control himself. He had to be strong. He had to think clearly if he was going to have any chance to save Tony.

***

Tony awoke and immediately rolled onto his side and vomited. He opened his eyes. He might as well have saved himself the trouble. It was absolutely pitch black. He could see nothing. He felt the fear tug at him that he might be blind.

What the hell?

He could smell chloroform. Bhatt had knocked him out with it, obviously. He didn't remember anything after opening the back door to the sedan Bhatt had led him to, so the director must have put him to sleep with it there, as he climbed into the back seat.

Tony could tell he was lying on sand or gravel or some kind of coarse material. He reached down, being careful to avoid what he had thrown up, and ran his hands through it.

It was corn. Tony had seen kids playing in "sandboxes" of the stuff, when he had gone to a local farm each fall to buy pumpkins and wind his way through a giant corn maze.

He was baffled about where he could be, about what kind of place would have a floor covered in corn and no windows to let in the light. The realization of the obvious answer came quickly, followed by a growing sense of terror. Tony had also read the stories of men dying in grain bins. He worked, after all, for a rural newspaper that carried such stories.

He wanted to stand, but he wasn't sure if he should. What if the corn was deep? Would that increase his chances of sinking into it? He wanted to run but didn't know which way. Were there other dangers he couldn't see? He tried to remember what he knew about grain bins. Did they even have doors to the outside? Obviously, Bhatt had found a way to get Tony inside. But maybe he had been dropped in from the top. He hadn't noticed any particular pain. *Maybe I'm hurt, but the chloroform is masking the pain. Or maybe I didn't fall very far. Does that mean it's a small bin, or that I'm close to the top of a big bin? If it's one of the big ones, is there ladder somewhere?*

Tony didn't know the answers, but the idea he might be perched at the top of thousands of bushels of corn petrified him. He knew he had to do something. He couldn't just lie here until he died of thirst or some farmer decided to dump another few thousand bushels of grain on his head. He decided to try moving on his hands and knees, sweeping his right hand across the corn in front of himself as he moved, covering wider and wider arcs until he found something, anything. He quickly realized crawling was a poor strategy. His hands and knees kept sinking deep into the corn. He stretched out on his stomach and tried more of a swimming motion. He fought hard to control his panic.

***

Charles pulled his Lincoln into the farmyard. As his headlights swept past the grain bins, he immediately saw Bhatt silhouetted against the shiny steel exterior of the first bin. He parked his car, shut off the lights and ignition, and stepped out onto the dirt.

The area was illuminated by a single light mounted on a pole near the barn about fifty yards away. As Charles's eyes adjusted to the low light, he could see Bhatt waiting in a casual stance, his hands behind his back.

Raising his hands so Bhatt could see he was unarmed, he said, "Okay, Ramesh. I'm here. I'm alone. Now where's Tony?"

"Shut up, Charles. Keep your hands in the air like that and come over here."

Charles did so. As he approached, Bhatt pulled an automatic pistol from the belt behind his back. Charles stopped.

"Wondering where I got this gun? You shouldn't be surprised. I work in the movies. We have warehouses full of guns. However, in this case, I didn't need the props department. This is more fun. I got this from the case in the back of your son's Explorer. Did you know Tony carried such an elegant and deadly weapon?"

Charles nodded, and Bhatt said, "Put your hands as high as they can reach and don't move. I'm switching off the safety…" he did so, "…and I swear I will shoot you if you even flinch."

Charles stood stock still as Bhatt searched him.

Using his free hand, Bhatt removed Charles's phone and keys

from his pockets. He checked to be sure the phone was off, then tossed it into the weeds behind the grain bins, followed quickly by the keys.

"Okay, Charles. This is the good part. You get to visit Tony now." He gestured toward the steel staircase. Take that to the top. It's the bin on the left. Remove the hatch, and you'll be able to see him."

"You son of a bitch. If you've hurt him, I'll…"

"Shut up, Charles," Bhatt said wearily. "I'm the one with the gun. You'll do nothing but walk up those stairs and talk to your son. If you try anything else, I will shoot you in the leg. Then you'll have the pleasure of climbing the stairs with one good leg while the other bleeds out."

"Why, Ramesh? Why are you doing this? All because of one night I spent with Harriet? It meant nothing to her. It was just a last fling. She was in love with you and couldn't have cared less about me."

"That's right, you fucker," Bhatt said. "She was in love with *me*, and you took her anyway. You shit on your best friend and you destroyed her life."

"Destroyed her…? What are you talking about? It was just one night."

"No, you despicable bastard, it was *not* just one night. You didn't just fuck her. You impregnated her."

Charles was stunned. He had been friends with Ramesh and Harriet for thirty-five years. He had never seen nor heard a hint of this before.

"Pregnant? No, I couldn't have. How could I not know…?"

Bhatt spit out the words. "She terminated it. She couldn't bear to tell me, to tell anyone. It would have ended her career. It would have devastated her family. She ended it, and that ended her ability to have children. She never recovered, not really. It destroyed her,

Charles. It destroyed us."

The rage in Bhatt was terrifying. Charles worried the gun would fire by accident. He looked at the stairs. He needed to know Tony was okay. He strode quickly to the side of the bin and started up.

As he climbed, he shouted down, "What is the point of all this? If you want your pound of flesh, why not just shoot me?"

From below, he heard Bhatt confirm his worst fears.

"I don't want to kill you, Charles. I want you to suffer. In a minute, you're going to wish you had been convicted of murder and were sitting in a prison cell."

Charles knew what Bhatt meant. If Tony was dead, or dying, the anguish would destroy him. It would destroy Carlotta, Rita, and a lot of other people as well. Tony was loved by so many, like Ben and Darcy and Doug and... Who knew how long the list was? But for Charles, it would be unbearable to know his selfishness and physical desires from decades earlier had cost his son his life. Spending life in prison would have been an infinitely preferable fate.

When he reached the top, he was forced to stop and catch his breath. He bent over to suck in air, his hands on his knees.

"Hurry!" he heard Bhatt yell from below. "Tony is waiting. He could be dying!"

Charles stood, walked to the center of the bin's roof, and kicked open the four latches that held the top hatch in place. He lifted and flipped it over, exposing the round opening. The mechanism normally mounted inside that dispersed grain evenly as it flowed into the bin had been removed. Charles knew this because he had written the murder scene for the movie. In doing so, he had done his research. He knew far more about grain bins than Bhatt could ever guess.

Because the mechanism was missing, Charles's view was unobstructed. It was also meaningless because all he could see was a pitch-black hole.

He put his face to the opening and shouted "Tony?"

The response was immediate. "Dad? Thank God! Yes! I'm here!"

Charles's relief was intense but short-lived. Before he could say another word, he heard the sound and felt the vibration of the auger starting.

Into the opening, Charles screamed, "Run! Tony, get to the side! Move!"

"I'm trying. It's hard… I can't…"

"There's a ladder mounted inside the bin," Charles yelled. "You have to find it. You have climb up out of the corn. The flow of grain into the auger will suck you in! Hurry!"

"I'm trying. Dad, I'm sorry."

Tony was crying.

Charles knew that once his son was waist-deep in the corn, no amount of effort could pull him out. He had to get to the auger switch. He had to turn it off before it was too late. He turned, hurried to the steps, and started down.

A shot rang out as a bullet struck the metal next to his feet. He froze.

Bhatt yelled, "I think it would be better if you stayed with your son! You'll want to say goodbye before he dies!"

"Dammit, Ramesh! Stop this!" Charles screamed.

The response was another shot and another bullet striking the stairs.

Charles ran back up and knelt in front of the open hatch. He yelled, "Tony! Have you made it? Did you find the edge? The ladder? Something to hold onto?"

"No," Tony sobbed, "I can't move! It's pulling me under. Dad, I'm sorry. I can't."

"Tony! No! You must! I'm sorry. I'm so sorry. My God, what have I done?"

Tony's sobbing subsided. He shouted, "Dad, save Darcy! It's Darcy you have to think about now. Bhatt has her! You have to save her!"

"I will, I promise. But Tony, you have to…"

Tony's shout cut him him off. "This isn't your fault. Bhatt did this. Don't blame yourself. I love you! Tell Mom, tell Darcy and Rita, I love them."

"No!" Charles screamed. "Tony, listen." He lowered his voice, hoping Bhatt couldn't hear him but Tony could. "There's one other chance. Can you hear me? If you go under, try to get to the bottom before you pass out!"

"What?"

"I know it sounds crazy, but there's a chance. There was a case where a boy was saved because he was on the floor. The floor has holes in it, where air is pumped into the bin. If you can get to the floor, you have a chance to stay alive until we can get you out!"

"I'm scared. Daddy, I don't know if I can do it."

The word "Daddy" ripped through Charles's heart like a chainsaw.

"You can, Tony. You're the bravest man I know. You can. Just hang in there. I will get to you. I promise."

There was no response. "Tony!" Charles screamed. Only the sound of the auger's grinding came back to his ears.

Crying and weak-kneed, Charles stumbled back down the staircase. He collapsed on the ground in front of Bhatt.

"He's gone. You worthless piece of shit. You killed my son. I hope you're happy now, because you're going to burn in Hell for eternity for this."

"Happy is not the word," Bhatt said, backing away toward his car. "Satisfied, perhaps. At least for now. I'm realizing even this may not be enough. It doesn't make up for three decades of pain. We'll see. Have a nice walk back to town."

He tossed Tony's gun into the dirt thirty yards away, climbed into his car, and drove away.

As soon as the car turned out of the farm lane, Charles jumped up and ran to the control panel on the side of the bin. He was glad to see the Sukup logo. It was the same brand of bin he had studied when writing the movie script. He glanced over the electronic touch-control screen. Thankfully it was backlit, so he wasn't working blindly in the dark. He found the screen for the air blower, selected the highest setting, and pushed "on." His hopes rose a little as he heard the air pumps start, knowing huge amounts of air would be pumped up through the floor of the bin every minute.

He prayed it would be enough. He also prayed Tony had been strong enough. He prayed the weight of the grain had not crushed the life from his son before he'd made it to the bottom. He prayed for forgiveness.

As he prayed, he searched for the auger control screen, found it, and shut it off. With luck, Tony had avoided being mangled in the mechanism designed to pull the corn from the bin.

Charles ran between the bins to the patch of weeds at the back where Bhatt had thrown his phone. Even in the low light, Charles had been able to see roughly where the phone had disappeared into the darkness. Charles was desparate to find it. He knew the GPS tracking device on his ankle would lead authorities to him eventually, but he couldn't wait for that. Every additional minute Tony was in the bin increased the chances he would die.

Charles tried to estimate where the phone would have landed and dropped to his knees. After several minutes of clawing through the thick foliage and pleading for divine help, his fingers found the smooth edges of the phone case.

"Now work. Please work," he said aloud, as he held the power button.

The screen lit up. Charles could see the glass was broken, but he hoped it wouldn't matter.

"Hey Siri," he said, the tears erupting again, "call 911."

***

The first responders arrived in less than ten minutes. By the end of the hour, the farmyard was lit up like a California canyon fire. Fire trucks, an ambulance, sheriff's patrol cars, and state troopers' cruisers were joined by steelworkers' pickups carrying cutting saws and other tools and semi-trucks with empty trailers ready to load and haul away the grain as it was pumped from the bin.

The MercyOne helicopter, traveling 180 miles per hour, was on its way from Des Moines. However, it was headed to Sheffield, Iowa, first to pick up one of the structural engineers who worked for Sukup. The engineer was already connected over Zoom, working closely with the people on site. The rescue team had planned for grain bin accidents. No effort would be spared to extract Tony, though no one at the scene besides Charles believed he could be alive.

Rich Davis stood at Charles's side as he watched the flurry of activity. Sheriff Mackey was directing everyone with precision, his voice at a volume that could be heard two counties away.

"We can't fault the effort," Davis said. "If there's any chance to save him, these folks will find it."

Charles didn't look at him, but said, "Shouldn't you be chasing and arresting the bastard who did this? Or better yet, chasing and shooting him?"

Davis said, "Believe me, there's an army of people looking for him right now, including the police, sheriff's deputies from ten counties, and a bunch of state troopers. We already know his stuff is gone. His motel room and his office at the community center have been cleaned out, so he must have planned this for tonight."

Charles wasn't surprised. Bhatt planned everything carefully. He said, "We should assume he had an escape plan ready. He wouldn't have left me alive to tell about this if he wasn't already certain he would get away."

"We'll get him," Davis said.

"Don't be so sure. Remember, he had access to costumes, makeup, props, and most importantly, money. He could be a ninety-year-old lady boarding an airplane in Des Moines by now."

Someone they couldn't see shouted, "Clear?"

"Clear!"

An ear-splitting sound erupted, and sparks flew. A huge, specially-designed saw was cutting into the side of the bin.

The helicopter landed in the farmyard just as the workers completed the third of four needed cuts. The pressure of the grain inside the bin was causing the steel panel to bulge out slightly. The fourth cut would be the most dangerous for those outside the bin.

Charles walked away. He desperately wanted to watch, to help, to tear the bin apart with his bare hands to save his son. But he knew he couldn't. The agony of watching helplessly was more than he could stand.

Davis followed Charles to the other side of the farmstead. They sat on a low row of bricks, probably a part of the original farmhouse's foundation.

"We have to prepare ourselves for the worst," Davis said. "I wish I could be more encouraging, but I've seen these before."

"I know," Charles said. "I did my homework. No one ever survives one of these situations. Except for that one time. That means there's a chance, right?"

The agent nodded. "Sure. I'm not giving up, but…" his voice trailed off.

The agony was apparent in Charles's voice when he added, "I just didn't know it would take so long. I didn't know they would have to cut into the bin."

"There are guys inside too," Davis said. "They're in harnesses to protect themselves, but you can imagine the difficulty of searching when every hole you dig immediately refills and you don't know where to look. Getting the grain out usually is the only way we find the…" he stopped short of saying the word "body."

Charles put his face in his hands and sobbed. "How am I going to tell his mother? His sister? How will any of us survive this?"

Davis didn't comment. He put his arm around Charles's shoulders and held him close.

***

A short time later, a silver Chrysler 300 arrived, driving fast up the lane and stopping near Charles and Davis. Ben Smalley jumped out of the driver's seat, followed by Darcy Gillson from the passenger side and Doug Tenney and Alison Frank from the back seat. They ran up to the two men, who stood to greet them. A flurry of questions, expressions of horror, tears, and cries of anguish followed.

Once he understood the situation at the grain bins, Ben suggested the others wait where they were. He went back to his car, popped open the trunk, and retrieved his camera bag. He strode toward the activity, snapping a series of photographs as he went.

Darcy was aghast that Ben would, or could, take pictures while his friend was dead or dying inside the bin, but Doug and Alison understood. It's what journalists do.

Doug sounded almost tender as he explained to Darcy, "He has to do it. Whatever happens, the paper will need photographs, and the Associated Press will want them too. And if… I mean when Tony recovers from this, he'll want to have them. People always react negatively to the photographers at the scenes of tragedies, but later they often treasure the photographs."

Darcy wasn't convinced, but she kept quiet.

Doug added, "I'm just glad he didn't ask me to do it. I don't think I could…" His voice broke and tears rolled down his cheeks.

Another hour of agony passed before Charles gave up. He struggled to stand, weak from exhaustion and despair. His voice was raw from the previous screaming and the continued crying. He said, "I have to call Carlotta. I can't risk her hearing this on the news or from one of our friends."

Davis nodded. "We'll give you some privacy." Darcy, Doug, and Alison returned to the car, leaning on the trunk as they watched the workmen.

Davis walked toward the activity at the bins. Another semi full of grain had just pulled away, giving him a clearer view than he'd had in a while.

A woman in a bright yellow jacket with "Quincy County Rescue" emblazoned on the back in reflective letters turned and shouted, "We've got him!"

Davis glanced back to be sure Charles had heard, then took off at a run across the yard. Charles arrived at the gaping hole in the bin at the same time as Davis, the other three close behind.

The rescue workers gingerly pulled Tony's body from the bin.

"Careful!" someone said. "Watch the edges. Don't tear his skin."

"Oh my God," Charles moaned, falling to his knees.

Tony was covered in grain dust. Dried blood covered the side of his face and neck. What little skin was exposed was as white as unused printer paper.

The EMTs placed him on the helicopter's patient gurney. The nurse was at his side in an instant, with a stethoscope.

She turned and looked directly at Charles, still on his knees, crying.

"He's alive," she said. "He still has a chance."

Town Crier

Reporter rescued from murder attempt

Heroic efforts saved the life of Tony Harrington of Orney
Manhunt underway for movie director charged in the crime

Ben Smalley, Editor

ORNEY, Iowa – Tony Harrington, 29, of Orney, is hospitalized at MercyOne Medical Center in Des Moines with multiple injuries following an attempt on his life early Thursday morning. No report of his condition was available from the hospital at press time.

Ramesh Bhatt, 54, of Piñon Hills, California, has been charged with attempted murder, according to Quincy County Sheriff George Mackey. Bhatt is the director of a movie currently being shot on location in Orney.

Sheriff Mackey said Bhatt also is a person of interest in the murder of actress Charlotte Andresson, 28, of Santa Clarita, California, who was found dead at the Orney County Club June 21.

Charles Harrington, 57, of Iowa City, the father of Tony Harrington, was previously charged with Andresson's murder. The sheriff said he expects those charges to be dropped in light of new evidence uncovered in the investigation, but he did not elaborate.

In the case of the attempt on Tony Harrington's life, Mackey said Bhatt is suspected of using chloroform to render Harrington unconscious, then placing him inside a grain bin on a farm six miles northeast of Orney. Bhatt then turned on the bin's unloading mechanism, causing Harrington to be pulled beneath the grain, the sheriff said.

"Our victim is lucky to be alive," Mackey said, noting that deaths occur by accident in grain bins nearly every year. "His father was on the scene and had the foresight to turn on the air flow mechanism. It appears Tony Harrington was pulled or dug his way to the bottom of the bin, where he was kept alive by the inflow of air."

At about 1:45 a.m., after Tony Harrington was believed dead, Bhatt left the scene driving a gray, late-model Buick sedan, the sheriff said.

Bhatt's personal effects had been removed from his motel room and from his temporary office in Orney, indicating he had fled to avoid arrest, according to Special Agent Rich Davis of the Iowa Division of Criminal Investigation. "A multi-state, intensive search is underway for Mr. Bhatt," Davis said. "Anyone with knowledge of his whereabouts should contact the local authorities immediately."

The sheriff noted Tony Harrington was unconscious when removed from the bin. Investigators have not yet had the opportunity to speak with him. He was transported to Des Moines by a MercyOne helicopter. Assisting in Harrington's rescue were...

Chapter 27

Des Moines, Iowa—Friday, July 10

He could hear Darcy calling his name. She was crying, asking for help. He wanted to reach her, but he couldn't move. He was stuck, buried. "I'm coming," he screamed.

The terror of the nightmare woke him. Tony's eyes popped open and he cried, "Darcy!"

There was a rush of movement. He spotted her blonde locks and caught a whiff of her scent before the people in green scrub uniforms asked her to step back.

Tony shook his head angrily. "Darcy!"

He heard her voice. "I'm here, Tony. I'm right here. Let the doctors and nurses do their thing. I'm not going anywhere."

"But you're… safe? He didn't hurt you?"

"What? No, I'm fine. Try to relax. We'll talk soon."

Inside Tony's brain, a battle erupted between confusion and relief. Relief won. He relaxed back into the pillow and patiently let the green-garbed people poke and prod him.

When they had finished, one of them pulled a pair of chairs to Tony's bedside. Darcy sat in the one closest to his head. She took his hand in hers and kissed it. He felt moisture from her tears.

He couldn't quite make out who was in the second chair. Then he heard Doug say, "Just my luck. The bastard woke up. Darcy was just starting to like me. I could've been her gigolo, living a life of leisure in Hollywood."

"Bite me," Tony and Darcy said in unison, huge smiles breaking out on both faces.

"Thank God you're okay," Tony said, taking his turn to kiss Darcy's hand.

"That's an odd thing to hear from someone who's just had a near-death experience. We're the ones worried about you."

"But Bhatt told me he had you tied up somewhere. He said you were going to die."

"Really? Well, I'm happy to say that wasn't true. You mean Wednesday night, right?"

He nodded.

She said, "No, nothing happened. I mean, he came to my trailer on the lot at the end of the day. He told me you and he had decided to meet to discuss your dad's case and suggested I go back to the motel. He said you would call me in the morning. Witt gave me a ride. I didn't know there was a problem at all until your dad called me in the middle of the night. He asked me if I was ok, and then told me you were trapped. Ben came by soon after to pick me up. When I arrived at the farm and saw that bin, I just… I… Oh, I don't want to talk about it."

"That's fine by me," Tony said.

Charles burst into the room. "Tony! Thank God! Oh… Tony! They told me you were awake."

His father leaned over the bed and kissed his son on the forehead. He added, "They said I shouldn't hug you. Something about you getting multiple bruises from wrestling with six thousand bushels of corn."

"It felt like six million, but thanks for sparing me the squeeze. Am I in Des Moines?"

"Yes. They flew you here by helicopter. You appeared to be dead, or nearly so. I was so scared. It turns out your injuries are minor. One cracked rib, the cuts on your face, and a few hundred bruises. I can't believe you did it. You really did it."

"Thanks to you, Dad. If not for you, I wouldn't have known what to do."

"It was a long shot, the Hail Mary to beat all Hail Marys. But you did it."

"How are mom and Rita? Are they here?"

"Rita's with your mother in Iowa City. Carla didn't want to come yet. She said she couldn't bear to see you unconscious in a hospital bed. She'll be so thrilled to hear you're awake."

From behind Charles, Darcy said, "If you'd like, I can go out and call her while you boys talk."

"That would be great," Charles said, not turning away from Tony for even a moment.

Doug followed Darcy out, and father and son were left alone for the moment. Charles said, "Tony, I am so sorry. This is all my fault. Bhatt told me…"

"I know all about it, Dad. I got confirmation of Harriet's medical issues Wednesday night, right before Bhatt took me."

Charles shook his head. "You are a wonder. You're going to have to tell me later how you managed that bit of detective work."

"I will, but you won't believe it," Tony said, grinning at the thought of Montay slinking around Rome in the middle of the night.

He added, "And you won't like it when you see the bill."

Charles shrugged that off and sat down. Looking his son in the face, he said, "Tony, when I thought you were gone, I wanted to die. I don't know how I ever could have survived, knowing my despicable behavior caused your death."

"Well, as I tried to say before, you didn't do this. Bhatt did. He's a true sociopath. Which reminds me, have they arrested him?"

"Not yet. There's a manhunt underway, but so far, he's eluded it."

Tony tried to sit up, panic creeping back into his voice. "We need to protect you and Mom, and everyone! Rita and Darcy and Doug, everyone we care about is a potential victim until he's caught."

"Take it easy," his dad said, placing a hand on his arm. "They've got people with big guns crawling all over us. Even Ben has a tail, which he doesn't like much. Rita, on the other hand, thinks the U.S. marshal guarding her is hot."

Charles smiled, and Tony finally joined him. "Tell that marshal to keep his hands off my sister. I have a gun too…"

Apparently, the sleep and pain medications were kicking in. Tony drifted off, but Charles stayed in the chair, taking his son's hand and saying another prayer of thanks as he began to weep for the hundredth time that day.

Town Crier

Charles Harrington innocent of murder

All charges dropped; nationwide manhunt underway for movie director

Ben Smalley, Editor

ORNEY, Iowa – Ramesh Bhatt, 54, of Piñon Hills, California, has been charged with two counts of first-degree murder in the slayings of actress Charlotte Andresson, 28, of Santa Clarita, Calif., and Geoff Warbler, 78, of Solon, Iowa, according to Special Agent Rich Davis of the Iowa Division of Criminal Investigation.

Davis said new evidence uncovered in the investigation of the two deaths proved the previous suspect in the killing of Andresson, Charles Harrington, 57, of Iowa City, is innocent and implicated Bhatt in her death as well as the killing of Warbler. Andresson was killed at the Orney Country Club June 20. Warbler was killed a few days later when his car was forced off the road near Solon, Iowa.

"Mr. Bhatt apparently has fled in an attempt to escape arrest," Davis said. "The FBI and the United States Marshal's Service are assisting in a nation-wide manhunt. Because Mr. Bhatt has dual citizenship in Great Britain and is a frequent traveler in Europe, Scotland Yard and Interpol have also been notified."

Bhatt was the director of a movie filming on location in Orney this summer. Andresson was an actress in the cast of the movie, and Charles Harrington was the writer of the screenplay.

Bhatt is also charged with the attempted murder of Tony Harrington, according to Quincy County Sheriff George Mackey. Tony Harrington is Charles Harrington's son and a reporter for the *Orney Town Crier*.

Tony Harrington was rescued from beneath an estimated 6,000 bushels of shelled corn inside a grain bin on a farm northeast of Orney on Thursday morning. Sheriff Mackey described Harrington's survival as "a miracle." He credited the quick thinking of Charles Harrington, who was at the scene when the incident took place, as responsible for saving the younger Harrington's life.

Agent Davis said the new evidence in the case of Andresson's murder indicates that Bhatt killed her in an attempt to frame Charles Harrington for the crime. "When that didn't work, Bhatt attempted to kill Charles Harrington's son," Davis said.

When asked why Bhatt would do these things to the Harringtons, who previously had been reported to be friends of Bhatt's, Davis said that information is still being gathered.

Geoff Warbler appears to be an unfortunate victim in the events related to Andresson's murder, according to Sheriff Mackey. The elderly man was...

Chapter 28

Orney, Iowa—Monday, July 13

Doug Tenney and Alison Frank sat on a bench in the Orney Town Square, watching the crew members from the production company pack the last pieces of equipment into a sixteen-foot straight truck and disassemble the movie sets in an effort to salvage and return as many of the building materials as possible.

It was warm and muggy, but the sun was muted by a thick layer of clouds, keeping the temperature from becoming unbearable. Doug's light skin burned easily, so he was happy whenever cloud cover allowed him to keep the sunscreen in the glove box of his Toyota RAV4.

Doug and Alison had completed their interviews and had taken their photos for the *Crier's* article about the exodus of the film company. The financial backers had decided to end the production and put *Murder Beyond Them* on the shelf for now. With one of the stars dead and the director on the run, no one had been surprised.

"By tomorrow, everyone will be gone," Doug said absently, enjoying the chance to relax next to Alison.

"Everyone but Darcy Gillson," she said. "I heard she's gonna stay with Tony for a while to nurse him back to health."

"Yeah, he told me. Y'know, I might've climbed in that grain bin myself if I'd thought Darcy Gillson would come live with me for a while."

"Hey!" Alison scowled. "I'm right here. As long as we're going out, you're gonna have to keep those kinds of thoughts to yourself."

Doug shook his head. "Oh, man. You're talkin' about changing a lifetime of smart-assiness. I'm not sure I can do it."

Alison took his chin in her hand and turned his face toward hers. "Remember that thing we did last night? The thing you really liked?"

He grinned. "Oh yeah. Absolutely."

"Well, if you ever wanna do that again, learn to treat me with a little respect."

"One warehouse full of respect, comin' right up!" Doug saluted, and Alison laughed. "C'mon," he said. "We got everything we need for tomorrow. Let's go see how Tony's doing."

They stood, stretched, and headed for Doug's vehicle, holding hands as they walked.

Tony had been released from the hospital the day before. His father had driven him home, with his mother riding in the passenger seat and Darcy beside him in the back. He still had considerable pain, especially from the broken rib, but the pills helped. The fingers Darcy ran through his hair as he leaned against her in the rear seat helped even more.

She hadn't asked whether she could stay with him. She had simply announced it, saying he shouldn't be left alone for the first few days after discharge. Tony hadn't argued, thinking it was the best idea he'd heard in a long time.

More importantly, Tony's mother hadn't resisted either. She hadn't stopped smiling all day as she had helped Tony get settled back into his house and had prepared a dessert for dinner. Darcy had cooked pork chops and baked potatoes for a welcome-home meal.

Today, Tony's parents were back in Iowa City, and he and Darcy were alone except, of course, for Deputy Tim Jebron, who sat in a fully-loaded Sheriff's Department cruiser in front of the house and periodically made walking inspections of its perimeter.

Tony was on the couch most of the day, occasionally dozing off and waking when pain or hunger fought their way through his nightmares to wake him.

At 4 p.m., he heard two quick raps on the side door by the carport and heard someone come up the three stairs into the kitchen. He pushed himself up into a sitting position and turned to let his feet drop to the floor. Darcy got out of a chair across the room. She was headed toward the door, but when she saw who it was, she joined Tony on the couch.

Doug and Alison walked into the room.

"I tried to tell him to wait until someone answered the door..." Alison began.

"Bah! Between Ms. Frank and the deputy outside, I thought I'd never get in," Doug said, smiling. "You've restocked the beer by now, I trust?"

"Hi, guys. Nice to see you too," Tony said. "It's okay, Alison. Doug's been a pain in my ass for so long, I hardly notice anymore."

"I heard that," Doug called from the kitchen as he pulled a beer from the refrigerator. "Who else wants one?"

No one responded.

"Okay, suit yourselves."

Doug and Alison settled into chairs facing Tony and Darcy.

"Must be weird having a deputy outside your house all the time," Doug said.

"Yeah, but you should know, right? You have one too."

"Well, yeah, but ours aren't full-time. They've got a couple of Orney cops doing regular drive-bys and wellness checks on several of us who work at the *Crier* and the radio station, but they aren't sitting on us twenty-four seven."

Tony wasn't sure he liked that. Surely Bhatt had proven the extent of his insanity and willingness to do harm.

"Dammit, guys. You have to be careful. Bhatt's still out there."

"Sorry, Tone-man. Didn't mean to upset you."

"We're being very careful," Alison said. "After seeing what happened to you, I'm not letting that guy get anywhere near me."

"Any news about the search?" Tony asked. "I've been asleep most of the day."

"Nah, he's in the wind," Doug replied.

They talked about that for a while, wondering where he could have gone and how he had escaped so quickly and effectively. They also discussed how Bhatt had access to everything he needed and a propensity to plan everything in advance.

"They may never pick up his trail," Doug said.

Darcy shivered. "I hope they do. I hate the idea of living the rest of my life wondering where and when he'll show up."

"I wonder if there's another way," Tony pondered aloud.

"Another way for what?" Darcy asked.

"I think Doug's right," Tony said as all eyes in the room turned to him. "I know it seems unlikely, but it could happen."

"I could say something," Doug replied, "but I hate to kick a man when he already looks like he's had the shit kicked out of him."

Tony was unfazed. "I agree with Doug that picking up Bhatt's tail is unlikely. He's too smart, too prepared, and, quite frankly, too rich. So if we can't follow him, is there another way to find him?"

Alison said, "I'm sure the authorities are pulling out all the stops when it comes to things like tracking cell phones, checking on his residence and usual hangouts... All that typical investigative stuff."

"Again, I agree," Tony said. "Bhatt's not ever going back to his old life. He must have planned all along that if his plot against my dad failed, he would bail and start a new life as someone else."

It was Doug's turn to respond. "If he does that, won't it be impossible to find him, at least in the short term? As you said, he's rich. He literally could be anywhere on the planet."

Tony mulled that over, finally saying, "We have to try to think like him. Where would he go? Darcy, you probably know him best. Did he ever comment about loving a particular place or wanting to vacation or live somewhere new someday?"

"Not really. I mean, jeez, he's been everywhere. He once told me he's filmed on location on four different continents. He was fascinated by history, so we had a mutual interest in that. He admired the accomplishments of ancient Egypt, but also those of the Aztecs, the Chinese, the Vikings... I could go on, but you see what I'm saying. He's shown interest in dozens of places, not just one. Sorry, but I don't think I can be very helpful."

"How about this?" Tony asked, sitting up straighter. "What's the one thing he has proven he loves more than anything else in the world?"

"Killing?" Doug asked, only half-joking.

"I was thinking something much more personal. Something worth killing for."

"Harriet!" Darcy said. "Of course!"

"What day is it?" Tony looked at his watch. "Today's the fourteenth."

"Sorry, Tone-man, you lost me."

"Harriet died a year ago on July 28. She's buried in Milan. Think about that. We may not know where Bhatt is, but I have a damn good idea where he'll be in two weeks." Tony turned to Darcy. "How would you feel about taking a vacation to Italy?"

A broad smile crossed her face, but it disappeared just as quickly.

"It sounds wonderful. But you can't go to Italy now. You can barely breathe. You groan when you walk. The idea of traveling overseas—and doing it to catch a murderer, no less—is just absurd. I'd love to go to Italy, especially with you, Tony. But let's wait until Bhatt's behind bars and you're healed. Then we can really enjoy it."

Tony was about to respond, but Doug beat him to it.

"Have you even met this guy?" Doug asked. "He's got a hunch, and he's already convincing himself he's right. He's not gonna stay home just because his lungs and legs don't work."

"Tony, please," Darcy said.

"Okay, okay, I tell you what. Let's wait a week and then decide. If I'm feeling better, we can agree to go. If not, I'll share my idea with Rich Davis, and he can talk with Interpol or the Italian Polizia, to see if they'll follow up."

"Why not do that anyway?" she asked, obviously dreading the thought of Tony putting himself in harm's way again.

"Three big reasons," Tony said. "First, the police may not buy it. They could easily dismiss it as a silly idea coming from some nobody in America. Secondly, if the police do take it seriously, their response will be to mount some kind of big operation. Bhatt will be watching for that. Also, he lived a big part of his life in Italy. He'll know who to call to find out what is or isn't being done to find him. Lastly, it will be hard for the police to prepare for how clever and purely evil he is. One of them could be hurt or killed because they're not used to dealing with someone who will react violently to being found and is able to kill without remorse."

"And you are?" Darcy retorted. "I don't know anything about Italy, but I'm not sure you give the police enough credit."

Doug laughed, "That's because Tony's full of shit. Don't pay any attention to that B.S. he's spewing. He wants to go because he's Tony. He can't stand the thought of the puzzle being solved and the bad guy being brought to justice, if he's not leading the charge."

Tony didn't laugh. He glared at his friend.

Doug was still smiling. "Go ahead. Deny it, and I'll apologize."

"I.. Shit. I can't," Tony shook his head and broke into a smile.

"You boys think it's funny," Darcy said, "but if Bhatt's too dangerous for a police force, just how is Tony supposed to avoid joining Harriet in one of those graves if he finds the bastard?"

"I just have to be smarter, more clever, and maybe a touch more evil than him," Tony said.

***

"I'm scared," Darcy said.

"About what?" Tony asked, wondering which of a dozen things would be top of mind for her.

They were lying on their backs side-by-side in Tony's bed. It was late. Tony was having trouble sleeping, a result of his pain, his difficulty breathing, and his day filled with naps.

"I don't want to lose you."

It's *inevitable*, Tony thought glumly. Aloud, he said, "If I go after Bhatt, I'll be careful. I promise."

"I wish I could believe that. I'm beginning to realize what Doug said is true. You like playing the role of the hero."

"Every kid dreams of being a hero," Tony acknowledged. "But that's not why I do these things. It's not why I'm going after Bhatt.

I'm scared, too, but he has to be stopped. He's wicked and dangerous. He tried to destroy my dad, and he tried to kill me. And the two people he killed…"

"I know," she said, turning onto her side and speaking quietly into his ear. "Charlotte and Geoff were both so alive and so innocent. It's horrible to think their lives were ended by some crazy person pursuing his revenge on someone else."

"Exactly," Tony said. "I'm going to find him and stop him, no matter what."

Darcy ran her hand across his chest. She said, "You have to be careful of yourself, too, you know. Don't let Bhatt become an obsession. In trying to stop him, don't get pulled into that same black hole of revenge."

Tony thought about that. *Where is the line between doing the right thing and simply wanting to inflict punishment on someone who's hurt you?*

He wasn't sure how to explain it, but he did know the difference. "I don't know how to define it, but I know I'm not like him. I don't want to hurt anyone. I just want to be sure he doesn't get a chance to hurt anyone else."

He smiled in the darkness and continued, "I'm a nice guy, remember? I'm a lover, not a fighter."

Darcy sighed. "Sadly, you're neither one tonight."

"I'm sorry to say you're right," Tony said, sighing louder than she had. "If I tried to make love to you in my current condition, it might kill me." He turned his head, kissed her, and added, "Though, based on experience, I can say with confidence it would be worth it."

She giggled.

My God, I love that sound, Tony thought.

She ran her hand down past his stomach and between his legs.

"Maybe there's a thing or two I can do to make you feel better, without taxing your poor battered body too much."

He could feel himself growing erect in her hand. "Darcy…"

"Shh… I'm sure I can figure out something you'll like." She did.

He did.

Chapter 29

Orney, Iowa — Sunday, July 19

Tony and Darcy were packing for their trip to Italy. For Darcy, it was a matter of refilling the suitcase she had packed to come to Iowa. The clothes weren't ideal for Italy, but she would make do, knowing she could buy any needed outfits or accessories once she was there. Shopping in Milan wasn't exactly an unwelcome task for a woman with plenty of money.

Tony's wardrobe was equally limited. He had traveled to Italy many times to visit his mother's hometown as well as to vacation and tour. He had no trouble deciding what to throw in a bag.

He was excited and happy. He had been working out at the dojang every day for the past week. While physical contact had been extremely limited due to his injuries, he had been able to gradually increase his workouts using weights and inanimate opponents. He felt good about how much his breathing, stamina, and reaction times had improved. With the purple splotches hidden beneath his clothes,

Tony looked almost normal.

He was especially pleased Darcy had agreed to go with him. Once he had decided, she had suppressed her objections and had been supportive. *One more reason to love this woman*, Tony thought.

They would fly out tomorrow morning, first from Des Moines to Chicago O'Hare, and from there to London. Because Italy had been hit so hard by the pandemic, flights in and out of the country were more limited than in the past. Tony had been unable to get a direct flight to Milan, so he'd chosen to fly to Heathrow and catch an Alitalia flight to Milan from there. It would be a full day of travel, but with luck, he and Darcy would be settling into their hotel in Milan by the end of the evening Monday.

Ben had been surprised when Tony had asked for another full two weeks off. Tony had explained that he wanted to be in Milan a week early to prepare. He wanted to be ready so as to avoid detection in case Bhatt chose to visit Harriet's grave a day or two early. Assuming he succeeded in catching Bhatt, he would need a couple of days to deal with the authorities. Then he wanted to take Darcy to Amalfi to meet his Aunt Martina and his young friend Amedeo.

Ben had expressed the same misgivings as Darcy but had agreed to the time off. With the movie production at a halt, he could spare a reporter for a while. However, it did mean Doug had to stay and work. Ben couldn't do without them both. It would be odd for Tony to be going into a risky situation without Doug at his side.

Ben had concluded their conversation about the trip by saying, "Hey, maybe when you're done with this, you could actually write a story for the *Town Crier.* I'm kind of tired of writing everything while you're busy getting your ass kicked."

Tony had laughed and had promised he would. He had ended the conversation as he often did, by thanking Ben and expressing his belief that Ben was the best boss on Earth.

"I feel like I'm taking too many shoes," Darcy said from the bedroom as Tony was getting his shaving kit assembled in the bathroom.

"Don't bring anything uncomfortable," Tony said. "We'll be doing a lot of walking."

"That's what I mean. I have my tennis shoes and sandals for sightseeing, but I have to bring dress shoes for dining. I'm not gonna wear Reeboks with that black dress you love. And I *am* wearing that dress to the Osterin... Ostepri... What was it again?"

"The Osteria Del Binari. My favorite restaurant in Milan. The food is great, and the outdoor patio is on the second floor overlooking the Palazzo Reale. The Duomo, uh, the Cathedral of Milan, looms over the site. You practically have to share your hors d'oeuvres with the ghosts of saints and sinners reaching out from its spires. That would be bad, by the way, because the hors d'oeuvres are tiny. I promise you'll love it."

As he concluded his reassurance, she came through the bathroom door and put her arms around him.

"I know I will." She smiled and kissed him. "As long as you're not dead, I know I'm going to have a great time."

"The first night after Bhatt is behind bars, we'll go there to celebrate. We won't let anything stop us. Deal?"

"Deal," she said.

Twenty minutes later, as they stood at the kitchen counter fixing tacos and rice for dinner, Darcy's cell phone began singing a tune from the back pocket of her jeans.

"Crap," she said, rinsing and wiping her hands. "I know that ring. It's my agent."

Tony tensed but tried not to show it. He continued stirring the taco meat on the stove.

"I'd better take it," Darcy said. "Someday I may want to work again."

"Of course," Tony said, trying to keep his tone upbeat.

Darcy stepped into the living room to answer the call. As she chatted, she gradually worked toward the front of the house. When she stepped through the doorway into the bedroom, Tony stopped cooking. He turned off the stove, washed his hands, and sat at the kitchen table nursing a diet soda.

When Darcy walked into the room, her face was visibly pale. She tried to smile. "What, no food?"

"It can wait," Tony said. "Tell me."

"Tony…"

"It's okay, really. Just give me the facts, and we'll go from there."

"He wants me back in L.A. right away. He'd prefer I leave tonight, but I said absolutely no to that."

Tony stared straight ahead, not really seeing anything.

She said, "Ang Lee wants to meet with me. Wants me to star in the next Marvel extravaganza. My agent said it was urgent, so I'm guessing whoever Lee cast in the part originally has died or broken a leg or something."

Tony tried to smile. He failed.

"I said no, but…"

"I understand, really," Tony said, and he meant it. How could she not go? It was Ang Lee. It was fucking Marvel, for God's sake!

"He insisted," Darcy said. "He said I couldn't risk passing this up. They were talking ridiculous numbers, like maybe a five million guarantee."

"That had to have been an easy decision," Tony said, holding his hands in the classic pose of weighing two options. "A few days in Italy with Tony versus five million dollars. I'm gonna win that contest any day."

"Tony, don't," she said, irritation creeping into her voice. "I have a career. You know that. You know I have to go back to work at some point. I didn't ask for this call, and I don't want to go, but you can't expect me to walk away from the hottest director in Hollywood and a chance to star in what might be next year's biggest blockbuster."

Softly, calmly, Tony said, "I already told you I understand. You're right. I knew this day would come. I just hoped it would come a lot later."

"Tony, please don't be upset. I told you, I don't want to lose you. I need you."

Tony stood and looked down at her. "It's nice to be needed," he said. "It would be nicer to be loved." He walked into the bedroom, picked up his suitcase and shoulder bag, and walked back through the kitchen to the door. "As you know, my flight leaves really early in the morning. I'm gonna get a motel in Des Moines tonight. Do you need a ride?"

"No," she said, barely above a whisper. "They're sending a plane here for me."

"A private jet. Of course, I forgot. You're Darcy Gillson. Lock up the house when you leave."

"Tony…"

He walked down the three steps and out the door.

Chapter 30

Milan, Italy — Tuesday, July 21

Despite all his flights departing and arriving roughly on time, it was 1 a.m. Tuesday morning by the time Tony checked into the Moxy, an ultra-modern hotel near the Aeroporto di Milano Linate, or Linate Airport, east of downtown Milan.

His room was small but comfortable and equipped with all the latest electronics. Tony wondered if he would be able to sleep with the airport nearby and the bright purple, pink, and maroon décor shouting at him. He needn't have worried. Ten minutes after taking his medicine and crawling into bed, he was sound asleep.

He woke to the sound of the maid knocking on the door, inquiring in Italian if she could clean his room. He groaned, realizing he had forgotten to tell the front desk or hang a notice on the door instructing the staff to leave him alone.

He rolled over and touched the screen on his phone. It said 9:44 a.m. He suppressed a second groan, knowing it could have been worse. He padded over to the door and spoke through the wood, "Uno ora." Translated, it was "one hour," that is, if his rusty Italian hadn't failed him. In any case, the maid departed, and Tony headed for the shower.

After a light breakfast in the hotel's café, Tony hailed a cab and asked to be taken to Cimitero Lambrate, the cemetery in Milan in which Harriet had been interred. Tony figured he had three or four days at most to make his preparations, and he wanted to get started.

Once the cab dropped him off, Tony walked up the long, paved road that wound through the trees. He had no particular destination in mind. He was just getting a feel for the lay of the land. When he spotted an empty bench under a huge shade tree, he strode to it and sat.

He knew what he needed to do next. Ever since walking out of his house in Orney, he had felt embarrassed and a little ashamed of the way he had acted. Darcy deserved better. He sent her a text.

Sorry about reacting like a five-year-old. I'm not used to having to behave like a grown up. I hope your meeting goes well—really! I can't wait to see you in a spandex superhero suit.

He pushed send, then tried to put the entire relationship issue out of his mind. He needed to stay focused on what he was doing, or he could end up in real trouble at the hands of a madman.

His next task would be unpleasant, and perhaps dangerous, but he couldn't think of an alternative. He needed help.

He couldn't face Bhatt, and certainly couldn't subdue and hold him for the police, without the benefit of some gear. He knew a lot about Italy, but he didn't know where to buy weapons or any of the other things he might need. He did, however, know someone who would know. Unfortunately, that person despised Tony and had instructed him to stay away.

"Oh, well," Tony said to himself. "Nothing ventured, nothing gained." He opened the web browser on his phone and quickly found the number.

A voice answered in Italian, announcing he had reached Lastra Construction and Development. The company was based in Naples and was one of the largest builders in southern Italy. What the voice didn't announce was that its founder and CEO, Angelo Lastra, was rumored to be the most powerful don in the Camorra.

Tony said, "Signore Lastra, per favore."

The phone line clicked, and another woman's voice asked how she could help. Tony knew from experience that everyone in the office spoke English.

"May I speak to Mr. Lastra please?"

"I'll check to see if he's available. May I say who's calling?"

Tony was tempted to say no, but he knew that wouldn't help to get him through to the boss. If Lastra was going to refuse to talk to him, he might as well know it now.

"This is Tony Harrington, from Iowa, in the U.S.A."

"Mr. Harrington! I remember you well. This is Bridget. Our receptionist is out sick today, so I'm answering the phones."

"Hello, Bridget. It's nice to hear your voice. I hope you are well." Tony remembered Bridget. She was Lastra's personal assistant. She was extremely smart and normally tended to the company's most important tasks. She was probably capable of running the place without Lastra. She couldn't be happy about being stuck to a desk answering the phones.

She said, "Yes, I'm fine, thank you. We're all glad that things are finally returning to something like normal. And how are you?"

"I'm okay," Tony said, but quickly amended it. "Actually, to tell you the truth, I'm tired, jet-lagged, and sore from being crushed inside a grain bin."

"My goodness."

"To make matters worse, I'm in Italy, and I need a favor."

"And you're calling Mr. Lastra?" Bridget laughed out loud. "I seem to remember he didn't care for you much and asked you to leave him alone."

"Yes, I remember. But if he knows how that other matter turned out, and I assume he does, I'm hoping his disdain will have subsided a little." Tony was referring to an incident the previous year in which a member of the family was found to be a serial rapist and murderer. Tony had helped put a stop to it without causing any trouble for the man's associates, either in Italy or in New York.

He continued, "More importantly, I think Mr. Lastra will want me to succeed in my current, uh, quest. Whether he likes me or not, I think he'll want to help me. At least I hope so."

Bridget said, "I'll ask him, but please tread lightly. Mr. Lastra is not someone you want to... how do you Americans say it? Uh... piss off."

"I get it," Tony said. "Thanks."

Lastra picked up the call quickly, his voice booming. Tony didn't know where the man was, but pictured him as he had last seen him, sitting at a huge oval conference table in the company's board room.

"Harrington, you have balls the size of my company's bulldozers. What in the hell do you want?"

"Thank you for taking my call," Tony said meekly. "I'm chasing a murderer, and I need your help."

"Again? Jesus Christ, that's the same bullshit you fed me the last time you were here. I seem to remember being very offended by your insinuations and throwing you out of my office."

"This is different," Tony said quickly. "This man has no ties to you or your business. At least not that I'm aware of."

"Neither did the other one," Lastra sneered. "Try to remember that."

"Right, of course." *Strike one*, Tony thought. *I've already offended him a second time, even if he is lying through his teeth.*

"The man I'm chasing grew up in Italy, but he lives in California. He's a movie director..."

Lastra cut him off. "Why in the fuck do you think I care about this? Why are you calling me?"

"I'm calling because, to be honest, I don't know where else to turn. I thought you might care because this man has killed at least two people in cold blood, and now he's back in Italy—at least I think he is. If I'm right, well, I thought perhaps you wouldn't mind helping me take a killer off the streets of your beautiful country."

"You are so full of..." Lastra let his voice trail off, then said, "So what is it you want from me this time?"

"Just a contact. If I'm going to confront a sociopath who's proven how violent and deadly he can be, I need some things... Things I can't buy at the Galleria Vittorio."

"And again, you think I can help? Why would the CEO of a construction company know such things?"

"I mean no offense or implication by asking," Tony said. "You've done business in Italy all your life. I'm confident you know someone who can help me."

"You're talking about the underworld. I can't just send a stranger to them, even if I knew how to do it, which I don't."

"There must be some way."

"Shut up. I'm thinking."

Tony waited, his hopes rising.

"This kinda crap can't be talked about on cell phones. Can you come see me?"

"Well, actually, I'm in Milan."

"Milan! Jesus. That's a million miles from here. How am I

supposed to help you up there?"

"I don't know," Tony said, his confidence growing despite Lastra's tone, "but I'm confident you can."

"Where are you staying?"

Tony told him.

"I'll think about it. And Harrington…"

"Yeah?" Tony said, cringing at what was coming.

"If you ever call me again, I'm going to feed those giant balls of yours to my bulldog."

The call ended.

***

Tony spent the next two hours walking the cemetery's grounds, which were extensive. It was about one-third burial grounds and crypts, one-third chapel and outbuildings, and one-third semi-public park. It was well-kept, and at this time of year, the shrubbery and flowers were beautiful.

As he walked, Tony made a mental map of the place. He had an actual map he had picked up at the entrance. However, the map didn't show him the topography, or the locations of trees, hedges, giant tombstones, or any of the other details necessary to develop a plan and, hopefully, save his life.

He had no trouble finding Harriet's grave. A beautiful slab of marble covered the entire plot. The engraving at the top said, in English, *Harriet Danziker Bhatt, Beloved Wife, Daughter, Sister, Aunt. The World Misses Its Most Beautiful Gem.*

Tony knelt and said a prayer for her. It occurred to him to also pray for her forgiveness for what he hoped to do. He stopped short of asking for her divine intervention. Even if he believed in such things, he was pretty sure Bhatt's beloved would stop short of helping

Tony capture him.

By mid-afternoon, Tony was starving. Outside the cemetery, he caught a bus headed toward the center of the city. He got off in front of the huge downtown park called the Giardini Pubblici Indro Montanelli.

On the other side of the street, he immediately spotted a restaurant called Napiz Milano and entered through its ten-foot-tall double doors.

As his eyes adjusted to the darker interior, a man's voice immediately said, "To dine, yes? For one? Now?"

Speaking English. How do they always know immediately that I'm American?

"Si," Tony said.

"This way," the man said. "Very lucky to be so early. No tables tonight."

Based on the aromas coming from the kitchen, Tony wasn't surprised.

It was only four in the afternoon, so the dining room was nearly empty. Tony saw no one on duty except the man who had greeted him. He didn't know if the man was a maître d', a waiter, the manager, or the owner. Post-pandemic, he could have been all four.

Once Tony was seated, the man extended a menu for him. Tony held up a palm. He said, "I'm hungry, and I trust you. Bring me what you would like me to enjoy of your fine food."

The man beamed. "Very good! You will feast like a king."

By the end of the meal, Tony was pretty sure kings didn't dine at Napiz Milano. If they did, they would weigh six hundred pounds and be unable to move. He was stuffed to the point of discomfort with pastas, breads, cheeses, vegetables, and berries. There were some meats, fish, and other things, but Tony couldn't identify them all.

When offered dessert, he was forced to decline.

"For later? At your hotel, yes?"

"Sure," Tony said, trying not to groan. "That will be great."

The cheesecake and pastry delight filled an entire bowl. The man insisted Tony take the dish with him in a carefully sealed cardboard container.

"Is pleasure to serve a man who knows good food."

"It is a pleasure to dine in such a fine ristorante," Tony said. "My Italian mother would be proud of you."

"Italian? I knew it!" the man chortled. "You may dress like an American, but you have the heart of a Milano."

***

Tony spent more than an hour walking the streets of Milan, trying to work off a few of the ten thousand calories he had consumed. He avoided the duomo and the palazzo, not wanting to be reminded that Darcy hadn't responded to his text. Eventually, he grew tired of lugging the box of dessert around. He hailed a cab and went back to his hotel.

It wasn't yet 7 p.m., but Tony was exhausted. As he unlocked the door to his room, he wondered if he should nap or try to stay awake until bedtime. Despite all his trips to Europe, he still hadn't mastered overcoming the seven hours' difference in time zones.

He needn't have wondered. When he flipped on the lights and strolled into the room, he immediately spotted a white sheet of typing paper taped to his mirror.

Printed on it, in large letters, were five words: *Piazza Mentana Statue, nine o'clock.*

"Lastra, you old goat," Tony said to himself. He was smiling, choosing to believe Lastra had come through with a contact for what was needed, rather than arranging for his abduction and a trip to a nut-crunching bulldog. "I bet you're loving this."

***

Tony wasn't familiar with the Piazza Mentana. When he looked it up on his phone, he quickly realized why. It was a small courtyard in what was called the Old City. There was one statue in the center, behind a waist-high fence.

Tony arrived shortly before 9 p.m. He had spent the previous two hours planning and making a list.

Precisely at nine, as the last daylight disappeared behind the ancient buildings and scattered trees, a heavyset man in a dark suit strolled into the piazza and up to the statue. The man's face struck Tony as odd. His features were small and narrow but were set in an oversized head with fleshy cheeks and a protruding brow.

It looked, Tony thought unkindly, like a thin man was trying to escape out of the fat man's head.

The odd man spoke very good English.

"I am told you have needs." He turned away, as if admiring the statue.

"You were told correctly."

"I may be able to help. It depends, of course, on what you seek. If you want a bomb, for example, our conversation is over. I love my city and have no wish to be a part of that."

Tony smiled and shook his head. "No worries. I'm not a terrorist nor a criminal."

"If you buy weapons on the black market, you may have to reassess your opinion of yourself."

"Point taken," Tony said. "But I am here only to apprehend an evil man who has killed at least twice and may kill again if I fail. In other words, I want to protect this beautiful city as much as you do."

"We shall see," the man said, "but I suspect you are mostly trying to protect yourself."

"I won't deny it. I prefer to capture this man without losing a limb, or worse, in the process."

"You have a list?"

"I do." Tony pulled the piece of hotel stationery from his pocket and handed it to the man.

The man noted the name and address of the hotel, printed clearly on the paper.

"I hope you are better at find and capture than you are at spycraft."

Tony chuckled. "Hey, my instructions were posted inside my locked room. It's not as if my hotel is a closely-guarded secret."

"Point taken," the man said, mimicking Tony and smiling.

He glanced through the list, not seeming too surprised or concerned about anything he saw. That is, until he got to the last item.

"This could be a challenge," he said. "Even if I can do it, the cost will be considerable."

"I'm not a rich man, but please see what you can do. I'll proceed either way, but I'll be much more confident if I have everything on the list."

"You have cash? Now?"

Tony had brought a thousand dollars in hundred-dollar bills with him from his bank at home. He knew it would take more, but he didn't want to carry a larger amount until he knew what was needed.

"How much?" he asked.

"You are, shall we say, renting, rather than buying some of this, right? Obviously, you're not going to be taking this back with you on an airplane."

"Yes. If I can do that, it will be ideal."

"I won't know the final amount until I know what's available and talk to my boss. You brought something for a down payment?"

Tony pulled out his wallet and tugged out the bills. The wallet instantly went from very fat to very thin. He told the man the amount, adding, "As you can see, it's all I have with me."

"I hope you still have cab fare," the man jibed. "You don't want to walk these narrow streets alone at night." He pocketed the money and added, "But then, getting robbed now would be no big deal."

Tony didn't find it very funny. He asked, "So how does this work from here?"

"By six o'clock tomorrow, you will have a message at your hotel telling you where and when to meet and how much more money to bring. I assume you have a car rented?"

"No, but I will by then."

"Rent it starting Thursday. I'm sure we won't be meeting before then."

"It can't be any later than that. I need…"

The odd man cut him off. "I was told you were a horse's ass. Just be quiet and do what you are told. No one is exactly sure why we're helping you, so it won't take much to tip the scales the other way. One wrong remark, and my boss could decide we're just going to take this pocket change you handed me and disappear."

"I'm sorry," Tony said. "You're right. You're doing me a big favor, and I appreciate it."

The man nodded, still not looking at Tony, and said, "Walk away now. Don't look back. I'm admiring this statue."

Chapter 31

Milan, Italy—Monday, July 27

By 5 p.m. the following Monday, Tony was having trouble remaining still. After two days of watching Harriet's gravesite from a perch in a nearby tree, his muscles burned, and blisters had formed a line along the back of one calf. His body screamed at him to move, to stand, to do something to relieve the aches in his back and limbs.

He had, of course, taken breaks to eat, sleep, and relieve himself. But he had spent as many hours as possible in the tree trying to remain motionless, knowing that remaining undetected was his best chance for success and survival.

Worse than the physical discomforts were the mental gymnastics. His mind went from long stretches of boredom to bursts of high anxiety whenever someone walked near Harriet's resting place. He tried not to torture himself but couldn't help it. One minute he worried all of his efforts had been a waste of time—that Bhatt wouldn't show. The next minute, he worried that he would.

These thoughts were interrupted periodically as he chastised himself for choosing to hide in a tree. Originally, he had assumed he would wait behind the hedge at the edge of the property, or in the caretaker's tool shed a couple hundred yards away. But when he had spotted the tree, he had immediately realized it was in the perfect location and had the ideal branches and foliage to enable him to observe the site without being seen. He had modified his plan and his equipment order to take advantage of Mother Nature's gift.

Now he was kicking himself, metaphorically speaking, as the act of actually kicking himself would have felt better than he was feeling now.

Despite his pains and frayed nerves, thinking about the equipment order caused Tony to smile and shake his head for the hundredth time. Thursday evening, he had returned to his hotel room hoping to find instructions about where to pick up his gear. Instead, when he'd entered the room, he had found everything already there, carefully stowed in canvas backpacks. The note taped to the mirror instructed him to return the equipment to his room when he was finished with it and leave it there along with the additional money he owed.

I know some American companies that could learn a lesson or two about service from the Camorra, Tony thought.

As another hour ticked by, Tony's anxiety grew. The cemetery stopped allowing visitors to enter at 6 p.m. Those already inside might be able to linger for a while longer, but they would have to be out by seven, when the gates would be locked to prevent passage in either direction.

If Tony was right that Bhatt would insist on visiting Harriet on the anniversary of her death, it would have to be soon. On the other hand, wasn't it just as likely he would choose the anniversary of her burial, or her birthday, or their wedding anniversary, or any one of a dozen other dates?

Harrington, you're an idiot. You've spent half your life savings, lost the girl of your dreams, and gotten mixed up with one of the most powerful criminal organizations in the world, all for nothing. Get out of the damn tree and go home.

As soon as the thought had passed, everything changed. Tony saw movement on the ground by the gravesite. He lifted his binoculars and saw a priest dressed in a full black cassock and hat, called a biretta, kneeling to pray at the grave. He couldn't see the priest's face, but the height and the build looked right. He assumed it was Bhatt.

He placed the binoculars in his bag and extracted a safari-style khaki vest. He slowly and quietly slipped it on and reached back into the bag to retrieve an Axon Taser. It was the gun-style electronic weapon that fired darts into the victim, rendering them immobile with 50,000 volts of electricity discharged between a pair of electrodes. The Taser went into the right pocket of the vest.

Next, he removed a pair of handcuffs and placed them in his left pocket. Finally, he pulled his smart phone from his jeans. He set it to "Record" mode and fastened it to the vest just below his left collarbone with the garment's Velcro straps.

He glanced up. The "priest" hadn't moved.

Tony opened the flap of a second backpack affixed to a large branch behind him. From it he removed the rope he used for ascending and descending the tree. The rappelling hardware was already in place. Only the rope had been coiled into the bag to keep it from falling to the ground. Tony slipped the rope into the belay device attached to the harness he was wearing around his waist, and slowly lowered the free end to the ground below. He pulled on a pair of leather gloves and did a final quick check to ensure that everything was in order. It was. He took a deep breath, leaned out, and allowed himself to glide down to the lawn at the base of the tree.

The entire operation had taken only seconds and had made minimal noise. Tony was confident he had remained undetected. Staying behind the tree for cover, he removed the ropes. He took off the gloves and stuffed them into his back pocket, took a moment to stretch, then removed the Taser from his pocket.

He stepped around the tree and strode quickly down the hill and up behind the man in the priest garb. Stopping fifteen feet away, Tony held out the Taser in firing position and said, "Hello Ramesh. I was hoping I'd see you here."

The man stood and turned. It was Bhatt. He said, "And I was hoping you would come, Tony. I don't know how you escaped the grain bin, but I've been looking forward to setting it straight."

Before Tony could comment, or think, or pull the trigger on the Taser, Bhatt's hand came up from the folds of the cassock, holding a large, chrome automatic pistol. He fired once without hesitating, shooting Tony in the heart.

***

Bhatt looked around to ensure the cemetery was empty. A noise suppressor on the end of the gun made it unlikely anyone had heard. He reached up under the cassock and placed the gun in a holster affixed to his thigh. He straightened the folds, took one last look at Tony's body sprawled on the grass, spoke a few words of farewell to his wife, and began walking to the exit. He wasn't sorry and didn't apologize for leaving a body next to his wife. There was a certain poetry to the idea of Charles Harrington's son dying next to the woman Charles had destroyed.

When Bhatt arrived at the gate, the caretaker was there. He was an elderly man dressed in coveralls.

In Italian, the caretaker said, "Hurry up. You are the last one. I want to get home for my dinner."

Bhatt didn't reply and hung his head, hoping to obscure any opportunity for the old man to identify him later.

Because he was staring at the ground as he walked by, he noticed, but too late, that the caretaker was wearing nice shoes. Not the shoes of a man who mowed grass and tended to flowers. More like the shoes of a...

Before Bhatt could react, the old man's arm was around his neck. Bhatt opened his mouth to protest, but didn't get the chance. The old man pushed something into Bhatt's mouth and forced his jaw shut.

In twenty seconds, Bhatt was dead from the large dose of cyanide.

Without missing a beat, the caretaker lifted Bhatt over his shoulder and carried him back to Harriet's grave. As he approached, he saw Tony sitting cross-legged in the grass, rubbing his chest. His khaki vest lay on the ground beside the Kevlar vest that had been under his shirt.

"You're lucky he didn't shoot you in the head," the caretaker said in Italian.

Tony couldn't translate perfectly, but he got the gist of what the man had said.

"I don't feel so lucky," Tony said in English, not knowing or caring whether the man could understand him. "That hurt like a son of a bitch. I may have another cracked rib."

The caretaker switched to English. "No complain. Not dead."

"Yeah, well, there's that."

As Tony stood, the old man asked for his help in setting Bhatt's body on the grave.

"Not to drop. Post-death injury raise questions."

Tony understood. He pulled his gloves back onto his hands and helped to lower Bhatt from the man's shoulder. He was careful not to sweat or drool or allow his hair to get near the body. After a few moments of arranging the body and removing Bhatt's gun and holster from his thigh, they were done.

Watching the caretaker, or whoever the man was, do his work thoroughly and efficiently made Tony doubly glad he had included the last item on the list of things he had given to the odd man. He had written, "Backup, in case I fail." He hadn't known they would send an assassin, but if Tony was honest with himself, he knew he should have expected it.

"I'm sorry it came to this," Tony said. "I purposely didn't bring a gun because I wanted to turn him over to the polizia. He never gave me a chance."

"Is okay. Better for you. Better for us. Maybe better for him."

"Maybe," Tony said, doubtfully.

The two men quickly went to the tree to retrieve and pack Tony's gear. Tony kept looking around, worrying about being seen, but the old man told him not to be concerned. He had made sure all the visitors were gone from the cemetery before taking care of Bhatt.

"Night watchmen? Polizia?"

"Please to give some credit," the man said. "All accounted... uh, arranged, yes?"

"If you say so," Tony said, lifting the packs onto his shoulders. "I'll still be glad to get out of here."

Before the two men reached the entrance, the old man took Tony's arm and stopped him. He held out a piece of paper.

"Here is one other thing you want, from list."

Tony glanced at it and smiled. One of the items on his "order" had been an alibi. The paper he took from the caretaker contained an itinerary of the times and places Tony supposedly had been, in other parts of Milan, that afternoon and evening.

"Is good," the old man said. "Plenty witnesses saw you."

Tony shook his head, amazed again at the efficiency of the criminal organization. "Thank you," he said. "I owe you."

"No!" the old man barked. "No say that! You no want owe debt to Camorra. Pay and forget. Understand?"

"Yes, I understand."

Chapter 32

Milan, Italy—Tuesday, July 28

Tony slept late and enjoyed a long bath. While in the tub, he memorized the fake itinerary, then soaked the paper in the water until the ink was gone. Finally, he tore it into tiny pieces and flushed them down the toilet.

He also spent a long time thinking about the events of the previous few days. He couldn't deny he was glad Bhatt was dead, but every ounce of relief and satisfaction was accompanied by a pound of guilt. Was he responsible for what the Camorra had done? He hadn't asked for Bhatt to be killed. He had been careful to order a taser, and only a taser, as his weapon. It must have been clear to them that he hadn't intended to kill his target.

On the other hand, he had asked for backup, and a part of his mind had suspected the type of person they would send. *Does that make me an accomplice to murder? Am I now a criminal? Have I crossed the line that Darcy begged me not to cross?*

In the end, Tony knew these were questions that couldn't be answered. He also knew that the only way he could cope with what had happened was to push his guilt back into a dark recess of his brain, and force himself to resume his long-held self-image. He was a good person. He was committed to the law, to professionalism, and to his faith. No one could ever suspect otherwise—least of all himself.

As he toweled off, he watched the water drain from the tub, and prayed that his sins and remorse were being carried away with it.

Before leaving his room to get something to eat, he made sure everything was in place as instructed. The gear was on the bed in exactly the way he had found it. The only difference was an envelope full of money stuffed in one of the side pockets.

As he exited the hotel, a police car was pulling to a stop under the front awning. A uniformed male officer and a woman in plain clothes stepped out of the car. When the woman spotted him, she said, "Mr. Harrington?"

Tony stopped and turned, fighting to control the expression on his face. The woman was holding up a badge in a leather case. Her name and rank were there, but he couldn't read them from a distance.

Tony smiled and said, "Yes, I'm Tony Harrington. May I help you?"

The woman explained she was an investigator with the Milano Polizia and would like to ask him a few questions.

"I'm happy to help," Tony said, still smiling but inwardly thinking about the damning evidence sitting on the bed in his room. "I haven't eaten anything yet today. Would it be possible for us to chat over food?"

The detective seemed reluctant but agreed. They took the police cruiser to a nearby outdoor café.

As Tony was released from the rear seat, he found himself hoping it would be his last ride behind locked doors.

Tony ate an omelet, fresh bread, and a bowl of mixed fruit, while the officers sipped on coffee and asked him about his movements the day before. Tony was smart enough not to just rattle off the times and places that had been created for him. He feigned a struggle to remember everything, but eventually helped them assemble a list.

When finished, he said, "I have to admit, you're making me nervous. May I ask what this is about?"

She said, "This is about coincidence, Mr. Harrington, and a police detective's natural suspicions when one occurs. May I ask why you are in Milan?"

"Well, sure," Tony said, looking put out that his question hadn't actually been answered. "I guess you could say I had three reasons to come, four if you include the fact the tourist business is slow, and I thought it would be fun to visit when the city was less crowded."

"We appreciate that," the detective said. "What were the other three reasons?"

"Well, first, my girlfriend and I planned the trip together. It was to be a romantic getaway."

"Was?"

"Yeah, she got a better offer the day before we were to leave. She went to California without me, so I decided to keep my tickets and come by myself."

The detective made some notes and looked up at him.

Tony said, "The second reason is that I have family in Italy. My mother is from Amalfi. I'm going there next to visit my aunt."

"And third?"

"The third is I'm looking for Ramesh Bhatt. I thought he might come here because his wife is buried here. She died a year ago."

"Ahh," the detective said, nodding and making a note.

Tony knew, of course, that this was what she had been waiting to hear.

"And you found him, yes?"

"No," Tony said. "I've been here all week and haven't seen any sign of him. I've given up. I'm planning to head south tomorrow."

"You're sure you haven't seen him?"

"I'm sure. Why do you ask? Have you seen him? I assume you know he's a fugitive. That he's wanted for murder back in America."

"Yes, I'm very aware," the detective said. "I'm also aware he tried to kill you before he disappeared."

Tony shrugged, trying to give the appearance he expected her to know this.

"Mr. Harrington," she said, "Ramesh Bhatt is dead. So you can see why I'm uneasy."

Tony noted the shift in her language from "suspicious" to "uneasy." He tried to look shocked as he responded. "Dead? Here? How? What happened?"

The detective looked at her notes, decided she had what she needed, and said, "He was found dead this morning on his wife's grave in Cimitero Lambrate. It appears to be a suicide."

"My God. I never would have guessed that Bhatt would shoot himself. I mean, I assumed he was mentally ill after everything he did in the states, but didn't think…" he let his voice trail off, as if lost in thought.

The detective said, "Just so you know, he didn't shoot himself."

"Then how…?"

"It appears he swallowed a massive dose of cyanide. If the autopsy confirms this, I can tell you death would have been nearly instantaneous."

Tony nodded slowly. "Wow. I don't know what to say to that.

I was really hoping he would be returned to Iowa for trial and be convicted there. The publicity about his trial would have helped put an end to anyone's remaining thoughts that my dad was involved in one of the murders."

"I'm sorry you didn't get your wish," The detective said. She closed her notebook and said, "I think that is all we will need from you, Mr. Harrington. I simply felt it was important to, shall we say, scratch that itch. I hope you don't mind."

"I don't, and thank you for telling me. I will travel easier knowing I don't have to worry that Mr. Bhatt is out there somewhere."

"Yes," she said, eyeing him closely. After a long pause, she stood. "Enjoy your remaining time in our beautiful city, and have a safe trip to the south."

"I will, thank you."

Once the officers were back in their car and pulling away from the curb, Tony sucked in a deep breath and wondered if it was his first since the conversation had begun.

***

Tony spent the afternoon sightseeing, being careful not to visit any of the places he had supposedly visited the day before. Fortunately, that did not prohibit a stop to see "The Last Supper," the masterpiece by Leonardo da Vinci, in the refectory of the Convent of Santa Maria delle Grazie. Tony had seen it only once before and was thrilled to have a second chance. It was even more stunning now, thanks to amazing restoration work that had been done in recent years.

When he was finished there, he checked the time and called Ben to report on Bhatt's death. This was one time the *Crier* should be able to scoop the other media with breaking news related to the murders.

It was only 7 a.m. in Iowa, but Ben sounded glad to hear from him. "You sound good," he said. "I hope that means everything is going okay. Have you had any luck with Bhatt?"

Tony explained that Bhatt had been found dead at the cemetery.

"You didn't…?" his boss began to ask.

Tony laughed. "No, I swear I haven't killed anybody. A police detective came to see me at lunch today. She said his death was an apparent suicide by poison."

"I'll be damned," Ben said. "I know I should feel bad for him, but I can't bring myself to do so."

"I know. I feel the same way. I would have liked to have brought him home for trial, but it may be better that it's all over and done with. We don't have to worry about extradition, or God forbid, him getting acquitted on some technicality."

"All true," Ben said. "You're sure you didn't…?" He let the insinuation hang in the air.

Tony didn't respond. He simply filled Ben in on the few details he had from the police, then talked about his plans for the next few days. "I'll be back at my desk on Monday at the latest," he said, "assuming you haven't given up on me and hired my replacement." "Well, there is that high school kid who keeps asking me for an internship. He's pretty sharp. You may not want to delay your return by too many days."

"Got it. I'll consider myself on notice. See you Monday."

Ben laughed and said, "Have a good time, and travel safely."

Tony's next call was to his parents to let them know about Bhatt, primarily so they wouldn't have to keep looking over their shoulders.

"Maybe we'll finally get those armed guards out of our hair," his father said after expressing both relief and deep regret about Bhatt's death. "On the other hand, Rita's going to be very disappointed. That U.S. Marshal is..."

"I don't wanna hear it!" Tony squawked with a nervous laugh. His last call was to Rich Davis also giving him "the official version." Rich was even more pointed than Ben in questioning what had happened. Tony put on his best "how can you think that of me" voice and assured him he had killed no one. "C'mon, Rich. The guy swallowed a cyanide capsule. I wouldn't know how to get one of those in the U.S., let alone in Italy. And even if I had one, I wouldn't have been able to get close enough to Bhatt to make him take it. Trust me, you can stop worrying about this one. I didn't do it."

The fact that everything he said was technically true was all that enabled Tony to get through his spiel without revealing his misgivings.

Tony asked Davis to keep the news to himself until morning so the *Crier* would have a chance to publish the story before word of Bhatt's death leaked out.

Davis agreed but wasn't happy about it. He said, "The protection we're providing your family and friends is costing a fortune. I hate for it to continue when I know it's not needed."

"Think of it this way," Tony retorted. "The people of Iowa can pay for all of it with what they're gonna save on Bhatt's extradition, trial, and incarceration."

"Fair point," Davis said. "Okay, I'll give you twenty-four hours, then I'm calling everybody off."

"Thanks."

Tony spent several hours strolling around the city and its eclectic mix of ancient and modern architecture. At the end of the afternoon, he took a cab to his hotel to clean up. He smiled when he walked in the door and saw no sign of backpacks, envelopes, or notes on the mirror.

After his shower, he put on a dress shirt, slacks, and a coat and tie. He walked down to the lobby and hailed another cab.

At 8 p.m. he walked through the doors of the Osteria Del Binari, and asked the maître d' for a table on the patio. He had promised himself a celebration when his pursuit of Bhatt was over, and he was going to enjoy the food, the views, and the service of his favorite restaurant—even though he was alone—before leaving Milan in the morning.

The maître d' seemed excited to see him and led him toward the corner of the second-floor patio with outstanding views of both the Duomo and Palazzo Reale.

As they approached the table indicated by the host, Tony stopped, feeling his breath catch in his throat. At the table, sipping a glass of wine, sat Darcy Gillson. She was wearing the black dress with red flowers. This time no scarf obscured any part of her neck, or her cleavage.

She looked up at Tony and smiled. "There you are! I thought you'd never get here."

Tony sat, taking the menu from their host without even noticing he had done so. Struggling to find his voice, he croaked, "I'm surprised. You look wonderful." He furrowed his brow and said, "Wait. That didn't come out right."

She giggled.

"Thank you for being here, but *why* are you here?"

"It's the twenty-eighth. I figured you would be finished with your work one way or the other."

"Not that. I mean what's happened? Why aren't you in California?"

She waved away his question and said, "We'll talk about me later. I want to hear about you. Have you had any luck? Is that why you're here? I hoped you would keep your plans for the Ostep... the Osheri... Oh crap, however you pronounce the name of this place."

Tony smiled and reached out to take her hand. "It could have been the McDonald's on the corner across the piazza, and it would have been perfect as long as you were sitting there waiting for me."

She blushed but said, "Is there really a McDonald's over there?"

Tony nodded, still smiling.

"That's... that's criminal, don't you think? Maybe that should be your next quest—removing all fast-food restaurants from the great cities of Europe."

"Hmm, I think that's a better job for a movie star. Nobody knows me over here."

"Ooh," she said excitedly. "That's what's so great. Nobody knows me either. I shopped all afternoon and hardly got noticed. Well, I got a couple of whistles from construction workers, but not one request for an autograph. I love it! Now stop changing the subject, and tell me what's happened, if anything."

Tony once again related the official version.

She said, "Not to wish bad things on anyone, but isn't it good news, for you I mean? Bhatt is gone, and you didn't have to capture him and deal with the authorities. You don't have to worry about him ever again or deal with the nightmare of a trial and all that."

"Hey, it would have kept the *Crier* in big news for months," Tony said, feigning outrage. "The bastard cheated me again!"
She smiled. "Well I'm glad he did. I'm so relieved we can relax and enjoy Italy."

"We? So you're staying?"

"Of course. You promised to introduce me to your aunt and to that young boy who worships you. What was his name?"

"Amedeo, and I'm pretty sure I never used the word worship."

"Whatever. I bet he does. Can we stay in Rome for a night on our way? I bet the train passes right through there."

"It does, and we can. We can do whatever you want."

"Whatever I want? Hmm, you'd better be careful what you offer." Under the table, she began running her toe up and down his calf.

Tony winced as her foot passed over the blisters.

"Oh! What did I do?"

"It's nothing," he said. "Perhaps we should order before I pull you under the table and tear off your clothes. I don't want to get thrown out of here before I've enjoyed at least some of their food."

She stuck out her lower lip in a faux pout and sighed. "If we must."

As they feasted on shrimp and pasta, Tony returned to the issue of her movie offer. "So tell me about L.A. How was your meeting?"

She set down her fork and dabbed her lips with a napkin.

Stalling for time, Tony thought. *Trying to figure out how to give me the bad news.*

"It was great. Perfect, really," she said. "They offered me the part of this super-person from some comic book I've never heard of and offered a four million guarantee. My agent said no way, and they countered with six million, just like that."

The numbers were mind-boggling to Tony, who still was trying to figure out if he would have to get a bank loan to pay for what this trip was costing.

"Everyone in the room hated me when I said no."

"You said… Wait, what did you say?"

"I said no. I wasn't interested. It may be the most fun I've ever had in a meeting. They all thought I had lost my mind."

Tony leaned back in his chair. "That's easy to believe because I agree with them. You *have* lost your mind." He had a horrible thought and said, "God, I hope you didn't do this because of my childish behavior back at home?"

"Relax. It's not you. Of course your opinion matters to me, but you made it clear you understood, at least intellectually, even if it hurt you emotionally."

"Well, I…"

"Shh. Let me finish. I looked through the script before the meeting began. It wasn't terrible, but it wasn't great. There were all these references to a fantasy reality I've never studied and don't understand. More importantly, I realized I didn't even like the part."

She continued, "It also called for a couple of months of filming in Bolivia. Apparently part of the story takes place on a barren world, so they went looking for a remote, unforested, and forbidding place. I'm not afraid to work hard or to do it in challenging locations, but not to make a movie I don't really like in the first place." She took another sip of wine. "Mmm, that's good. Finally, I didn't want to risk being labeled as an action hero. It can be so hard to break out of that once you're there. So I told Mr. Lee I would love to make a movie with him someday. I said I would do it for less than half what he offered for this if he found the right part in the right vehicle. He said I was making a mistake walking away from this, but also that he admired me for doing what I thought was best. I don't know him well enough to be certain he meant it, but at least he didn't seem offended and didn't call security to have me escorted out."

"So I was right," Tony said, grinning. "You weighed a trip to Italy with me against a multi-million dollar move role, and chose me. Well, Italy rather."

"Don't get all full of yourself. My actual choice was between Italy and Orney, Iowa, or worst-case scenario, Malibu, California. Filming for the movie doesn't start until September."

He laughed. "Touché."

𝕿𝖔𝖜𝖓 𝕮𝖗𝖎𝖊𝖗

Movie director dies of apparent suicide

Trail of murder, attempted murder, revenge ends in Milan

Ben Smalley, Editor

MILAN, Italy – Ramesh Bhatt, 54, of Piñon Hills, Calif., was found dead Tuesday morning at the site of his deceased wife's grave in Milan, Italy, according to sources close to the case who reported details exclusively to the Town Crier. Italian police said Bhatt died of cyanide poisoning in an apparent suicide.

An autopsy was scheduled to be conducted in Milan today to confirm the cause of death. The timing for the release of the autopsy results was not known at press time.

Bhatt's wife, Harriet Danziker Bhatt, was a former fashion model and actress. She was American by birth, but worked for years in Milan and often referred to it as her first love. She died of cancer a year ago and was buried in the Milan cemetery. People close to Bhatt said he was very distraught about her death.

At the time of his death, Bhatt was the subject of an intensive search throughout the U.S. and Europe. He was wanted on two counts of first-degree murder in the killings of actress Charlotte Andresson, 28, of Santa Clarita, California, and Geoff Warbler, 78, of Solon, Iowa, according to Special Agent Rich Davis of the Iowa Division of Criminal Investigation.

Bhatt was the director of a movie filming on location in Orney this summer. Andresson was an actress in the cast of the movie. She was found dead of a severe head wound at the Orney Country Club on June 21.

Warbler's only involvement in the case, Davis said recently, was his agreement to assist in holding some evidence related to the murder weapon in Andresson's killing. The actress was killed with a golf club, and Warbler worked for a golf course in eastern Iowa.

Bhatt was also charged with the attempted murder of Tony Harrington, according to Quincy County Sheriff George Mackey. Harrington is a reporter for the *Town Crier*.

Harrington was rescued from beneath an estimated 6,000 bushels of shelled corn inside a grain bin on a farm northeast of Orney July 10. Sheriff Mackey described Harrington's survival as a "miracle." He credited the quick thinking of Harrington's father, Charles Harrington, who was at the scene when the incident occurred, with saving his life.

Agent Davis said the new evidence in the case of Andresson's murder indicates Bhatt killed her in an attempt to frame Charles Harrington for the crime. "When that didn't work, Bhatt attempted to kill Charles Harrington's son," Davis said.

When asked why Bhatt would do these things to the Harringtons, who previously had been reported to be close friends of Bhatt's, Davis said the animosity stemmed from an incident between the two men that took place 35 years ago. He said no other details were available to the public.

Authorities expect Bhatt to be interred in Milan, near his wife's burial plot. The movie he was filming in Orney has been put on hold. When contacted about the film, a spokesperson for Prima Racconto Films said…

Chapter 33

Orney, Iowa—Monday, August 3

As he had promised, Tony was back at his desk in the newsroom on Monday. It had not been easy.

The remainder of his travels in Italy with Darcy had been a whirlwind. They had spent nearly four days traveling to Rome, to Amalfi, and back for the long flight home. As a result, they had only been able to enjoy one day of sightseeing in Rome, and one day in Amalfi to visit family and explore the beauty of the mountains and sea around the coastal city. Darcy had loved every minute of it, and Tony had promised her they would return soon.

Tony hoped Ben's expectations of him on day one would be modest. He wasn't sure he could put two coherent sentences together. His body was a mess, wracked by jetlag, an itching calf where blisters were healing, a sore chest where a bullet had struck his vest, and sore muscles everywhere else from all that had happened in recent weeks.

If possible, his mind was in worse shape, filled with conflicting emotions of relief, sadness, love, disdain, and more than a little guilt. He wondered whether the Italian police would decide to really go after his story. If they checked his bank accounts, they would know something significant had drained them. If they checked his alibi, well, he had to hope the Camorra were as good as they appeared to be.

And then there was Darcy—the bona fide movie star who was back at his house right now, unpacking his suitcase and doing his laundry. He grew more incredulous every time he thought of it. He loved the woman to the depths of his soul, but he also remained convinced it couldn't last. Thinking about it made him crazy.

So stop thinking about it, dumbshit.

He was struggling to update an obituary for a former Orney mayor. The man wasn't even dead yet. The paper kept draft obituaries on file for local people of interest, in case one of them died close to deadline. It could be a real godsend for a skeleton crew late at night faced with a death announcement. Ben had indeed decided to go easy on him his first day back. There was no more mundane task than this.

Despite that, Tony's mind kept wandering. He pondered what it would take to get back in the groove. He reached down to scratch his itching calf. His cell phone rang. It was Darcy.

"Hey, hotshot movie star, what's up?"

"Nothing much, farm boy," she said brightly. "I just remembered something I meant to tell you. I love you too." She giggled and was gone.

***

An hour later, Tony was still completely befuddled by Darcy's call. He was happy, of course. He had desperately wanted to hear her say it—but now that she had, what did it mean? Could he move to Hollywood to try to build a long-term relationship with her there? He couldn't see it. Could she stay in Orney and settle for a life in rural Iowa? That seemed even less realistic. Was there a "neutral" third option? Someplace that could serve as home base for both of them? Maybe back in Chicago? San Francisco? Phoenix?

He sighed and made up his mind to stop fretting about it. No solution was going to magically appear. In the end, he knew he needed to do exactly the same as he had done since their first date— enjoy his time with her, do the best he could to cope with the insanity of her world, and let happen whatever happened. It wasn't a great answer, but it beat the hell out of losing her.

Tony couldn't sit still any longer. He stood, stretched, and headed for the break room. He needed another Diet Dr. Pepper.

The good news about the vending machine at the *Crier* was that it only charged one dollar for a bottle of soda. The bad news was that the machine was old and only took quarters. Tony patted the front pocket of his slacks and realized he was out of change. He strode over to an old Tupperware container on the counter, dropped in a dollar bill, and extracted four quarters. The container full of quarters was part of an honor system developed by the staff so people didn't have to waste their time begging for change around the building whenever they were in need of a beverage.

Tony's hand was reaching for the change slot in the front of the dispenser when he noticed the quarter he was holding between his finger and thumb was unusual. He stopped to examine it.

"Huh," he said. It was a 1964 quarter. It looked new, but the date on the front was clear. It had caught his eye because the entire coin was made of silver. In 1964, U.S. coins hadn't yet made the transition to being minted from less expensive metals.

Tony wondered if a sixty-year-old coin in pristine condition would be worth something to a collector. He put it in his pocket, retrieved another dollar from his wallet, and went back to the Tupperware for more change.

"Well, I'll be…" he said aloud. Among the four quarters he pulled from the container, another one was old—this one from 1959. He thumbed through the dish of coins to see if he could find any others. He didn't, so he purchased his soda and headed back to his desk.

Once there, he laid the two old coins on the surface in front of him and examined them closely. "Where did you come from?" he asked the coins. "And where have you been all these years?"

Tony decided to pay more attention to the coins he handled in the future. Would more show up? Even if they did, would it matter? It couldn't mean anything, could it? It couldn't be important.

Could it?

He took a deep breath and told himself it was probably nothing. Most likely, someone short of change had dipped into an old collection, or even a cookie jar from grandma's kitchen counter. Still, it made him curious. Even if the answer was something simple like the cookie jar, it might result in an interesting feature for the Sunday paper.

And just maybe, it was something more. There was no way to know until you did the legwork. So Tony would do it. Not because he expected great things, but because it's what journalists do.

Once again, he was feeling the tingle at the back of his brain. He would soon find out that, this time, the tingle should have been an entire head full of alarm bells.

Afterword

I must admit it was fun bringing Hollywood to Iowa for this book, the fourth in the Tony Harrington series of mysteries/thrillers. The idea is not as far-fetched as it may seem to some people who live elsewhere. The state has been privileged to be the setting for the plots of several major motion pictures, including Meredith Willson's *The Music Man* and the original *State Fair* starring Will Rogers and Janet Gaynor.

More to the point, Iowa has hosted the on-location filming of many popular movies including Dick Van Dyke's *Cold Turkey*, filmed in Greenfield, Clint Eastwood's *The Bridges of Madison County*, filmed in Winterset (home of John Wayne), and Kevin Costner's iconic *Field of Dreams*, filmed in the Dyersville/Dubuque area.

Happily, no murders occurred during the filming of any of these movies (at least none of which I'm aware).

While I had no direct experiences with any of the movie companies that filmed in Iowa, I spoke with several people who did as I attempted to understand how the people in rural communities react to the presence of film crews and movie stars. I learned a lot from others' observations, then ignored most of what I'd learned in order to create an atmosphere in the fictional Orney, Iowa, that I thought would be the most entertaining and helpful to the story.

The return to Italy (see book three, *The Third Side of Murder*), for part of the backstory and for the resolution at the end, was a surprise even to me. As I began the story, I knew I wanted the perpetrator to be someone from the Harringtons' past. Having this person's connection to and hatred for Charles Harrington stem from his years in Italy didn't occur to me until I wrote it. However, once the story took that turn, I was glad it did. It was fun to revisit a country I've grown to love, and to have Tony risk, once again, asking for help from the Camorra.

In short, creating *Performing Murder* was a real pleasure for me. I hope you enjoyed reading it as much as I enjoyed writing it.

Lastly, regarding that mention at the end of the old coins… I'm sorry, but you'll have to read the next Tony Harrington story, called *The Sophocles Rule*, to find out whether they are tied to anything significant. If I had to guess, I would say they are.

– JL

Acknowledgements

The dedication at the beginning of this book is unusual in that it lists a large number of people. This was done to acknowledge that whatever successes I've enjoyed in my life are due to many people who've helped me in numerous ways. Most of them would refuse to take credit for anything related to my careers or my creative endeavors. However, as the dedication indicates, I know with certainty that without them, I would not have all the wonderful things with which I've been blessed—a beautiful and loving family, great friends, good jobs, a series of published novels, incredible experiences making music, and on and on.

The list in the dedication includes some friends, former bosses, mentors, bandmates, siblings, and two Religious Sisters of Mercy. (It could include the names of all the nuns with whom I've worked, but that's a dedication for another day.) As I'm sure is true for most people, the list could be much, much longer. Undoubtedly, I'll revisit it later and wonder how I could have left off another dozen names or more. I simply have to hope that everyone who has helped me will understand the intent of the message: I love and appreciate them. I will never take them for granted or forget how lucky I have been, or forget how strongly they have supported me, even during the times when I didn't earn it or deserve it.

The same can be said for my immediate family. My wife, Jane, and our six children have been steadfast in their support of my efforts to be a writer.

I also want to thank you, the readers and purchasers of books. Supporting authors and booksellers continues to be critically important to our society. It certainly has added to my list of blessings. My appreciation also goes to the crew at Bookpress Publishing. I couldn't ask for a better partner in getting my stories from manuscripts to finished products in readers' hands.

Another word of thanks goes to Steve Sukup, President and CEO of Sukup Manufacturing in Sheffield, Iowa. I've known Steve for many years, as a business leader, as a state senator, and as a generous supporter of community projects and organizations. Steve was incredibly helpful when I called on his expertise related to modern grain bins. His company makes high-quality and technolog- ically-advanced products for storing and managing grain on farms.

When I decided to have the murderer add Tony to his list of victims by throwing him into a grain bin, I knew I would need an expert's help. I was aware grain bins could be deadly, but I didn't know much beyond that. I wanted to be as accurate as possible in describing Tony's near-death experience. As impossible as Tony's escape may seem, especially to those who understand the mortal danger posed by stored grain, it is based on a real incident. None of what happens in that key part of the novel would have been possible without Steve's willingness to share his time and knowledge.

Lastly, to repeat an acknowledgement I've made before, I suggest we all thank the men and women who strive every day to keep daily and weekly newspapers, and other forms of news media, alive and available to everyone. The economic and operational challenges of running a viable news organization are enormous, as evidenced by the huge number of newspapers that have downsized or closed in recent years. Many communities are fortunate to have people in them who continue to work hard to keep local news coverage alive. Thomas Jefferson said democracy cannot exist without a free press. He was right. As a result, we owe our friends in the media a tremendous debt of gratitude.

I hope my tales of Tony Harrington and his friends and co-workers in the world of small-town newspapers pay proper homage to the journalists doing this work in the real world.

– JL

 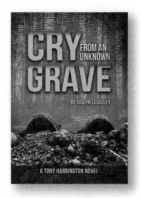